The Last Alliance

The Mercian Ninth Century
Book 9

M J Porter

Cover and map design by Flintlock Covers

ISBN: Ingram Paperback 9781917374040

ISBN: Paperback 9781917374002

ISBN: Hardback 9781917374019

ISBN: Kindle 9781917374026

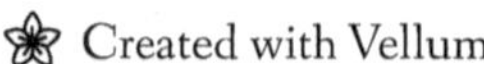

Contents

GAINSBOROUGH
TORKSEY
CHESTER
GWYNEDD
BARDNEY
REPTON
LICHFIELD
TAMWORTH
THETFORD
POWYS
PETERBOROUGH
ELY
EAST ANGLIA
OFFA'S DYKE
WARWICK
NORTHAMPTON
MERCIA
GRANTABRIDGE
WORCESTER
PASSENHAM
HEREFORD
KINGSHOLM
DYFED
GWENT
GLOUCESTER
ICKNIELD WAY
LONDON
KENT
WESSEX
WINCHESTER
MAP OF EARLY ENGLAND
0
50 Miles

Prologue

The kingdom of Wessex, AD875

'Attack,' I roar. With Hereman to one side, and Icel to the other, we move into the enemy. They're too cowardly to take the first steps. I've never been one to shy away from a fucking big fight, and if it's unlikely that we're going to win, then all the better.

My shield before me, seax to hand, I advance on them. There are small gaps between my men. We can't stand shoulder to shoulder and counter our opponents. But that doesn't concern me. All we need to do is keep the bastards from breaking through and attacking us from behind as well as from in front.

I meet the first foeman with a crashing blow from my seax. The blade isn't perfectly weighted for my hand, but brute strength will still make it perform as I want. My adversary, who thought he was surely to succeed, falters at the attack. It takes him precious moments to perfect his hold on the shield and in that time, I'm too close for his spear to be useful. Fucking arse.

My seax blow is elevated, aiming for his neck. He lifts his shield high. I punch with my shield into his almost exposed belly. The spear clangs to the ground as I graze his hand. He collapses around the pain in his belly. It takes but a moment to stab into his exposed throat with my blade.

'Daft bastard,' I glower, watching him stumble. I spit the taste of his blood from my mouth and menace the next bastard. He watches his ally fall, eyes on stalks. Like the first man, he's too slow to stop me from landing the first blow. I aim for legs, and he shoots his shield low, knocking it against the bucking legs of the dying man. I grin as I reverse the action, stabbing into his belly, only for the blade to come up against the protection of his byrnie. A grimace, and I hack towards his neck again.

He might be slow to start, but he ducks out of the reach of my seax blade. I arch an eyebrow as a sign of respect. Not that he sees it.

In the back of my mind, I'm considering these events. I decide whoever's in command will have done one of two things. They've either sacrificed the weaker warriors, allowing those with more experience to attack us when we're already bloodied and sweated, or they've not given it a moment's thought, and the men are intermingled. I imagine the latter, but I'll make my judgment when the enemy are all dead.

My adversary steps in to meet my next assault, his war axe in one hand, his shield in the other. He glowers, lips downcast, beard splattered with the blood of his dead ally. But his eyes show his fear. Fear will make a man piss himself in fright when faced with a lethal warrior. I am that lethal warrior.

I surge towards him, mindful of the man who's dead or dying and will soon be dead. I extend my seax, elbow high. He has his shield there to protect his neck, leaving legs exposed once more. Not that I go for them. He'll be expecting that. Instead, I repeat the action and then punch out with my shield, driving it against his shield and forcing both close to his body. I see his eyes bulge as the angle of his elbow is too extreme to be comfortable or maintained. He'll drop the blade or break his own arm unless he steps back.

He holds firm. I smirk at that, pushing more and more weight behind the shields. Any moment now, he'll remember the war axe in his hand. I lash out with my seax. He watches it coming closer and closer. I toy with him, a slice to his unprotected chin. I've drawn first blood.

With a cry of thwarted pain, he finally steps back. My shield gives. He crashes into the man behind him. The damn arse doesn't watch his ally's efforts, instead jeering at those fighting Hereman and Icel. With nowhere to go, my foeman finally remembers his war axe, lifting it to crash it against my shield. I lift it to hold the blade away from me and step ever nearer. He was stuck with his shield too tight to his chest. Now, he's wedged between me and his ally, and neither of us is going anywhere.

He shouts to his fellow warrior, but the man is oblivious. I lower my seax and stab into his body, angling it this time so that it has the chance to get beyond the byrnie. But his protection is good. It withstands the assault. I grimace. Overhead, my shield keeps his axe away from me. It means we're closer than we could be. I pull my arm ever higher, my foeman struggling to keep hold of the shield. He focuses on that and not on me. I step forward and nut him on the nose. My head reverberates with the blow as his nose explodes with a sharp snap. He veers away, only to hit the man behind him once more. His war axe hand trembles, dropping away, as he brings his shield up to try and protect himself.

A muffled conversation, nasally. I imagine he demands the man move or aid him. He does neither, and now, with tearing eyes and streaming nose, I slide my seax blade into his open mouth, deep until it impacts the back of his throat. The bastard dies with his snot and blood mingling on the edge of the blade.

'Stupid bastard,' I offer, yanking back the blade, allowing him to fall to the ground. To either side of me, I sense Icel and Hereman overpowering their foemen. This is too easy. I expect some fiercer defence from the next man. But he eyes me with surprise. Did he think his ally still blocks his path?

'You should be paying more fucking attention,' I inform while his mouth settles into a firm line of determination. He also has a shield.

The two abandoned boards at my feet get in the way. He has a sword. I eye it. His equipment shimmers. I consider if he knows what he's doing, and have my answer soon enough.

Shield before him, he meets my attack, sword raised high to chop down on my shield. I consider if that will work as I guide my shield forward. I'm mindful of the dead and dying below my boots. The number's growing almost by the breaths I take. The shouts and cries of my allies mingle with those of the enemy. I detect Rudolf's shriek of triumph, Pybba's grunt of effort, even Icel's quieter but more determined attack against our foemen. If I closed my eyes, I could determine where my men fought. But I don't close my eyes. I need to kill the bastard and his bloody flashy sword.

So far, my opponent hasn't given me much cause for concern, but I'm always prepared to be surprised. This isn't to be one of those rare occasions.

The sword swings before my eyes. I bat it aside with my shield, menacing with my seax. I don't go for the killing blow yet. The equipment he wears is much better than anything the other two had. I'll need to be craftier and use more skill to kill this fucker.

He brings his sword back with a soft grunt. His beard is trimmed with trinkets, and his tunic is dyed brightly red beneath his byrnie. This man has wealth—or rather, he did. Soon, he'll be dead, and whoever takes his wealth is damn well welcome to it.

I thrust my shield towards his sword again, holding it at bay. The amount of time it's spent in the air, being ineffective, he might as well have a fucking war axe. A sword shouldn't be swung almost overarm at the enemy. I'd use mine with far more skill, but it's not a weapon to be employed when men press tightly to one another as they do now. A seax is much better. Or a war axe. Or a shield. Not a bloody sword.

Once more, he repeats his tactic. This time, I'm quicker, fiercer. I thrust the shield against his sword, pressing tighter and tighter so the blade's held against him. He can't lift it to employ it again. I jab with my seax, aiming for the upper arm of the hand holding the sword. His byrnie doesn't extend down his arms. Again, I'm fascinated by men who fight in such a way. I stab and then stab again. A well of blood erupts. He grunts in pain, unable to move his sword to counter me, although he tries to batter me with his shield. I feel it hit my back once, twice, three times. For every blow he lands, I jab into his arm. Any moment now, he'll drop his weapon. He won't be able to hold it as I hack through the flesh of his upper arm.

'*Skiderick*,' he screams, going from a man able to contain his pain to one who fucking can't between blows. Blood streams from his arm. He drops his sword. It lands with a clang on the shield of one of the dead men. I'd not expected that. It must have rolled this way. Not that I look down. My eyes blaze into his. He spits at me. I don't move aside. I keep my gaze steady. His shield hits me despite his pain, knocking me closer and closer to him. I allow it. I can smell his fear and sweat. Fuck, I can smell what he drank that morning.

I lift my seax from his arm. The edge shimmers wetly in the sunlight, a gleam of his lifeblood. I think he's mine. I believe I'll kill him, but he shocks me.

He steps back. I redouble my grip on my shield and follow him, eyes alert to what he's doing. Is he trying to escape? Does he have someone else to fight this battle for him? Or is he just wounded and desperate to leave here with his life? I follow him, mindful of where I place my boots, not wanting to be rushed. His shield's held before him, his right-hand drips with blood, his arm's useless at his side. He won't be lifting anything with that, no matter the shimmer of his well-made byrnie. He has other weapons. I see him fumbling for a seax from his weapons belt, but his right hand can't grip the blade.

Close enough to smell him again, he jabs with his shield. I'm expecting it. I counter with my shield, fingers firm on my seax. Any moment now, I'll get the chance I need. I'm mindful of walking too far from my allies. We don't fight in a tight shield wall, yet we must all protect one another. I can't let him leave either.

I watch him, sensing him, licking my lips, waiting for the right moment.

His lifeless hand flops against his weapons' belt, tears or sweat dripping into his beard from beneath his helm. His eyes flash with fury and pain. He's a wounded animal, and wounded animals are as lethal as that bastard Hereman is lucky.

'Come on, arsehole,' I menace with my seax blade. There's no one behind him. Whoever was there, if anyone was there, faces one of my warriors, or has run away. I wouldn't be surprised if they've run. They thought they had the numbers, but this is a fucking blood bath.

'Who are you?' the man asks through white lips.

'I'm King Coelwulf of Mercia, the second of his name,' I offer, my voice soft and menacing. 'And I'll be your death.' Quickly, I run at him, seax high once more. At the last moment, as he moves his shield to protect his head, I thrust my weapon low, striking against his byrnie in a shower of sparks. I force it upwards, thrusting my seax beneath the arm holding his shield, piercing the unprotected part of his underarm despite the glimmer of iron and silver.

His eyes open even wider, but it's the slow grin on his lips that temporarily distracts me, and then a blow lands on my shoulder. I whirl, realising I'm too far from the rest of my warriors.

I've done what I said I wouldn't do. Now I'm the fucking arsehole.

'Coelwulf,' my name rings through the air, but five bastard enemies surround me.

'Well,' I huff through tight lips. 'This just got very fucking interesting.'

Chapter One

Kingsholm, the kingdom of Mercia, Summer AD875

'Bollocks,' I exclaim, riding Haden through the familiar gateway allowing entry to Kingsholm. The smell of smoke taints the air, but it's not as obnoxious as it was within Gloucester.

My eyes are everywhere, Haden twitching beneath me. He's not forgiven me for what happened to him. Fuck. I've not forgiven myself, either. I may never do so.

I was so bloody confident, so assured, so certain I'd done the right thing—but no more.

Frightened eyes look my way. I see Werburg. She stands with young Æthelred, who looks terrified. I look to the other children and the women who count me as their lord and king. I've failed them.

My aunt's beside me. We've come together. Jethson behaves himself beneath her legs. I'd question that, for the beast never did that for Edmund, but it would be churlish in the circumstances. I have much more with which to concern myself.

I hold myself rigid, my fellow warriors, with all of their bruises and cuts, following me inside. I don't wish to look at the people responsible for ensuring Kingsholm remains intact. I don't fucking want to, but I know I must.

'My lord king, Coelwulf.' It's Ealdorman Æthelwulf who inclines his head to me. It's his sister who's wed to King Alfred of Wessex. And it's Ealdorman Æthelwulf's warriors, more West Saxon than Mercian, who've secured Kingsholm for me. The horses might have ended up in the hands of our enemy, on their way to the Severn Estuary now in what ships remain to them, but my people were protected.

'Lord Æthelwulf. It's a surprise to see you here, and you have my sincere thanks for preventing my home from being ransacked by the enemy.' I'm astounded the words don't stick in my throat, even as I'm grateful that they don't. I'm even more astounded that they sound so sincere.

'You are my king,' he inclines his familiar head as I dismount and hand Haden's reins to Rudolf. Rudolf leads him and Dever to the stables. I'm surprised he doesn't wish to stay and watch this, but perhaps he's too exhausted. Or maybe he doesn't wish to witness my humiliation, for this feels like that.

Behind me, Bishop Wærferth's joined my aunt. He dismounts quickly. My aunt remains mounted. I'm unsure why. Perhaps I realise she needs some assistance. I look at her, noting her scowling face and furiously tight lips. I hold my hand towards her, but she doesn't take it. Her gaze remains fixed on Lord Æthelwulf.

It seems I'm not the only one unhappy to see him here, within Kingsholm.

'Why are you here?' I question, walking forward to grip his forearm in greeting. I stink of smoke and blood and probably other things as well. For a man who's been protecting Kingsholm, Lord Æthelwulf has not a single hair out of place. That annoys me. On the other hand, his warriors are more ragged where they catch their breath at his side. Someone's done some fighting. I don't believe it was Lord Æthelwulf.

'King Alfred bid me seek you out again. He'd like to hasten your meeting. It was agreed for Cricklade in three weeks' time. Alas, Wessex is once more beleaguered. The enemy are at Wareham.' His words are bland. I manage to show no culpability for that. I wanted the enemy to look elsewhere, other than Mercia. I admire him for dismissing the state I'm in, and for not asking me about what's befallen Gloucester and Kingsholm. Or do I? He's a man with only one thing on his mind.

'The jarls?' I ask, content to play his game. For now.

'We don't know their identity,' Lord Æthelwulf states. The men and women of Kingsholm are bleeding away, busy with their tasks. Bishop Wærferth has hurried to the church, no doubt to offer prayers for our victory, if it should be called as such. My aunt remains mounted. Unsurprisingly, Icel stays close as well. He's handed off his horse. I don't know who took the animal.

'Where would King Alfred like to meet now?' I manage to speak without contempt.

'Cricklade, but in a week's time. He requests you bring your warriors with you. He hopes that you'll ride to war with him against a combined threat.'

I open my mouth to immediately deny that, but somehow, Lord Æthelwulf has intervened here and fulfilled the task that should have been mine. He's protected Kingsholm. While that should be his bloody role, after all, he is an ealdorman of Mercia and not Wessex, I feel churlish denying King Alfred's wishes which Æthelwulf has brought to me. Perhaps, I realise, I'll have to make this journey. Maybe, I muse, there will be strength in working together. But it very much depends. I'll need to hear from Ealdorman Ælhun and determine if Northampton is secure. I've also half a mind to discover what's happening at Grantabridge.

I look at my aunt, who is still mounted, but she offers me nothing, which is bloody astonishing.

'Come, we'll talk more inside,' I indicate the way forward. Lord

Æthelwulf bows his head and walks behind me. I listen to hear what my aunt will do. It's not like her to leave me alone to make such decisions. But all I hear is her soft murmur and Icel's answering one.

I know what Icel will caution me to do. I want to do so, but I can't deny being in Lord Æthelwulf's debt on this occasion, as much as it rankles.

Werburg has already returned to the hall, encouraging the women there to resume their labours. She brings me a jug of cool water and a jug of ale for Lord Æthelwulf. I drink gleefully, savouring the flavour of the cool liquid. I want to throw water over my head as well, and remove these clothes which mark me as someone other than Mercia's king. I've been employing a rouse. But Lord Æthelwulf won't know of that. It's probably better that he never does.

'The enemy are gone?' Lord Æthelwulf questions.

'Yes, back to their ships. Alas, they retrieved Jarl Guthrum.' I don't miss Lord Æthelwulf's astounded look. I scramble for an explanation because he can never know why we allowed that to happen.

'We've not long arrived from Northampton. I intended to speak with Jarl Guthrum about his allies and ask him to dissuade them from further attacks.' Whether he believes me or not, I'm unsure. I don't think I care either way. I do not need to explain my actions to a man who's never within Mercia. His holdings in the ancient kingdom of the Gewisse could be entirely overwhelmed, and he and his sister couldn't do anything about it. Or so I console myself.

'A pity. He was a valuable hostage.'

'He was,' I concur, even though I don't think he was. He should have been, but with Jarl Halfdan kicked out of Northumbria, we'd merely replaced one arsehole of a Viking raider with another one.

'Did he truly accept baptism?' Lord Æthelwulf's intrigued.

'He did, yes, deciding on the baptismal name of Æthelstan.'

Silence falls as Lord Æthelwulf absorbs this.

'And did he adopt the faith willingly?' I consider this.

'It seems so. As we escorted away, he held up his hands as though to praise God.'

Lord Æthelwulf visibly shudders.

'Our enemy should be pagans,' he intones sanctimoniously. I shrug.

'It doesn't matter what they are. We still need to kill the bastards.'

'Perhaps,' Lord Æthelwulf murmurs. I can see he's trying not to annoy me. He's learned something, then.

'So, King Alfred wishes to meet me at Cricklade, and the Viking raiders are attacking Wessex?' I resume our conversation.

'Yes, at Wareham.'

I feel my forehead wrinkle. I'm not sure I know where Wareham is. I probably should. If Icel were here, he'd tell me more; I'm sure of that.

'Wareham's on the south coast,' Lord Æthelwulf offers, sensing my confusion.

'So, it's a coastal location, not a river one?'

'Yes,' he answers slowly.

'So, they might simply leave?'

'Well, they might, but they show no intentions of doing so. King Alfred's very concerned.'

'I imagine he is. Surely, he must have the warriors to counteract a single attack?' I leave unsaid that Mercia has managed to do so to the north, west and east, well, not quite to the west, but that's our secret and not for Lord Æthelwulf to know.

'Well, the Wessex forces...'

'Yes,' now I'm elongating the word as he tries to counter my argument.

'Lack the skill of the Mercian ones.' I laugh at his statement.

'I bloody doubt that. The Wessex warriors have been fighting all over the place? Haven't they?'

'They've suffered heavy losses.'

'And what, Mercia hasn't?'

'I don't think the king considers it a game of one-upmanship as to who's lost the most men.' Lord Æthelwulf offers a pained smile.

'Perhaps not, but surely King Alfred has his warriors and those of his ealdormen? Wessex is vast, perhaps not as huge as Mercia, but it has much good land and portable wealth. The population must be similar?' Again, Lord Æthelwulf hesitates with his reply.

'My lord king,' his reluctance is telling. 'Forgive me if I speak out of turn, but I'm aware you were not often at the court of King Burgred, Alfred's brother by marriage.' I try not to allow my lips to curl at the mention of bloody Burgred. What an arsehole he was. 'I believe,' Lord Æthelwulf continues, 'that you're unaware of the, let's say, 'special relationship' enjoyed between the two kingdoms.'

Now I'm aware of my aunt and Icel entering the hall. They watch me keenly. I see where Icel's fist clenches. He's pissed. That makes me feel better because I'm certainly pissed with where this discussion is going.

'Do tell,' I encourage, hoping Lord Æthelwulf doesn't sense my growing anger. Any moment now, if he's not careful, my seax will be in my hand or my first on his chin. And if not mine, then Icel's. I'd like to see that. Lord Æthelwulf is about my age. I think every man with as many winters as me to his name should face Icel's wrath. Only that way will they truly become a man.

'As you know, the marriage alliances were forged.'

'Yes, two of them.' I agree.

'And as you know, the king, and his brother aided King Burgred at Nottingham a few summers ago.'

'Yes.' Bloody hell, this is akin to getting Haden to show me his hoof when he's trodden on something that makes him limp.

'Well, King Burgred forged a treaty with Wessex, one of mutual support.'

I glance up, my aunt even closer now, listening carefully to the words being spoken.

'And now, regardless of who is king in Mercia, that agreement stands.'

I furrow my forehead, opening my mouth to speak, but my aunt's there before me.

'Lord Æthelwulf,' she inclines her head towards him respectfully. 'I think, perhaps, you were not often at King Burgred's court either. You're the one who's mistaken, or at least, your king is. The treaty between Mercia and Wessex wasn't one of mutual support. It was one of subordinate to master. King Burgred was the overlord of Kings Æthelred and his brother, Alfred. He ordered their assistance outside Nottingham. He agreed to the union of your sister with Alfred only as a means of dispensing some largesse on Wessex. Nothing else.'

I watch a multitude of conflicting expressions cover Lord Æthelwulf's face. His mouth opens and closes. His hands clench and relax. My aunt has placed an entirely new perspective on what he was told to say. I see that even now he knows the truth of her words. King Alfred is a bloody bastard.

'I'll meet with King Alfred, at Cricklade,' I confirm when the silence has become uncomfortable and I can't stand Æthelwulf's squirming any more, the only sounds to be heard those of the wounded being tended to and the occasional angry whinny from one of the horses. No doubt Rudolf's busy helping those that have been wounded.

'Very well, my lord king,' Lord Æthelwulf inclines his head respectfully, evidently deciding now isn't the time to contradict my aunt or the hulking menace of Icel. 'I'll inform my brother by marriage of this, and we'll meet you in Cricklade.'

'And tell him to bring as many warriors as he can spare from defending Wareham. I'd like to see how his men match up to mine. No agreement or assistance will be forthcoming unless I can see the strength of Wessex. But you may take my personal thanks for what you did here today. Mercia's grateful that *her* ealdorman could defend Kingsholm from the Viking raider menace. I hope none of your men have been wounded.' This I offer as an afterthought. It should have been the first thing I asked. Lord Æthelwulf's presence here is unwelcome and has unsettled me when all I wished to do was drink, get clean, and check on my men to assure myself no one has died because of the ruse we've orchestrated on the Viking raiders.

A glow suffuses Lord Æthelwulf's face. Despite everything, he's a prideful man. I can only imagine how insufferable his brother by marriage will prove to be when we meet in person.

I can hardly bloody wait.

Chapter Two

Not that Lord Æthelwulf and his warriors turn tail and leave immediately. I leave instructions for them to be fed and watered, the horses as well, and make my way through Kingsholm to survey the damage.

It's not as bad as I feared. I might have offered my thanks to Lord Æthelwulf and his men, but it seems much of their fighting took place outside the walls. But that means there are dead and wounded Mercians who need tending.

My aunt and Werburg move amongst those brought into Kingsholm, either for burial or to be aided. Content the horses' wounds are also being treated, I survey what a mess we've made of Gloucester and Kingsholm.

Walking, despite my exhaustion, around the outer walls of Kingsholm, I look to the river. Ship Commander Æthelred hails me from the river bank, a jaunty grin on his face. I can see he and his sons have ensured the Viking raiders couldn't make it further inland, as planned.

'Did they come this way?' I call to him, unable to tell either way.

The river's filled with ships, but not as far as I can see, with any wreckage.

'The ones who took your horses tried their luck here first. When they couldn't take the ships, they went for the horses.' I glower at that. Shipmen shouldn't have been able to overwhelm my Mercians, but then, the men were riding and leading unfamiliar horses.

'You have my thanks, as well as for your help at the attack point, the other side of Gloucester.'

'Is it a mess?' Commander Æthelred asks gleefully. I smile, the first time since the battle finished.

'It's a right bloody mess. We'll be picking bodies out of the water for days.'

'We might go and have a look,' he offers with a gleam in his eye. 'There'll be good sails and treasures, I would have thought. Unless, of course, you wish to retrieve them.' I shake my head, laughing.

'No, I've seen enough of the water for one day. You can venture south by all means. Be careful. It's not exactly blocked, but it'll take some skill to get through the wreckage.'

'The enemy managed, though?' he checks.

'They must have done, yes. They've not returned this way, and no one has reported another attack.'

'Then the ploy worked.'

'Mostly,' I admit. 'Alas, it was a Wessex force under Lord Æthelwulf that protected Kingsholm.'

'I saw it all,' he informs me confidently. 'They didn't do as much as you might think. Be careful how much you reward them. Kingsholm would have stood, no matter their input.' I grin ever wider and reach over to grip his forearm in thanks.

'You're a good man. You serve Mercia well.'

'Well, you're a good king. The best Mercia's had for many winters. I do what I can.'

Parting ways, I walk along the river despite my complaints that I've seen enough of it. I'm checking for any sign of the enemy. I need to be reassured that no one hides in the undergrowth. Eventually,

Hereman joins me. I notice his bleeding nose with a wince. He smirks.

'It didn't hurt,' he offers, and I wince again.

'It sounds like it should.'

'Where there's no sense,' he laughs, a tendril of blood trickling into his beard before he sobers. 'What did that bastard Lord Æthelwulf want?'

'We're going to Cricklade, to meet a king,' I murmur unhappily.

He growls. He's only the first of many who will complain about the necessity of what I've agreed to do. I don't like it either. And, in light of Ship Commander Æthelred's words, I question whether I should feel indebted to Lord Æthelwulf after all. He wasn't quick to assure me he'd done little to save Mercia. And he tried to pull that trick on me about the relationship between King Burgred and Alfred and his brother.

I need to be very wary of them. I might, admittedly, have enticed the Viking raiders to sail around his kingdom, and it might potentially be my fault that they're besieging Wareham, but in this game of words, King Alfred and his brother by marriage intend to play dirty, offering me half-truths. I'll have to take my aunt with me and Icel and Bishop Wærferth, and two of that number aren't going to be pleased.

Even the fact I'm irked with it all, won't make them go easy on me.

I rub my hand over my forehead, wincing as I knock some previously unknown bruise. I don't want to do this, I really fucking don't, and if I want to know what really happened in Mercia before I became king, I need to speak to someone other than my aunt and Icel. Bishop Wærferth, I hope, will offer me some truths—better ones than Lord Æthelwulf and, perhaps, more reasoned ones than my aunt and Icel.

* * *

I find Bishop Wærferth within Gloucester itself when I fail to find him within Kingsholm. I note that the Norse Christians are helping with the cleanup. I see young Knut. He glowers at me, and I nod in return. He's a feisty bastard. When he's older, I'll welcome him into my war band if he wishes to join. I really must find some youngsters to replace my lost men. I don't welcome the thought of it. New members always upset someone.

His grandmother also watches me. Her gaze is difficult to decipher.

'Bishop Wærferth,' he meets my appraising gaze and approaches me. His monks are busy tending to the wounded. The people of Gloucester eye me with something between respect and anger. I hope they appreciate the reason for all the subterfuge. The bishop's robes are smoke-stained, and he still wears a byrnie. I shake my head on seeing it, but he stands proudly. I shouldn't berate him for such bravery.

'My lord king. Is everything well within Kingsholm?'

'Yes, it is, and Lord Æthelwulf will return to Wessex soon.'

'That pleases me,' the bishop sighs. 'This went almost as we'd hoped.'

'It did, yes, but as so often happens, we now have a new problem.'

While Hereman escorts me, he moves aside to speak to a collection of young lads riffling through the collection of bodies awaiting burial.

'King Alfred wishes an alliance?'

'He does, but Lord Æthelwulf alludes to the agreement forged between King Burgred and his sister's husband. I would know the truth of it from someone who might be less biased.' I need not say who will be biased.

For a moment, he's still, and then grins. 'Your aunt will be proud of you for being alert to her feelings and those of Icel's and King Alfred's.'

'Perhaps. I'd welcome your assessment of it all. I fear I wasn't present at that time.'

'Well, we all know what you were doing,' Bishop Wærferth offers, but there's no rancour to his words which pleases me.

'As you know, the Viking raiders attacked the kingdom of the East Angles and made some inroads into Mercia. King Burgred had warriors at his command. He was convinced he'd drive them away again. This was long before the enemy took Repton and Torksey. Back then, Ivarr led the attacks. He was a bastard,' the bishop growls, surprising me and enjoying it as he smirks. 'The ealdormen of Mercia and King Burgred's warriors laboured to eject them from Mercia and were largely successful. But then young Alfred came to Mercia on his brother's behalf.'

'Was Burgred already married then?'

'Yes, the marriage occurred when Burgred had been king for only a short time. Wessex would say it was a marriage of equals, but it wasn't. It was a political match. She was, for much of the time, almost a hostage for the good behaviour of her brothers. Until, of course, she became more Mercian than West Saxon in her outlook.'

'And then what happened at Nottingham?'

'Little and nothing. The king decided to offer the enemy money to leave Mercia. They accepted it, and the West Saxons did little but march here and back to Wessex again. They came as a subordinate party. If they'd arrived more quickly, Burgred may well have overrun the invaders. He decided against it. It led to some bad blood between the two kingdoms. Burgred exacted a heavy tribute from them to counter his payment to the enemy.'

'So, my aunt and Icel are right to be angry with the West Saxons?'

'Perhaps, yes. I'm perplexed by the desire of Wessex to ally with Mercia. There was a time they were said to have more links with West Frankia, but West Frankia is also struggling under the onslaught of the same enemy we face.'

'I don't like it,' I murmur.

'There's little to like, my lord king. The West Saxons are inherently untrustworthy. We bishops must play lip service to them because of the archbishop's residence in Canterbury. Perhaps he should also be invited to this meeting?'

'I doubt a week would allow enough time for him to arrive.'

'Perhaps, but I imagine a day or two late will have little impact on the gathering. I don't see any agreement being reached quickly.'

I consider this. Perhaps it would be good to have a third party there, someone who looks to every Saxon kingdom as opposed to just Mercia.

'Shall I send a messenger, or will you?' I decide quickly.

'I will, my lord king. Cricklade, you say?'

'Yes, close to the crossing and the ford.'

'Then you'll be within the kingdom of Wessex?' he cautions.

'I suspect so,' I concede, not quite sure about that, but happy to accept it if Wærferth states as much. 'With my warriors and some of my ealdormen. I assume you'll join us?'

'Yes, I will.'

'Are you happy to leave Kyred in your absence to ensure no further attack here?'

'I'll see it done. And your aunt and Icel?'

Now, I pause, unsure about this aspect. 'I'll allow them to decide what they wish to do. I won't force them.'

'I meant more in terms of their conflict to anything you might want to agree with the West Saxons?'

'Ah, well there, I might have to exert myself over them, but I'll heed their warnings. For now, and aside from Lord Æthelwulf's actions to defend Kingsholm, which I've been assured were not as heroic as he portrayed, I look to the West Saxons as an enemy, just as much as the Viking raiders.'

'At least the enemy have left Mercia.'

'For now, although I'll wait to hear from Ealdorman Ælhun. Jarl Halfdan was still there when I left for Kingsholm. I hope he's left by now. Grantabridge must be denuded of men and women, and I can't imagine they've thought far enough ahead to plant crops to feed them this coming summer.'

'The Viking raiders are not known for being farmers,' Bishop Wærferth chuckles. 'And, of course, when King Burgred paid them to leave Mercia, they'd not have been able to eat the silver given to them.'

'Hum, perhaps it wasn't the best idea, or maybe it was. It certainly resolved the issue temporarily.'

'It also revealed that Mercia was wealthy and her king desperate not to fight. That, my lord king, is why King Burgred eventually lost his kingship.'

'A weak man?'

'A strong man, but one who misunderstood how to reveal it to his enemy. I assure you, King Coelwulf, that you can never be accused of that. You reveal your strength, and as bloody as your battles might be, you've never yet appeared weak, not even here, today, with Jarl Guthrum. I believe he'll do much good with his new faith and also much damage with it. But, at least, it'll be as we planned.'

I consider all the bishop shares with me. There's much to be wary about. All the same, I don't like this. Not at all.

Chapter Three

The following day, we begin our journey south. Gloucester's protected. The Viking raider ships haven't been seen since the fight, which forced them to leave. Jarl Guthrum has escaped as intended. The rest of this shit show is very far from what I envisioned.

'We ride south,' I advise my men. My aunt watches me pensively from her seat on Jethson. Why she won't ride her usual mount bedevils me. Jethson's a bloody handful. He always has been. Yet Hereman and Gardulf make no objections. Surprisingly, neither does Icel. That boils me, but I hold my tongue.

'Will we never be still?' I complain to Haden as I prepare to mount. Admittedly, my thoughts are counter to my usual intentions. I don't like to be still. I don't like to be in one place. All the same, there's a difference between choosing to be on the go all the time and being forced to do it.

Bishop Wærferth's with me, alongside some of his scribes, including the nun who seems to be responsible for much of the record-keeping required to run Mercia.

'She has the finest hand of anyone,' the bishop assured me

when I questioned him about it. 'No matter how much the others labour, they simply can't produce such high quality under time constraints. They're good for copying and writing letters. They're not good for recording the matters discussed in the witan. For that, I need her.' I'm sure my aunt would have much to say about why women are better under pressure than men. I'd probably agree with her. Men are too quick to snatch up blades and wreak bloody vengeance.

The weather's mild, and the sun's bright overhead. The summer's well underway; indeed, it's almost too late to name it summer, but I will anyway. I'd like to visit Northampton on my journey south, but it's somewhat out of the way. Instead, we'll follow the Fosse Way south. The journey should take two days at a gentle pace. We won't be haring anywhere with my aunt and the bishop in our entourage.

My aunt's insisted on bringing young Æthelred with her. Now, they talk as they ride. He's mounted on my aunt's gentle mare, the animal she should be riding. The animal is far too tall for him. I fear he'll fall, but my aunt doesn't share my concerns.

'He's good with her,' she informs me. I suspect I know where her thoughts have taken her. I suppress a grin of exasperation. My aunt's never one not to look to the future, even when we should be contending with the here and now.

Pybba keeps me company, only he can endure my long silences. I don't welcome this meeting with the Wessex king. He knows it. The others also appreciate it but want to talk and joke. I shouldn't blame them for enjoying the momentary tranquillity.

Later, a cry from those ahead assures me we've come to the location we'll be stopping overnight. I expect it to be a roadside campsite, and it is, but in the distance, I smell smoke and even hazard I can see a few dwellings.

'Why stop here and not there?' I question. My aunt doesn't respond. No one else seems to think anything of it which arouses my suspicions further.

When we've eaten, and the guard duties have been set, I turn towards the few lights from the settlement, biting my lip in consternation. I know exactly who I need.

'Come with me,' I mutter to Rudolf. He startles from where he's been nodding to sleep. I whisper to him, hoping he won't reveal my intentions.

For once, he holds back his hundreds of questions and merely disappears into the darkness surrounding the fires. I've been waiting for the daylight to bleach from the sky. It's taken a long time when I want to be exploring.

'What are we doing?' he whispers when we're far from the campsite, the glow just that in the distance.

'I want to know why we stopped there and not at this settlement.'

'Ah,' Rudolf says. I expect him to tell me more, but he shrugs his shoulders. 'I didn't even consider it,' he confides, surprising me. Together, we make our way along the roadway, carefully keeping a thin line of the paler stones in view as a guide. Without them, we'd probably find ourselves knee-deep in manure.

Cows and sheep graze in the nearby fields, their farts and snores filling the air, as well as the sound of hooves moving over the ground

'Why didn't you just order us onwards,' he queries when we've been walking for a long time and don't seem to be getting any closer.

'That was the designated campsite,' I counter. 'I didn't want to argue about it. I'm not a petulant man.'

'But you're a bloody nosy one,' he smirks, his teeth white in the darkness. I'd give him a smack for that, but finally, I see the dwellings up ahead. The settlement's small but evidently quite prosperous if the smell of the woodsmoke is anything to go by. It's not enclosed, but that's not unusual for such small places. Indeed, enclosures have only recently been erected in Worcester, while one is under construction in Hereford. The defences at Northampton are recent as well. Mercia's not needed imposing defensive structures before.

I expect to be hailed by someone on guard duty, but other than the shuffle of the few animals in the sheds, we see and hear no one.

'They don't fear an attack?' I question,

'Well, there are only two of us,' Rudolf hisses. I can tell he's long since grown tired of following me, but he won't leave me. After all, Mercia's king should be accompanied by many of her warriors, as the only one, Rudolf knows his duty.

In what little light there is, I look around me. There's one main roadway, and on either side are homes or workshops. I can smell animals as well as the smoke. I stop and squint. I'm amazed we've not spent the night here. There's even a bloody, great hall within which I could sleep instead of on the hard ground. Admittedly, I don't always enjoy being indoors, but all the same, my confusion grows.

And then I hear a voice I'm not expecting to hear. It's impossible to mistake Icel's dulcet tones coming from within the hall. I rotate towards Rudolf. He looks at me, the same confusion evident on his face.

'What the fuck?' I glower, striding towards the closed door. 'Why does Icel get to rest in comfort, when we don't?' Rudolf hurries to catch me. He doesn't urge me to stay away. I lift my hand and raise it to hammer on the firmly closed wooden doorway.

Unexpectedly, the door opens, emitting a line of warm yellow light, and I fall forward, the force of my intended blow unbalancing me.

'Why don't you come in, my lord king.' Icel's firm hands on my chest hold me upright. I gaze into his face, sensing not dismay but wary acceptance of my presence.

'Thank you, I will,' I counter, righting myself and pulling my cloak tight around my body in an effort to feel more in control. He steps aside and welcomes me and Rudolf inside.

It's a fine building. The rafters' overhead are blackened with smoke from the hearth fire, but the room itself is spotless. Even in the gloom of the fire and few candles, every surface gleams. It's been polished to within an inch of its life.

'My lord king, Coelwulf,' Icel inclines his head, beckoning for food and water to be brought for me. Three servants hasten to obey him. I feel the furrow on my forehead deepen as he indicates I should sit before the hearth. Rudolf is all wild-eyed and open-mouthed. I don't imagine I look much better.

'Well, my lord king, welcome to Budworth.' Still, I don't understand it.

'This is my home, or it would be. I spend my time with you at Kingsholm. My tenants manage the settlement in my absence.'

Now, my mouth drops in shock. I always suspected my warriors had homes and dwellings away from Kingsholm, but this is the first time I've ever seen one. It's a rich hall. There are shields and even tapestries hanging from the walls. It smells of age and also home. There's the faint scent of sawdust overriding everything. Perhaps all isn't as old as I suspected.

'Why?'

'This is my home. You would always be welcome, but we have other things to focus on at the moment,' Icel admits grudgingly. 'I thought a better time could be found to welcome you here.' I feel my eyes narrow at his explanation. It's not a terrible lie, but I sense it's not entirely true.

'This is your home?'

'It's been in my family for many decades.'

'Family?' I find myself squeaking. If there's one thing I never suspected, it was that Icel had a family. 'Are you married? Do you have children?'

'No, I don't. This was left to me many summers ago.' For a moment, sadness tinges his lips and eyes. Once more, I'm reminded there's much about Icel I don't bloody know.

'And so, you thought to spend the night here?' I counter, trying to recover myself. I feel uneasy. I appreciate this, which has long been Icel's secret, and he doesn't welcome me here. My eyes survey the shields and tapestries. They're thick with eagle images, the emblem of Mercia. I consider that.

'My uncle was lord of Budworth before me,' Icel continues. 'He died when I was younger than Rudolf.' Rudolf's mouth drops ever lower. He's not alone in being amazed. I can't imagine Icel ever having been young. He's always been a gruff, miserable bastard, able to kill with a look. Almost.

'I visit when I can,' Icel continues. The goblet of water in my hand wobbles, reminding me of its presence, as I place it back onto the table. I'm too astounded to drink.

'I,' I begin, but I don't know what else to say.

'It's a small place. We breed good sheep and cows, the occasional pleasing horse. There's wealth here, but not too much. It keeps me fed,' Icel offers with a small smile.

'There's no need to explain,' I manage, even though I really think there bloody is.

'Your brother knew of my home,' Icel continues, as though I've not spoken. 'Alas, I believe you never gave it much thought. Most of your warriors, including me, spend the majority of our time at Kingsholm.' I nod again. My warriors. I do pay them in more than just clothes, food and good horses. I know I could gift them land, but I also know they don't want it; I've tried it before. Icel, then, is altogether different.

'Why?' Rudolf begins.

'Why do I fight for the king when I could be here, tending to my home and not risking my life for Mercia?'

Rudolf nods. Icel's better at voicing our thoughts than we are.

'I have responsibilities to Mercia that exceed any desire to simply retire away to my little corner of it. I'd be a fraud if I refused to fight for what's mine and what belongs to my king.' The words sound correct, yet Icel's tone is also slightly bruised. Perhaps he does wish to be here? I wouldn't blame him. With what little I've seen, it's a good place. It's wealthy and far from any rivers upon which the Viking raiders might seek to attack.

I open my mouth to ask more questions, only for another disturbance.

'Ah, this will be your aunt, I imagine,' Icel intones, his eyes looking towards the door quickly opened by one of the servants.

'Have you seen...' the words begin, but my aunt's familiar voice stops abruptly as she sights me. 'You have then,' she answers, coming inside, her eyes fixed on Icel and not on me.

'He always was a nosy boy,' Icel comments as my aunt settles on another of the stalls available. She doesn't look at the shields or the tapestries. A suspicion forms that she's been here before.

'I see you've discovered Budworth,' my aunt offers, her light voice betraying the look in her eyes. 'Icel's home,' she continues.

'Yes, it's a fine hall,' I offer. 'I've not been able to see much outside.' From outside the walls, I can hear others traipsing down the street.

'I'll just tell them you're here,' Icel offers, standing once more. I eye my aunt as he goes to the door and steps outside. Her face shows resignation at what I've discovered. She offers no further explanation. I want to ask how she knows, but perhaps she's always known. She and Icel have been acquainted for many long years.

'Now, Coelwulf, I've sent the rest back to the others. I'm sure some of them will stand guard outside. You may sleep here, as it seems you don't crave the damp ground, but instead, solid walls to surround you.' I open my mouth to argue with that, but already, the servants are bringing in bundles of mattresses stuffed with fresh straw. Icel's comments broker no arguments, and before I know it, I'm lying close to the hearth, my boots abandoned to the side of me, my cloak as well, as I look up into the rafters, chasing tendrils of smoke towards the smoke hole.

I want to ask Icel about this place. I want to ask my aunt about it, too, but Icel has taken himself away once more, and my aunt's back is turned towards me. She doesn't want me to question her. I could ask Rudolf, but he's already snoring.

I squint into the gloom. I've always known Icel was a law unto himself. Now, he's become even more of one. Before we ride out, I'll inspect this settlement. I want to know more about it. It's evident Icel's not going to tell me anything. I'll have to draw my own conclusions.

* * *

I sleep poorly. I'm woken early by some disturbance. Aching, despite the straw mattress beneath me, I scamper upwards, well, I creak upright, force my feet into my boots and then swirl my cloak around me before escaping through the doorway. Outside, I catch sight of Leonath yawning wildly. He nods towards me, but doesn't demand to escort me.

The gentle glow of dawn illuminates my surroundings as I walk along the roadway, my eyes focused on the church ahead. If this place has long belonged to Icel's family, I expect to find many graves within the churchyard.

The church itself is half built of stone and half of wood. It's slightly smaller than the great hall, but still big enough to welcome everyone who lives within Budworth. I open the small wooden gate and step inside, taking in all I can see.

To the far side of the church, I see many graves, not all of them with markers, although a large proportion do have flowers on them. The people who are buried here are well remembered. I find that comforting. People visit the dead, just as I like to pay my respects to my brother in the churchyard at Kingsholm.

The grass is dewy underfoot, but I don't let it stop me. I walk around, seeking something, although I'm not sure what exactly. I see small stones, some with names and some without names, but instead with small carved emblems. I see nothing out of the ordinary though, not until I turn a corner to be greeted with a tomb made of some black rock. I gasp at the splendour of it. It's clear of weeds and grasses, and a fresh collection of bright blue flowers is nestled over it. I swallow against a sudden burst of sorrow.

This reminds me of my mother's grave at Kingsholm. There, I revered her, even when I was too drunk to care for myself. I never knew her. I've often wished I did. My aunt has long assured me my mother loved me, but I don't see how she could have done when I was the cause of her death.

I run my hands along the fine engravings, marvelling at their depth. This tomb was created to last and be a living testament to whoever lies beneath it. I suspect this is where Ice's mother is buried. It's funny that I've never considered he had a mother when he most certainly must have done.

I move aside, feeling as though I trespass here. This is Icel's home. I had no right to come here. I should not have pried, only, of course, he's there, watching me, his grey hair festooned with the brightening glow of the sun.

'Have you seen everything you need to see?' he demands gruffly. I wince at the fury in his voice.

'My apologies, Icel. I shouldn't have done this. I'm sorry.'

'No, you shouldn't,' he counters angrily, his eyes raking in all those buried or entombed here. 'When I'm gone, this place will no longer belong to my family, for I've no one to leave it to. In time, no one will remember us.' His anger's quickly given way to grief.

'But you can leave it to anyone you wish. It's yours to hold. You hold the landbook.'

He inclines his head, perhaps considering who that person might be.

'Perhaps, but I'd sooner not saddle someone with such an inheritance.' I open my mouth to argue and accuse him of contrariness, but Icel moves aside and strides to the gate.

'Come, my lord king. We have to get to Cricklade.' The suppressed fury in his voice brokers no argument, and not for the first time in my life, I feel like a small child, berated for meddling with his father's sword, cutting my fingers in the process.

I go where I'm instructed, hoping I've not lost Icel's trust by being a bloody nosy bastard.

Chapter Four

My aunt watches my return, alongside that of Rudolf and Icel with an icy gaze from atop Jethson. It appears everyone's waiting for me, even Haden stamps his front hoof in impatience.

'Bloody come on then,' I growl, anger at myself making me grumpy.

Icel doesn't look at me. I sense Rudolf's gaze and offer him a small smile of complicity. He nods, no doubt relieved to see I feel like a naughty child as well.

We move off. In the distance, I watch the settlement of Budworth grow larger until we skirt around it and then move ever south. I can see why I've never really noticed Icel's holding before. It's both close to the road and far enough away that it would always have appeared to be one of any small holdings throughout Mercia, all of which I've sworn to protect.

Pybba joins me. His expression is guarded. Perhaps, I realise, he knew about Budworth. Maybe I'm the only one who didn't. Once more, my single-mindedness might well have blinded me to the fucking obvious.

'My lord,' he begins. I growl. He smirks. I appraise him and really see him. My ally is old and broken, and yet, there's a keenness around him. I know he's going to want to talk about King Alfred.

'Pybba.'

'Alfred.'

'Yes?'

'Is... not the man you think he is, and yet, he is as well.' I shake my head, astounded by Pybba's ability to make something sound so complicated.

'So, he's not an arse, but he also is?' Pybba grins, revealing a row of yellowed teeth.

'I'm pleased you listened so carefully,' he offers. I smirk as well, then.

'Spit it out?'

'He says things in a laboured way. He's not a man of quick action. You'll be fed up by the time he finishes saying hello.'

I laugh now, Pybba joining in. I'm aware others look at us with surprise.

'I'm already looking forward to it.' I chuckle.

'He doesn't laugh, either,' Pybba adds with a martyred sigh.

'What does he do?'

'Fuck all, but he wraps it in a whole world of pain for you.'

'I already know I'm not going to like him.'

'Um, but you also might like him. He is charismatic. I don't understand it,' Pybba admits. 'He's an arse and a right royal arse at that, but also someone you probably would quite like if he wasn't the king of Wessex and you weren't the king of Mercia, and he didn't want your warriors to fight his battles for him.' I meet his keen gaze. I can see how conflicted he is about our trip to Wessex. He's a good man. I admire him afresh.

'And Icel, he might not like the West Saxons at all, but he isn't entirely blinded by his hatred. He knows stuff only you could ever dream of knowing. Don't dismiss his cautions out of hand.'

I survey Icel. He and Samson ride far to the front of the line of warriors. His back's rigid. He looks like a thundercloud. That's probably my fault, although it could be because of our meeting with Alfred and the West Saxons.

'Has Icel met Alfred before?'

'Not as far as I know. But Icel did 'enjoy' knowing his father, King Æthelwulf, as he became.'

This shouldn't surprise me, and yet it does. I try to recall what I know about King Æthelwulf.'

Pybba rolls his eyes at me. 'Four sons, a daughter, married Judith of Flanders, as did his son after his death.' Now I know to whom he refers. I find myself smiling, and also juddering.

'I wouldn't want to bed a woman I knew my father had had,' I offer, quelling the nausea in my belly.

'Aye, well, if you'd done that, you'd have bed your mother, so yes, I doubt you'd want to do that.' I grimace once more while Pybba chuckles softly. I can sense my aunt close by, listening to our conversation. I imagine she might have a few choice words for Pybba, but she holds her tongue.

My mother. Icel's mother. These women give their lives for their children and never get to see them grow to adulthood. I wish there were more that could be done. It's one battle I never want to fight. It's one battle I never want to inflict. And with that thought, I consider young Æthelred.

I've not had time to get to know my brother's son. I won't anytime soon either. I call to my aunt.

'Aunt.'

'Nephew.' I meet her eyes. They remain icy. I'm still in trouble. I shake my head.

'Æthelred?'

'Is a good boy.' The implication is that I'm not.

'You're happy he is my brother's son?'

'Well,' she hesitates. And I wait. I need to know her opinion. She knew my brother better than I did. Indeed, any of my warriors who served him did. 'Well, yes, I am convinced he is. He has some of his mannerisms and also looks very much like you. So, I'm content that he's your nephew, just as you're mine. Why?'

I shrug my shoulders. My mind's busy, but she doesn't need to know where my thoughts have gone.

'I'd like to get to know him better,' I waver. 'I'd welcome the opinion of others as to whether he's truly part of our family or not.'

'Then you should ask someone with less to gain from unexpectedly finding a great-nephew. I know you don't wish to wed. Æthelred could be the solution to all our problems.'

I harrumph in reply. He really could. But first, he needs to become a man, and at the moment, he's little more than a boy.

'Very well,' I acknowledge, unsure if she's following my thoughts or whether she's being less far-sighted. Her appraising glance tells me nothing.

We ride in comfortable silence for some time. I'm alert to the landscape of Mercia that surrounds us. Lush fields and fat animals catch my attention. As do the hearty welcomes called by the inhabitants of the farms and villages we pass through. I realise this is why I fight as I do. This is a scene I wish to see repeated all over Mercia. This is what I want for Mercia.

As the day ends, I find myself once more camping by the side of the road. This time, I don't wander off to explore the local villages. I don't know what else I might discover, and quite frankly, I don't want to know any more bloody things about my loyal warriors than I already do. After all, they don't ask to know everything about me. Not, I realise, that I have many secrets. Well. I don't think I do.

* * *

The following day, the River Thames quickly comes into view. But here, so far from London, it's not much of an impediment to our desire to cross it. Further east it would probably involve ships or getting wet feet, well, more than wet feet. There's a crossing here, and it's shallow enough for the horses to cross it without getting their legs wet. It wouldn't be possible later in the year. Not far from here, and I'll officially be inside Wessex. A shudder of unease runs down my spine.

'Be wary,' I instruct my warriors, trying not to stare at Icel but doing so all the same. His lips are curled, revealing his teeth, surprisingly complete for a man who's fought for so much of his life. I'm unnerved by how simple it's been to pass over the River Thames. I always thought it was more of a deterrent, but far from London, I'm mistaken. I might need to do something about that. I turn to the east, thinking of glimpsing that large settlement, but I can't. Not from here. Not even a trail of smoke rising into the air reveals its location, which I know is far to the east. The enemy, Viking raiders or Wessex, could find this place and exploit it. Then, the lush landscape I've just ridden through would be overwhelmed by them. Admittedly, the river's little more than a trickle. I consider how far east I need to go for it to swell and become navigable. I open my mouth to question Icel but then snap it shut once more. He's still not speaking to me.

Icel rides with his byrnie, enclosing his large frame. I look to my other men. They're not wearing byrnies, but they have donned grim expressions. I don't blame them. My teeth are gritted. If not for the fact my aunt, nephew, and Bishop Wærferth were with us, I might be tempted to ride north once more. I don't have time for bloody King Alfred. I don't think I ever bloody did.

'Come on, nephew,' my aunt instructs me. She and Jethson are ahead. I realise then that I'm purposefully holding Haden back. I don't want to reach Cricklade and King Alfred. I really bloody don't. I shouldn't have agreed to this. I sense Icel's scrutiny, and meet his gaze. He glowers at me, and only that makes me encourage Haden onwards. Icel doesn't want to be here, but he'll stand as my ally. The poor bastard. If he has to do it, then so can I.

Ahead, I see smoke from cook fires, and then the small settlement comes into view. I glance around but see no sign of King Alfred. Admittedly, we've arrived early. It's not taken us a week to get here. I only wish I could speak to him and then turn around and be gone from here. But no, I need to linger and wait for him to arrive, should he do so. Not, I realise, that there's any chance of him changing his mind. Unless, of course, the Viking raiders renew their attack on Wareham or any other part of Wessex. I wish they'd bloody hurry up and do so. I'd sooner be fighting than brooding.

King Alfred doesn't appear the next day either, or indeed the one after that. With my campsite erected, I spend time with my warriors.

'We need to train,' I advise them. We've just come from one fight, of which I still carry cuts and bruises, and soon, we might be in another one.

'Can't we rest?' Rudolf complains. I think to round on him, but Icel gets there first.

'No, we can't bloody rest. There'll never be any rest. Not until the enemy are all dead, and Mercia's safe.' I wince to hear the rawness of Icel's fury. It speaks to me of a man who's been at this game for too long. But I don't berate him for his anger. Instead, Pybba beckons Rudolf to him, and they begin to work together. I consider Icel, but I'm not minded to fight him today.

'Gardulf,' I order the younger man to face me. He smiles, standing with his shield and blunted blade before me. For a moment, I'm reminded of the loss of Edmund, but I hold myself together. Edmund was a mean fighter. Gardulf's shaping up to be the same. I'm sure we can learn things from one another.

'What do you think is your weakest point?' I ask. The young man shrugs but then gives the matter some serious thought.

'I struggle in the shield wall. I'm better at fighting outside one. I need to learn to trust my fellow warriors more.' I nod at this. It is a problem. And for someone like Gardulf, who's not been a true member of my war band for long, I can understand why he thinks it needs more work.

'The man to your right will help you with his weapon, and the man to your left with his shield.'

'I know that,' Gardulf confirms. 'But what if the shields fall, or the man to my right takes a wound.'

'There'll be others to replace him.'

'Hum,' Gardulf says, holding his shield before him, inspecting the weapon's rim, which shimmers in the daylight. 'But how do I know that?'

I grin. 'Because that's how my warriors fight.'

'But there might not be enough men to replace the fallen one.'

'Or there might be.'

'I want to be able to pivot regardless of what happens.'

'So, you wish to know how to fight alone and with your fellow warriors and also how to trust them even when you're in the thick of the battle?'

'I do, yes.'

'Then you need to have eyes everywhere. The focus should never be on what's happening in front of you.'

To somewhat prove the point, Pybba moves in towards Gardulf, a wry smirk on his lips, as he taps him with his shield. Gardulf understandably jumps, already turning to meet the unexpected blow.

'Not like that,' I advise him. He grimaces. 'You always need to be alert. No matter what. You could be taking a piss, and you'd need to be aware of your fellow warriors or even what the leaves are doing on the tree in the far distance.'

Gardulf's mouth drops open.

'Or you can be like your uncle, who gives no thought to anything but is a lucky enough bastard that it rarely matters.'

'Hereman does have his own particular way of fighting,' Gardulf admits.

Pybba's grin widens, while Rudolf stands with him. I realise Rudolf's panting heavily. What has Pybba done to him, for Pybba's barely broken a sweat?

'He does. Your father was the same. He didn't lack for skill, but luck was also often on his side.'

'And you, my lord,' Gardulf asks. 'Were you always so good at fighting?'

I shake my head immediately, only for Pybba and Icel to both chorus a 'yes.'

I look at them both. Pybba grins. Icel doesn't.

It falls to Pybba to speak, for Icel remains pissed with me.

'From a young age, Coelwulf was alert to everything around him. He could beat anyone and often did. His brother most of the time. And then, when he was older, although he forgets this, his brother's warriors.'

'I would say,' Icel offers, a gleam in his eye. 'That he once used to drink away this awareness.'

I consider his words. There was a time when they would have shocked me. I'm not so convinced they do. I know what I was. I have my regrets, and there are more than I'd like, but Icel has summarised my rebellion well.

'Perhaps,' I offer.

'Definitely,' Pybba interjects quickly. 'Your king, your lord, whatever you want to call him, has always been blessed and cursed with quickness, precision and skill. He can be no other way. He often fails to understand that not all men are made in such a way.'

Gardulf meets my eyes. Respect flashes on his face.

'There's a lesson to be learned there,' Pybba cautions. 'Men like the king are unusual. Most will have some weakness. It might be that they believe themselves to be too good at fighting. They're the ones to fear. Those who think they're weak may often prove themselves wrong. Those who think they're good will also prove themselves wrong, but first, they'll do their damnedest to make you suffer.'

'I shouldn't hope to be as good as my king then?'

'Oh yes, you should,' Icel growls. 'We should all want to be as good as him. Lacking his natural talent, we must work harder at it.'

'Is that what you do?' Gardulf questions Icel. Hereman has joined us. Some of the men sweat at their endeavours. Hereman seems to be about to go for a jaunty walk, although poor Gyrth is down on one knee, puffing through pink cheeks after their brief encounter.

'You ask the wrong man,' Pybba cautions. 'There are few who can fight like Coelwulf. One of them is Icel. A rare thing indeed.'

Gardulf opens and then closes his mouth, dropping the weight of his shield as he considers how to reply. I'd smile at his consternation, but Pybba and Icel are correct. I do struggle to understand how my fellow warriors can be so weak, so blind to the obvious, and so immune to their fellow warriors' needs. This leads me to impatience and makes me impetuous, the most recent being concerning Jarl Guthrum.

I look to Rudolf.

'What sort of warrior is King Alfred?'

Rudolf shrugs his narrow shoulders, his face pensive. I don't ask Pybba. Pybba has too much experience.

'My lord, I truly don't know. I didn't see him fight. I barely saw him do more than sit and stroke his bloody beard.' I smirk at the image presented to me. 'He's an arse, as I said. However, he does have the appearance of a warrior, although it might just be he has the best equipment.'

I appraise my other warriors. I know that Icel and Pybba were supposed to fight for Mercia alongside the West Saxon forces at Nottingham, led by Alfred, before he was king. But have they actually ever fought with Alfred?

'King Alfred knows one end of a sword from another, and which end is the pointier one on a spear,' Icel comments slowly. 'I wouldn't like to say whether he knows more than that.' And yet, for all Icel offers no opinion, his tone is easy enough to decipher. King Alfred, it seems, might look like a warrior, but whether he is one is very bloody doubtful.

Not for the first time, I consider how a man who's not a warrior can become a king. Alfred should have been taught to fight from a young age. I know I was, and I was so far from the ruling line, it should never have been an option for me to become king. If Alfred, as the fourth-born son of a ruling king, wasn't taught to fight, then what exactly did he spend his bloody childhood doing?

Alas, it seems, I am about to bloody find out.

Chapter Five

Reports of the arrival of the West Saxon king arrive long before he does.

'He's cutting it bastard fine,' Pybba complains from where he waits beside me. We were practising once more, two more days have passed, but my aunt pulls us away, saying we should make ourselves presentable. I'd sooner have a sweating forehead and a stinking tunic, but it appears that's not the way 'these things are done,' or so my aunt informs me in her martyred tone.

Of course, Pybba and Rudolf have met Alfred before. As has Ealdorman Ælhun. But for now, Ælhun remains in Northampton. I know Jarl Halfdan has left the immediate area, a messenger found me and informed me of that yesterday. I'm not entirely sure I trust Halfdan to fully bugger off though. After their last meeting, I hardly think Ealdorman Ælhun will regret not being here to witness me speaking to the West Saxon king.

'Stop fidgeting,' my aunt slaps my hand from where I try to find room for my arms in the too-tight tunic. I glower at her. She offers me a bright smile. She's contrary these days. Then again, she probably always was, I didn't feel the force of it.

Bishop Wærferth offers me a smile of solidarity. He too is wearing his best robe, while overhead, the sun beats down on us. It's too bloody hot, and I'm thirsty.

'Bastard hurry up,' I huff. Rudolf's bark of laughter brings a wry smile to my lips. It seems we're all thinking the same. I'm trying to strengthen myself for whatever will come of this meeting. I don't expect it to be pleasant. I consider Archbishop Wulfhere. He's returned to Northumbria gleefully when he learned Jarl Halfdan was no longer there. I don't wish him any ill. I'm just glad he's out of my bloody hair.

'Finally,' I sigh. We're waiting for the king's entourage before a great hall. Inside holds the promise of cold water and cool air. But I can't enjoy it until this little bit of pomp and ceremony is over and done with.

But, at last, a rider appears, in fact, a few of them. The one ahead carries a banner. I squint into the brightness of the day, but I can't tell what the banner depicts because the red, yellow and black banner hangs limply in the oppressive heat.

'A wyvern,' Rudolf offers me. He has keen eyes, but I think it's more that he's seen it before.

Behind the banner comes another man, this one holding something else. I glower and then look apologetically at Bishop Wærferth, but his face holds the same expression.

'A bloody cross,' I complain.

'Aye, my lord,' Rudolf confirms. 'A religious fanatic, or so they say.'

I hear Icel's growl. I don't look at him. This must be hard to tolerate. It is for me, and I only hate them. Icel detests the West Saxons.

While I cast a glance along the shimmering wood that holds a dazzling golden cross aloft, I'm really interested in seeing King Alfred. I consider what he'll look like. Will he be broad-chested with a full head of hair, or will he be weedy and bald? I smile to myself at the thought. I've been told he's younger than me. So, perhaps he won't have fallen foul of hair loss just yet. I almost run my hand through my hair, but I know it remains long and, thankfully, blond. I've even been forced to groom my beard and moustache, although I notice that Icel hasn't been prevailed upon in such a way.

His glowering face, grey beard, and long, grey hair, alongside his rippling muscles, make him a scary proposition. And that's to me. Despite annoying him the other day, I know he remains my firm ally and friend.

Behind the first two horses, come more and more animals. I shake my head. I thought Viking raiders beleaguered the Wessex kingdom. And yet there seem to be enough men here to protect her unless these men are for show and little else.

The bannerman stays close, but the rest move aside, allowing me to finally catch sight of King Alfred.

I eye him. He rides well enough, and the horse beneath him is a beautiful chestnut stallion, high-stepping and glittering with wealth on the reins and bridle. The animal is bright-eyed but obedient. It's also very tall. Perhaps not quite as tall as Haden, but not far off. I think of my foul-tempered beast and this placid animal before me, upon which sits a man of medium build with a shock of brown hair, complete with a neat beard and moustache. I'd sooner have my horse and his many little arguments.

Beside King Alfred is Ealdorman Æthelwulf. He inclines his head to me with what he must think is respect. Behind him are others on horses, the names of men I don't know, and also a cart driven by horses, where I catch several women's shimmering hair. It seems the king of Wessex has brought his entire family with him, including his wife. Admittedly, my aunt and my nephew are accompanying me. But they both serve a purpose.

I try not to glance at my aunt, but it isn't easy. I know she thinks little of Lady Ealhswith, Alfred's wife.

'My lord king,' I intone, a helpful elbow to the midriff from Rudolf reminding me that I have a part to play here other than a gormless bystander. 'And your family and warriors are welcome to Cricklade.' I don't miss the tight grimace on King Alfred's face. He looks around, no doubt counting my warriors and assessing my strength, before twisting and dismounting. He pulls riding gloves from his hands.

'Well met, Lord Coelwulf,' his voice surprises me. It's deeper than I expected. It also seems to carry well. I don't miss that he names me as 'lord' and not 'king.' My aunt doesn't either. I can tell just from the way she stands.

We shake hands, all the same.. His grip is firm and dry—a good grip. Closer now, I look at his face. It lacks all battle scars, not even the hint that his nose might have been bent in a fistfight. He offers a small smile, and I notice his straight teeth. I'm used to dealing with warriors missing half their teeth. I'm not sure what to make of the man before me. I've heard a great deal about King Alfred. It seems much of it is true. I confess I'm disappointed.

Alfred isn't a warrior. Far from it. I thought him a young man, well, younger than me. I suppose that doesn't necessarily make him young. How strange it is to see those who are younger than me seem aged. His eyes flash dull blue, and some wisps on his cheeks and above his lips attest that he can't grow a full beard. Lucky bastard.

But more than anything, his lack of muscles tells me the truth about who this man is. How, I think, has he fought the Viking raiders for all these years? Like Mercia, Wessex has faced the enemy for over a decade, and before that, the pestilent bastards were likely to crop up all over the place.

'King Alfred,' a smile tightens his lips. I lightly grasp his forearm, feeling less muscle than I'm used to encountering. I employ the title 'King Alfred' once more as though it might prompt him to offer me the same respect. It doesn't.

I tower over him, able to see his growing bald spot easily. My arms could crush him if he were my enemy. My beard is as light as the day, my long hair reaching beyond my shoulders, no hint of grey or even white to be seen. My skin is shaded in a permanent warm shade. I spend all of my time outdoors. It's almost impossible to get me beneath the shadow of a roof, apart from during the winter months, when there's no choice but to seek shelter from the extreme weather.

I'm dressed as a warrior, the only jewellery I condescend to wear is a symbol of my claim to Mercia, the two-headed eagle brooch, an ancient family heirloom. My true claim is the sword I carry, crowned with the self-same symbol. It marks me for who I am and what I stand for. I am Mercia.

While King Alfred doesn't wear his crown, he's a man of a civilised court. His tunic seems dipped in molten gold, his neck adorned with a golden cross, and he even has clean shoes! It's the final point that makes my eyebrows furrow. I can't remember the last time I had clean shoes. Hiltiberht has more important things to worry about than whether my boots are muddy. He must care for my mount, Haden, and see to his needs, which are many and varied and likely to change on a day-to-day basis. That horse is a monster of changeability.

I almost smirk at the thought of him kicking the stable doors, even as I left him this morning.

I consider what King Alfred sees when looking at me. I'm at least half a head taller than him, and my body is much bigger, rippling with muscles. He certainly doesn't have a warrior's physique, but some of the best bastards are the smaller, wiry ones. His eye is drawn to my neck. The red of the wound that nearly killed me has long since faded, and yet, I know it's there, and so do others.

'I thank you for your warm welcome to Cricklade,' King Alfred intones. 'Please, meet my wife and children. You know Ealdorman Æthelwulf.'

I incline my head politely as I turn to gaze at the Mercian woman wed to Alfred. I can see some of her brother in her fierce eyes. They share a long, slim face. She's somewhat small in stature, and I suspect the bulge of another child growing in her belly as she twists side-on and grips the hand of a young girl. The girl has a mischievous glint in her eyes as her gaze wanders over the Mercians. I consider where

Alfred's son is, but then another woman appears, carrying a squirming bundle in her arms.

'My lady, my lady, and my lord.' I'm pleased not all of my manners have deserted me, even if my aunt thinks I'm as coarse as a pumice stone. King Alfred beams with pride.

'I think you know my aunt, Lady Cyneswith,' I continue to make introductions to Lady Ealhswith, 'and of course, this is Bishop Wærferth from Worcester.' King Alfred pays no heed to my aunt, but the bishop does arrest his attention.

'Come,' my aunt takes control of the conversation. 'We'll seek shelter inside.' I hasten to follow where she directs Lady Ealhswith and her children, but my aunt hisses at me. 'Not you.'

I stop and rotate once more to Alfred and Ealdorman Æthelwulf.

'We've much to discuss.'

'We do, yes,' Alfred agrees, his voice once more carrying. 'But first, I would inspect your warriors.'

I scoff at that. His eyes widen with surprise.

'Why would you inspect my warriors?'

'To assess their strength,' King Alfred replies, as though it's self-evident.

Behind him, I realise the West Saxons are forming up in some grid pattern, no doubt to reveal their strength and skill. I've not advised my warriors we'll be doing anything like that today. I don't need to show off my men. Their skills speak for themselves in the wounds they carry.

'Ah,' King Alfred mutters, sensing my uncertainty. 'Then perhaps I'll introduce you to my warriors.' I catch sight of Icel's face, glowering and furious, and feel very similar. Only Rudolf, who's once more beside me, seems interested in the force the West Saxon king has at his command.

'Come on then,' I reluctantly agree, licking my lips and swallowing.

'Perhaps your men could prepare in your absence?' King Alfred suggests.

'No, it's too hot for them to stand around in byrnies and holdings shields. If you wish to see them, then tomorrow morning, at dawn, will be a good time when they're practising their skills against one another.' I can tell King Alfred's unhappy with that suggestion. Perhaps, I reason, he should have sent word of his pompous ambitions to amaze me with the force he has with him.

With my closest warriors in attendance, alongside Bishop Wærferth, who I suspect my aunt has instructed to stay with me and ensure I remain civil, we make our way beyond the piles of horse shit from the animals who journeyed here and onto a flattish piece of land. This area would flood in the winter if the River Thames burst its banks. Every step I take releases the smell of slightly stagnant water. I wrinkle my nose. The West Saxons must be finding it unbearable.

'This is Commander Blæcca. He's in command of my household warriors.' I incline my head at the tall man, marvelling that someone so slim can hold the weight of the byrnie, shield and weapons belt that wrap his body.

'My lord king,' his words roll with the West Saxon accent, even more than King Alfred's. He must be from a different part of the kingdom than Winchester. I notice that he names me as king and that Alfred's lips purse at the honorific.

Behind Commander Blæcca stretch several rows of warriors. I know Rudolf will be counting them, so don't bother to do so. If this is the king's strength, then despite my earlier thoughts, it does seem to be smaller than I anticipated. That said, the men have fine equipment. All have polished helms on their heads and shields against their legs.

I eye them, offering some a smile, but my overwhelming thought as I follow King Alfred as he names every one of the men and offers me a small detail about their lives is that these men aren't battle-hardened. Like their king, they lack the physical marks of having fought battles. Only one or two carry a scar, and they're the slightly older men. And that's another thing. These warriors are young, even

Commander Blæcca. No one here is as old as Icel, Pybba, or my more experienced warriors. There's no one here that I judge to be my age.

I smile and shake hands, but all the time, I'm considering their lack of experience, their youth and their fine equipment. None of it is battered or shows signs of being repaired. None of it seems to be aged and passed down from father to son. And, I notice that all of these men speak with the same roll to their words as Commander Blæcca and not that of King Alfred.

I can't imagine these men will be the ones to protect the men and women of Winchester, let alone Wessex as a whole.

I don't believe they have it in them to do so.

At the end of the inspection, King Alfred looks me in the eye.

'A fine collection of warriors,' he looks pleased with himself.

'Have they seen much fighting?' I question. People can look the part and be as much use as a hot knife through butter.

'Well, of course they have,' he stutters. I notice he makes no mention of where or when.

'Rudolf here began as my squire and is now a member of my war band. He recently fought at Gainsborough, Grantabridge, and Northampton, as well as in Gloucester. Pybba, here, you might notice lacks a hand, but he's been with me since I became ealdorman and also fought at Repton. A missing hand doesn't stop you, does it, Pybba?' I wink at the pair of them.

'No, my lord king,' Rudolf's bright with his reply. 'We know our task is to kill the bastards,' he announces. I swear King Alfred winces at the term.

'Well, of course,' King Alfred rumbles to a reply. 'I've not told you all these men have accomplished.'

'No, but you've told me of their families and where they live.' It's not truly a complaint, but as much as I care for my warriors, I know their pride comes from what they do to protect their families. They don't need me to know all the details of their lives.

'I have yes,' and now King Alfred looks conceited and pleased with himself. 'The oath sworn lord of these men should know that about them.' I want to argue that point, but my tongue's too dry.

'Come, we'll go inside. I'm parched,' I offer, noticing Ealdorman Æthelwulf's uneasy look. 'Tell your men to stand down and drink and eat before they fall down.' I can see a few of them swaying while sweat drips down their noses.

'I believe that's for me to decide,' King Alfred complains, grimacing as he does so, and giving no indication that he intends to follow my suggestion. The crash of one of the men falling forwards, brings a furrow to his brow.

'Then I suggest you make that decision,' I counter with annoyance. 'There's no enemy here, as far as I can see.' And with that, I direct my path towards the hall, my warriors and Bishop Wærferth accompanying me. I don't hear Alfred following on, but I'm not about to wait. I'll be on the ground with his warrior next if I do. It's too damn hot, and my tunic is too bloody tight.

Immediately, the roof takes the heat from my head, and I turn to Rudolf.

'No more than ninety-eight of them,' he says promptly. I look to Icel then, even as I summon a servant dressed in the colours of Mercia to bring me water, and quickly. I scan the room. My aunt sits with Lady Ealhswith. Her lips are pursed. She's enjoying this meeting as much as I bloody am. I take comfort from that.

'And those blades are fresh from the blacksmith and have never been tempered with blood,' Icel comments. His lips are as sour as my aunt's.

Quickly, I swallow a beaker of water, and then refill it myself. The water's cold and fresh on my tongue. I feel my tension start to ease away.

Pybba speaks next, his tone wry. 'Did you see that four of them held their shields the wrong way round.'

I hadn't done so.

'Nerves?' I question.

'Bloody incompetence,' he counters. We huddle close to the door.

I spin to see King Alfred lingering outside, his men continuing to stand to attention. The shimmer of their iron almost blinds me as I squint against the brightness.

'Is that the best they have to offer?' Bishop Wærferth surprises me with his dour comment. I would expect him to be more conciliatory.

'It seems that way,' I reply, and then affix some sort of welcome on my face as Alfred comes closer, only giving his warriors an order to stand down when he's almost beneath the roof of the building.

'Come, we'll join your wife and my aunt,' I offer, wincing at my tone. It's not as welcoming as it should be, but my shoulders are prickling with unease. If this is King Alfred's strength, then I'm entirely unsurprised that he seeks assistance outside his kingdom. But, if this is all he has to offer, then it's no surprise he falters. I've not brought every warrior of Mercia to Cricklade. Ealdorman Ælhun's in Northampton. Bishop Deorlaf and his men remain in Hereford, ensuring the border with the Welsh kingdom stays quiet. Even Ealdorman Aldred's in Gainsborough, keeping a watchful eye on events in Northumbria. Kyred is also at Gloucester.

But Alfred's offered me no sense of where more of his men might be, and he's only accompanied by Ealdorman Æthelwulf. Is that because he's a Mercian by birth? Or is there something else afoot?

My mind busy, I join my aunt, bending to offer her a kiss on her cheek, an uncommon occurrence, but one that lets me mutter to her. 'I don't like this.'

'I agree,' she responds, smiling around the words.

Lady Ealhswith sits with her son on her lap, her daughter busy with some small toys before her. King Alfred plants a kiss on the top of his wife's head and that of his daughter and son. I consider if he does it to match the way I greeted my aunt, and it isn't his usual way. Certainly, Lady Ealhswith's eyes open wide at the action.

Unease prickles along my shoulders. I really don't like this.

Chapter Six

Despite my physical advantages over King Alfred of Wessex, I confess to feeling uncomfortable.

While I respect and hate my Viking raider enemy, I feel I have the upper-hand when forced into tedious exchanges with them. I expected to feel the same here, but I'm not sure I do.

A long silence stretches between us. What happens now? I'm not entirely sure how to react to a man who not only wants to be my ally but is unarmed. I can't even see an eating dagger on his belt. This man is supremely confident, yet I believe he's weak.

King Alfred's face is strained, and I presume his courtly manner has deserted him. I never had any, so I feel better about that.

'Talk to me about your proposals,' I find the words from somewhere.

This seems to recall him to our purpose.

'Of course,' his deep voice, so at odds with his appearance, thrums. 'Sit with me,' he offers, turning to indicate the two chairs set out for our meeting. When the request was made that we bring our chairs to this meeting of kings, I found it ludicrous.

But given King Alfred's elaborate wooden chair, which is so

heavy I imagine an ox, not a horse, was forced to bring it to our meeting place, it's taken altogether more planning that I've put into my stool. It's the one I use when fighting Viking raiders and camping on some god-forsaken hill. And that's only when Hiltiberht remembers to pack it. I'd be just as happy with the ground beneath my bloody arse.

Here, King Alfred wins the game of diplomacy. Or perhaps he doesn't. We might be on neutral territory, with Cricklade poised between Mercia and Wessex, with the River Thames slightly to the north, but this smacks of desperation. King Alfred hopes to impress. But having a great big chair doesn't influence me. Not at all. Just as having warriors who gleam in their armour doesn't. If anything, that makes me doubly suspicious. I'd rather he carried the heads of those he'd killed or, at the least, brought his sword to this discussion.

Yet, as I settle on my stool, our heads now level, I appreciate the subtleties that Alfred is trying to employ.

He must know what I look like; my reputation speaks for itself. In place of that, he has nothing but a title, or rather a chair, with which to taunt me.

'Your reputation as the man the Viking raiders are scared of interests me,' he begins. I'm sure it bloody does. I wait for him to say more, but when he merely waits, hands resting in his lap, I realise he expects me to repay the compliment. I flounder. What can I say about him? He's survived more by fortune than skill, and I can hardly acclaim him for that. I've always thought derisively of it. Or perhaps he deserves my respect. There's little about him to win the trust of others, to make them pledge their lives to him—nothing, other than his birthright and tenacity. I wouldn't think it was enough, but evidently it is.

'Your reputation for survival interests me.' I have no idea if I'm saying the correct thing. His facial tells are far from reassuring. I hear a sigh from my aunt. She doesn't approve. I'd like to know what she'd have said. '*Your wife's a bitch. Your father was an arsehole.*'

'The Viking raiders are rarely terrified of anyone,' King Alfred states, ignoring my feeble efforts with a brief downturned twist of his lips. 'They believe they're the most fearless warriors ever to live. They don't expect to encounter anyone who can beat them, and certainly not here. They believe our island is ripe for the taking. And we have shown them that's not always the case.' He tries to sound firm and assertive, but it appears despairing, even with his deep voice.

'Individually, we've been effective, but we could be much more together.' King Alfred's eyes light up at the thought. I wish the idea of an alliance filled me with as much delight. I've been alone since King Burgred abandoned Mercia and I was declared its king.

'If we worked together, how would we reach decisions?' I'm used to deciding and having my warriors follow my commands without argument. I don't think King Alfred would do that. Neither do I believe his fresh-faced, gleaming warriors would agree to follow my instructions.

King Alfred seems to consider my question carefully, his eyes narrowing in concentration.

'When King Burgred ruled Mercia, we had an alliance of mutual support,' he speaks slowly.

'But how were decisions reached about what constituted mutual support and what situations required reciprocal support?' I decide to go along with him, for now. I'll argue about the nature of their alliance when it behoves me to do so.

'Mercia was under almost constant attack from the north and the east. Wessex did what it could for Mercia. Mercia never once came to the aid of Wessex.' King Alfred's tone has grown sharp, his blue eyes reflecting his anger, even though I'm not accusing him of anything, and indeed, I've been told something very different.

'Mercia is still under attack.' The fact I have to reiterate this surprises me.

'Mercia still stands,' King Alfred retorts hotly. I want to laugh. Why are we arguing about this? Does he think Mercia 'owes' him and Wessex something? What that might be, I don't know. If anything, he's stolen a Mercian woman for his wife and done bugger all to aid

Mercia during my kingship. He might even have conspired against it with the little lamented Bishop Smithwulf.

I sigh, running my hand through my hair. I didn't want to come here. I knew it would be a waste of time. I meet the eyes of Icel. He nods at me as though agreeing with my thoughts. I don't look to my aunt or Bishop Wærferth.

'Wessex still stands as well, and while I fight the Viking raiders, you seem to do little but beget children and make alliances with our enemy.' There, I've said it. It brings me no joy. I speak in a flat voice.

A murmur of conversation swells amongst those observing us. It might only be King Alfred and I who speak, but more witness our discussion.

Do we argue about our kingdoms' future, or is something else at stake?

I know war and battle, not politics. Violence has allowed me to hold onto Mercia. It's not the same for Alfred, as far as I can tell. If it is, it's through battles fought in his name, not by him. He's not stood and battled as I have. He's not bled as I have. He's not lost close friends and allies. He's not battled men and women hungering for his death. He's not worn the blood of others as his warrior-helm. He's not been hunted by three hundred Viking raider warriors intent only on his death, as I have.

'You and I are more alike than different. We've both been forced to use compromise when we didn't want to do so. What matters is people's lives and livelihoods. How that's accomplished is of less importance.' King Alfred flutters his hands, apparently dismissing my statement. That boils me. I can see Icel growing frustrated with this man who thinks of using words as weapons rather than weapons as words. I know what I'd bloody do.

'So, you propose an alliance of mutual support where the prize is maintaining what we currently hold?'

I feel I have to force the issue.

'An alliance of mutual support where the prize is the knowledge that others will fight for your kingdom if it's overrun.'

I don't believe this is worth my time or consideration. The Mercians support me. Always. They will take up arms to protect what belongs to them. They'll not do that for the kingdom of Wessex. I know that.

Still, I'm curious.

'And how would we announce such? How would the people of Mercia and Wessex know of this accord, and know not to take up arms against one another?'

'A symbol of our alliance should suffice.'

'What sort of symbol?'

And now King Alfred's eyes cloud. Already, I don't trust him and his ambitions. I'm sure that the next word out of his mouth will be London. What is it with the bloody Viking raiders and the kings of Wessex? They covert London above all else. I would much sooner have Gloucester, Tamworth or even Northampton, but all they want is London and the stinking river beside her.

'A coin.'

'A what?' Of all the things he could have said, I'd not have expected him to mutter those words.

'A coin,' and he places an object into my hand.

I almost don't want to look, to drag my eyes away from his, trying to determine the truth behind such a simple demand, but the weight of it forces me to eye the object placed there.

It is a coin. I'm not entirely sure what's so special about it.

'A mark of unity,' King Alfred states, pointing to the object's surface. Only then do I peer closer, and then even closer.

Ah, I understand now.

'It's been done before, and now it would be a mark of our alliance against a common enemy,' King Alfred urges. I'm aware that it has been done, and I'm also conscious that it doesn't need to be done again. Once was surely enough?

King Alfred has tried an alliance with Mercia by marrying a Mercian woman while his sister married the Mercian king, and now he's devised a new ploy.

'King Berhtwulf of Mercia and King Æthelwulf of Wessex, my father, together, on one coin.' Alfred's voice is very excited, but I confess his words fail to impress me. What use is a bloody coin against the Viking raiders? What good will such a trinket gift to me? Will it replenish my lost numbers? Will it drive the Viking raiders from my lands?

Will it make my people yearn to fight for Wessex? Will it make the Wessex warriors keen to fight to protect Mercia? I can't bloody see it.

What I do see causes a tight smile to touch my lips.

'Who will be first?' I ask, focusing my gaze back on King Alfred, enjoying the slip of his eager smile. He's like a child who thought to gain something by only mentioning half of what they wanted, hoping the other wouldn't appreciate what was being arranged. It's similar to giving away something you only desire a little to gain something you genuinely hunger.

King Berhtwulf wasn't my ancestor. He was one of the kings who should never have ruled Mercia. My aunt's dog carries his name. That tells me all I need to know about him. I hardly think it fitting to wish to emulate him.

'First?' King Alfred questions. 'It will merely represent us, side by side. Neither of us will be first. They would be struck and distributed from London.'

'But London is Mercian.'

'London is Mercian, but it is the centre of England's trade. Those from far and wide know of London's great wealth. Such coins will be used by traders from all over Frankia and the northern kingdoms. They'll spread the word that Mercia and Wessex are united. That Mercia and Wessex will defeat the Viking raiders. Together.'

I can't see that any of those events will occur. Why would traders speak of a simple coin? Coins are for buying and selling, not for proclaiming an alliance.

But my attention's caught by Bishop Wærferth. He's heard every word King Alfred has spoken. I can see he finds the proposition appealing, which surprises me. He was so against this meeting.

And really, what am I giving away?

This isn't an alliance that offers anything other than a promise. I know that such is far more potent than King Alfred truly understands. The hope of ridding the twin kingdoms of the Viking raiders will be beguiling and enticing. I can almost appreciate how King Alfred has stayed in control of his kingdom, even though his hands are softer than a child's. Has he ever killed a man? Does it even matter when he thinks such clear thoughts?

'I'll consider your suggestion.' I sit back on my stool as I speak, only then realising just how far forward King Alfred has been sitting and how eagerly those in his entourage listen to his words.

Alfred needs this token far more than I do. That much is evident.

I'd sooner he allied with me than with the Viking raiders. And, it would perhaps stop me from feeling some remorse for enticing the enemy to attack Wessex instead of Mercia. Other than the coin, King Alfred has spoken of little else.

'But what of warriors?' I remember the men outside and how they gleamed and shimmered beneath the sun. 'What numbers do you have?'

King Alfred's smile drains from his face. It seems he's happy to talk of bloody coins, but the specifics of how we'll support one another aren't as appealing.

'My warriors are at Wareham, holding back the Viking raiders.'

'All of them?' I almost squeak. 'I didn't realise there were so many enemies attacking Wessex.'

'Yes, all of them, apart from those outside. Those men are my personal guards or under the command of Ealdorman Æthelwulf.'

'How many do you have? How many of the enemy are there?' I'm thinking of the six ships that came to Gloucester. I know two of them were destroyed and the men killed. 'Is it Jarls Oscetel and Anwend?'

King Alfred looks perplexed by my question.

'They're the enemy in ships who come to kill my people. I've not spoken to them.'

'So, you've not seen them?' I notice how he evades my question about the strength of his force.

'I came here to meet with you.' He concedes. I look to his wife; her eyes are downcast. Does she hear the truth of her husband's cowardly response?

'You have ealdormen fighting on your behalf?'

'I do, yes. Fine men. They'll eject the enemy from Wareham soon.'

'And how many warriors do your ealdormen have?' I will get a bloody answer. All well and good, King Alfred, and his desire for a coin with both our faces on or something like that, but what about the number of swords and shields?

'Enough to counter the enemy.' His answer is belligerent.

'Which number how many?'

'Really, Lord Coelwulf, you seem determined to ask me about this, and I don't know. Enough. Too many. Not enough. We'll overwhelm them. You need not fear that.'

I consider my response to this. I'm not convinced he will overwhelm them, and it's starting to really bloody frustrate me that he insists on naming me lord, not king. How bizarre when I berate others for naming me as Mercia's king?

'At Gloucester there were six ships. Two of them were scuppered.' I like the use of that term. 'The ship men were killed. My warriors performed their duty for Mercia.'

'And yet, Jarl Guthrum escaped?'

'He did, yes. A most determined man. But as you know, he's been instructed by Bishop Wærferth in the Christian faith and accepted baptism.'

King Alfred's eyes alight on the bishop, a nod of regard directed his way.

'He'll quickly forget all that.' I open my mouth to argue, but Bishop Wærferth speaks first.

'He was fervent. He could see the errors of his ways. I'm hopeful that even now, amongst his heathen allies, he'll continue with his faith and spread the word of God.' I try not to glower at Bishop Wærferth's sanctimonious tone, mainly because King Alfred seeks to belittle him, and I don't like that. I can think what I like about Wærferth, but no one else is to do so. Certainly not a man who wears no weapons belt. I know Bishop Wærferth would fight for Mercia. I've had to prevent him from doing so, after all. I don't think I can say the same for King Alfred.

'We will see,' King Alfred comments, his lips downcast. I take a calming breath to prevent myself from saying something I might regret. Or would I? I don't think I like King Alfred. I fear I actually like my Viking raider enemy jarls more, well, apart from Jarl Halfdan, who I'd happily sever limb from limb if I ever had the chance.

'And, of course, there's the matter of a marriage union to discuss.' I feel my eyes widen at this. How can he go from talking of war to marriage without taking a breath?

'I'll not wed.' I counter quickly. 'A marriage union will not seal our alliance. Your daughter is far too young.' I try not to look at the small child as I speak. The thought of being tied to her makes me want to gag. She's little more than a mewling babe. Well, she's not, but she might as well be.

'No marriage union?' King Alfred counters with a gasp.

'No marriage union,' I reaffirm. 'Any alliance will be one of military might, perhaps with some fiscal arrangements. But not one of marriage.'

I see his face cloud at my firm tone. I also sense him looking to Lord Æthelwulf. Whatever he said to him, it was a downright lie.

'But you'll teach my engineers and builders how you construct walls and ditches to protect your settlements?'

'I'll ensure they know how to do it, but I understand it's not really that complex. Do you have walls? At Winchester?'

'They're old and tired. And the area around Winchester is vast. And I lack the men to protect a city of such size.'

'My lord king,' Icel stands as he speaks, inclining his head as he does so, terming me his king.. The respect astounds me. We've still not reconciled since my missteps at Budworth. 'If Wessex lacks the men to protect Winchester itself, then Wessex lacks the men to protect Wessex, and indeed, anywhere else.'

King Alfred's cheeks whiten at those words. But Icel hasn't finished.

'I was in Winchester many years ago. I know only too well the size of those walls and the shape of the settlement within.'

'I doubt that,' Lord Æthelwulf huffs. I find myself watching the two men, unable to take my eyes from their furious faces.

'You doubt what?' Icel barks. I sense my aunt watching me, perhaps hoping I'll interfere, but I don't want to do so. I want to see what happens.

'That you've been to Winchester. You're a Mercian.' Lord Æthelwulf snarls the words.

'I visited Winchester decades ago. Ask me about it if you don't believe me. I know more than you suspect.' He pauses then. 'I've also been to Canterbury and the Island of Sheppey, amongst other places. I'm no stranger to Wessex-held land.'

The words are spoken softly and filled with menace. Icel tells me more about his anger against Lord Æthelwulf than he does when I ask him direct questions.

'Alas, since your visit, Winchester's walls have been largely robbed,' King Alfred seeks to temper the blazing rage between the two men.

'Then you should bloody rob it back,' Icel announces decisively. I try not to smile. I look down at my scarred hands, holding them firm until I can trust my expression. I didn't think I'd enjoy this meeting, but I am.

'The stones have been used to build churches, from which we can sing praises to our Lord God.'

'And will he and his bloody angels come and fight for you, or will you expect others to do so?' Icel's words are sharper than a blade. I wish I could speak as boldly as he does.

King Alfred shoots a look my way. I sense he wants me to berate my warrior, but I'll do no such thing.

'I think the point is fair,' Bishop Wærferth hastens to mediate. Coming from him, this means a great deal. 'If Winchester can't be defended with its own walls and men, why should Mercia risk hers? If it's a simple matter of building walls and digging ditches, then you, my lord king, must do as King Coelwulf does. Spare the settlements from taxes and feeding the king's horses and servants while the defences are constructed. That seems a sensible course of action, doesn't it?'

Lord Æthelwulf's lips compress in a tight line. King Alfred opens his mouth to speak and then closes it again. His next words are far from unexpected.

'So, you won't share your expertise?' He's a petulant arse. I mean, I've always bloody suspected it, but to have it laid so bare before me is astounding. He's a king. A leader of warriors. He's a bloody father. If nothing else, he should want to protect his children. And his Mercian wife. I can't help thinking she'd have been safer had she remained within Mercia than wed Alfred of Wessex.

'We will, of course, but we'll not take men from Mercia to build walls for Wessex.' I concede when the silence between us has grown uncomfortable.

I gaze at King Alfred, curious to see how he'll respond to this. It's evident he didn't expect me to be so difficult to bend to his will. His arrogance astounds me, especially in light of his ineffectiveness. Why, I consider, would he expect me to drop everything and do as he bid?

King Alfred licks his lips and reaches for wine. He should drink water, not bloody wine, I think, but he drinks the red fluid, savouring it. I consider where it came from and just how expensive those mouthfuls might have been. He would do well to spend his coin on weapons for his warriors. And on bloody stone for his damn walls.

'It appears we've reached an impasse.' His tone is lighter than it should be. 'I suggest we take some time apart and reconvene tomorrow. We've travelled a long way today and would welcome some rest.'

I turn to my aunt, and she stands, and quickly summons servants to assist her in tending to the king of Wessex, his family and his brother by marriage. I stand and incline my head to Lady Ealhswith and King Alfred, if not to Ealdorman Æthelwulf. After all, he's my ealdorman. He should be bending the bloody knee to me.

Silence rings through the hall as Bishop Wærferth and I wait for the Wessex contingent to leave. I sense Icel's simmering fury and even Pybba's unease. Rudolf told me Alfred was a bloody arse. He was fucking right.

I sit when they're finally out of the hall, nursing a beaker of water in my hand, and twirling it around on the table, watching where droplets are pushed aside by the container. I don't know what to say. I know what I want to say, but I shouldn't bloody say it here. But, of course, there are men with me who have less compunction in holding their tongues.

'What a fucking bastard cunt,' Wulfstan glowers, and I grin, raising my eyebrows to meet his gaze.

'I couldn't have said it better myself.' I reply.

Chapter Seven

Not that I remain sitting for long.

'Come with me,' I beckon Icel and Pybba to join me. Bishop Wærferth has already made his excuses and taken himself off to pray. I imagine his prayers will be conflicted.

Outside, the daylight's just starting to bleed away. But it's light enough to see without the need for brands. I make my way to where King Alfred's warriors are camping.

Icel and Pybba are silent at my side. No doubt, we're all thinking the same thing.

King Alfred isn't what he seems. Or rather, he's exactly what I think he is, a king in the mould of King Burgred.

The men are busy tending to fires or making themselves comfortable for the coming night. I realise a few of them are on guard duty, but no one stops me from entering the encampment. They've no doubt been told I'm an ally already. That couldn't be further from the truth.

I dredge a smile onto my face as I amble down the rows of neat tents, the guide ropes shimmering brightly. These tents have never been used before. Or, if I'm being generous, they've been given new rope. But I suspect the former.

The canvases reek of pigs' fat. The linen has been greased recently as well to make it water-tight. Even the boots the men wear shimmer with freshness. Is there nothing here that isn't new?

I consider all I know of King Alfred. Once, he ruled beside his brother. But then his brother died, and Alfred became king in his place, the fourth of four brothers to be proclaimed as king of Wessex. The older brother, I know, had two small sons. I consider where they are now and where the brother's wife is, for I know she still lives. There are some rumours that King Alfred has done these children and his sister by marriage out of their inheritance. Looking at the warriors, this wouldn't surprise me. King Alfred has coin to spend on his men. I wonder how much he's paying them.

The year of his brother's death, he and Æthelred, his brother's name, engaged the Viking raiders on multiple occasions, and one of those battles led to the death of Æthelred. By the end of the year, weakened and lacking his brother's military reputation, Alfred bought off the Viking raiders using West Saxon silver. The next thing we knew, the bastard Viking raiders were making inroads into Mercia.

Since then, I'm unaware of any attacks by the Viking raiders besides this new attack at Wareham, for which I might be partly responsible.

'Where does the money come from?' I murmur to Icel.

'From wherever he can get it,' is his response. I spin to Pybba instead.

'Where does the money come from?' Pybba considers his response.

'When we met before, his court was rich and furnished with many tapestries and pieces of silver and gold. I assume, my lord, that he's calling on reserves of wealth left by his predecessors.'

'I thought he used his wealth to buy peace with the Viking raiders.' Icel interjects.

'It seems he didn't use all of it, then.' I mutter under my breath, unhappy with that answer. It doesn't sit right with me.

'What do you suspect?' Icel asks. We're at the end of a line of tents. It's not as long as I'd like it to be, and it's not of great depth. These few warriors are very well provided for, but with blades and equipment that have seen no use before today. I realise King Alfred has been planning this little show of strength for much longer than I've been prepared to countenance it.

'I don't know. Do you think he might be in league with the bastards?' I don't elaborate on which bastards I mean. That's obvious.

'They killed his brother?' Pybba reasons, although he's not outraged.

'And?'

'He says he's under attack at Wareham.'

'But we only have his word for that. What if he's not? What if this is another of the Grantabridge jarls attempts to get to me? Does a bounty remain on my head?'

'Of course, it does. I imagine it's even more valuable than it once was.'

'And so, why wouldn't King Alfred want to get involved in that?' I'm thinking back to Bishop Smithwulf being in league with Jarl Guthrum before his death inside Grantabridge. Certainly, Jarl Halfdan was also involved in that. They spoke of dividing Mercia between them. Icel believed it would happen. What if this is just another step towards doing so.'

'My lord,' Pybba breathes deeply. 'I don't know how to bloody reply to that.' I appreciate his honesty. Icel's already shaking his head. He doesn't believe my ideas are quite as ludicrous as I feared he would.

'King Alfred and his whole bastard family are fuckers,' Icel rumbles. He's watching everything before him carefully. 'But, his obsession with this coinage makes me believe he does have the wealth to make it a worthy endeavour. He must have silver to make these coins, or why else would he be so committed to the cause?'

'So, you believe he's wealthy and not that he's working with our enemy?'

'I didn't say that, my lord. I believe he is wealthy *and* capable of working with the enemy. What better way of paving the way for him to claim some of Mercia than to have his head on a coin next to yours?'

Now, I'm the one grumbling unhappily.

'You make a good point. It might be more than I suspect.'

'It might also be less,' Pybba interjects.

'I don't believe that, do you?'

'No, my lord, I bloody don't, and even Ealdorman Ælhun was unsettled by the way we were received earlier in the year.'

I hunch my shoulders and then drop them slowly, trying to reduce the sudden tension thrumming through my body. I'm not fucking good at politics. I'm bloody good at skewering the bastard Viking raiders. This task of trying to outthink King Alfred isn't an easy one for me. I need my aunt and Bishop Wærferth to ensure I don't take a misguided step. I also need Pybba's reasoned approach and Icel's fucking fury. If Edmund were here, he'd be fuming as well. I still think the best action would be to ally with the Welsh, but I won't do that because with Edmund gone, he can't argue against an action he would despise. I'll not sully his name by running roughshod over his feelings.

'What should I do?' I question forlornly, like a small child unsure which parent to run to for comfort.

'You need do nothing for now, my lord,' Pybba mollifies.

'You could send warriors to determine the truth of matters at Wareham.' I turn, surprised by Icel's suggestion.

'Have Mercians ride through Wessex?'

He shrugs his massive shoulders.

'It wouldn't be the first time,' he assures me. I find myself smiling once more.

'Icel, you're one fucking bastard,' I grin, enjoying the sensation.

'Not that you could come with us.' He confirms.

'What?'

'You couldn't be one of those who went to Wareham.'

'I don't see why fucking not,' I complain.

'Because you're the damn king of Mercia, and you must not travel any further from Mercia than these few steps here, at Cricklade.'

'But.'

'My lord, you're no child to stamp his foot when thwarted. You bloody know where you should be.'

I look away, my eyes affixing on the battle standard of Wessex, with the lifeless wyvern depicted on it. Even that piece of cloth looks new. It also shimmers. Has the bastard used golden thread on it?

'We will wait,' I eventually announce. 'And not just because you say I can't go to Wareham,' I state before Icel can further insult me.

'Then why?'

My eyes are busy before me. I don't immediately answer.

'Because, before we do that, I suggest a few men make friends with the West Saxon warriors. I'll provide ale and good food. I don't expect you to do it,' I direct towards Icel. 'And when they're drunk and relaxed, some questions can be directed to them. After that, we should know more about what King Alfred is planning.' Neither Pybba nor Icel immediately answer. I'd take that to be because they agree with me, but it might be the very opposite.

'Who?' Pybba asks.

'The young lads, Rudolf, Hemming, Hiltiberht, Gardulf, the ones who aren't quite as jaded as we are,' I decide. 'The ones who've seen some action and might like to brag a bit.' Pybba nods. I can detect he likes the suggestion. I don't look to Icel. He won't like it. Not that I think any less of him for that. I realise Icel's hatred of the West Saxons isn't without foundation. Indeed, I'm hardly enamoured with them, and King Alfred is the first of the bastards I've met. He won't be the last. If he proves to be like the Viking raiders, then I'm likely to hate them even more with familiarity.

I don't believe King Alfred is worthy of allying with Mercia and me.

No doubt, he wishes he could think the same about me.

* * *

When I return to the hall, Rudolf, Hemming, Hiltiberht, and Gardulf do not take my new instructions well.

'For fuck's sake, my lord,' Rudolf grumbles. I can see he's angry. I think he has every right to be. Being one of my youngest warriors is somewhat of a curse. Rudolf has had more than his fair share of difficult tasks to perform for me. From setting fire to Grantabridge to swimming the River Trent, oh, and swimming across the River Nene as well.

Hemming and Hiltiberht have less to complain about, and Gardulf probably has slightly less.

'Will you do it?' I repeat. I won't order them, although I'd like to do so.

'Yes, we'll bloody do it,' Rudolf answers in a martyred tone, running his eyes over his fellow warriors to ensure they agree.

Pybba and Icel appear, both carrying jugs of ale and beakers. Well, Pybba carries one jug, and the beakers are trapped between his handless arm and his body. Rudolf hastens to take them from him with a grimace on his face. Hemming relieves Icel of his load. I realise how young they are in the flickering firelight within the great hall. For a moment, I reconsider, but all they need to do is drink. I've risked their lives often enough in a shield wall. How dangerous can it be in an encampment that should be friendly?

'Come on,' Gardulf huffs softly, reaching to take a jug of water from my table. I frown at him, and he raises an eyebrow at me. It seems I'm not the only one who avoids ale. Perhaps that shouldn't surprise me.

'What do you want us to find out?'

'Everything.' I inform them.

'Specifics.'

'We need to know about Wareham and who King Alfred's been talking to, other than us.'

'And when we know?'

'Come and find me.' This seems obvious.

'So, you want me to wake you?'

'If it takes you that long, then yes, wake me.'

The four lads, I can't really think of them being more than that, move off and I watch them, noticing that Icel shadows them.

I'd call him back. But what's the point? He'll only find another means to evade me.

'Don't give them away,' I urge him, then settle at the table again. It's getting late. From outside, I can hear the shouts of men and women bringing their daily tasks to an end. The guard changes, and hungry men troop into the hall to be fed. They eye me or try to avoid my scrutiny. I'm not truly looking at any of them.

My aunt joins me, Bishop Wærferth trailing behind her.

Pybba is also sitting with me. The rest of my men have either been sent to get pissed or are sleeping or on watch duty. None of us feel comfortable with the West Saxons here, but they're all taken themselves into their campsites, not even King Alfred deciding to sleep in the rooms prepared for him. I'd be angered by that, but I'm grateful he's not here.

'What are you thinking, nephew?' My aunt questions me. Beside her sits Berhtwulf, her remaining hound. The animal is slower than he used to be. He's not the only thing to feel the years pressing down on him or to miss his friend. I keep meaning to find her a replacement for Wiglaf, but I confess, I do fear she'll name the dog after me, and I don't want to endure that humiliation. Or perhaps she won't. Or maybe she will, in a fit of spite. I still need to speak to her about riding Jethson and using Edmund's weapons. I fear she'll think of using them with the skill he once possessed.

'I'm thinking that I don't trust any of this. I've sent the young lads to get drunk with their counterparts in the West Saxon encampment. Of course, Icel's keeping an eye on them.'

'And what do you want them to tell you?' Here I pause, feeling Pybba's gaze on me.

'I want to know if there's truth to this attack on Wareham and, more importantly, where King Alfred gets all his money from.'

'Wessex is wealthy,' my aunt says slowly. 'As wealthy as Mercia.'

'It might well be, but Mercia has suffered. I know the taxes have fallen, because you tell me as much. And for this coinage, he's so desperate to produce, he must have silver.'

'And you think the enemy is paying him off?' I bite my lip now. My aunt, as ever, has divined my thoughts quickly. I consider whether it's because she's thinking the same.

Bishop Wærferth speaks next.

'He might have silver to make the coins, or like in Mercia, he might just be determined to have them melted down and recast.' I shake my head at that.

'I don't believe any king in his right mind would welcome a coinage with another man's head on it. Not within his own kingdom. I doubt his intentions. I suspect he means the coinage to make it easier for him to take part of Mercia, just as Bishop Smithwulf suggested to the Grantabridge jarls.'

Bishop Wærferth doesn't immediately deny my suggestion. I'd sooner he had. That means he and my aunt don't believe my worries are far-fetched.

'King Alfred himself is no warrior king.' I say that as though it explains everything else.

No one offers an opinion, and this also worries me.

'Bollocks,' I exclaim. 'We shouldn't have come here.'

'You came to acknowledge your thanks for Ealdorman Æthelwulf's actions at Kingsholm.' Bishop Wærferth speaks.

'Yes, but the more I hear about it, the more I suspect them. And

Ealdorman Æthelwulf is a bloody Mercian. He should be defending his bloody kingdom and not his sister's adopted home.'

Mention of Lady Ealhswith has my aunt pursing her lips. How I'd dearly love to know more about their relationship before Ealhswith's union with Alfred. And if not hers, then that of my aunt with the woman's mother and father. I'm convinced there's a good reason for my aunt's dislike of the family.

'I'll see what Rudolf can find out for me,' I huff unhappily, running my hand through my long hair and beard. 'And if he doesn't find out anything, I fear Icel will be haring off to Wareham.'

'And you'll not go with him,' my aunt's words are sharp. I glower at her. Her ability to make me feel like a small child in trouble for dirtying his boots astounds me.

'I'll not go with him,' I parrot, noticing a grin on Bishop Wærferth's face, even as he looks down at his hands to mask it.

'The archbishop will arrive soon,' he eventually manages to say. 'He'll have his own thoughts on this alliance, as it were.'

'Not that it has anything to do with him.'

'Not that it has anything to do with him other than a desire to keep the religious establishment within our island free from attack.'

'Well, yes, there is bloody that,' I admit, taking great delight in saying 'bloody' before my aunt. If she's going to chastise me like a child, then I'll bloody well act like one. I catch a glower on Pybba's face, and I'm reminded of Icel's complaint against me. I am being petulant. Once more, I breathe deeply and try to expel the increasing tension from my shoulders. Give me some fucking bastard Viking raiders to kill and not this bloody bollocks with King Alfred and the sodding archbishop.

'Then you have a plan of action,' my aunt confirms, standing, which I mirror. 'Good night, nephew,' she offers but comes closer, extending her neck so that I kiss her cheek. 'Behave yourself this night,' she cautions me with a knowing look before sweeping away. I watch her go. I'm convinced that beneath her dress she wears

Edmund's weapon belt. I'm sure I heard the clink of metal. I really do need to speak to Hereman and Gardulf about it.

Bishop Wærferth also rises. 'Goodnight, my lord king,' he offers, taking his leave without a backward glance.

That leaves me with Pybba. He takes one look at me, shakes his head ruefully, and doesn't reclaim his seat.

'Bloody come on then. We'll find Icel and find out what the fuck the Wessex bastards are up to now.'

Chapter Eight

It's cooler outside, and the day's heat is thankfully bleeding away. Overhead, the sky is clear, a gibbous moon offering some light with which see.

Pybba's silent at my side. My hand reaches for my seax. I don't normally need to check my weapons. Tonight, with unease rippling down my back, I require the reassurance.

Those on guard duty at the doorway to the hall, note me. I offer a smile for Wulfstan and Osbert. They don't have the most enviable task.

'Remember to step fucking quietly,' Wulfstan mutters. I glower at his bright eyes and veer aside. Do my warriors know me well enough to determine my thoughts before I do? It seems they bloody do. Perhaps I should be grateful, I admit grudgingly.

Through the next guard post, where Goda and Sæbald perform a similar task, Sæbald points off to the right. I direct my steps that way. It appears he's been watching Icel.

Within a few steps, darkness covers us, as does a helpful ridge in the land, blocking the sightline from the West Saxon encampment. It's not the best place to erect a military camp. My feet crush sweet grasses, releasing a pleasant smell, but above it all, the stink of men and horses can be detected. Pybba's a silent companion, walking far more quietly than I can manage. The sound of the West Saxons laughing and joking, luckily, covers the noise of my passage, and then we find Icel.

He doesn't even turn to look at me. He can decipher my bloody steps as well.

'Nothing yet,' he growls softly. I can hear Rudolf and Gardulf laughing. I'm not sure the other two will enjoy it quite as much. But then, they're younger than Rudolf and Gardulf. They might not delight in associating with the perceived enemy.

I listen. Gardulf hasn't smiled much since his father died, but now he's chuckling violently. It's a relief to hear him so joyful, even if it's also somewhat forced. The rolling voice of a West Saxon is engaged in some tale of brave daring do. I listen and then look to Icel. He shakes his head, white teeth visible to show the movement.

'Bloody hell, they can sprout some arse and bollocks,' he murmurs. 'No one can bloody do that. Not even the great King Coelwulf. They're all at it. Most of them, I suspect, don't know their arse from their elbow.' This is hardly filling me with confidence. I consider my warriors of Mercia, the men of my war band and the greater Mercian force. Do they speak such bollocks when oiled with good ale and mead? I don't think so, but perhaps we do. No, I don't, I decide. Nothing I say is ever bollocks. I smile at my refusal to accept anything other than that.

'Ah, now we might have it,' Icel mumbles. In the darkness, a question that could bring us some answers is finally asked.

'We fought Jarl Guthrum at Gloucester. What do you know of him?' I'm impressed Rudolf's managed to bring the conversation to this. 'I think he's a devious bastard.'

'Which one's he?' a West Saxon questions.

'Arsehole, with owl tattoos and helm. Thinks he's in charge of all this.'

'Don't know him,' the same voice replies. 'The bastard with the snake tattoo on his face, I've seen him in the flesh.'

'Oscetel,' Gardulf answers confidently. 'What an ugly thing that tattoo is. I wouldn't want to be marked with that piece of shit.' Gardulf chuckles darkly and hiccups violently.

The other voice laughs too vigorously. 'I've been told it looks like it's erupting from his mouth.'

'I thought you'd seen him?' Gardulf queries.

'Oh, I have, yes, certainly, but not close enough to see all the details of his tattoo. I'm not the bloody king to sit and dine with the bastard.'

I wince to hear that. I'm impressed Rudolf has the wherewithal to speak quickly, so the warrior doesn't realise his mistake in admitting that so openly to the Mercians.

'Aye, well, I can tell you it looks like shit.' He chuckles darkly. 'Really shit. Here, have some more ale.' I glance to Icel. His triumphant glance is visible in the moonlight.

'Fucking hell,' I explode as softly as I can, rage flooding through me. It is as we suspected.

Some might think it just a turn of phrase, but this rings with too much conviction. Not only does King Alfred have about as much military might as a swarm of butterflies, he's been in contact with the enemy. The only thing we need to discover now is when that took place. But I suspect Rudolf and Gardulf won't be able to find out the details. Indeed, I'm unsure how we can.

My mind buzzing with the revelation that's far from unexpected, I stand and listen until my knees start to ache and I yawn uncontrollably.

'Go to bloody sleep,' Icel orders me. He's alert. How he can stay awake for such a long amount of time is beyond me, but I decide sooner he's knackered tomorrow than me.

With a final glance towards the smouldering fires and with the chuckles of Gardulf and Rudolf ringing in my ears, I slip back inside the complex, greeting my warriors quickly, but thinking only of what I've heard.

So, the Viking raiders are at Wareham, or so King Alfred says, but at some point, he's met the snake-daubed Jarl Oscetel before seeking me out. I consider what other Viking raiders Alfred's met before. Certainly, he forged a peace with them after his brother's death. Was that just the first of many such alliances with the enemy?

I think I'll worry about the matter throughout the night, but fuck it; sleep is more important. Banishing my thoughts of the oily King Alfred from my mind, I turn over and settle to sleep.

* * *

On waking, I remember all I learned the night before, and immediately determine to find Icel to discover what else he discovered, but instead, I come upon the four youngsters, sitting at board and trying not to inhale the rich aroma of a meal cooking.

I smirk at them. Rudolf winces. Gardulf doesn't even lift his head.

I look to Pybba. He's enjoying this as well, a huge grin splitting his face.

Carefully, ensuring I scrape the stool as loudly as possible over the wooden floorboards, I sit and wiggle my arse until I'm comfortable, eliciting some more shrieks and screams of outrage from the pieces of wood meeting.

Pybba does the same, his eyebrows rising high.

Rudolf glowers, his eyes red-rimmed, his tunic askew. He looks at me with loathing and then twists to Pybba with a complaint on his lips. Only he winces once more at just opening his mouth to speak.

I sense movement in the hall and see my aunt coming to join us. She brings a jug with her, and two servants trail her. I imagine she's already seen our young friends and thinks to aid their aching heads.

'Morning,' I bellow as loudly as possible. My aunt shakes her head, a smile on her lips. I even see my guards, Beornstan and

Ingwald, chuckling at my antics. I'm pleased to see Beornstan enjoying himself. It's taken him a few months to recover from being held captive by the enemy within Grantabridge. It's taken his face almost as long to lose the slow-to-fade bruises.

Gardulf lifts his head, eyes even more red-rimmed than Rudolf's, his face ashen. He looks like he's been sick recently. He smells like it, too, and here I thought he only drank water.

Hemming and Hiltiberht merely wince. I see then that all four of them have buckets at their feet, ready for when they vomit whatever ale and mead they threw down their throats last night. They'll certainly suffer for my orders. It delights me. One day, they might even thank me for sore head instead of a weeping wound.

'My lord,' Rudolf mutters. 'I'd sooner fight the bastard enemy, than drink that much again, in order to protect Mercia.'

I chuckle. The others join me. Even my aunt, although she gives me a sharp look. I consider if she approves of my tactics to discover all there is to know about King Alfred and his alleged warriors.

She's busy handing foul-smelling concoctions to the lads. I gag on seeing the raw eggs floating on the surface of whatever it is she's giving them. In my mind, I remember all the bastard bad heads I've ever suffered. Too stubborn to seek aid, I've forced myself through some torturous days after nights, drowning my sorrows. I'm unsure whether my aunt would have ever been as helpful to me as she's been to the lads.

'I hope it was worth it,' she hisses wrinkling her nose at the foul miasma the four are extruding. It really does stink like a tavern in the great hall.

'It was,' Icel announces even more loudly than I spoke before. It's my turn to shake my head at the sight of him. He looks fresh and relaxed and not as though he's spent half the night listening to other conversations while hiding. Even his bloody tunic is freshly washed. He shimmers with good health. Rudolf's downcast face makes me laugh once more. I can't deny it pleases me to see others suffer in such a way. I remember only too well how it felt to have a sword striking a shield resounding in my head, and the sour taste of a dog's bollocks in my mouth after a night of heavy ale-drinking.

Icel screeches back a stool. With a smirk on his lined faced, he seats himself beside Rudolf, offering him a smack around the head at the same time. Rudolf glowers and half-heartedly balls his fist, even as he swallows to hold his nausea down.

'Now, now, play nice,' Icel intones. The sound's so booming that I wince, and from close by, I hear the hens squawk in shock. 'Down your drinks, and I'll train that ale out of your body. What you need is to work up a good sweat.'

'Urgh,' shudders Hemming. Hiltiberht's eyes plead with me. I shake my head. I won't make them do it. Well, I probably won't make them do it.

'Spill it,' Pybba suggests.

Rudolf gazes from me to Icel to Pybba and swallows again. 'I don't know. I don't remember anything.' Now, even my aunt is laughing as she places food before the four lads. It's a delightful mixture of eggs and sausages, but Hiltiberht looks fit to vomit at it and, indeed, dashes from the room while we older men, who obviously have never fucking vomited up the contents of our bellies after a good night of imbibing, laugh at his faltering steps. He just makes it out of the doorway, but not without crashing into it first. The sound of his retching and the way Hemming holds his hand over his mouth only make us laugh even more.

'Well, one of them let slip that he's seen Jarl Oscetel, but not close enough to view his snake tattoo because, and I repeat his words, 'he wasn't sat having dinner with him,' so clearly King Alfred has done that.'

'I fucking heard that,' I glower, my humour leaving me in the wake of the memory.

'Later, they also made mention of what's happening at Wareham.'

'Which is what?'

Icel winces at my sharp tone.

'A shit show. The Wessex king and his ealdorman were caught sleeping, so Jarls Anwend and Oscetel took the settlement when they were supposed to rescue Jarl Guthrum from Gloucester. They thought a little deviation from the plan would refill their coffers after what happened at Grantabridge. Even now, while King Alfred is here, the enemy's trying to break through the West Saxon forces led by ealdormen Cuthred and Bucca.'

'And what of the other ealdormen?'

'They've been slow to react. They're more concerned with protecting their own holdings than helping the king. There are rumours the king will forge another peace with the Viking raiders, regardless of whether you make an alliance with him.'

'So what's the purpose of this summons, then?'

Icel winces. 'I have my suspicions,' he suggests. I sense I'm not the only one glowering at him.

'And they are?' It's like forcing Haden to lift his hoof when its sore.

'If I know my Viking raiders, it was to ensure the recovery of Jarl Guthrum while you were otherwise engaged.'

'Bollocks,' I explode, standing and scraping my stool over the wooden boards intentionally. My three brave, ale-addled warriors and squires groan in unison, but there's no longer any humour in the situation.'

'You're bloody lucky the ships arrived before Ealdorman Æthelwulf came to Grantabridge,' Icel continues.

I growl low, thoughts of what I'll do to bloody King Alfred and Ealdorman Æthelwulf forming in my mind.

'And that's not all.'

'Fucking hell. How much worse can it be?'

Icel offers me a pitying look.

'The warriors suspect that one of the ealdormen has been dispatched to delay the archbishop. They mean to hold you here for even longer.'

'Why?'

'So the jarls will be able to take Gloucester. Of course, that won't happen now. The jarls are gone. I imagine the entire force is on their way to Wareham even as we speak. If Oscetel and Anwend even went to Gloucester. They might just have sent ships.'

Any remorse I might have had for encouraging the Grantabridge jarls to leave that location and take back Jarl Guthrum is evaporating quickly. It was impossible for them to take ship around Wessex without being reminded of the wealth of the kingdom. It wasn't impossible for King Alfred to stand aside from offering them any form of alliance, if that is what he's done.

'So, we're lucky to have prevented all that from happening then?' Pybba suggests, his tone aggrieved.

'Yes. But it puts the king in a difficult situation, even so. After all, we're here. The rumours amongst the West Saxon warriors are of these things being agreed between the king and the jarls, but they're not confirmation that it actually happened.'

I take a deep breath and resume my seat. Icel's correct. I mean, I know what my own warriors can conjure in their minds about my intentions, and they rarely let me out of their sight.

'So, these warriors suspect King Alfred is in league with the Grantabridge jarls, and that he has no compunction in allowing Mercia to suffer the consequences. But we have no proof either way, and I'm here, with the fucking bastard, supposed to be forging an alliance with him? Does that summarise all you learned last night?'

'That's about it, my lord,' Icel offers inclining his head. At the same time, I catch sight of Rudolf. He's regained his senses remarkably quickly, although he looks like a dip in a water barrel wouldn't go amiss.

'How am I to play this, then?'

'The fact the jarls aren't attacking Mercia is a mercy,' my aunt interjects. 'They've failed and won't be trying their luck again anytime soon, not now they have Jarl Guthrum once more amongst them.'

'Yes, but what of this alliance with King Alfred, which we've come all the way here to discuss?'

No one speaks. I know what I want to do with it, and it involves my fist up someone's arsehole and, perhaps, my fist poking out of their throat, but I don't say that. No doubt, I don't need to do so.

Icel coughs.

'Alas, I believe the only way to have any answers is to send some of your men to Wareham to have a little chat with one of the Grantabridge jarls.'

'What? You'd sooner trust them than the king of Wessex?' I question with a wry twist of my lips.

'I'd sooner trust the damn devil himself than King Alfred of Wessex.'

I don't like the idea, not at all. I certainly don't like the thought of being stuck here while I await news from Icel or whoever I send to Wareham to discover the truth.

'Who will go?' I don't want to agree, but once more, it seems I'm being forced to make the decision. One day, I'll be able to make decisions free of the imperative to react.

'I will,' Icel announces.

'And me,' Rudolf offers, as do a few others. I'm pleased Pybba doesn't suggest himself.

'Then it's agreed, Icel, Rudolf, Hereman, Wærwulf and Lyfing will go to Wareham,' I announce softly, checking to ensure we're not being overheard.

'And you, my lord king, will promise to remain here,' my aunt cautions. I offer her a mirthless smile. I'll not be making that fucking promise today.

Chapter Nine

But first, I have to speak with King Alfred again.

I've dismissed my men, and sent the lads to bed with sore heads. Rudolf and Gardulf aren't that grateful. Hemming and Hiltiberht are. Icel has adopted his customary glower.

'You'll have to slip away in the bloody night,' I inform him. 'It's not like you can just leave now.'

'I don't see why not,' he grumbles.

'Well, you can't,' I counter belligerently. I hasten outside, keen to evade my aunt's scrutiny. She knows me too well. I suspect that while I'm busy with politics and generally wasting my time with King Alfred, she, Pybba and Icel will cook up some means of ensuring I remain at Cricklade. They can fuck off. I want to see this alleged enemy with my own eyes. Only then will I truly know where I stand with King Alfred.

'My lord,' Alfred greets me while leaving the encampment where he and his family have spent the night. He seems to shimmer beneath the sun. I feel my forehead furrow. Whenever I've slept in a tent, I've not woken and looked quite so well put together. But then, I rarely sleep in a tent. I prefer the blackness of the sky above my head, the scattering of shimmering stars and the rustle of leaves. Unless it's bloody raining, of course. Then all of that can fuck off.

'My lord king,' I greet him, conscious of my aunt and Bishop Wærferth hurrying to join us. Alfred's escorted by Ealdorman Æthelwulf. He looks as well put together as his king. I prevent myself from peering down at the state of my clothes.

'I trust you slept well,' I offer.

'Of course, other than some loud singing from some of my warriors. There will be some sore heads today.' Alfred fixes me with a pointed look. I smile benignly in reply. If he believes I sent men to get his warriors pissed so they'd slip up and tell the truth of his interactions with the enemy, then he'd be bloody right. He should have done the same.

'Bishop Wærferth,' King Alfred greets him next.

'Lady Cyneswith.' I hear her murmuring pleasantries. Then I sense King Alfred's gaze on me.

'I would hear Mass this morning. Where's the church?'

'Of course, my lord king,' Bishop Wærferth smoothly interjects before I can express my thoughts. 'A service has been arranged for every morning. More can also be organised if you prefer to pray later in the day as well.' Bishop Wærferth turns and indicates the small wooden church nestled in the corner of Cricklade.

I don't miss the look of dismay on King Alfred's face at where he'll have to offer his prayers while he remains here with me. I consider if it might be enough to push him back towards the heartland of Wessex. Considering his determination to meet here, I might have expected him to know more about this place. After all, it is a Wessex settlement.

'I'll summon my family,' King Alfred announces peremptorily.

'Surely not the children?' I find myself speaking without realising.

'Of course, the children. They must be raised in the virtue of our Lord God.' My eyes boggle at his pompous tone.

'Very well,' I try and move aside. I've no intention of enduring another tedious Mass. I'm sure I only sat through one a few weeks ago.

'You'll join us, King Coelwulf?' Ealdorman Æthelwulf interjects. I close my eyes, and fix a smile on my face.

'I'd be delighted,' I offer. I swear, I hear my aunt laughing behind me.

Once in the church with my aunt sitting beside me, I watch Bishop Wærferth and the local priest perform the Mass. I'm itching to be doing something, anything else, but my aunt's hand on my arm every time I fidget forces me to stillness.

Bishop Wærferth, sensing my impatience, speeds his way through the service, for which I'm grateful, although the priest isn't quite as well attuned to my needs. He tries to speak at his normal pace, only for the bishop to hurry, and in the end, the priest is almost breathless by the time I can once more step outside.

I've heard the small child being hushed throughout the service, although Alfred's daughter has been well-behaved and attentive. She seems far too serious for a child of less than ten winters. Certainly, with my experiences of young children amounting to Rudolf, she's very unlike him. My aunt also summoned young Æthelred to attend the Mass. He was about as patient as me, making me smile, while my aunt tried to ensure we were attentive.

I wish I could sleep through Mass, but I really wouldn't want to face my aunt's wrath if I did so.

I hasten to leave the small church, confidently side-stepping King Alfred to make my way to the paddock where the horses are temporarily corralled. Haden hears my heavy tread and rushes to my side, his eyes expressive.

'Aye, lad, I know,' I say, running my hand over his black and white nose. He looks as fettered as I feel. Not for the first time, I wish I'd been less hasty in agreeing to this. Admittedly, the events that have brought me here were set in motion at Northampton over three weeks ago. 'Not everything is as it seems,' I mutter to my horse.

Pybba joins me alongside a yawning Hiltiberht.

'Sorry, my lord, I'll tend to him,' he gabbles.

'No need, I can see to my own horse. I told you to rest.' Hiltiberht still looks green. He smiles, or rather winces, at me.

'My head hurts too much, my lord. I'd sooner be doing something.'

'Then, by all means, tend to Haden. I wouldn't want to deprive you,' I offer with a smile. He grins, or rather grimaces, and moves to fetch the shit shovel. Pybba chuckles darkly.

'Poor lad. I think they took your instructions too literally.'

'I agree. They were supposed to get the other bastards drunk, not themselves.'

'You do know you can't go to Wareham,' Pybba cautions me conversationally. Now, it's my turn to grimace.

'I can do what the fuck I want.'

'Not in this, you can't. It's not like you're just popping down the road,' he cautions. 'Even Icel says it'll be difficult to accomplish in four days of hard riding. You can't bloody disappear for ten days when you're here to discuss whatever the hell it is you're going to do with King Alfred.'

I scrunch my nose at his words. I don't need to tell him I've no idea how far Wareham is from Cricklade. Perhaps I should have asked Icel before, but he'd be the one having this discussion with me instead of Pybba.

'It's not as though I can stay or keep King Alfred here for ten bloody days either.'

'So, better to disappear, is it?'

'My aunt will cope without me.'

'She won't thank you for that. She hates him.'

'So what, while the others go to Wareham, I have to remain here and try to avoid letting King Alfred know I don't trust a bloody word that erupts from his lying mouth?' Pybba grins in delight at my furious words.

'That's exactly what you have to do, my lord king. Exactly what you have to do,' he repeats, while I growl again.

Surely, there must be a quicker way of determining what's happening at Wareham. I don't much want to be stuck here with Alfred and his family. I feel my hands clenching in fury.

'Lady Cyneswith has bid all of your men prevent you from leaving.'

'It's not really for her to command my warriors, is it now?' I grumble.

'Really? Is that the hill you'll die on? I think you know more than anyone just how loyal your warriors are to your aunt. They'll do as she says.'

'Bollocks,' I exclaim. 'Do none of them have the stones to follow my orders?'

'It seems not, my lord king. It really bloody does.'

And then Rudolf appears, and my eyes narrow.

'What now?' I scowl. 'What is it?' I march to where he waits, indecision on his pale face. 'Icel means for us to leave immediately,' Rudolf informs me, a hand over his mouth, no doubt to stop himself from vomiting.

'He's such a shit,' I stamp my way to the far side of the paddock and find Icel and Lyfing already mounted. Wærwulf looks less pleased about it, whereas Hereman's engaged in a war of words with the other man.

'What the fuck?' I demand.

'Better to just go,' Icel mutters. His face is clouded with fury. I don't miss the angry look he directs towards Rudolf.

'We said tonight.'

'And we all know why you said that. And, as I told you, you're not bloody coming to Wareham.'

'So, you're just going to fuck off without saying goodbye?'

'Well, I was, yes, but Rudolf has fucked that, hasn't he.' I'm aware we're attracting unwanted attention from the West Saxons.

'You really are a bastard,' I glower. 'Go on then, fuck off, and remember, if you fucking die, I'll be forced to avenge your bloody death.'

Icel grins at my tone.

'And remember, if you fucking die here, from boredom, or eating too much venison, I'll have to do the bloody same.'

I laugh then. Icel is such a bastard, but he's probably right, and that rankles more than it should.

'I'll be here when you return,' I reassure all of them. Rudolf, despite his pale face and lack of sleep, is hustling to prepare Dever for the long journey.'

I look from Rudolf to the horse and back again. Samson is an old boy now, but Dever is even older.

'Do you want to take a different horse?' I suggest. 'Dever's still recovering from his wound. And you might want someone a bit quicker.'

'Who?'

I bite my lip, considering my next words carefully and thinking of my aunt's reaction.

'Take Jethson. He needs a good ride out to blow the cobwebs from his ears.'

'What of your aunt?'

'She won't need him, and she'll understand. I'll make sure Hiltiberht sees to Dever as well as Haden.'

Rudolf spins and hastens back to where the saddles are being kept within the stables, although there's not enough room for the horses as well.

'Is that wise?' Icel demands. I'm sure he's considering Jethson's intractable nature.

'I want to know he can escape if the enemy comes after you or the bastard West Saxons.'

'Dever won't like it.'

'Dever will be well,' I reassure Icel. My warriors and I are all connected to our horses. They keep us out of trouble. It behoves us to treat them well, but Dever's an old boy. He should, by rights, be allowed to do little more but graze at Kingsholm and perhaps teach the youngsters how to ride.

'Well, help me,' Rudolf calls from where Jethson's eyeing him warily. I hear a nicker from Haden, and scowl in his direction. His lips are pulled back from his teeth, and I think he's laughing at me.

'Here, boy,' I approach Jethson confidently. I'm aware my aunt has claimed him and that Hereman and Gardulf find the arrangement acceptable, just as they do her having Edmund's sword and seax. But Jethson's a warrior's horse. He's been trained to obey instructions and has enough stamina to ride all day, take only a bag of oats, and then ride the following day. The same can't be said for all horses.

But, Jethson and I aren't exactly friends. He moves away, eyes on me and not Rudolf. Rudolf, with his talent for getting all horses to like him, hovers close, ready to fling the saddle on him and the reins.

Hereman, the shit, chuckles. I'm sure he could help me, but instead, he chooses to watch me struggle with his dead brother's horse.

'Come on, boy,' I try again. My aunt would bloody kill me if she found me here, tempting her horse. The ground is liberally splattered with horse shit, despite the best efforts of the squires to keep the ground clear. Horses don't really understand the idea of shitting in only one place.

I can't watch my feet and Jethson, as I shuffle towards him. I'm wary of having to change my boots, or clean them. Hiltiberht, with his bad head and weak belly, won't be available to chisel the crap from them.

'Come on, boy,' I repeat. Jethson's nose flares, his eyes filled with fury at my attempts to place the reins over his head. We might have been allies in our grief for Edmund, but we're not united in this attempt. I know how tricky the bastard can be.

'Hurry up,' Icel bellows, just as I'm within touching distance of Jethson's long nose. Jethson rears a little in the fight, and I dash away. I turn to glower at Icel, who smirks and offers me a shrug of his wide shoulders. He's a bastard as well.

Rudolf's getting closer, but not close enough.

I take a breath and try again. 'Come on, boy,' I soften my voice and encourage him towards me. I walk confidently, trying not to take my eyes off him. I need to hold the contact or I may as well give up and send Rudolf on old Dever.

'Come on, boy,' my voice is even softer, enticing. I hold his reins out to show them to him, and he sniffs with his huge nose. I reach out and run my hand along his familiar nose, almost but not quite managing to reach and place the bit in his mouth.

'Hurry the fuck up,' Icel roars. Jethson rears for real this time, his hooves coming up as though he'll punch me with them. I veer backwards, foot connecting with a steaming pile of shit, and my legs goes from beneath me. I land on my arse, a whoosh of air leaving my mouth, my hands and arse now in the shit, while all I can hear is Icel pissing himself with laughter. The fucker.

I make to stand, noticing my boots, trews, and hands are filthy now. I yank the reins into my hand and turn to face him.

Tears stream from his face and from Hereman's, who's also mounted. But what absolutely takes the piss is that Rudolf's managed to place the saddle over Jethson's back and now cinches it into place, adjusting the stirrups as he goes.

The laughter brings Eahric running, eyes wild, hand half on his seax. He must think the horses are being stolen. His eyes rake in all before him, and he grins as well. I bend and wipe my hands on some stray pieces of hay, and march to hand the reins to Rudolf rather than towards Icel and Hereman, who I've half a mind to force from their saddles and fight me with their damn fists.

'Fucking marvellous,' I glower. Rudolf wrinkles his nose at the sight of me, but hastily forces Jethson to take the bit before threading the reins over his ears.

'Sorry, Jethson,' I mutter.

'Take care of him and yourself,' I urge Rudolf. 'You can't trust those bastards to do so.' His face splits in a grin, replacing the one of consternation.

'And you look after Dever. And, my lord, I'd change your trews and your boots before your aunt sees you.' With a smack on Jethson's shoulder and cupped hands to help Rudolf mount, I face my men. Hereman and Icel still roar with laughter. Wærwulf wears a small grin, although he's keeping himself busy with his horse. Lyfing shakes his head at Icel's antics.

'Fuck off, the lot of you,' I roar, taking some delight in startling the usually placid Samson. 'And if you get fucking killed, you'll have me to answer to,' and with that, I stamp from the paddock, trying to find grass to wipe the crap from my boots, hoping against hope that I don't look as bad as I think I do.

Only then, I see my aunt, watching the actions of the horses and my men. Her lips are pursed with annoyance. I see her whisper something to a servant who rushes away.

'Why have you sent Rudolf on my horse?' She asks, eyes appraising my appearance.

'Jethson needs the exercise,' I counter. I don't want to argue with her about it.

'So, why did you take it upon yourself to apply his reins? You could have asked me. I know the way to that horse's heart.'

'I thought you were busy with King Alfred.'

'I wouldn't have needed to change my fine dress after saddling him,' she informs me, an eyebrow arched high.

'Then next time, I'll be sure to call for you.'

'Very well. Remove those boots and your trews, and dunk your head in water. You can't discuss an alliance while you look like the stable boy.' She runs her hands down my blue tunic, as though to flick dust from it. She grimaces.

'At least you've not got shit on your shirt. You really are a terrible king,' she mutters. 'You don't look even half as formal as King Alfred.' I open my mouth to argue but realise she's laughing. I kick my boots free, then my trews, and stand there, allowing the heat to work along my legs.

'Bloody hell,' I mutter as I stamp to a waiting water barrel and thrust my head into it, and then pour water down my legs and feet. I wrinkle my nose. I smell a bit ripe, but it'll half to bloody do.

With ill grace, I watch my men ride out. I'm still pissed off, and my aunt has chosen to make herself scarce. It's been a tedious day already. King Alfred is an arse. I'm already tired of deflecting his requests, and it's really only just begun. I hope he doesn't notice that my warriors are missing. Not, admittedly, that he seems to notice much about anything he deems beneath his attention.

But, with Icel, Rudolf, Wærwulf, Lyfing and Hereman gone to Wareham, following Icel, who assures me he knows the way very well indeed, I feel marooned here without them. I have my aunt to complain to, and Bishop Wærferth, and of course, Pybba remains, but I feel the loss of Icel and Rudolf keenly, even Wærwulf and Lyfing. And of course, Hereman can make light of even the most disastrous of events.

That night, my thoughts turn to what might be happening in my absence in Mercia. When my aunt came back from meeting Bishop Burgheard of Lindsey, she told me, as he'd assured her, that the news from Northumbria was that Jarl Halfdan had bitten off more than he could chew in the lands of the Picts, killing the son of one of their many kings. With the wrath of an entire kingdom against him, he'd ridden for Northumbria, only to find King Ricsige had risen against him there, killing some of his shipmen and effectively blocking him from remaining there. At least, I realise, it means Archbishop Wulfhere has returned home. I endured more than enough of his bitching and complaining.

I consider what drives these men to seek outside assistance against the enemy. I've not done so. I've fought many battles. I've protected my kingdom. Why the fuck can't these useless turds do the same?

The following day, ill-tempered and grumbling from lack of sleep, Hemming rushes to me with news that Archbishop Æthelred of Canterbury will arrive shortly. I growl into my morning pottage.

'Just another of the bastards to lie to my face.' I know Alfred did much of that yesterday. He really can use four hundred words to say something that I could enunciate in about twelve.

'Perhaps, my lord king,' Bishop Wærferth startles me by replying. I've not seen him enter the room. 'But he, at least, isn't here to demand you protect him from the enemy. That, by right, is King Alfred's role to fulfil.'

'What's he like?' I ask Bishop Wærferth. I feel no remorse for questioning what the archbishop might be like. Bishop Wærferth's loyalties are split. I'd like to know who else holds his allegiance.

'A devout man with political acumen. I'm sure you'll enjoy meeting him,' Bishop Wærferth offers with an unexpected laugh. My growl of fury only makes him chuckle all the more.

'Come on,' my aunt summons me. 'You look like you could do with a shave and a bath.'

'I don't need...,' I mutter, but my aunt has already gone.

'We should all clean behind our ears before meeting the archbishop,' Bishop Wærferth announces and follows her.

Pybba, beside me, stands and waits.

'Bloody hell,' I explode.

'Aye, there's where you'll be going if you don't clean behind your ears,' he chuckles. I mutter beneath my breath about bastards and holy men.

I can see this is going to be a terrible day. Already, I'm half-minded to follow my men to Wareham, even though I'd be a day behind. I'd sooner be fighting than listening to men extol their virtues as though they're somehow better than me. Bloody arse. I'd sooner be anywhere but here.

Chapter Ten

Yet, I'm pleasantly surprised. Archbishop Æthelred arrives without fanfare. He's accompanied by a small force of warriors wearing his emblem on their equipment but carries no banner or even a holy cross proclaiming who he is.

He's older than I suspected he'd be, yet his brown hair is intact. He has no tonsure. I can see that he's shaved recently, with small cut marks on his thick neck.

Archbishop Æthelred dismounts fluidly and greets me and my aunt. King Alfred also stands to welcome the archbishop. Alfred's clothes are so threaded with gold thread that I wince to look at him. He'll be visible from a bloody good distance, perhaps not as far as where the River Thames meets the sea, but not far off.

I'm not alone in avoiding looking at him beneath the heat of the shimmering sun.

'My lord kings,' Archbishop Æthelred speaks with a deep tone, inclining his head as he stands before us. I'm pleased he greets me as a king. Alfred has still not grasped that he owes me as much respect as I give him. My aunt hastens to offer the archbishop cooled wine to quench his thirst, which he accepts gratefully.

'It's going to be a hot one,' he comments, looking up at the sun overhead.

'You're welcome to Cricklade,' I offer before King Alfred can speak and offer his extravagant welcome. I notice that the archbishop gazes northwards, over the dividing line of the River Thames.

'I don't believe I've ever been to Mercia,' he comments. I don't correct him that this isn't strictly Mercia, although King Alfred clearly intends to, but the archbishop speaks first. 'Looks just like the rest of Saxon England,' he offers without conceit. 'I can see why the enemy has no care for where they beach their bloody ships.'

Already, I find I like him. He speaks his mind. Men should either speak their minds or back up their actions with blades. King Alfred appears incapable of doing either.

'Come, let's take this inside,' my aunt smoothly takes control of the situation. 'It's too hot to stand beneath the sun.'

With a quick glance to ensure my warriors are keeping to the shade, or at least aren't baking themselves to leathery skin, I follow her within.

Lady Ealhswith and her brother await the archbishop inside. She curtseys and he bows, and I watch the young girl follow suit. I'm still outraged that there was ever mention of me marrying her. She's too young, far too young, to even be considering marriage, let alone to a man who's at least four times as old as her, and possibly nearly five. And yet, in her calm demeanour I already detect the bearing of my aunt. I can't deny that Æthelflæd intrigues me. I consider what sort of woman she'll be when she's fully grown.

The archbishop greets them kindly, a soft word for Æthelflæd, making me appreciate he sees it as well. I might have to speak to my aunt about her. After all, she is half-Mercian. I should have a care to her future. I don't miss that it'll annoy the hell out of King Alfred and Ealdorman Æthelwulf if I show interest in the older daughter instead of the mewing son.

'If you'll allow me a few moments,' and the archbishop sweeps from the hall. I settle on one of the benches, with Bishop Wærferth joining me. My aunt's busy ensuring all happens as it should, while King Alfred speaks to his wife and children.

'My lord kings,' Archbishop Æthelred shortly greets us once more, and then settles on one of the waiting chairs. I notice that in my absence, Alfred's had his chair draped with a cloth revealing the emblem of Wessex, the wyvern. I don't look at my aunt. She'll be annoyed to have missed such a trick, compounded with my failure to even bring a royal chair with me.

'I'm most grateful to have been invited to this meeting. It's a pity that Archbishop Wulfhere of York couldn't attend, but I understand he's somewhat busy elsewhere. At least the Viking raiders have left Northumbria.' I try not to smirk at that far too polite description of Wulfhere's recent actions. Bishop Wærwulf was as good as his word, and did convene a meeting to discuss matters with the York archbishop. But, as soon as he heard Jarl Halfdan was gone from Northumbria, Wulfhere hurried back to York as though powered by the force of his own farts.

'And of course, we must pray for Bishop Smithwulf's soul. A terrible loss.' I smirk at that as well, but it's really more of a grimace. Smithwulf. What a bastard he turned out to be. I consider if Archbishop Æthelred knows the truth of Smithwulf's intentions. I find myself peering at King Alfred, keen to make an assessment of how he reacts to the archbishop's pious words.

If King Alfred knew of Bishop Smithwulf, he makes a very good artifice of appearing as though he doesn't. That reawakens my suspicions. I'm sure he was involved. I'd almost stake my fine double-headed eagle seax on that, but my blade remains embedded in the church roof within Northampton. It'll be there until the thatch needs replacing, which might not be for many years. At least I have my sword once more. I didn't enjoy fighting outside and within Gloucester without it.

'But,' and the archbishop's voice is surprisingly cheerful, considering his previous words. 'We meet to discuss how to unite to drive the Viking raiders from our shores once and for all. I understand,

King Coelwulf, that you've bettered the enemy at Gloucester, although, alas Jarl Guthrum was able to escape.'

'He was. However, as Bishop Wærferth will tell you, he undertook baptism and converted to our faith, taking the baptismal name of Æthelstan before his escape.' I don't like admitting we allowed Guthrum to escape, especially as I can't temper that by adding that I wanted him to escape.

'Baptism?' I'm sure the archbishop must know this, but he sounds surprised.

'Indeed, the witan thought it would ensure he sees the error of his ways.' Wary respect flashes in the archbishop's eyes. I don't look at King Alfred, but I sense his scrutiny. I consider if he wishes he'd thought of such a thing, rather than just paying off the Viking raiders after his brother's death.

'And now,' Bishop Wærferth interjects. 'It's hoped Jarl Guthrum takes his new faith and spreads it amongst his fellow Norse. Indeed, as he departed Gloucester, we all witnessed him praying to his Lord God.'

The archbishop's face is pensive, his long hands crossed and held under his neck as he absorbs the information.

'It could work,' he admits. 'It really could. If they understand our faith, it might stop them attacking their fellow Christians.'

'But it now means we fight men and women who might share our faith. Where will our Lord God be in that battle?' King Alfred intones pompously, refusing to be awed by what we accomplished with Guthrum. I keep a quirked grin from my face. Where was this fear for Christians fighting Christians when Wessex was trying to overrun Mercia?

'It's merely one of many strands,' Bishop Wærferth moves to smooth the furrow from King Alfred's brow. I personally don't think he should worry himself about that.

'So, my lord king, do you have intelligence that all four jarls are now at Wareham?' This the archbishop questions King Alfred, assuring me he is well-appraised of events within Wessex.

'No, we don't. I'm unsure who's at Wareham,' King Alfred announces. I feel my eyes narrow. He's not mentioned that before.

'I understand you knew Jarl Oscetel was there,' I find myself unable not to gainsay him, especially after all I've been told by my young warriors and squire who earned bad heads for their endeavours.

'Did you now?' King Alfred retorts, his eyes blazing. 'I don't know from whom you heard that. I don't believe we know the identity of the shipmen at Wareham. All that's known is that there are seven ships, and however many shipmen that implies.'

'Three hundred and fifty,' I offer quickly. It's not many. I mean, it is, and it isn't. They sent almost as many men to kill me when taking Repton from King Burgred. It's hardly an insurmountable number of enemies. Unless, of course, you have no warriors to counter the attack.

'You've not spoken with the Viking raiders?' the archbishop clarifies.

'My two ealdormen are there, now, Cuthred and Bucca. They ensure the safety of Wessex.' That's not an answer at all. I think the archbishop should press for more details, but he disappoints me by not doing so.

'And the enemy means to attack inland?'

'It's enough that they hold Wareham,' King Alfred offers darkly. 'It's too close to Winchester. They need to be ejected from Wessex, just as they've been from Northumbria and Mercia.' King Alfred's face is determined, his lips pursed, his eyebrows rising.

'Your ealdormen will not be able to do that?'

'My ealdormen do what they can. We seek assistance from our fellow Saxons, the birth kingdom of my dear wife, to ensure the Viking raiders are dealt as mighty a blow as they have managed. Or rather, had managed until Jarl Guthrum was lost.'

I'm grateful he can't see my curling fists. I consider how he has the audacity to cast aspersion against Mercia, even while calling for her assistance.

'Then, if Mercia is too weak to restrain Jarl Guthrum, perhaps you shouldn't seek her assistance,' my aunt interjects, honey-sweet. If I'd said that, she'd have glowered at me. It seems she can speak with honestly.

I enjoy watching King Alfred open and shut his mouth while beside him, Ealdorman Æthelwulf glowers in my aunt's direction. Despite my outrage that she's spoken as she has, and only because, as I said, she'd berate me for such feeble attempts at forging an alliance, I'll have to congratulate her on infuriating King Alfred after this discussion has ended.

'Mercia isn't weak,' Ealdorman Æthelwulf speaks over anything King Alfred might have been about to reply. 'Mercia is strong. She's revealed that on many occasions recently. Despite the loss of Jarl Guthrum,' and here he pauses, as though just realising something, 'Mercia still has the warriors and the knowledge to overwhelm our combined enemy.'

'Mercia isn't weak,' I echo. 'Her strength lies in her warriors. We can't denude Mercia of that strength to aid another kingdom that's not endured as Mercia has. Mercia has lost her king. Her queen.' Pointedly, I glare at King Alfred. He forgets his sister very easily.

'And yet Mercia has a new king. A warrior king,' King Alfred counters, chin raised as though to ward off blows.

'Are you saying you're not a warrior?' I question, enjoying the flurry of emotions that descend over his face.

'I'm saying, in the last decade, Wessex has aided Mercia, and now merely asks for a reciprocal agreement.'

'Did Wessex aid Mercia, or did Mercia call on her subordinate to fulfil an obligation from not one, but two marriage treaties? An obligation, I fear, about which you've forgotten.' As I speak, I glance at Lady Ealhswith. She has no place at this discussion, unlike my aunt. She's in the room, but she's busy with embroidery and tending to her children. She should be here, speaking for herself. I tighten my lips.

I expect King Alfred to be furious with my suggestion.

'I fear, my lord, that you've been misinformed.'

I turn then, from the archbishop to Bishop Wærferth, to Ealdorman Æthelwulf, and then my eyes rest on my aunt.

'Have I been misinformed?' I ask the group at large. 'Lady Ealhswith?' perhaps I shouldn't involve her, but I'm stubbornly determined to do so.

'My lord king,' she gasps, meeting my eyes. She's not an attractive woman, but she's regal. I admire that. I note that she calls me her king, much to Alfred's annoyance, which flashes in his eyes.

'Tell me of the marriage treaty that brought you to Wessex.'

'My, my lord king,' she stands unsteadily, holding the back of the chair she sits on, the embroidery clutched tight, the many threads hanging down in confusion of riotous colour. 'The agreement was forged between my father, King Burgred and King Æthelred of Wessex. I don't know all the details,' she demurs. King Alfred bristles. I consider if it's because his wife lies so poorly or because he realises I'm not the pushover he thought I was going to be.

A flurry of vellum and I spin to Bishop Wærferth. I sense Lady Ealhswith resuming her seat, her sigh of relief audible that I won't ask her for more details. Perhaps she's even grateful that Bishop Wærferth holds the answer, and she need not lie to me.

'I have a copy of the agreement here,' the bishop comments. 'I've examined it in some detail. It makes it clear there is a payment to be made from Wessex for the marriage union, and also an instruction that Wessex will assist Mercia if she's attacked. Alas, I see no reference to a reciprocal agreement.' A heavy silence falls. I avoid scrutinising King Alfred. I do eye the archbishop. I consider what he'll make of this development.

'Then there's no basis for Mercia sending her warriors to Wessex, but perhaps that's something that could be agreed upon. Or, at least, an agreement that Mercia could assist Wessex in defeating the enemy on this one occasion. That might be all that's needed. The Viking raiders, once ejected may well leave our shores for all time. Certainly, the triumphs in Northumbria and Mercia do suggest that.'

I nod, admiring the archbishop for his ability to find some middle ground. But King Alfred is having none of it.

He stands, eyes fiery, his calm demeanour burning from his body.

'I'll seek out our copy of this agreement,' he states in an ice-cold voice. 'I don't say that you lie, Bishop Wærferth, but my understanding of this matter differs. Mercia is to assist Wessex, as part of the marriage accord. If not, I wasted myself with this marriage.' I wince to see Lady Ealhswith blanche with horror but don't watch the king stamping away like a small child who's been caught shitting in the house and means to deny it, although the evidence is obvious.

'Well,' I offer. 'That went fucking well.' Already, I'm wishing my warriors were back here, but they only left last night. The sooner they return with details of what's happening at Wareham, the quicker I can end this charade and return to Mercia. I might even get to enjoy the hard-won peace this time.

I might even bloody enjoy doing so.

Still, I can't keep the small smile from curving my lips.

My aunt thinks I lack all diplomatic skills. It seems she's not met King Alfred. No matter what others say about him, he has about as much tact as a fucking ox.

Chapter Eleven

Far from unexpectedly, the meeting breaks apart, with bows and promises to reconvene at an unspecified 'later.' As everyone strides away, I eye my aunt. She quirks an eyebrow in my direction, but it's Ealdorman Æthelwulf who speaks.

'That was well done,' he glowers, his intent the very opposite of his words. I look down at my hands while he faces my aunt. I can't allow him to see the amusement on my face.

'I said what needed to be said,' she offers haughtily. I consider for how long she's wanted to speak so bluntly to the king of Wessex. I believe it's been brewing for a long time. Not that I blame her. Again, I'm reminded that Rudolf termed Alfred an 'arse,' he was right to do so.

As Ealdorman Æthelwulf storms from the hall in a parody of his brother by marriage, I indicate my aunt should join me. She threads her arm through mine. Together, we leave at a steady pace. No one needs to witness us stamping like small children.

I take her to the paddock. She eyes the horses, lips pursed.

'Jethson?'

'Needed the exercise,' I remind her.

'Icel is set against this alliance,' she cautions me. 'He'll find what he wants to find.'

'And King Alfred is set for this alliance. And he tells me what he wants me to think. Somewhere, between the two of them, there'll be a balance.'

'What if Wessex is genuinely beleaguered?'

'I'll fight for her, but not in any means that King Alfred expects.'

Pybba joins us. His eyes take in the horses. His stance is as belligerent as my aunt's.

'That went bloody well,' he comments sourly.

'As well as can be expected.' For the first time in my life, I feel as though I'm the one who can see reason here and not the others. My aunt means to make this as awkward as possible. I wish I'd known that before.'

'So, you'll send us to fight for Wessex?' Pybba questions, even though I've said no such thing. No doubt, he again knows my mind better than I do.

'If we can be assured of banishing the Viking raiders once and for all, I'll seriously consider it, despite King Alfred.'

He sucks his lips and crosses his arms. This, then, doesn't please Pybba either.

Once more, I wish I'd known this before. It would have made things much simpler for me.

'King Alfred hardly cloaks himself in glory.'

'Does he even know what glory is?' my aunt counters aggressively.

I watch Haden rather than let either of them see my smile.

'We'll see what the next discussion brings,' I suggest.

'Or shall we terminate this now and return to Kingsholm?' Once more, it's my aunt who speaks.

I shrug my shoulders. 'We're here now. We should at least see how this plays out.'

'You're the king,' she offers, but I genuinely think going back to Kingsholm would please her.

'My men have gone to Wareham. I'll remain until they return.' My aunt's face is thunderous.

'That could be two weeks.'

'It could, yes, and in that time, King Alfred might prove himself less of an arse.' But I confess, I'm smiling as I say it. I don't think he'll do so. I don't think he can. King Alfred of Wessex isn't at all the man I thought he would be, and I hated who I thought he was. He's proving himself to be even easier to despise.

* * *

However, Archbishop Æthelred isn't an arse.

While the discussion doesn't resume that day, I invite him and all of the delegates to dinner. He sits beside me, but King Alfred and his wife do not.

'I confess, King Alfred can be an unreasonable man,' he offers in an undertone. 'I'm unsurprised by his reactions today.'

I wish Bishop Wærferth had told me of this before. Somehow, I'd assumed that the archbishop and King Alfred were closely aligned. That goes to show what I bloody know.

'He causes me some difficulties and is always slow to respond to any request for help.'

I consider this, and also why the archbishop is speaking to me about it.

'He lacks warriors?' I question.

'I didn't believe so, but perhaps he does. If they are defending Wareham, his ealdormen might have all the men. Those outside in the encampment have little or no battle experience. I doubt some of them know which end is the pointing bit.' He chuckles, but I detect some unease. 'Tell me,' and he makes a visible effort to turn the conversation. 'Was it your suggestion to convert Jarl Guthrum?'

'No, my aunt's. It was a good idea, and he does appear to be a genuine convert.'

Archbishop Æthelred shakes his head, clearly torn between amusement and respect.

'I wouldn't think of such a thing.'

'Then, let me share with you that all three jarls seemed most concerned about the baptism. They asked me how it would change Jarl Guthrum.'

'Genuinely?' again, I realise his interest isn't feigned.

'Yes, we had to make some reassurances. And Jarl Guthrum's not alone in his conversion. Some of the displaced Norse from Grantabridge also sought sanctuary with us, and our Lord God.'

I'm sure Archbishop Æthelred would be stroking it if he had a beard. His eyes are somewhat unfocused, considering the possibilities.

'I believe I'll send this information to the Pope. He'll welcome knowing that the Norse are open to conversion. He might even send missionaries to work amongst them.'

'They'd need to be brave men.' I'm quick to argue.

'Ah, King Coelwulf, all men of the cloth are brave men. Never doubt that.'

'Even to walk amongst those who would kill them, given half a chance.'

'Perhaps them more than any others.' He chuckles again. I mirror him, but I'm far from convinced that sending men amongst the Norse to convert them is wise. Perhaps it's better if one of their number converts first. Not, I realise that I believe the answer to the problem of the Viking raiders lies with conversion to Christianity.

No, the way to solve the problem of the pestilent bastards is with swords and seaxes.

Chapter Twelve

King Alfred remains truculent. I'm not alone in enjoying his refusal to accept he might be at fault and not Mercia. Even Archbishop Æthelred is far from soothing when we resume discussions.

The days drag, becoming a week, and nothing is agreed. The days drag once more, and finally, I realise my men should be back soon. The weather's on the change and the harvest well under way. I've a desire to back my way back to Mercia and end this tedious process.

I find time to speak with Lady Ealhswith. She's not at all what I expect.

'My lady,' I greet her. I find her and the children watching the horses. Her face is pensive—her sharp words urging Æthelflæd to return to her side repeatedly from where she gets close to the animals. I find myself more and more intrigued by her daughter. She seems nothing like her father. She is, perhaps, similar to her mother.

'My lord king,' Lady Ealhswith's face is unsmiling. Instead, lines already mar her lips and eyes. She seems to spend much time frowning, but I can't see that she spends it laughing.

'Your daughter's an energetic child.'

'My daughter will be the death of me, my lord king. She's head-strong and takes reprimands poorly.' I smile. I've little experience of children at that age. I feel I shouldn't recall my memories of Rudolf. He was a pain in the arse unless, of course, he was spending time with Haden.

'Your son is more placid?'

'My son is still a baby. He's yet to form an opinion of himself.' I'm surprised she speaks so openly with me. I thought she'd be more like her husband. And her brother. 'My husband assures me he'll be a fine king one day.'

I feel my face furrowing now. I'm sure King Alfred has nephews who should be king after him, but I hold my tongue. It's the conceit of men to believe their sons will be fine warriors. As a small baby, I won't yet decide about Lord Edward's likely future.

'Lady Æthelflæd likes horses?' I ask instead, trying to find a means of smoothing the fury that's settled over her mother.

'She likes anything she can use to get away from me. Today, it's the horses. Tomorrow, it might well be a ship. It might be merely a cow or ox a week from now.' I find myself laughing, even though I determined not to do so.

'You present an image of a very determined young lady.'

'I speak only as I see it,' she complains.

'Does she have a horse or a pony?'

'She does, but the animal isn't here.'

I consider that, my eyes drifting towards Dever. The horse is content, not seeming to miss Rudolf. But he's huge compared to what I image Æthelflæd's pony looks like.

'Perhaps an animal could be found for her to ride here,' I suggest. Lady Ealhswith purses her lips, a familiar reaction to anything I suggest from that family.

'It depends whether we linger or not. For now, she can merely content herself with speaking to the animals.'

I nod, although I'm unsure whether I agree with that statement.

'Then, at least let me introduce her to some of the horses.'

Before she can say no, I beckon for Hiltiberht to come closer. He approaches with a familiar smile.

'My lord.'

'Bring Dever to meet Lady Æthelflæd,' I ask of him.

'Of course, my lord,' Hiltiberht is perhaps too pleased that's the summary of my request. I watch the older horse raise his head when called by Hiltiberht. He comes easily to him, and together they walk towards me.

'How old is your horse?' Æthelflæd questions, already standing beside me, her intrigued words startling me because I thought she was by the fence.

'Older than you. Not quite as old as me.' She nods with understanding.

'He once belonged to my brother, but that was many years ago.'

'What happened to your brother?' the simple question makes me wish I'd not started the conversation.

'Now Æthelflæd,' her mother quickly comments. 'You shouldn't ask questions such as that.'

'Why not?' And now I've brought it upon myself.

'My brother has been dead for over a decade. Longer than you've lived.' Her forehead furrows, her mouth opening and closing.

'And that's why I shouldn't have asked about him?' she speaks carefully. I'm once more surprised by her astuteness. I find it strange that her father is so bumbling.

'Perhaps, although you weren't to know, so the fault lies with me, not you.' She nods, but already, her attention is focused on the horse. Hiltiberht has a handful of oats with him, which he offers to Æthelflæd. With delight, she laughs as Dever whiffles the oats from her hand. It's always a strange experience to feel the roughness of a horse's tongue over my hand.

She pats his nose, gazing into his eyes. Lady Ealhswith's silent at my side until she's not.

'I've vague memories of your brother, but alas not of you. I recall your aunt much better.'

'I wasn't often to be found at court. I had other matters that required my attention.'

'Yes,' she mutters. 'I remember the comments about those as well.' I refrain from an immediate response. I've never given much thought to how people spoke about me when I refused to claim my birthright: when I drank and laboured to bring forth the harvest like any common man. Those days were ones of freedom and also, I confess, denial. I didn't wish to be who my father, brother and aunt wanted me to be. I doubt I am, now, if I'm honest. But my aunt puts up with me.

'Then you know more than I do,' I offer, watching Hiltiberht speaking to Æthelflæd. Young Edward sleeps in his mother's arms. He seems to be heavy.

'Do you want me to take him?' I question. I don't know if I've ever held a child before. I'm sure I must have done it. Or have I? My family is far from fertile. I don't know when a child's cry was heard in my own hall. Amongst the inhabitants of Kingsholm, certainly. But not for my brother and not for me. And certainly not for my aunt. I appreciate that she took a lover only when a child wouldn't be born from the union. She truly has put her emotions on hold for my family. Unlike Lady Ealhswith.

'No, it's fine.' A rare smile touches her cheeks. 'As a mother, you somehow get used to the weight. It's a relief that he sleeps. Although my one arm is much stronger than the other these days.'

'He's only your second child?' I question as we share a moment together.

'Unfortunately, I've been unable to carry many of them until they were old enough to be born.' She speaks with lightness, but I detect much sorrow there. I refuse to ask more questions. Instead, I allow Hiltiberht and Æthelflæd's words to wash over me. Despite where I am, and the woman at my side being wed to the arsehole King Alfred of Wessex, I enjoy the moment. It seems peaceful. It seems too peaceful. I absorb it all the same. Until I don't.

'Bloody hell,' I glower; Edward startles to wakefulness with an angry cry as someone shouts my name, the voice stringent. Somehow, I knew this would end bloody badly.

Chapter Thirteen

'Icel,' I spin to meet him. Samson steams beneath him. The others I sent with him aren't far behind as the horse thunders to a halt before me, mud flying into the air. Instinctively, I step before Lady Ealhswith to shield her and her son from Icel and his sweating mount.

Icel's face is wracked with fury. I count my men and name them in my mind; Rudolf, Hereman, Wærwulf and Lyfing. All present and correct.

'Good to see you, too,' I comment. Icel sweeps a gaze behind me, but he's already speaking.

'This is no time to fucking arse about,' he shouts. It's so unlike him to lack control that I feel my eyes startle open.

'What is it?' I demand. Behind him and the other warriors I sent south, I see others racing. I think to reach for my seax, but Icel speaks quickly.

'The enemy's overwhelming the West Saxons from Wareham throughout much of Wessex. Even now, one of the ealdormen chases me here to demand action from King Alfred.'

'Tell me everything,' I demand, even as Lady Ealhswith calls for her daughter to join her. Æthelflæd complains, but I don't interfere. If Icel's here, there must be some calamity.

'Did you make it to Wareham?' I question. Icel shakes his head.

'Within sight, nothing more. The place is aflame. The West Saxon ealdormen can't do anything to counter the attack. It makes me doubt our fears that King Alfred is in league with Jarl Oscetel. If that's what allies do, I wouldn't welcome them.'

I nod decisively, absorbing that.

'Who leads it?'

'The jarls, all of them. I saw the emblems of all four men, including Guthrum's. It's been altered. He's added a winged-dove to his owl. But since then, we've been hastening back to you. The jarls are on the march. They've destroyed Wareham, and now they make their way inland. The ealdorman will tell their king. Wessex is threatened. I understand that one of the ealdormen has been entirely overwhelmed, his men dead, while he's held in captivity. But the jarls mean to do more than torch a few places. They intend to claim the entirety of Wessex.'

Grateful that Lady Ealhswith has hurried away, I eye Icel aghast.

'Just like that?'

'Just like that. The West Saxons are bloody useless. They don't know how to fight, not to win, anyway.'

Hiltiberht hastens forward, taking Samson from Icel, who's dismounted in a waft of stale sweat and bad breath. He winces on hitting the ground and bends to rub his hands over his inner thighs.

'We've been riding almost non-stop. My legs are rubbed raw,' he offers ruefully.

I look from Rudolf, to Hereman, taking in Wærwulf and Lyfing. They wear expressions of fury. That surprises me. I'd expect them to welcome Wessex being overrun. But, of course, they're not bloody fools. If that happens, Mercia will again have the bastards for neighbours.

'Shit,' I glower, running my hand over my face, feeling my beard underneath my hand. It's remarkably well-kept. That's what wasting my time listening to King Alfred bitch about his proposed alliance has done to me. Even my damn beard is in better battle-readiness than King Alfred.

'What do you propose?' I ask my warriors. Pybba's come running. Hiltiberht, Hemming and three others have taken the horses to be offered water and brushed down. I note Jethson's gleaming after his brisk journey. At least it's done him some good. More and more of my men run from their activities as well, as the cries of the approaching Wessex ealdorman and his warriors make themselves known. Even my aunt steps towards me, Bishop Wærferth following on behind.

'There's little choice, my lord. Unless the West Saxons have a force of thousands to call upon, they'll be bloody overrun. Mercia and its warriors must come to their aid, especially as we can be confident all four of the jarls are a part of the attack. As they did at Repton, they've reunited to drive a king from his kingdom.'

'Bollocks,' I exclaim, resenting the fact my joy in the day has dissipated. The quiet was calming. The serenity was fulfilling. Or was it? Shit, I was bored out of my head, talking of children with Lady Ealhswith and other such bollocks. I almost felt as though I cared for her.

'King Alfred demands your attendance,' my aunt offers, eyebrows arched. I notice her appraisal of Jethson. No doubt, she's relieved to see him in one piece.

'I just fucking imagine he does,' I mutter, reaching out to grip the forearms of my five brave warriors who've ridden to Wareham and back, returning with the growing scent of smoke in the air from the south, or so my imagination has me scenting.

'Let's get this bloody over and done with,' I stamp, marching towards where Archbishop Æthelred watches my approach from his position within the hall. I take in the West Saxon horses and warriors, noting that the animals are good quality, the warriors, as ever, well provided for. And yet, with all that wealth in horse flesh and iron, King Alfred can do fuck all to stop the Viking raiders.

The bastard is much like his worthless brother by marriage, King Burgred.

But, on this occasion, I'm here to bolster him. And I bloody will.

But I don't like it. Not at all.

Chapter Fourteen

I eye the man before me. He sweats from more places than I believed a man could bloody sweat. I've not yet determined his name, but he's one of King Alfred's ealdormen. They stand within the hall, well, he stands, King Alfred remains seated. I see no sign of Lady Ealhswith or her son and daughter. I'm unsure where they've gone.

Archbishop Æthelred's also standing. I'm standing. My aunt's standing beside Bishop Wærferth.

The ealdorman gabbles, but King Alfred has eyes only for me, and Icel standing at my side.

'You sent your warriors into Wessex?' he demands, eyes blazing. 'You didn't believe me?' he shouts. No one speaks. From outside, the sound of horses and men finally taking their ease after a long day in the saddle can be heard. I look from King Alfred to the archbishop's neutral expression. Then I drag a smile onto my face.

'I fucking did, yes. I wanted to see the truth of your strength, and it seems I was correct to do so.' I walk arrogantly, taking myself to the table to pour water into a cup and drink deeply from it. I look to the

Wessex ealdorman. His mouth opens and closes, unsure what to make of this.

'How dare you,' the Wessex ealdorman finally emits, and I stamp towards him so that I'm so close, I can smell him. Shit, I feel damp just being so close to him. He's wetter than a dog after a swim.

'I am King Coelwulf of Mercia. Not that your 'king' honours me as such, and I will speak as I fucking see fit.' His lips clamp shut unhappily, eyes raking in Icel as though much now makes sense. I should have questioned Icel and my warriors about their contact with the West Saxons. 'King Alfred's accusation of something that's eminently obvious isn't the way to garner my assistance.' King Alfred's face is red with fury, his eyes ablaze. I hold his gaze evenly.

Now his mouth opens and closes while no sound comes forth. Fuck. I hate him. He should be a man of action, a man of quick thinking. But he's as soggy as his sweating ealdorman.

'You are?' I ask the man, drinking deeply once more. I see where he licks his lips and beckon one of the servants to give him water as well.

'I'm Ealdorman Wulfhere of Wiltshire.'

'And I'm King Coelwulf of Mercia, and these are my warriors, Icel, Lyfing, Rudolf, Wærwulf and Hereman.' I indicate my men. They're sweating and dust-stained, but nothing compared to Ealdorman Wulfhere, who's a tall man but with a belly that strains against his equipment. He's probably older than I am. He should practise with his blades more to keep that belly at bay.

'They inform me that Wareham has been overrun. The Viking raiders move towards Winchester and northwards. Do you agree?'

'My, my lord king,' but Ealdorman Wulfhere doesn't address me. Behind him, Ealdorman Æthelwulf has made a late arrival. I consider what he's been doing.

'Speak,' King Alfred mutters darkly. He looks perturbed—hardly the epitome of a warrior king.

'We encountered the enemy at Wareham. As you know, ealdormen Cuthred and Bucca were already there. We held them for some time between us, but then they managed to come around the back of us to fight on two fronts. Many were wounded. We retreated. Our line of defence didn't hold. We retreated again. As King Coelwulf says, the enemy move northwards. Winchester's taken.'

'And what of the other ealdormen?'

'Sorely tried, my lord king. Cuthred's been wounded. Eadwulf and Garulf track the enemy. Cuthred's been taken within Winchester. He must be surrounded. Bucca, I fear is dead as well.'

'How many?' I demand, but I look to Icel. He shrugs his massive shoulders.

'We've seen seven ships, as we were told, but there are more of them than that,' Rudolf answers instead. 'I would say thousands, three, maybe four.'

I wince.

'Where have all the bastards come from now?' I mutter, although I expect no response. There were fewer than that at Grantabridge.

Archbishop Æthelred surprises me by answering. 'There have been reports, delivered to me only this morning, of ships seen with the enemy emblems, skirting Kent and making their way west.'

'How many?'

'Ten, perhaps fifteen. They're staying far enough out at sea to make it difficult to count. Port Reeves sent me the news, pleased the enemy didn't come ashore.'

'How many men do you have?' I question King Alfred. In my mind, I'm considering what I should do. Ealdorman Ælhun protects Northampton. Ealdorman Aldred holds the land to the north, close to Lincoln and Gainsborough. The other ealdormen are scattered throughout Mercia. It'll take them days to arrive, and it seems we don't have those days.

I look to my warriors. Icel's firm in his resolve despite hating the bastard West Saxons. Rudolf also stands with his chin held firm in defiance. My aunt looks belligerent, arms crossed over her body. Wærwulf looks fit to growl or howl, living up to his namesake. The rest of my warriors appear as fiery in their resolve as I'm becoming.

'I have over a thousand,' King Alfred stutters. 'A few hundred here, and others close by, towards London.' I glower at him for this admission. His obsession with London has left him exposed once more. The fucking arse should learn to look to protecting his kingdom and leaving mine the fuck alone.

'So, the enemy has thousands, you have a thousand. What of the other ealdormen? You named them Eadwulf, Cuthred, Bucca and Garulf?' This I direct to Ealdorman Wulfhere.

'Ealdorman Cuthred took heavy losses before his capture. His men have divided between the remaining ealdormen. Eadwulf and Garulf have fewer losses. Perhaps, between us all, another thousand.'

'So, at most, you, as in Wessex, have two thousand warriors.'

I see Ealdorman Æthelwulf swallow heavily.

'And you, Ealdorman Æthelwulf?' I've forgotten about him.

'A hundred and forty-seven,' he answers quickly. I absorb all this, thinking of London. London is the closest place to us here, although Gloucester is a three-day ride.

'King Alfred, have your men from London summoned. I'll call for Kyred and his warriors. We'll also muster Ealdorman Ælhun and his, but they'll take days to arrive. In the meantime, we need a location to confront the enemy. I don't know, Wessex; where should it be? Where will their attack naturally funnel them?' I don't believe the Viking raiders plan to attack London. No, I think they mean to rush through Wessex in the hope of reaching Mercia, perhaps even directing their attack here, to where the River Thames can be easily forded. They intend to take their revenge against me. No doubt, Jarl Anwend seeks vengeance for his son's death. Perhaps Jarl Guthrum wishes to cast aside the taint of his Christianity. Or perhaps, this is all about King Alfred and his shit defence. He should have been at Wareham, organising his men, ensuring the enemy couldn't slip beyond their guard. Instead, he was arguing with me about the terms of the treaty with Mercia.

He really is fucking crap at being king.

'I know the perfect place,' Icel offers when no one else speaks. I meet his gaze, seeing a glint in his eye as his eyebrows rise. Now, I consider how the fuck Icel would know the perfect place to face our enemy. Icel must be referencing something that happened long ago.

I really must ask him about it. But not fucking now. Now, I have to ride to war, essentially to protect Mercia, but really, to ensure King Alfred has a bloody kingdom to pass onto his squalling son. I hope it's bloody worth the risk. I really bloody do.

Chapter Fifteen

Bishop Wærferth and his fast-working cleric write down my instructions, my aunt hovering nearby. I want to send her to Gloucester to summon Kyred. She determines to stay at Cricklade. On this bloody occasion, I'll have her obey my instructions, or I might just bind her and have her forced back to the safety of fucking Gloucester atop Jethson. She really doesn't know how bloody determined I am about this.

Icel, Rudolf, Wærwulf, Lyfing and Hereman eat hungrily. I eye their mounts. They need rest. I can't see that Icel will take kindly to being told he can't join us. As always with these things, a sense of urgency permeates everything, but it also slows down time. There's much to organise and throughout it, I can't help glowering towards King Alfred's encampment. He's hardly summoning his men with the urgency that Icel and his own ealdorman imply needs to be taken.

'I'll ride with you,' my aunt announces defiantly. I bark a laugh.

'You bloody won't. On this, dear aunt, you'll act in the best interests of Mercia. You'll hasten back to Gloucester, taking young Æthelred with you, and order Kyred to ride out. Indeed, it might be best if you take Lady Ealhswith and her two children with you.' I almost enjoy the sour cast of my aunt's lips at that suggestion. The fact she doesn't argue about that assures me it's sound policy, even if she doesn't like it.

'She'll slow me down,' is all my aunt complains. I'm grateful that worry stops her from debating more about my restriction on her involvement.

'Then you ride on ahead with Æthelred, leave Lady Ealhswith with her small escort, and make Kingsholm ready for her.'

'Who'll protect her?'

'I've no idea. But it won't be her brother, and it won't be the king of Wessex, for he'll be joining the fight.' On this, I'm determined. Bishop Wærferth and his female cleric take my orders and then hasten to find fast horses. Ealdorman Ælhun needs to be mustered. My aunt will inform Kyred. London perplexes me. Perhaps I should send men to protect her. I consider Archbishop Æthelred's words about the enemy ships. Could they have been travelling towards Mercia and not away from her? Is London threatened by the Viking raiders or just by King Alfred and his arrogant belief it should be his? I shake my head, once more frustrated that news takes too long to arrive and is subject to the vagaries of whether people deem it important. It makes me wish I had more warriors and could send orders far more quickly than I can. Perhaps I need a ship army to patrol the waterways of Mercia.

'You're taking Haden,' my aunt distracts me by asking. I consider her question. Haden was wounded in Gloucester. It's been little more than three weeks since then. Can I ride him at a greater pace than the gentle trot we employed to reach Cricklade?

'I am, yes,' I announce quickly, not considering it further. If I don't take him, my horse will be pissed with me.

'Then you must ensure his wound is kept clean,' she offers with no more than a gentle shake of her head, perhaps for my stubbornness.

'And you'll take Dever home with you,' I inform her. 'Rudolf will ride Jethson.' This she opens her mouth to argue about, but then relents.

'That's sound policy,' she confirms. 'But Jethson's mine. After this, you'll need to find Rudolf a new mount. Dever must retire. You know it. I know it. Dever knows it, for all he fights it, like so many of your warriors. Of them all, only Tatberht appreciates that men's reflexes slow and they can't fight as they did when they were young and sprightly.' I realise her gaze rests on Icel. I, too, think Icel knows no limits to his physical prowess. I hope it doesn't bite him on the arse one day.

'Why does Icel know Wessex so well?' I ask softly, trying my luck. My aunt's chin lifts, but her eyes sparkle.

'As you well know, dear nephew, that's for Icel to tell you, not me. But trust him. He does. He'll not direct you to a poor location. And be mindful of King Alfred. As useless as he seems, he and his brother did fight the enemy four years ago at Wilton and Ashdown.'

'But were they successful?' I ask callously. I know the answer to that. My aunt huffs softly.

'Do I really need to welcome Lady Ealhswith to Kingsholm?' she whines. I grin.

'We must both do things we don't want to do, dear aunt.' She grumbles softly but accepts it without further complaint.

I take myself to where my warriors are preparing.

'It's a bloody good job we came with all our equipment,' Wulfstan huffs as he readies Berg.

'Aye, we'd have been fucked if we hadn't,' Ingwald choruses.

'We came to make a bloody peace, not ride to sodding war,' I call to them. A few chuckle, others lift their heads from beside horses and offer me varying degrees of incredulous looks.

Goda asks what they're probably all thinking. 'Where are we meeting the bastard enemy?'

'You need to ask bloody Icel about that. I've no idea.' Icel might well have announced he knows where we should face the Viking raiders, but so far, he's remained tight-lipped about it, tending to

Samson. The horse is winded and now stands, the sweat slicked from his body but still breathing heavily. Icel's entirely preoccupied with his horse.

'Icel,' I call to him. 'Where are we meeting the bastard enemy?' I get no reply. I look to Rudolf. Jethson's in much better condition, but he's not been as badly used as some of the other horses since Edmund's death.

I hear chuckles from my men. I fix them with a lour and stamp my way to Icel's side.

'You can't take him, you know that, don't you?' I say lightly, noting the concern on Icel's face.

'He will be well.'

'He won't. Look, the others are exchanging their mounts as well. All apart from Jethson are exhausted. You need to allow him to return to Gloucester with my aunt.'

Icel rears up before me; his familiar face creased in a fury, his lips tightly pressed together beneath his thick grey beard. Only then Samson nudges him, and the anger leaves his face.

'I know,' he admits unwillingly. 'But I still need to ensure he's well enough to make that journey before I find myself another horse to ride.'

'In the meantime, we need to know where you think we should fight the enemy.'

Icel nods, his hands busy brushing his horse, although his eyes are far distant.

'The woodlands, not far from the Portway. That's where we'll make our stand. The enemy knows the area well. They've fought there enough times before, but it's still a good location.'

'Thank you,' I offer, turning away.

'My lord,' his voice is only just loud enough to hear. I look back. He hesitates for a moment as though thinking better of it, but then speaks again.

'The enemy is vicious, as you know. But your allies, they're not all as ineffectual as they make out. And, it won't take a man with much skill to end your life, my lord king. Be wary of them. Be very wary of the traitorous bastards. It won't be the first time the West Saxon royal family try to kill a Mercian king.' My eyes narrow on his words. I absorb the warning.

'Then Icel, you must always have my back: you, Rudolf, Pybba and Hereman. I'll rely on you to keep me safe for the future of Mercia. It can't rest only in the hands of young Æthelred. He doesn't even truly understand who he is.'

'Aye, my lord,' he confirms, a slap to Samson's rump having the animal move aside, but only a little. Exhaustion steams from him.

'And my thanks, Icel, for the warning and for your endeavours to determine the truth of events in Wareham. I don't want to ally with the Wessex bastards, but it appears I might be much to blame for this. I'll contend with it, and then King Alfred can fucking bend the knee. If we save Wessex from the bastard enemy, he'll be my subordinate.' I grimace at the thought, but a rare smile touches Icel's lips.

'I like the fucking idea of that,' he confirms, eyebrows high. I grin again, mirroring his actions, only for Rudolf to shout for my attention.

'Bloody hell,' I huff. 'A man can't have a moment's sodding peace these days.' Not, I realise, that I want a moment to myself because, and I confess this to myself easily, while I'm busy, I can't think of Edmund and how he seems to walk at my shoulder through every action I take.

I know I'll never not miss him.

The fucking cock.

Chapter Sixteen

Rudolf stands beside Dever. My aunt beside him.

'You'll have Jethson again,' I inform him.

'But,' my young former squire argues.

'Dever was badly used, and he needs to rest. He's bloody old, Rudolf.'

'But.' And I look from him to my aunt, seeing how her lips curl in a sad smile.

'Look, you can take him with you and risk him, or you can allow him to go back to Mercia and spend his remaining years taking it easy. A quick death or a slow one, you can decide.'

Mutiny shimmers in Rudolf's eyes as he rubs his hand over Dever's inquisitive nose. He doesn't seem unduly concerned if Dever realises what's under discussion.

'Take Jethson,' I speak again. I really don't have time for this, and yet, I also do. This is Dever, after all. He was once my brother's mount. I'm as mindful of this last link to my brother as I am that Jethson ties me to Edmund.

'I,' Rudolf tries once more. I know what he's thinking.

'Dever really won't take offence,' I comment, sensing the time for soft words is short. We need to be ready to leave. We're not going to get far today, but it's better to start the journey and disperse this gathering. Archbishop Æthelred will return to Canterbury. Lady Ealhswith will come to Mercia, not that Alfred knows that yet. I'm not looking forward to that conversation.

'Let Æthelred ride him,' I urge Rudolf, and finally he relents.

'I'll just find him and tell him a few things,' Rudolf confirms, a little happier. I roll my eyes at my aunt. She fixes me with a look.

'Tell me you wouldn't be the same about Haden? He's hardly fit to ride, and yet you're taking him with you.'

'That's different,' I begin, but my aunt smiled wryly.

'Come on, you need to speak to King Alfred about your plans for his wife.' Now I grimace. I'd rather not have to endure this conversation.

With a parting shot for my men and horses, an eye on Haden to ensure Hiltiberht is tending to him, I stride back to the main hall, the sound of angry voices greeting me before I'm even halfway there. I wince as I recognise King Alfred's voice from inside.

I listen to his words, and quickly realise what this argument is about. My fury towards him intensifies. I clench my fists and then release them slowly. It doesn't settle my anger as much as I'd like it to do.

King Alfred faces Ealdorman Wulfhere. The ealdorman wears a pained expression.

'You'll remain here and protect her,' King Alfred argues. Behind them both, I see Ealdorman Æthelwulf and Lady Ealhswith. She clutches her sleeping son to her breast. Æthelflæd's watching wide-eyed.

'What's this?' I interject forcefully. 'Why aren't you readying your men to leave.'

A look of loathing covers King Alfred's face, but he quickly banishes it.

'I'm ordering Ealdorman Wulfhere to remain here and protect the royal family.'

'What, here?' I state, looking around and raising my hands to indicate the building. 'With no walls and defences. I think that's somewhat foolish. Anyway, I've made arrangements for your Mercian wife and her children to journey to Kingsholm alongside my aunt. We'll keep her safe.' The implication isn't lost on King Alfred. The flash of relief on Lady Ealhswith's face is impossible to ignore, although luckily, her husband glowers at me and doesn't see it.

'She's not Mercian. She's West Saxon.'

'For the time being, she's both,' I console, feeling the urge to slap the arrogant arse for quibbling when the capital of his kingdom is threatened. I really don't understand his fucking priorities, but then, I don't have children to worry about. Perhaps if I did, I'd embroil myself in such tedious arguments. I've hardly had time to get to know Æthelred, and anyway, he's not my son. I certainly don't yet feel the regard for him that my aunt extends to me.

'Lady Ealhswith,' I incline my head towards her. 'My aunt will make you welcome within Kingsholm. There are strong walls to keep you and your children safe.'

'Are you sure of that, Lord Coelwulf?' King Alfred's determined to argue with me. 'I believe my warriors aided your men only a few weeks ago.'

'The enemy didn't gain entry to Kingsholm. The Norse prisoners we had within escaped and met their allies. It's somewhat different to how you perceive it. Kingsholm, with the enemy Norse gone, is more secure than anywhere within Wessex at this time.'

'What of London?' King Alfred demands. I breathe deeply, working to stop my fists from clenching and my shoulders from tensing.

'The walls in the old part of the city are precisely that. Since the death of the bishop, there's no one in overall command. Ealdorman Ælhun will come south. He'll not linger at London. And, you will summon your force from there as well. If Lady Ealhswith's meagre body guard can protect those giant walls, then of course, she may go there. But, Kingsholm, or Northampton, is safer at this time.'

The swift look of triumph on King Alfred's face slides away.

He doesn't have the men to send with his wife. His wife's warriors will be unable to hold those walls and any potential weaknesses I'm ignorant about. I'm sure there'll be some for those who look hard enough. I don't believe the enemy will attack London, but if they did, I won't guarantee her safety or that of her children. Kingsholm's more heavily protected. I don't lie about that.

'My dear wife.' The bastard directs it to her. I shake my head now that King Alfred can't see me. 'Wouldn't you rather go to London?' His tone is honey-sweet and beguiling. It's pure pretence. How Lady Ealhswith doesn't wince, I'm unsure.

'I'd sooner be with Lady Cyneswith,' she speaks hesitantly, but I admire her, all the same.

'Then that's agreed,' I announce, done with this conversation. 'Now, my lord king, perhaps we could prepare to ride out to counter the enemy marauding through our island.' I almost say 'your' but stop myself. The Viking raiders are the enemy of every person on this island.

How I hate the fuckers.

And yet, at the same time, I detest King Alfred just as much.

He really is a bloody arse.

* * *

I stride from the hall, once more bellowing instructions to all and sundry. Bishop Wærferth and his cleric are left behind. They have their tasks to attend to, and I have mine. I don't wait for the ensuing argument that might or might not break out between Alfred and his wife. My unease with that union grows with every interaction. King Alfred doesn't respect his wife. I'd be unsurprised to discover he takes his pleasure elsewhere as well. There have been rumours he has a bastard son. Admittedly, one who's older than his marriage, but a man with one bastard will also have many more.

King Alfred regards Lady Ealhswith only as the means of

securing his believed alliance with Mercia. More and more, I'm understanding that much of what I thought happened might have been wrong. I've always considered King Burgred to be a weak king. I mean, he was in the end, but what if, before that, he was wise to the ploys of Wessex? I'll consider that, but not now. Now, I hasten to Haden and mount up, sharing a look with Icel and Pybba. Icel's left Samson aside. He rides a tall, fine horse, but I can tell from his tight lips that he doesn't like the sudden change.

'Ready?' I question Pybba, not wanting to give Icel an opening to object. He knows I speak the truth. Only Jethson has the stamina to make the return journey so quickly. Icel's not fool enough not to realise that, but I don't expect him to like it - not at all.

'As we can be,' Pybba confirms. His eyes sweep everywhere, resting somewhere over my shoulder. I don't need to ask him to know he's watching King Alfred. I hope he doesn't comment about the man. Even now, I can detect the cries of the men in the encampment as they struggle to dismantle tents and prepare to journey south This expedition will be strung out along the road we must take.

'I can't say the same for others,' he offers more darkly. I look down at my hands and smile. I don't want to be the one to show King Alfred how war is actually conducted. But there's no other option. If I left it to Alfred, we might leave to counter the enemy at any point during the coming week or even month. By then, the bastard jarls would hold most of Wessex under their control. The jarls might well be ruing their determination to take Mercia from us. They should have stayed within Wessex. Then, they'd have a kingdom of their own to command.

'They can bloody catch up,' I counter quickly. I sweep my gaze over my warriors, ensuring they're all well and prepared. Tatberht raises his arm in farewell, where he's ready to go back to Kingsholm. I offer him a grin. Tatberht's a miss, but I don't argue with him about his determination not to fight. He's spent his life battling for Mercia. He knows his time of doing that is at an end. But, he's not useless to me. There's much he can still accomplish on my behalf. Protecting my aunt, Æthelred, and Lady Ealhswith is sure to be fraught with tensions. I'd much sooner have a sword and seax to hand to contend with any who think to argue with me. He'll have to use words.

My aunt hastens to my side. Her gaze is serene as she reaches up to grip my arm.

'Go well, nephew. Remember, it's not worth dying for another fool's kingdom.'

'I know, aunt. I'll do just enough. And promise me you won't murder the king of Wessex's wife?'

'I'll do my best,' she offers haughtily. 'But I make no promises, as you never do. Now, be off with you. If you don't leave soon, it'll be dark and time for you to stop for the night and then resume arrangements in the morning.'

'Look after Mercia,' I urge her, turning Haden to where Icel and his new horse wait impatiently for me to urge my men onwards. 'Come on, you halfwits,' I call. A thunder of hooves, and then Icel leads the way, his grey stallion swishing its tale from side to side jauntily. The animal's neither fat nor thin; all the same, Icel dominates it, seeming to fill more than its back as he sits in the saddle. He was the largest animal to hand. Hereman has a smaller mount as his replacement and sits even more uncomfortably than Icel. I imagine they argued over who was to have the big bastard. I'm unsurprised Icel won.

Without looking back and pretending not to notice the disorganisation in King Alfred's attempts to leave, I hasten to Icel.

'So, are you going to tell me where we're going?' I question. He shakes his head.

'I'll show you, my lord. I can't do better than that.'

'And how do you know this place?'

'That, my lord, is for me to know and you to be desperate to find out. You should only be concerned that it's a good location for now. We'll have a good view of events to the south of us, and if the enemy come this way, we'll have plenty of options on how to counter them and stop them getting any closer to Mercia.' This should please me, and it does, but bloody hell, I wish the old bastard would tell me something.

I twist to consider Rudolf.

This, I decide, is something I can ask Rudolf to determine for me. He knows how to crack through Icel's regard with his persistent questions. I allow a smile to touch my lips. I'll have my answers. And we'll overwhelm the bastard enemy, and then King Alfred will be mine.

If I bloody want him, that is.

Chapter Seventeen

We stop for the night when it's too dark to see. My men divide watch duties, and others settle down to sleep. I roll myself in my cloak next to Rudolf and Pybba. The men who've travelled such vast distances aren't given watch duty, not that Icel likes that.

'You need to sleep, you grumpy bastard,' I glower at him when his querulous voice disturbs me. 'Now, stop your bitching and do as your king commands.' Hereman's delighted chuckle fills Icel's furious silence.

All night, I'm disturbed by the clatter of hooves and the shouts of West Saxon warriors arriving at the camp. Despite that, I'm kicked awake as soon as it's light enough to see by a grinning Sæbald. I meet his delighted smirk.

'Some of the fuckers have only just shut their eyes,' he offers me, grin widening with enjoyment at the discomfort those men must be feeling.

'Well, they're going to be bloody tired by the end of today,' I mutter without sympathy. Standing and stretching, I survey the scene. There are some fires, and the smell of pottage fills the air. The encampment doesn't stretch as far as I'd like. King Alfred doesn't have the numbers. I'm tempted to order everyone on their way, but the smell of the pottage makes my belly rumble, so I relent.

'We'll eat,' I instruct Sæbald and my warriors, who are waking and preparing to continue the journey. My aunt was correct. We hardly made any progress before darkness fell. All the same, I feel uncomfortable being so far from Mercia. I always vowed I'd never leave Mercian soil. The fact I've been forced to now sits uneasily on me.

Surprised, my men slow their preparations and hasten to eat. Even then, they're ready and mounted while some of King Alfred's men still struggle to wake. I march towards the yawning king. At least he's awake—or, at least, he's nearly awake.

'My lord king, we must hurry,' I announce without so much as a 'good morning.'

'My men,' he begins, affronted by my scathing tone, failing to greet me respectfully.

'Need to fucking hurry up, or all of Wessex will be lost, and you'll be king of fuck all.' I see Ealdorman Wulfhere wince but make no attempt to defend his king. He knows the truth of my words.

'My lord king,' King Alfred addresses me as I stomp back to my waiting men. 'You will not speak to me in such a way.' Just before I twist to face him, I see a grimace on Rudolf's face as he waits atop Jethson. He shakes his head. I'm minded of how alike Pybba he's becoming.

'King Alfred, if you don't want Mercia's aid, let me know. My men and I will return to Mercia and leave you to the coming fight.' I say nothing else. The words thrum through the air. Unfortunately, this public argument only slows down the West Saxon warriors, who all look from me to their king. King Alfred's all bluff and wounded sensibilities. I don't bloody have time for that.

When he makes no reply I continue. 'Then hurry the fuck up. We're riding on, but we won't attack the enemy without you, remember that.'

With ringing silence, I swirl on my heel and rush back to Haden. I don't want my warriors to say anything to me, but Hereman allows a low whistle of approval to escape his lips. With the silence of the encampment swirling behind me, the West Saxon anger making my shoulders prickle, I encourage Haden onwards.

If all I do is watch the enemy, it'll boil my piss, and I don't wish to spite myself just to make a point with King Alfred. I'll not allow good Mercians to die defending a kingdom their own bloody king can't be arsed to protect. I fucking will not.

The day passes quickly. Icel leads us onwards. Every so often, I encourage Rudolf to join him. I smile at the conversation that passes between them.

'You know the way well,' Rudolf begins.

'I do, yes. As you know, we followed this path only a few days ago.'

'But you knew it then.'

'I did, yes, and you asked none of these questions.' I look down as though some problem with my reins requires my attention. Icel perceives I've deployed Rudolf. I'll have some bloody answers.

'We rode too swiftly to speak of anything,' Rudolf complains.

'Or you didn't much care.'

'Oh no, I care, that's why I'm asking now. How many times have you been to Wessex?'

'More than enough,' Icel counters quickly. 'Too fucking many,' he offers more softly.

'Why?'

'Because I was ordered to do so,' Icel prevaricates.

'By who?'

'By whoever my lord was.'

'Before Lord Coenwulf?'

'Yes, Rudolf, before Lord Coenwulf.' Rudolf absorbs this. I think his questions might have come to an end.

'Then who was your lord then?' Icel's heartfelt sigh reaches even me. My eyes are wide now, taking in this kingdom of Wessex. It's a little different from parts of Mercia. Here, there are thick woodlands, rolling lands, and some peaks, which could provide a good viewpoint from which to see our enemy.

'I've had many lords,' Icel answers.

'And who were they?' I feel for Rudolf. Icel's being fiercely reticent.

'Men of Mercia. Good men of Mercia, mostly. Some died in battle, some in their beds.'

'Why did they send you to Wessex?'

At this, Icel turns and meets my gaze with a stern expression.

'Tell your lord, my young friend, to mind his own damn fucking business.' I crack a smile at this, as does Hereman. Rudolf elicits a cry of outrage but quickly slows Jethson and attempts to get close to me, not that Haden's having any of it.

'I tried, my lord,' Rudolf shouts from some distance. 'He's a damn fucking arse, and quite frankly, I don't give two shits about his damn secrets.'

I laugh; despite Rudolf's evident displeasure, he still knows how to rile Icel. If the damn arse, as Rudolf names him, refuses to share his secrets, Rudolf will try and entice him to do so. It might not be today. Indeed, it'll probably be one day when we least expect it, but Icel won't take kindly to Rudolf's naming of him as a damn arse. We will learn the truth. Eventually.

I keep my eyes on the well-defined trackway we follow. It appears to be an ancient road, similar to the many traversing Mercia, and every so often, Haden's hooves thunk as they hit some of the remaining stones that are no longer flat. I've sent Ingwald and Wulfstan to scout ahead. I keep looking in front, but I see only the occasional blot of smoke on the horizon. They're probably cook fires. I don't expect to see the enemy until at least tomorrow, if not the day after. The road's gutters are free from weeds and other summer growths. It could almost be pleasant. All the same, I can't shake the feeling of unease. I'm far from Mercia. With each gallop forward, I get even further away. I hope my aunt is nearly back at Kingsholm. I hope everything is as it was when we left it.

Soon, Rudolf and Pybba strike up a lively conversation. I grin as they speak. Rudolf is never one to be kept disgruntled for long.

'Pybba, have you been to Wessex before, other than when we went to meet King Alfred a few months ago.'

'No, Rudolf. Why would I, a good Mercian, have been within Wessex?' I catch sight of Wærwulf grinning, and some of the others are also chuckling.

Rudolf twists in his saddle. 'And the rest of you. Have you ever been to Wessex?'

A bubble of laughter starts to grow. I glance at Icel. But if he's taking umbrage at this, I can't tell. He still sits easily in the saddle, although he's not as comfortable as he'd like to be.

'I've been to Wessex,' Hereman calls. 'Only last week, in fact,' and again, the men roar with laughter.

But then Cuthwalh speaks, and I startle at his words.

'I've been to Wessex, and indeed, Frankia as well.' His eyes gleam with the knowledge as he shares a glance with Icel. Icel shakes his head, perhaps to dissuade him from saying more or maybe just in frustration at the whole conversation.

'It was many, many summers ago. I was a young man with about as much facial hair as Rudolf there.' Cuthwalh juts his chin towards Rudolf, who unconsciously rubs his hand through his small beard. It's yet to recover from the wound he took outside Gloucester. He's not the only one of my men to have slightly strange beards where they've been injured, and when healed, facial hair is likely to grow less fiercely.

'What was Frankia like?' Rudolf asks, a young boy once more, all wide-eyed and filled with awe.

'Much like Mercia and Wessex. It was good while it lasted, but I was pleased to come home.' I consider why I don't know this about Cuthwalh. I mean, he's bastard old. Perhaps older than Icel. How long has he been a warrior of Mercia? But, if he's a warrior of Mercia, why was he in Frankia?

'But you were born a stone's throw from Kingsholm,' Pybba states. 'Why were you in Frankia.'

'It's the way of kings and lords that some should find themselves in enemy kingdoms.' That Pybba's surprised by this revelation perplexes even me. It seems more than just Icel have their secrets.

'Where did you go?' Rudolf demands.

'Somewhere, I forget the name. I met the king, though.'

Rudolf barks a laugh at this.

'You met the bloody king of Frankia? Don't tell such bloody outrageous half-truths.'

'You think I shouldn't be known to kings? I'm known to King Coelwulf. And perhaps others as well.' Rudolf's mouth drops in surprise once more at Cuthwalh's proud tone. I snap my jaw shut. I'm aware I look like a small child, as astounded as my young friend.

'How long were you there?' Rudolf continues.

'Not long. Long enough. You see, Rudolf, you shouldn't make assumptions that we warriors do nothing but linger in Mercia. I'm sure I'm not alone, like Icel, in having visited other places.' And yet, none of the others speak up. Perhaps then, Cuthwalh and Icel are the exceptions.

'We've all been to the bloody Welsh kingdoms,' Icel calls, reminding me that, yes, I've just about left Mercia before. But other that? I've no recollection of being elsewhere, well, other than Grantabridge, which, by rights, lies in the kingdom of the East Angles if such a kingdom still exists.

Silence falls between my men. No doubt we're all considering Cuthwalh's revelations. From behind, I hear the Wessex force. King Alfred rides with his men. His skill in the saddle leaves something to be desired. Ealdorman Wulfhere leads the way. He at least can master his horse and warriors. Ealdorman Æthelwulf has been conspicuous by his absence. I assume he's there, somewhere. I presume he's not run to Mercia with his sister. Mind, I think King Alfred would like to do that if he felt he could get away with it.

When my scouts return, my thoughts are disturbed. I take one look at Ingwald's face and know the intelligence he carries isn't good. I hear Icel growl. I consider that we're some distance from where he intends to take us.

'The enemy, my lord,' Ingwald offers. 'They're not far down this road. No more than half a day.' This is unexpected.

'The bastards have horses and race this way.' I spin in my saddle and look to Ealdorman Wulfhere. His shoulders sag with defeat, and we've not even seen the enemy yet.

'Call a halt,' I order, threading Haden through the horses to reach the side of the road.

'Come with me,' I urge Ingwald, far from surprised when Icel joins us. I make my way to King Alfred. He rides in the middle of his warriors, face dusty because he lacks the stones to ride at the front. He yawns and I realise he's been sleeping. King Alfred is about as alert as a somnolent child. Or goat.

'What is it?' he demands. 'Why have we stopped? We must make quicker progress.' I bite down my bitter laughter at such an outrageous statement.

'The enemy has been sighted.' I state quickly. 'Half a day away. They've taken horses.' King Alfred shakes his head.

'No, that can't be right. We're barely halfway to Winchester. We've not even turned truly south.'

'I don't think you can argue that when my warriors have seen them with their own eyes.' A swift look from Ingwald to Icel's face, and King Alfred subsides.

'Perhaps not,' he demurs. 'I'll send outriders.'

'Don't you trust that my men have good enough eyesight?' I question because he's really pissing me off.

'I believe you're ignorant of the layout of this land. I would send men who can tell us how far they are from here.'

'Half a day, no more, and getting closer,' Ingwald speaks without inflexion. He's better at this than I am.

Ealdorman Wulfhere joins us. He doesn't speak. I see no sign of Ealdorman Æthelwulf. No doubt, he's hovering at the back of the line of men and horses. He's more craven than King Alfred.

'I'll be the judge of that,' King Alfred states stubbornly.

'Then get the fuck on it with,' I growl. 'I'll stop my men until you have your determination.'

King Alfred's face shades pink with fury. 'You'll not stop your men,' he demands, nose raised.

'I will because you seem to believe we don't know where we are. As such, you and your warriors can lead on. We'll move aside. But I suggest you hurry up, or the enemy will be amongst us, and you'll be entirely blind to them.' Without waiting for King Alfred to splutter an answer, I turn Haden and shout to my men.

'Move aside, the king of Wessex and his warriors will lead on. They know the way,' I order. My voice thrums with fury. Wulfstan twists to meet my gaze with one of icy resolve. I think he'll deny me, but then he moves his horse clear of the trackway, and my other men do the same.

Rudolf, ever alert to the potential to ease the horses' suffering, immediately finds a small stream. 'Let them drink,' he calls.

I dismount from Haden and lead him to where Pybba allows Brimman to drink deeply. I'm furious and also fucking fed up of being furious. I know King Alfred is an arse. I need to reconcile with that, or I'm never going to feel anything but anger in his presence.

'We'll be riding in their shit and piss now,' Icel sounds aggrieved.

'If the daft fucker weren't such a bloody arse, it wouldn't have come to this.'

'Perhaps, my lord.' Icel's calm tone annoys me as well. His next words assure me I'm not the only one angry with the West Saxon king. 'It'll mean we can get to the location I've decided upon. If the West Saxons stumble into a fight with the enemy, we won't be caught up in it.' I nod at that, working to ease the tension in my neck and shoulders. I really don't like this, and yet, what choice do I have?

The sound of horses and carts moving along the road continues for so long, I tell my men to eat and take their ease. Here, beside the road, is clearly an established camping place for travellers. There's a well-defined stone fire circle and evidence of several latrine ditches, or perhaps graves, beneath the few trees growing there. The sound of small animals and bird wings flapping assure me these creatures have no unease about warriors trundling by or the possibility of the enemy coming this way.

Icel stands and watches the West Saxon forces. He doesn't move or take his ease. Eventually, I cast my eyes over Ealdorman Æthelwulf. He rides to the rear with his warriors close to him. His gaze meets mine, his surprise is evident.

'Why are you here?' he questions, imperiously raising his right hand to call a brief halt.

'King Alfred doesn't believe Mercian eyes can see the enemy correctly. They're no more than half a day away. In fact, they'll be closer now. Alfred's gone to look for himself.'

Unease settles on Ealdorman Æthelwulf's face. I see that his hand strays towards his seax as though he might be able to defend himself.

'Half a day?' he murmurs fearfully.

'Less now. They have horses. Or so my weak-sighted Mercians inform me.'

'Then they're deep into West Saxon land, just as they were four summers ago.'

'So it seems, but don't take our word for it,' I can't keep the bitter bite from my voice.

'And it appears they know the area as well as the West Saxons themselves,' Icel comments sourly.

'Four summers ago, there were many battles?' I want the truth from Ealdorman Æthelwulf.

'Yes, nine of them. The enemy built a fort-like enclosure at Reading, to the south of the River Thames, and from there, they launched attacks on Wessex, first, at Ashdown. The king and his brother hoped to be victorious. Indeed, many of the enemy leaders died. King Bacseg, Jarl Sidroc the Older and Younger, Jarl Osbern, Jarl Fraena and Jarl Harald. Only Jarl Halfdan survived to hold the men steady. What a bastard he is. The West Saxon king, Æthelred, considered them defeated, but Jarl Halfdan rode to Boseng, south of the Portway, and did for many West Saxons. Not content, he then attacked Meretun and all before Easter of that terrible year. King Æthelred died only a few weeks later. It was a difficult time, and there were to be further attacks, most notably at Wilton. King Alfred was forced to pay the enemy to leave for fear there would be no Wessex left to rule.'

'All these battles were deep within West Saxon land and close to here.' I'm thinking. The current attack is different to what happened four years ago. I've my suspicions as to why. This time, they attacked from the sea, not a river. Ominously for Wessex, and if Jarl Halfdan forms part of this new attack, as he did the previous one, then he knows the lay of the land well enough to bring about complete and utter defeat for the West Saxons. With his gaze resting on Winchester, as he once tried to claim Repton, Jarl Halfdan intends to strike for the heart of the Wessex kingdom.

'Much deeper than they should have come, yes. I'm still surprised they made no attack on Mercia,' Ealdorman Æthelwulf concludes. I don't miss the caution there. Not that I have anything to offer. I spent much of that year close to Kingsholm.

'They did come to Mercia, and not soon after.' I can't keep the edge from my voice. 'I assure you, if you can get King Alfred to listen to someone other than himself, that Mercia has no intention of fighting nine battles against the enemy. Neither will we make any sort of peace with the enemy that doesn't involve the Viking raiders paying a great deal of money to Mercia and not vice versa. Bring him to heel, Ealdorman Æthelwulf, or my men and I will retreat and protect the border with Mercia and nowhere else. My concern is for Mercia, and yours should be. I'll offer my men to protect Wessex, but only when King Alfred appreciates we've fought many battles against the enemy. We've triumphed over them more often than not. On no occasion have we sought peace, other than when we held the upper hand.'

'Indeed, my lord king.' Ealdorman Æthelwulf bows respectfully. 'I'll do all I can.'

'It better be more than 'all you can.' I've already half a mind to return to Cricklade. Ensure your brother by marriage knows the king of Mercia isn't one of his ealdormen to bow to his commands or to fight his battles for him. I've got much better fucking things with which to be getting on.'

His gaze holds mine momentarily. I detect what I believe is respect in his eyes.

'My lord king,' he concurs, ordering his warriors onwards.

Chapter Eighteen

As soon as Ealdorman Æthelwulf has resumed his slow passage, I don't think the West Saxons do anything quickly, I summon my men to me, perplexed as to why the West Saxons show so little urgency.

'Do you remember the events of a few years ago?' I question them. A few nod their heads, Icel and Pybba amongst them, but most don't. I curl my lips.

'If what Ealdorman Æthelwulf said is correct, then Jarl Halfdan was the only one of our four jarls to be involved in that attack. He held the men firm despite terrible defeats and then reached an agreement with King Alfred.'

'King Alfred paid him to leave,' Icel confirms, as though I should know this, and I probably bloody should.

'Where are you taking us?' I direct to him. 'Is it close by?'

'Not that much further, but it's possible the enemy already hold the location. But if we can reach it, then there's an old fort there, one we can use as an ultimate means of defence, if needed.' I grunt to hear Icel speak like that. I'm pleased he's considering what might happen if we're not victorious. All the same, I don't plan on being hold up in a fort that lacks the defensive capacities of Northampton.

'Would it not be better to keep the woodlands at our backs?'

Icel considers this.

'It's another option available to us.'

'We must ensure the enemy doesn't reach this fort they once erected at Reading. It'll make it too easy for them to gain entry into Mercia, and it might also allow them access to London.'

Icel grunts, perhaps with approval for my thinking, or perhaps not.

'Come on, we ride on. Stay alert, and keep your weapons in hand. I wouldn't put it beyond Jarl Halfdan's ability to scythe his way through the West Saxon force to battle us. I don't want that to happen. We don't have the numbers. Not here. We must be wary.'

Without further caution, I turn Haden to follow the trailing end of the West Saxon force. I'm regretting my stubbornness, but equally, Ealdorman Æthelwulf has told me much I didn't know. He's also provided an insight into Jarl Halfdan and his motivations. I'm really wishing I'd killed the fucking bastard when I had the chance.

I choke on the dust of the passage of the horses and wagons, while Icel rides slightly to the side to get a better view of where we're going. Ingwald does the same to the other side. Both men are uneasy that King Alfred dismissed Ingwald's caution so readily. I agree with them. There's no bloody reason for them to lie. There's no bloody reason at all, but King Alfred, while demanding the aid of Mercia, is also content to dismiss her abilities. He's a contrary bastard. The more time I spend with him, the less I like him, and to begin with I thought he was a fucking cock. If he falls any lower in my estimations, I'll not be able to stop myself from speaking as I find before him.

'Ahead,' Icel murmurs a little later. The day's advanced, but it's still light. The night won't be long in arriving, although we can take advantage of the elongated summer daylight for a while longer.

The West Saxon force has slowed considerably. I didn't think it was possible to go any slower, but that shows what I bloody know.

'Smoke?' I ask, gazing up into the blue sky dotted with clouds. Thankfully, it's been a warm day, but not too hot that I'm sweating.

'Yes.' We're on a slight rise. Behind us, thick woodland spreads, reaching almost all the way back to Cricklade. Ahead, there are rolling lands filled with green and growth. In the distance, I fancy I could see the sea if the hills and trees would get out of the way.

I can hear men shouting at one another. I shake my head, push Haden close to Icel, and then continue along the line. We've been following the slow oxen that pull the supply carts. I don't ride to war in such a way. Apparently, King Alfred must have his special seat and bed to rest on. Not for him a hard floor and a cloak. I'd sooner be swifter and much less encumbered.

'What's happening?' I call to Ealdorman Æthelwulf. He remains with his few men, although he has come to the side to peer onwards, just as I have.

'The enemy is ahead,' he informs me. I consider how he knows when no one has thought to tell me, or perhaps it's just bloody obvious from the thin grey smoke. Why the bastards have to burn everything, I'll never know. When they fire the grain stores, they only ensure they go fucking hungry, as well as the people whose food they burn. And yet, well, Jarl Halfdan has surprised me with his thinking on this account. I thought him a fool who'd done himself so much damage in Northumbria that he'd been driven out. But he's found a means of undoing that harm. And his ambitions have grown somewhat. He means to take command of Wessex. Or, at least, he means to make King Alfred part with some hefty bags of silver to make him go away.

'And what are they doing?' I raise my hand to peer where he looks. It's futile. I can't see the specifics, just the general idea of green and grey; smoke and crops.

'Doing?' Ealdorman Æthelwulf questions.

'Are they preparing to attack, or are we just waiting to be invited for fucking dinner?' I growl.

Icel barks a laugh. Ealdorman Æthelwulf rounds on me, forehead furrowed.

'My lord king.'

'Don't 'my lord king' me. You know I speak the truth.'

'I believe King Alfred is assessing what should be done next.'

'Assessing? We either attack the bastards and drive them from Wessex, or we make this a protracted war.'

'And you would have knowledge of the second option.'

I glower at him. 'I would, yes, and I can assure you, and as your king should know, the first option is the best.'

'And yet the other ealdormen have been unable to withstand the assault at Wareham and Winchester,' he reminds me.

'Then we'll show them the delight of some shock tactics.' Frustrated with this useless conversation, I encourage Haden forward, mindful that Icel and Rudolf keep me company. No doubt the rest of my men are taking bets on how long it'll be until they're elbow-deep in gore, or I've severed King Alfred's head from his neck. Both possibilities currently exist.

I eye King Alfred's warriors and supplies as I go. I've not been paying enough attention because, on first look, I know they're poor warriors and not likely to be useful against the enemy.

These are King Alfred and his ealdormen's warriors. They're not the fyrd. Some of them have horses, some of them don't. Those we met at Cricklade, have shimmering blades that show no wear. Those that joined the king at Cricklade, have blades that have at least been bloodied. Some of them are clearly good warriors. I eye those that I wouldn't like to meet in a fight. A few are as well-built as me and as Icel once was. A handful are scrawny like Rudolf, but, no doubt, fast on their feet. They have faces and bodies that reveal they've bled for Wessex. The closer I get to King Alfred, the more these examples of warriors fade away, until I'm left thinking that the king has brought boys to the fight. I consider whether these men are actually members of the fyrd, dressed up to look the part.

I find King Alfred with Ealdorman Wulfhere. Æthelwulf has

remained to the rear. Alfred eyes me with contempt as Haden kicks a stone and announces our arrival.

'The enemy, my lord,' King Alfred indicates, sweeping his hand across the vista before us. He's remembered his manners, which surprises me, although he still doesn't name me as a king.

'I can bloody see that, my lord king,' I mutter, squinting at the sunset. 'I do recall my warriors brought the news to you.' King Alfred doesn't seem to hear my sarcasm. 'How many?' I question, after a lengthy delay.

I'm not surprised that Ealdorman Wulfhere announces, 'No more than a third of the force. I assume the rest have remained at Wareham or Winchester.'

'Or they might be running through the landscape far from here?'

'Perhaps,' Ealdorman Wulfhere acknowledges unhappily.

'So, we're still far from Winchester?'

'Yes, at least another day.'

'What do you plan?' I direct this to King Alfred, but again, Ealdorman Wulfhere answers.

'We need to overwhelm them and send them scurrying back to Winchester and then to Wareham and then to their ships.'

'How will you do this when your ealdormen have been overwhelmed once?'

I expect King Alfred to answer this.

Icel's behind me. I know he'll be accessing the landscape, using his knowledge to ensure we don't do something fucking stupid.

'We will encircle them and ensure they can't infiltrate further into Wessex, either through the countryside or along the Portway.'

'Thanks for stating the bloody obvious,' I mutter. It appears King Alfred is unsure how to proceed. I think back to what Ealdorman Æthelwulf told me. Was it, after all, Alfred's brother, Æthelred, who made all the military decisions in the year of his death? Has King Alfred been bloody lucky since then not to be overwhelmed by the enemy?

I expect Icel to offer some advice, but he remains silently contemplative.

'We'll split the force,' King Alfred announces decisively. 'Ealdorman Wulfhere, you'll lead your men to the west of here. I'll take the central location, and Lord Coelwulf, you'll have the east to block the Portway.'

I narrow my eyes at that, looking to Icel, who shakes his head. He doesn't like that suggestion.

'That'll leave us the most exposed,' I comment. King Alfred's evidently unhappy that I've realised this. I'm impressed I've interpreted Icel's response correctly. 'It's the most important area of defence?' I suggest, then, mindful that it could be quite easy to force King Alfred to change his mind.

'If the roadway is held firm, then the enemy will be penned in.'

'And you wish me to do that?'

'I do, my lord, yes. I do.' King Alfred announces decisively.

'Then we'll do so,' I agree, despite Icel's unease. He might not be happy, and he might have wanted to be at a certain place to attack the enemy, but I know the route of the Portway. If this is a shit show, we can run for the River Thames and not be hampered by the woodlands and trees we've travelled through to reach this location.

I don't like to consider a means of retreat when the battles haven't started, but in this, I feel some comfort in knowing my men and I won't be snared by the enemy and by the king of Wessex and his shit tactics.

'When will we attack?'

'Once we're in position, I'll send a delegation to the enemy,' King Alfred announces. 'They'll be offered the opportunity to leave.'

'Why?'

'That's the honourable way.'

'It's not the way to bloody win. Give them no chance. Just bloody attack them.'

King Alfred offers me a superior smile. 'And that, my lord,' he condescends, 'is why your face is covered in the remnants of cuts and wounds. In Wessex, we speak with our enemy.'

'In Mercia, we engage our enemies with blades and shields. We do the talking with the pointy end of our fucking weapons.' King Alfred remains serene despite my aggression.

'We'll see who's the better tactician,' he confirms, as though he's a bloody general of old.

'I think we already sodding know,' Icel announces. Ealdorman Wulfhere offers him a baleful glance, only for his expression to change almost immediately. I consider whether Ealdorman Wulfhere knows Icel. I wish I had the opportunity to ask him, but I don't.

'I'll take my warriors to our position, but King Alfred, be assured, if the enemy attack us, or there's an opportunity for us to defeat them, we will engage, no matter what you might arrange with them when you have a little chat. If you want the bastards gone, you need to make Wessex seem unappealing. I assure you we warriors of Mercia can accomplish that for you.'

Without waiting for a reply, I turn Haden and go back to the rest of the men.

'My lord, we really don't want to hold that position,' Icel informs me.

'And that's why we're going to hold it. King Alfred thinks to give us the more difficult task and hamper us by announcing the enemy must be given the opportunity to agree to a peace talk. We'll not be doing that.'

'If this is just to spite him and prove you're right, it's a dangerous gamble to take.' He cautions me. 'Especially when you know so little of Wessex.'

'Perhaps,' I acknowledge. 'But we're not going to fucking die, and we are the better warriors, so let's bloody prove it. If we can get our hands on Jarl Halfdan, we can slice his stones from his body and end this. He's plagued Wessex. He's plagued Northumbria. He's plagued Mercia. That bastard needs to die.'

Chapter Nineteen

Far from reconciled to what we're doing, Icel leads us away from the main body of the West Saxon force before it's fully dark. Overhead, the moon lights our path. I know he's uneasy. The rest of my men aren't, not even Cuthwalh.

We ride through a lush landscape before emerging onto an ancient roadway, clearly demarcated in the rubble and stones dotting the surface. Now that we're lower down, we can't see much of anything ahead, but we do have a clear view of what's at our backs. It might be some day's distance, but the River Thames is there, and we can make it to London if needed. I can't imagine we will. I intend to kill the bastard Viking raiders and keep Mercia safe. The thought of retreat is unappealing.

Icel pulls us to the side of the road, and dismounts from his horse. He moves without talking and I realise he's angry with me.

'We stay here for the night,' I call to my men. 'We keep guard and assess our options in the morning. Beornstan, Wærwulf and Ingwald, you'll have the first watch. Eahric, Goda and I will take the second. Icel, Rudolf and Oda, you get the third.' No one speaks against my commands, and I hurry to tend to Haden so I can leave him to his oats and then nibble at the grasses that encircle the campsite.

I consider speaking with Icel as I take bread and cheese from my saddle bags, but a shake of his head from Pybba, and I find myself in agreement with him. I don't want an unholy argument, and there will be one.

Instead, I join Pybba. The sound of a busy encampment slowly quietens. Men eat and sleep or piss and bitch, but no one is particularly uneasy, apart from Icel, and maybe Ingwald, who first saw the enemy. That's why I've given him the first watch. He needs to assure himself we can sleep without fear of attack.

'Well, this is a shit show,' I mutter to Pybba. He's also eating but nods, eyes gleaming beneath the moonlight.

'It involves Wessex, so it's going to be.'

'Icel's pissed.'

'Icel's always pissed. He hates the West Saxons. That won't stem from nothing.' I absorb that. And then I ask the question that's been plaguing me.

'Am I too overconfident?'

'Aye, my lord, you are. But that's never stopped you before,' he ends with a chuckle. I'm reminded of me and Icel's conversation on the bridge at Gloucester no more than a few weeks ago. He told me then that I took decisions and risks that he never would but that he couldn't complain because they always worked. Yet his unhappiness here makes me doubt the truth of that. Have I overextended myself? Should I return to Mercia? After all, King Alfred is taking the piss. I know that. My men know that. He's all hot air and little action. I've not even seen him lift his sword or seax in anger. Does he have any battle prowess? How many men has he killed, if any?

'Get some sleep,' I urge Pybba. I don't do the same. I'm tired but restless. Instead, I walk the perimeter of our encampment. We're hardly hidden. The closest trees are some distance away. If it rains during the night, we're going to get soaked. I don't think it will rain.

Wærwulf greets me with a knowing look as I approach. He peers into the distance toward where the enemy has been seen. His eyes blaze in the darkness.

'Fucking bastard,' he growls. I think he means the enemy. Or perhaps he means King Alfred.

'Anything?' I ask him.

'No, my lord, just the usual nighttime noises. If the enemy come over this road, we'll hear them long before they get close enough to take us unawares.'

'Would they even know we're here?'

'If they watched us arrive, then yes,' he suggests. I grin at that. I'm asking stupid questions, and the answers are suitably honest. Wærwulf's a good man.

'I don't believe we're being watched,' I comment, a slap to his back before I move on to where Ingwald also glares to the south.

'Ingwald.'

'My lord,' he replies immediately, as though he knew I was there, and no doubt, he did.

'Anything?'

'No, the fuckers aren't close. I don't expect to see them tonight.'

'Tomorrow?'

'Perhaps. Be wary, my lord. I don't trust that arsehole not to corral the enemy this way. Especially not after your discussion earlier.' I absorb that. It feels like a blow, but I think little of King Alfred. I can't imagine he thinks of me respectfully.

'Thank you,' I mutter to Ingwald, and again, slap his back and make my way to Beornstan. Beornstan looks north, along the Portway that would take us back towards the River Thames, with London on the far bank.

He stands alert and tense, hands behind his back, shield resting against a stone just to his left. He's ready to fight if the enemy comes from that direction.

'Anything?' I question.

'No, my lord. Nothing at all.'

Beornstan and I have had an uneasy relationship since his incarceration by the enemy at Grantabridge. They treated him poorly. I wish he'd not been so badly beaten by them.

'If they come, I'll kill 'em all, or die trying,' he growls. Despite the enemy we killed outside Northampton and also outside Gloucester, Beornstan, like many of my men, and I include myself in that, still hungers to exact the ultimate vengeance. I consider if we kill all of the enemy, if that will satisfy us. I'm not convinced it would.

'Beornstan, I wanted to apologise for what befell you within Grantabridge.'

I sense Beornstan stiffen at my words. When he speaks, his words are forced.

'There's no need. It was my responsibility to protect Lady Cyneswith—a responsibility I take seriously and at which I failed. I don't hold you accountable. It was the bastard enemy and at Jarl Guthrum's instigation.' I nod as he speaks. We've needed to have this conversation for some time.

'That might be, but I would have left you in that cage to rescue Lady Cyneswith.'

'My lord king,' his tone is formal as he turns to look at me. 'You would have done what needed to be done. If you'd risked her for me, I would have thought less of you. You know that. I know that. I'll kill the enemy, and I'll never be a prisoner again. Never fear on that account. And if I'm ever captured again, I'll kill as many of the fuckers as I can in trying to escape.'

His words thrum with conviction. I nod and realise I can't say anything else.

I've apologised. He's not accepted it. But he's my warrior, and he fights for Mercia. If I'm honest, I would expect all of my warriors to answer like he has.

'You're a good man, Beornstan. I'm honoured to fight at your side. Mercia is honoured to be served by a man such as you.'

So spoken, I take myself away to roll in my cloak and get some sleep. Beornstan wakes me what feels like moments later.

'Nothing to report,' he rumbles, kicking me aside so he can settle in his cloak. I stand and stretch, wiping grit from my eyes, and take his position. I'd sooner be looking south, but instead, I yawn and stamp life into my feet, eyeing the way back towards the River Thames.

The moon seems brighter, and I can see more and more. I feel I can see further than during the day when the sun dazzles my eyes. I walk along the road some distance, noting how it remains a constant width and how well-planted the surrounding landscape is. Then I turn back, looking towards the south, able to detect the men who keep guard with me but face the enemy.

I sense the openness of the location, the lack of tree cover, and the impediment of straggling bushes that demarcate much of the roadway. To the far side of them, I can sometimes hear the shuffle and snores of sleeping animals. This landscape is rich and vibrant, and undoubtedly, I'll be able to see steadings and villages close by during the daytime.

That makes sense to me. Such roads and waterways, like the River Thames, invite people to them, offering easy means of transport. They also entice the Viking raiders. I find myself considering Mercia. Is it as lush and vibrant as what I've seen of Wessex? I'm unsure. The parts I've seen mostly are the pathways alongside rivers or the Viking raider encampments. The actual people of Mercia are more difficult to find.

Icel relieves me sometime later. My thoughts are so busy, I've lost track of time.

'Get some sleep,' he growls at me.

'You don't like this?' I question instead.

'Not at all,' his face splits in a smirk, and I grin at him.

'Tell me what you fear?'

'I fear the Wessex king will send the enemy this way. I also fear that the enemy will want to follow this route. It'll give them much easier access to the River Thames and to the wealth that Wessex has to offer.'

'Which do you fear most? The enemy or our alleged allies?' Icel offers me a mirthless grimace.

'I don't think you need me to tell you that. We all know who the greater enemy is. Now, get some bloody sleep, and in the morning, we'll think our way out of this, or at least of a way to ensure your safety from our ally.' I swallow at the suppressed fury in his words.

Despite Pybba's assurances, I might have allowed my overconfidence to sway me into a perilous situation.

Fuck it. I will have to prevail.

Chapter Twenty

Bright sunlight wakes me again. I didn't think I'd sleep after the middle watch, but I have. Not, I realise as I wince against a growing headache, that it's done me any good. I shouldn't have been so stubborn. I could have allowed others to take the most uncomfortable watch, but I'm a contrary bastard and never likely to know what's best for me. I've proved that time and time again.

The campsite's busy. The shuffle of horses, their soft nickers, and the coarse cries of my warriors taking the piss out of one another have me sitting up and rubbing my hand through my ragged beard. A few days on the road, I'm already missing the thought of a decent shave and bath. I've grown bloody soft since becoming king. I try not to think about the dried sweat on my face.

'Get up, you lazy arse,' Icel calls. I know he means me. I groan, stand, stretch and then look around me. In the bright daylight, everything looks different to last night. It looks changed to yesterday when we arrived here, as well.

Kicking those who still linger on the floor, feigning sleep, and chuckling as I go, I find Icel, Ingwald, Pybba, and Rudolf surveying the road ahead. I can't see it, but somewhere there is Winchester – the capital of the West Saxon kings. King Alfred, I've been told before, does like Winchester. Why, I don't know. Ealdorman Æthelwulf was hardly filled with praise for the place, and it lacks decent walls. As I have at Kingsholm, a king's residence should have good walls to keep his people safe.

'What's been happening?' I question, yawning again. I wince at the smell of my sour breath when I catch it with my hand.

'Not bloody much.' Icel admits. I don't think he likes to do so. He'd like something to be occurring.

'Any news from King Alfred?'

'No, my lord. But I imagine they're still bloody sleeping.'

I grin at Icel's dour tone. He really hates the bastard, especially since some of our own men still sleep. Gardulf snores like he's in a bed with a new mattress and a feather pillow upon which he can rest his head.

'So, today we move deeper into Wessex-held land?'

'We do, yes,' Icel agrees. 'But I want everyone to know the way back to Mercia. The Portway, and if not that way, then towards that collection of trees over there, and straight through them back to Cricklade.'

'I think we can find our bloody way,' I offer reassuringly. Icel's silence on that point is telling.

'The smoke has stopped in the far distance. It appears the fires have burned themselves out,' Ingwald adds.

I shrug my shoulders and endeavour to drive away the sharp pain in my neck from lying in a strange position.

'Where was this place you wanted us to reach? Can we still get there from here?' I question Icel.

'Not here,' he shuts me down. I grin and arch an eyebrow.

'Then where is it, you damn arse?'

'Back the way we came, somewhat.'

'So between here and where we were yesterday?'

'Yes.'

'And what's there?'

'The remnants of an old fort, and tree cover for our backs.'

'So, rather than retreating along the Portway, we should go there?'

Icel doesn't immediately reply, but we're in no rush, so I wait for him to consider the response.

'Perhaps, my lord, yes. It would be better to be there than to be caught on the road, but then, we'd need to wait for reinforcements.'

I acknowledge that, but I'm still busy thinking about all this. Ealdorman Ælhun might well have received the message to get himself to London by now. But what of my other warriors? Kyred and his men might yet have come south. We have some options available to us. However, it appears Icel wants some decisions fixed in stone. I'm not sure I can give them, not yet.

'We need to see what happens,' I conclude.

'Perhaps, my lord. Or maybe we need to make something happen instead.' Ingwald's suggestion is intriguing.

'So, what, we set events in motion and then have them play out how we want them to do so?'

'If we can, yes. It would be better to predict what will happen when we meet the enemy.'

'I think we know there's going to be a bloody great big fight,' I chuckle, but appreciate his sentiment. Icel speaks then.

'Ingwald's correct. There's another location, not far from here, where even a few warriors could overpower the enemy and hold them at bay.'

'A river crossing?' I question.

'Something like that,' Icel is his usual forthright self. I wait. 'No, not a river crossing,' he eventually concedes. 'But the woodland is thick, and anyone coming to meet us would have to go through a tight and twisty section where it's impossible to see the way forward.'

'And King Alfred will know of this?'

'He should, but whether he does or not remains to be seen.'

'But, will the enemy know of this?'

'That rather depends on what happened here four years ago, and at the moment, we don't know that.'

Once more, I lapse into silence. Here, far from Mercia, I feel uncharacteristically out of my depth. All the same, I've long known that my strength is in knowing Mercia well. And one thing I appreciate is that Wessex is very much a mystery to me. But it isn't to Icel or Cuthwalh.

'We do as Icel suggests,' I announce, staking our future on his insights. I sense him startle at my easy, well almost easy, acceptance of his intentions. 'Icel knows this place better than the rest of us and, hopefully, better than the Viking raider jarls.'

'What of King Alfred?' Icel questions.

'What of him? He asked us for our help. He hasn't told us exactly how we must give it to him. At the moment, he thinks to have set us the most difficult task, leaving us the most exposed. We'll repay that bloody kindness by showing him how war should really be waged on our fucking enemy.' A slow smile stretches across Icel's face, and he looks the happiest since coming to Wessex. Whether his idea is the correct one or not, I don't know, but I'm content to find out. If Icel thinks I take unnecessary risks, I'll see how he does when that risk rests on his old head.

Eating hastily, we mount up and move along the road. Icel seems calm now he has more say over our endeavours. I wait for a messenger from King Alfred with some shit about how we should be doing what he orders. I'm surprised a messenger doesn't arrive. Well, I am until smoke once more clouds the horizon ahead, and Icel draws us to a halt with a raised hand. I've been riding to the rear, speaking with Pybba. Now, I rush forward, wondering how I've missed the growing smoke.

'Well, that's fucking marvellous, isn't it?' I complain. Rudolf's beside me.

'I take it that's a West Saxon force down there?' I point.

'It is, my lord, yes.' Rudolf announces quickly.

'Who leads them?'

'It's difficult to say, but as King Alfred said he wanted the middle ground, and we've not passed another force, I'm going to stick my bloody neck out and say it could be King Alfred and his warriors.'

Ahead, the Portway dips lower again, almost running alongside a river. And to our side of the river, there's a small encampment—or there was. Now it blazes, and smoke seems to jump from tent to tent. I can see a collection of warriors moving around, but I don't think it's a West Saxon force. They move with far more conviction than I've seen a single West Saxon warrior employ.

'Our leader has come undone already,' I explode softly. It doesn't surprise me. It really doesn't. What does surprise me is not knowing where he and his warriors have gone. It's evident they've not come to find us. It's also clear that it happened so quickly, King Alfred hasn't thought to send us a messenger to ask for our assistance.

Or maybe this is all a trick. I shouldn't be so suspicious, but I am.

'Are they Viking raiders?' I question Rudolf.

'It's impossible to tell from here,' he replies apologetically.

I look from the smoke southwards. There's another cloud of smoke there.

'Is that Winchester?' I direct to Icel.

'Yes.'

I gnaw my lower lip, trying to determine what's happened here. Has King Alfred been overwhelmed? Has he made a run for Winchester, although he was told it was compromised? Or has he gone further west to meet up with the warriors led by Ealdorman Wulfhere?

'What to do?' I mutter. Haden's quiet beneath me. He can't smell the smoke, so he has nothing to upset him. I wish I could say the same.

I look from Icel to Pybba to Rudolf to Ingwald.

'It appears we'll have to investigate,' I announce. None of them tell me I'm wrong, which isn't the fucking comfort I'd like it to be.

'Come on then,' I urge my warriors. 'Ride with weapons and shields ready. When we get lower, we'll be able to see even less. Don't engage unless there's no choice. And make sure you're not about to skewer one of the West Saxon warriors. I imagine the lot of them will be a bit flighty after whatever they've endured.'

'And then?' Icel asks.

'Then we'll make a new plan. For now, and with no information to aid us, we need to find out what's happened. If this is it, and the West Saxon force is overwhelmed, we'll return to Mercia. I can't face all four jarls with just a handful of men.'

'And we have your assurance on that?' Pybba demands.

I shake my head. 'There really is no fucking trust,' I chuckle, urging Haden onwards. 'The sooner we know, the sooner we can decide what we do next,' I inform them over my shoulder. I don't reach for my seax; I still miss the weapon impaled in the roof of Northampton's church, but I do ensure I can release my shield quickly if needed, and I curl Haden's reins up high in my hand. It'll take but a moment to tie them in a knot if I need to ensure he can gallop away without me. Not that I think it will come to that.

I have my suspicions about what's happened to the West Saxons. I almost can't decide whether I want to be bloody proved correct.

Chapter Twenty-One

The scent of smoke increases the closer we get. No one has run our way, either in terror or to meet our far-from-subtle approach. This many horses make a fucking lot of noise over the interchangeable packed earth and stone roadway.

Icel and Ingwald have taken themselves to the front. Goda and Sæbald hold the rear. I'm in the middle, although I'd rather not be, but I've determined to be almost sensible in this. Better to risk Icel and Ingwald than myself. Hereman's almost level with the front two. His hair streams beneath his helm as I fiddle with the knots to undo my own. Until now, I've not wanted to add the linen cap and iron helm to my head. It's been too hot, but I won't risk a blow to the head when I can prevent it.

The sound of the river close by grows in intensity. I thrust my helm onto my head, allowing Haden to ride without direction as it takes both hands to accomplish. The smoke grows thicker, and I stretch for my shield, ready to defend Haden, myself, and my men. I don't want Haden to be wounded again. The cut he took within Gloucester has yet to heal fully. It's left an area where I think his coat will never grow back.

'Ware,' Icel calls when we're on the edges of the encampment. The tents have been either set aflame or broken down. I can see from one end of the campsite to the other, and there are a good number of bloodied bodies lying with blades ripped from hands, or so I assume.

'Bastards,' Icel shouts, the first to dismount and stride through the ruins of the tents and men. I wince at the innards on display, noting these dead men weren't armoured. I imagine they had blades to hand, but no byrnies. They must have been caught with their arses out.

I dismount, Haden rearing back at the cloying smell of smoke and blood. I offer him a word of caution and bend to dip and examine the bodies. Ingwald and Icel stride through the camp, shields in hand, checking to see whether any enemies are lurking. We'd be able to see if there were, but I don't call them back.

I touch the face of the first body I come across, meeting the unseeing gaze of a man some indeterminate age with grey hair and a grey beard. He's not young, or he wasn't young. Neither was he particularly old. He's cold and marbled.

'They've been dead some time,' I call, perplexed. There's not a lot here to burn, so if the smoke still lingers, the campsite's been torched long after the men were dead.

'And he has,' Rudolf calls, hands already busy patting the man down for anything of value he might still have. Rudolf stands abruptly, a small coin bag in his hand, testing the weight before delving inside. I watch him. He pulls forth a handful of coins. They glint in what light there is.

'They didn't take this man's wealth,' he announces.

'Check them all,' I advise my men, striding to the next body and discovering the same. He even has his blade clutched in his dead hand. These people have been killed, but their wealth wasn't taken. That's not the way of the Viking raiders I know.

I stick my head in what remains of one of the tents. I rear back, lips twisted. There's another body inside, lying as though in sleep. It reminds me of when we killed the bastards outside Northampton. Not everyone was awake when they died.

'So, they've been dead a while but not been robbed, and the campsite was only recently burned.' I feel my unease grow. I look around. The river passes to the side of the encampment. It's not particularly far to the other side. I stride there, looking for some sign of a fording point, and quickly see it. Thick stone slabs line the river. There are signs that the ford often floods.

I rotate to look at Icel and Ingwald. They continue to march through the campsite, shields ready should they be needed. Icel suspects subterfuge. I'm with him on this. But who is the trap for? And who set it? That's probably the more pertinent question.

'Back to your horses,' I urge my warriors, rubbing my neck and peering all around. My unease is intensifying. We're hardly a full fighting force. Including me, I have twenty-eight men under my command and just as many horses. It's a good number, but that really depends on the force sent to hunt me down.

I mount quickly.

'Leave the dead, and their paltry treasures,' I urge Rudolf. He hastens to mount Jethson. Some of the others are slower to heed my caution, for once, Osmod isn't one of them. He offers me a grin from his horse. He's pulled his shield into his hand. I do the same.

'They killed the poor bastards but waited to bait the trap,' I murmur. If this is a tactic of the Viking raiders, then I confess, I'm impressed.

'Come on,' I urge my men. 'We need to leave here.'

Icel's finally mounted once more.

'Where to?' he questions.

'Through the ford and onwards until we meet where you want to stop. I can't imagine it'll be long until we know who killed these men.'

Rudolf scampers to Jethson's side, but first he places something into my hand.

I look down at it, and then I grimace.

The emblem is one depicting Jarl Halfdan's wolf.

'From one of the dead or from one of the living?' I question, but then I get my answer.

'Bollocks,' I huff. 'They're coming,' I shout, and from the other side of the river, I see a collection of leering Viking raiders approaching us, far from quietly. They fight with a wolf image daubed onto their shield. And there are at least fifty of them.

'Arse,' I exclaim. We could ride from this place because they're on foot, not on horseback, but then Goda's voice calls from behind.

'There are more of them,' his words are ominous as I turn Haden to eye those coming from behind. The men are well-equipped. They have shields, spears, and seaxes, while some have swords or war axes. There are at least another fifty of them.

'Fucking bollocks,' I explode. I won't be taken prisoner. I won't bloody die here. And I will kill all of these fuckers. I must determine how.

'Dismount,' I call to my men. The horses have the means to escape if we move quickly. I loop Haden's reins high and slap him heavily on the arse. He thunders towards the river, followed by Jethson and the majority of other horses, all apart from Icel's borrowed mount. I listen to the cries of the enemy and the crack as one of the bastards gets knocked over by the animals. I could have ordered us to go with them, but that would have resulted in a messy fight, and the horses would have been set upon as the easiest of the targets.

'To me,' I order my warriors. 'Form a circle,' I instruct quickly. I catch sight of Icel's furious face as he stamps to my side. Hereman's quick to take the space beside me. I move us out, away from the ruin of the tents and the already cold bodies of those killed earlier, perhaps days earlier. I'm pissed that I didn't realise the enemy was behind us as well as in front. I just need to live through this, and then I can be fucking furious with myself and every single one of my warriors. We all missed this. We can't bloody do that in enemy land.

I swivel my head from one side to the other. I'm trying to determine who'll attack first. I also glance at the enemy, deciphering whether I know these men. Were they at Northampton? I really can't tell.

'Wessex fools,' the one leading them through the ford calls in heavily accented Norse. I consider this. It seems they don't know my identity. Not even the double-headed eagle emblem on our shields has given us away. Perhaps these bastards weren't at Northampton. Maybe they've never encountered the Mercians. Admittedly, they can't be expecting to find Mercians within Wessex. I wouldn't anticipate finding West Saxons within Mercia.

'*Skiderick*,' Icel shouts. His voice thrums with fury but not rage. Whatever is at play here, we've not been sold out by King Alfred or hunted down by men loyal to Jarl Halfdan. I really should stop seeing conspiracy everywhere.

I sense my men falling into place around me, with Icel's horse in the middle of us all. The animal's making strange noises, undoubtedly terrified, and wishing it hadn't been so stubborn in not following the others.

I hear the Viking raiders shouting one to another in their own language, and then Wærwulf speaks.

'They mean to attack at the same time, from both sides.' I growl at that. They're confident they have the numbers. Now, we need to show them how wrong they are.

'Stay alert, and stay the fuck alive,' I order my warriors as the enemy encircles us from both sides. For the briefest moment, I allow a shard of doubt but then banish it. Fear will get me nowhere. We'll overpower them, or so help me, my aunt will fucking kill me, and what she'll do to King Alfred, I really don't like to consider. Or his wife.

Not that the Viking raiders come at us straight away.

'Cowards,' Hereman roars as they stand, spears extended towards us, but no one moving any closer. There's a growl of fury whether they understand the words or not.

'Can you only attack men who're sleeping,' Pybba demands next. A howl of rage greets that taunting statement.

'Damn bastards,' Wulfstan adds, and I grin at his less-than-original taunt.

'Come on then, you fucking chickens,' Wærwulf rumbles and must repeat the same in the Norse tongue. That gets the bastards complaining. But still, no one begins the attack.

'Hereman,' I call, and before the word is out of my mouth, he's thrown his spear. It skewers a man slightly to the front of the enemy line, who holds a shield but only loosely in his hand. The spear goes straight through his chest, forcing him backwards. Now, the wrath of the enemy increases. I can sense it'll only take one more thing for our opponents to attack us.

'Again,' I call. Hereman flings the next spear, and it too skewers another of the assembled warriors, this time behind where I stand. I watch the weapon, surprised that our foeman is caught so unprepared.

'Get ready for it,' I call. And then it happens.

The first of our opponents hasten forward, a roaring cry encouraging him. I eye them all. There are a hundred enemies. That means we have about four each to kill, give or take.

'A mancus for who kills the bloody most,' I shout, not that my men need such an encouragement. They bellow their appreciation all the same, and then shit gets real.

Chapter Twenty-Two

'Attack,' I roar. With Hereman to one side, and Icel to the other, we move into the enemy. They're too cowardly to take the first steps. I've never been one to shy away from a fucking big fight, and if it's unlikely that we're going to win, then all the better.

My shield before me, seax to hand, I advance on them. There are small gaps between my men. We can't stand shoulder to shoulder and counter our opponents. But that doesn't concern me. All we need to do is keep the bastards from breaking through and attacking us from behind as well as from in front.

I meet the first foeman with a crashing blow from my seax. The blade isn't perfectly weighted for my hand, but brute strength will still make it perform as I want. My adversary, who thought he would surely succeed, stutters at the attack. It takes my foeman precious time to perfect his hold on the shield, and in that gap, I'm too close for his spear to be useful. Fucking arse.

My seax blow is elevated, aiming for his neck. He lifts his shield high. I punch with my shield into his exposed belly. The spear clangs to the ground as I graze his hand. He collapses around the pain in his stomach. It takes but a moment to stab into his exposed throat with my blade.

'Daft bastard,' I glower, watching him stumble. I spit the taste of his blood from my mouth and menace the next bastard. He watches his ally fall, eyes on stalks. Like the first man, he's too slow to stop me from landing the first blow. I aim for the lower half of his body, and he shoots his shield low, knocking it against the bucking legs of the dying man. I grin as I reverse the action, stabbing into his stomach, only for the blade to come up against the protection of his byrnie. A grimace, and I hack towards his neck, repeating my earlier action.

He might be slow to start, but he ducks out of the reach of my seax blade. I arch an eyebrow as a sign of respect. Not that he sees it below my helm.

I decide whoever is in command will have done one of two things. They've either sacrificed the weaker warriors, allowing those with more experience to attack us when we're already bloodied and sweated, or they've not given it a moment's thought, and the men are intermingled. I imagine the latter, but I'll wait and see.

My foeman steps to meet my next assault, his war axe in one hand, his shield in the other. He glowers at me, lips downcast, beard splattered with the blood of his dead ally. But his eyes show his fear. Fear will make a man piss himself in fright when faced with a lethal warrior.

I surge towards him, mindful of the man who's dead or dying and will soon be dead. I extend my seax, elbow high. He has his shield to protect his neck, exposing his legs. Not that I go for them. He'll be expecting that. Instead, I repeat the action and punch out with my shield, driving it against the shield and forcing both close to his body. I see his eyes bulge, and the angle of his elbow is too extreme to be comfortable or maintained. He'll drop the blade or break his own arm unless he steps back.

He holds firm. I smirk at that, pushing more and more weight behind the shields. Any moment now, he'll remember the war axe in his hand. I lash out with my seax. He watches it coming closer and closer. I toy with him, a slice to his unprotected chin. I've drawn first blood.

With a cry of pain, he finally steps back. My shield gives. He crashes into the man behind him. The damn arse doesn't watch his ally's efforts, instead jeering at those fighting Hereman and Icel. With nowhere to go, my foeman finally remembers his war axe, lifting it to crash it against my shield. I lift it to hold the blade away from me and step ever closer. He was stuck with his shield too tight to his chest. Now he's wedged between me and his ally, and neither of us is going anywhere.

I hear him shouting to his fellow warrior, but the man is oblivious. I lower my seax and stab into his body, angling it this time so that it has the chance to get through the byrnie. But his protection is good. It withstands the assault. I grimace. Overhead, my shield keeps his axe away from me. It means we're closer than we could be. I pull my arm ever higher, my foeman struggling to keep hold of the shield. He focuses on that and not on me. I step forward and nut him on the nose. My head reverberates with the blow as his nose explodes with a sharp snap. He veers away, only to hit the man behind him again. His war axe hand trembles, dropping away, as he brings his shield up to try and counter my attack.

A nasally muffled conversation. No doubt he demands the man move or aid him. He does neither, and now, with tearing eyes and a streaming nose, I slide my seax blade into his open mouth, deep until it impacts the back of his throat. The bastard dies with his snot and blood mingling on the edge of the blade.

'Stupid bastard,' I offer, yanking back the blade, allowing him to fall to the ground. To either side of me, I sense Icel and Hereman overpowering their foemen. This is too easy. I expect some fiercer defence from the next man. But he eyes me with surprise. Did he think his ally still blocked his path?

'You should be paying more fucking attention,' I inform him while his mouth settles into a firm line of determination. He also has a shield, and the two at my feet are getting in the way. He has a sword. I eye it. His equipment shimmers. I muse as to whether he knows what he's doing, and have my answer soon enough.

Shield before him, he meets my attack, sword raised high to chop down on my shield. I consider if that will work as I guide my shield forward. I'm mindful of the dead and dying at my feet. The number's growing almost by the breaths I take. The shouts and cries of my allies mingle with those of the enemy. I detect Rudolf's shriek of triumph, Pybba's grunt of effort, even Icel's quieter but more controlled attack against our foemen. If I closed my eyes, I could determine where my men fought. But I don't close my eyes. I need to kill the bastard and his flashy sword.

So far, my opponent hasn't given me much cause for concern, but I'm always prepared to be surprised. This isn't to be one of those occasions.

The sword swings before my eyes. I bat it aside with my shield, menacing with my seax. I don't go for the killing blow yet. The equipment he wears is much better than anything the other two had. I'll need to be craftier and use more skill to kill this fucker.

He brings his sword back with a soft grunt. His beard is trimmed with trinkets, and his tunic is brightly dyed red beneath his byrnie. This man has wealth—or rather, he did. Soon, he'll be dead, and whoever takes his wealth is welcome to it.

I thrust my shield towards his sword again, holding it at bay. The amount of time it's spent in the air, being ineffective, he might as well have a fucking war axe. A sword shouldn't be swung almost overarm at the enemy. I would use mine with far more skill, but it's not a weapon to be employed now when men press tightly to one another. A seax is much better. Or a war axe. Or a shield. Not a bloody sword.

Once more, he tries the same tactic. This time, I'm quicker, fiercer. I thrust the shield against his sword, pressing tighter and tighter so the blade is held against him. He can't lift it to use it again. I jab with my seax, aiming for the upper arm of the hand which holds the sword. His byrnie doesn't extend down his arms. Again, I'm fascinated by men who fight in such a way. I stab and then stab again. A well of blood erupts. He grunts in pain, unable to move his sword to counter me, although he tries to batter me with his shield. I feel it hit my back once, twice, three times. For every blow he lands, I jab into his arm. Any moment now, he'll drop his sword. He won't be able to hold it as I hack through his upper arm.

'*Skiderick*,' he screams. Between blows, he evolves from a man able to contain his pain to one who fucking can't. Blood streams from his arm. He drops his sword. It lands with a clang on the shield of one of the dead men. I'd not expected that. It must have rolled this way. Not that I look down. My eyes blaze into his. He spits at me. I don't move aside. I keep my gaze on his. His shield hits me despite his pain, knocking me closer and closer to him. I allow it. I can smell his fear and sweat. I can smell what he drank that morning.

I lift my seax from his arm. The edge shimmers wetly in the sunlight, a gleam of his lifeblood. I think he's mine. I believe I'll kill him, but he shocks me.

He steps back. I redouble my grip on my shield and follow him, eyes alert to what he's doing. Is he trying to escape? Does he have someone else to fight this battle for him? Or is he just wounded and desperate to leave here with his life? I follow him, mindful of where I step, not wanting to be rushed. His shield's held before him, his right-hand dripping with blood, his arm useless at his side. He won't be lifting anything with that, no matter the shimmer of his byrnie. He has other weapons. I see him fumbling for a seax from his weapons belt, but his right hand can't grip the blade.

Close enough to smell him again, he jabs forward with his shield. I'm expecting it. I counter with my shield, fingers firm on my seax. Any moment now, I'll get the chance I need. I'm mindful of walking too far from my allies. We don't fight in a tight shield wall, yet we must all protect one another. All the same, I can't let him leave.

I watch him, sensing him, licking my lips, waiting for the right moment.

His lifeless hand flops against his weapons belt, tears or sweat dripping into his beard from beneath his helm. His eyes flash with fury and pain. He's a wounded animal, and wounded animals are as lethal as Hereman is lucky.

'Come on, you arsehole,' I menace with my seax blade. There's no one behind him. Whoever was there, if anyone was there, faces one of my warriors, or has run away. I wouldn't be surprised if they've run. They thought they had the numbers, but this is a fucking blood bath.

'Who are you?' the man asks through white lips.

'I'm King Coelwulf of Mercia, the second of his name,' I offer, my voice soft and menacing. 'And I'll be your death.' Quickly, I run at him, seax high once more. At the last moment, as he moves his shield to protect his head, I thrust my weapon low, striking against his byrnie in a shower of sparks. I force it upwards, thrusting my seax beneath the arm holding his shield, piercing the unprotected part of his underarm despite the glimmer of iron and silver.

His eyes open even wider, but it's the slow grin on his lips that temporarily distracts me, and then a blow lands on my shoulder. I whirl, realising I'm too far from the rest of my warriors.

I've done what I said I wouldn't do. Now I'm the fucking arsehole.

'Coelwulf,' my name rings through the air, but five bastard enemies surround me.

'Well,' I huff through tight lips. 'This just got very fucking interesting.'

Chapter Twenty-Three

'It seems I'm not acquainted,' I quip, resetting the grip on my shield before I do anything. But these bastards aren't here to have a chat.

A sword veers up before me. I batter it aside with my shield. The man who wields it is huge, perhaps taller than Hereman. Only a few men are that tall. He wears a slow grin, and I notice he doesn't sweat and no blood mars his blade as he recovers his grip to try again.

Behind me, the man I so nearly killed breathes louder than a bladesmith's furnace. At least he won't be resuming his attack. I have time, or so I console myself.

The next blow comes from a war axe. The blade shimmers wetly, and blood and severed hair adhere to it.

'At least you've been having a bloody good go,' I mutter, my lips taut, moving aside to evade the reach of the weapon which the Viking raider swings two-handed. If that blade hits me, I'll be winded. Instead, it scythes down behind me, doing little more than disturbing the warm air to allow a trickle of cool to bathe my face. I offer a smirk. I can't see my warriors, but they're there. The enemy hasn't overwhelmed us. There's only me that's made themselves vulnerable. I just need to hold until one of the bastards realises I'm not with them.

'Fuck this,' I wheeze, choosing my next target. I'll not stand here and allow them to take shots at me. I surge into a medium-sized man with more hair on his chin than his balding head. He carries no shield but has two seaxes. I don't think he'll be the easiest to defeat, but he'll confuse the others with that many weapons.

With my seax, I jab towards his chest, shield in the other hand, which I punch towards the man standing beside him. This warrior has a huge shield, so huge that I can't actually see his blade. The smack of my shield against his sends an uncomfortable thrumming situation along my arm, but it holds him at bay as I counter the double seax wielder. The bald warrior uses a seax to block my blow, but I knew he would. I veer around it, jabbing again at his belly, eyebrows high beneath my helm, showing him that two seaxes, despite what he thinks, are not better than a seax and a shield, which I have. I don't draw blood. I don't intend to, not yet.

His other blade comes closer. I thrust my shield towards the huge shield once more and feel the man behind me getting closer. It could be my wounded enemy. It could be the huge war axe wielder who needs two hands to swing it. I step into the double-seax holder. I see his eyes widen as whatever his ally is doing gets too close to him. A gabble of words, and I grin again, stabbing upwards with my seax, almost getting close enough to his neck, but he steps backwards, not to evade me, but to miss the blow from the war-axe.

Daft bastards are doing half the job for me.

Once more, I punch my shield towards the huge shield. Whoever stands behind it, and I can't actually see it's that fucking wide, he's made no move to do anything else.

The prattle of words sees the man with the huge war axe moving slightly away. I know what the double-seax carrier said, well, I imagine I know. 'Get the fuck away, or you'll kill me.' And that's what I want to happen.

I pivot, mindful I leave my back exposed and run at the man with the huge war axe. It's a fucking deadly blade in the right hands. I'm not sure he is the right hands. I threaten with my seax, and before he can recover himself from the failed blow, I land a strike on his arm, a deep gash that runs all the way to his elbow. He howls with pain, more akin to a pig on the way to be slaughtered. The sound's so loud and so bizarre coming from such a big man that it temporarily stuns me and those around him. Another babble of words and I stamp forward, once, twice, and my seax blade is at his throat and severing it before he can do anything else.

'A big fucking weapon isn't the answer,' I spit onto his slackening face, my gaze catching the already wounded man as I do so. Once more, his widening eyes alert me to an attack from behind. It's the man with two seaxes. Blooded weapon sweeping a path of red rain on those who fight me, I half-turn my body, raising my elbow, and stab into his chest, just about where his heart should beat. My blade shouldn't slide through his byrnie, but it does, the protection slipping with the evasive movement he attempts. The byrnie must have once belonged to a bigger man than him. His mouth opens and closes, hot breath making me gag. At the last moment, I snatch my blade back and duck below the sweep of his dying attack, seax high.

A shriek from behind me, and I realise the fool who thought to kill me earlier has absorbed that impact.

There were six of them, and now two of the bastards are dead. I feel a wolf grin on my face as I move my arm to wipe the sweat and blood from my exposed cheeks.

But it doesn't pay to be too cocky. Allowing a deep breath to prepare for the next onslaught, I feel the huge shield jab at me. It's vast. It knocks me, and I spin fully around. My feet are almost too slow to keep up with my upper body whirling. The shield, the man I've not yet encountered, the enemy who tried to kill me first and who now bleeds from a deep cut on his shoulder, all pass me in a whirl. I think to close my eyes and pray I don't fucking fall. Then, the final man is on me.

He's done little so far but stand and watch, or perhaps menace, I don't rightly know.

He doesn't have a seax or a war axe, but instead a bloody spear.

'*Skiderick*,' I gasp as the blade slices into my upper right thigh with a searing pain. 'Fuck me,' I mutter through stretched lips. But the heat of the pain refocuses my mind. I dismiss my victories to date. I'm far from done. I'm not even halfway done, and I still fight alone. Whatever my allies are doing, they're busy enough not to see my need or not be able to get to me to help.

'Fucking bastard.' I redouble my grip on the shield, position my feet and look at the man with the spear, or rather, the youth with the spear. He's so young, not even a first fuzz of beard shows on his face. His eyes are bright behind the elaborate eye guards of his shimmering helm. I know who he must be. No doubt, the son of the jarl who thinks to make a name for himself with his first kill. I'll show him the truth of that misguided belief.

His spear extended, although he's retracting it to try again; I follow the wood, stepping just slightly to one side to avoid a parting glance on my calf. The one wound is enough. I feel blood seeping down my leg, sinking into my sock and then into my boot, and I really fucking hate this prick.

The youth carries no shield, his faith in his spear misplaced. A spear is good for some things, especially in Hereman's hands, but not for this type of fight. He should have brought a seax and a shield, not a spear and a handful of sweet fuck all.

I slash across his chest with my seax. His eyes follow it, glittering with disdain. He shows me no respect. He thinks he's won this already. Damn arse.

My shield follows my seax, held before me and jabbing towards him. I turn the seax blade, grip uncomfortable and stab down into his left arm, the one he needs to help him steady the spear. His byrnie covers him down to the elbow. I leave a trail of seeping blood along it, all the way to his wrists. Leather gloves protect his hands. With my shield, I press against his main spear arm, holding it tighter and tighter to his body. The grip from his left arm falters, the right arm can't move, and the spear clangs onto the soggy ground, useless now. I grin at him. Well, I think it's a grin, but his head jerks back, fear showing on his pale lips. I lift my right leg and stamp down on the spear's haft. It cracks with a sharp snap, and now he has no blade, only half a broken stick with which to fight. I rush against him, mindful that his focus is entirely on me but that the others must be about to step into the fight to attack me from the rear. I'm putting a lot of faith in my byrnie holding against the onslaught. I stagger slightly due to the injury on my left leg but hold my balance.

He falls backwards beneath my weight. He almost wins by taking me down with him. I spring free, aware this is my way out of the circle of men who thought to kill me. His bleeding arm reaches for my leg as I skip over his body, but I stab down with my seax. I glimpse the light leave his eyes as his neck glistens wetly before me. A man downed will always inadvertently reveal the weakest part of his equipment with such a move.

A howl of rage erupts behind me, but I'm twisting, facing back the way I've come. The three men still want to kill me. The first man I fought is badly wounded. His pain had already made him angry, now fury streams from him as he pounds towards me, a pitying and grief-filled look on his face at the bucking body of the dying youth.

'Arsehole,' I offer him. 'You should have left the boy at home.' I scorn. I don't know if he hears me. All the same, I imagine he knows what I'm saying.

Blades to hand, he comes towards me.

My leg feels weak. I'm losing too much blood, but now isn't the time to stop and tie a tourniquet around my upper leg. I'll just have to hold on.

I didn't see how the rest of my warriors are faring, but I hope they're bastard winning.

My foeman has his shield held before him, a weeping wound on his face, and his hand is still fuck-all use. But a man crazed with pain and grief has other weapons at his disposal. An angry stream flows from his mouth, alongside a load of spittle as well, and he veers at me, shield extended, useless hand almost clenched in a fist.

I realise his intentions long before he does.

At the last moment, I move aside. As he rushes past me, I boot him on the arse. He lands in a clatter of rage and fury, his useless hand doing nothing to aid him as he thuds to the ground, his own shield hitting him with a clang. I watch his head sway backwards as though he can evade the blow from his shield. I stride towards him, well, half limp, and stab into the back of his neck.

He bucks like a fish on dry land. That leaves me with two foemen as I turn back to encounter them. It's the one with the huge shield and the other with the sword. Both weapons will be difficult, especially now I'm free from their encirclement, which sadly means they have more room with which to manoeuvre.

I offer them a smile, wishing they were the ones limping. I'm still alone, but I sense that it's my men who are close to my back and not the enemy. We've moved somewhat, or my men have, I'm unsure. We're winning, of that I'm confident as I hear the soft huffs from Icel, and the shrieks from Rudolf. I just need to end these two bastards.

A rumble of words from the sword wielder, and the other shrugs his shoulders as they both stride towards me, avoiding the dead bodies contemptuously.

'Just what I need. The two of you to work together,' I mutter. The pain from my leg is sharpening my senses. I can smell my sweat and blood. I don't like the blood aspect. I put my weight on the wounded leg. It seems to hold, but not it's not firm. I'll need to be careful how I counter this attack. I don't want my right leg to buckle beneath me and leave me the one flailing like a fish on dry land.

The huge shield comes first, held before them both, protecting the pair of them.

'Cowards,' I mutter, offering my shield simultaneously. I hold it close to my body, just below my eyes, to see what they plan next. If that shield strikes me, I'll fall. I test my right leg again, wincing as the pain redoubles. I'll have to rely on my left, but my right will still obey my commands. I'm not entirely fucked, I console myself. Not yet.

But it's not the shield that hits me, but the bloody sword. I see its sharpened blade coming at me and jab my shield to swing it away, high and wide. It's so fucking long. Perhaps it once belonged to one of these giants the bastards are always so keen to mention in their fucking scop songs. Bloody giants, what a joke. But this sword makes me reconsider my derision. As does the size of the shield.

The men behind both blades must be strong. I consider the foeman we killed outside Repton. He's the only one I can think of who would need a blade and a shield so huge. But, I can't see that these once belonged to him, perhaps a brother. But I distract myself. I need to remain focused.

With the sword high and wide, I jab into the other shield. It's like meeting the wall that surrounds the oldest parts of London. It's solid. There's no give in it, and even my shoulder thrums with the pain, my right leg wobbling alarmingly beneath me.

'Bollocks,' I gasp to myself. I don't believe I can be on the offensive with these two. But I don't want to wait for them to make a mistake either.

The sword carrier gathers the blade close to his body, the shield remaining extended. I eye it. It is huge. And it's daubed with the emblem of my enemy, but that gives me an idea.

It only protects them on one side. If I can move quickly enough, I can get behind them. I need to ensure my leg doesn't fail me and that my actions are precise and well-measured.

I hold for a moment longer. The shield is wedged against me. I can hear the wind around the sword as it comes towards me once more, this time from the right side of my body, which has no shield to protect it. I suck in a deep breath, almost gag on the fetid smell of the dead who've shit themselves in their final moments, and snatch back my shield and scamper around the enemy.

I almost make it. I sense the sword fall uselessly to one side, but the men are busy shouting at one another. By the time I'm almost to their rear, the shield's moving slowly to block my path. If the bastard was left-handed, with his shield on his right, I might stand a chance, but I'm not so lucky. I move quicker. Mindful of the bodies on the ground and the slickness of the churned mud and filth. My right leg isn't useless, but it's not bloody brilliant, either. I'm not quick enough to get ahead of the shield, and now the sword wielder has brought the blade about even more quickly from the other side.

'Fucking arse,' I explode. Now, I'm in the same situation, only with the enemy facing me from the position I was in. I hold my shield firm, determined to block their assault. And then realise I'm in a better position after all. I can see what's happening amongst my warriors now. I can see that almost all of the enemies are dead. Rudolf still fights a springy man, blows traded against one another. Wærwulf's also engaged with a tall warrior, blond hair streaming beneath his helm. But Icel has realised my predicament. So, too, has Pybba and Goda. The three of them march towards me, mindful of the dead at their feet. I need to hold the bastards off for a little longer.

I grit my teeth and try and urge my right leg and tired arms to obey me. I must hold them off, not necessarily kill them, because I'm not on my own any more.

I grimace, and thinking of how angry my aunt will be when she sees my wound, I thrust my shield firm against the huge shield. I keep my eyes on my enemy. I won't alert them to what's happening behind them.

I hold firm, my feet starting to slip on the wet ground, smelling the strong scent of death. I thrust my seax over my shield, wedging it so that I can put all of my remaining strength into working against it, holding the attention of my enemy until my warriors kill the bastards.

Time moves slowly, too bloody slowly. My arms shake with the effort, sweat beading my face. My right leg trembles so much that I realise even my seax arm is juddering.

'Hurry the fuck up,' I repeat time and time again, and then, it must be done. The shield collapses, and damn it, my right leg can't support my weight. I follow it down to the ground, just managing to let go of my seax before I hit the shield, and my shield arm is trapped beneath my body.

'Nicely done, my lord,' Icel huffs, offering his hand to pull me upright. The men beneath the shield are lifeless. I'm not sure how they died, but it's a relief they are fucking dead.

I hobble upright, wincing as I do so. Icel quickly assesses my wound, and fury descends over his implacable face.

'Fucking hell, my lord. You know, you do have bastard warriors that can help you. Two men, alone.'

'There were actually six of the fuckers,' I counter, wincing, even as I sag, my eyes appraising the battle site, relieved to see all of my warriors alive as I count them quickly.

'Six fucking enemies?' Icel glowers. He's already bent to rip a strip of cloth from one of the dead, scornfully moving the huge shield aside as though it weighs as much as a pea to tie a tourniquet around my upper thigh. His hands are rough. He has a cut on his left arm, which I notice dispassionately. He's muttering to himself while I eye Pybba and Goda. Goda has a weeping cut on his left cheek, his helm must have slipped. I watch him yank his gloves free to reveal a reddening thumb.

'That'll hurt,' I wince with sympathy, as Icel stands before me again. I expect him to berate me and continue his monologue against my foolishness. But damn the bastard, he does none of those things.

'Six, six?' And I smile, waiting for his praise. He shakes his head. 'Four, really,' he states. 'And my lord, I assure you, I once fought off twelve of the bastard enemy, alone, without my helm or byrnie, and I only took a wound to the tip of my fucking nose.' Pybba grins at Icel's words, Goda chuckling darkly, and fuck me, my fury spikes.

'Fucking hell, Icel. Can I never have a moment's praise?'

He looks at me, all humour gone from his familiar, lined face.

'No, my lord king, you bloody can't. Any praise from me, and you'll be even more fucking foolish in picking your fights than you already are. For a king, praise would be acceptable when he acknowledges that he has other men to fight on his fucking behalf.'

With that, he strides away. I find myself sinking to the ground, somehow sitting on the huge shield; my strength all but bled away.

'Fuck me, he's a hard bastard to please,' I huff, licking my dry lips.

Pybba bends low, running his hand over my shoulder as though to assure himself I'm well, other than the obvious wound on my thigh.

'Of course he is. And he's bloody right, my lord king.' He stamps away as well. I'm left facing Goda. He offers me a broad grin, steps closer, and speaks.

'He might be right, but fuck me, my lord. You fight like a demon from hell, and it's a bloody joy to witness.'

Chapter Twenty-Four

I haul myself upright, grinning at Goda's praise despite my pain. I'm damn thirsty. I wince and grit my teeth, turning to peer down at the huge shield. Icel's moved it aside. I finally appraise the man who tried to kill me. Goda stands at my side, hand resting on his seax, as though the dead might rise.

'Ugly bastard,' he juts his chin towards the body.

'Bloody ugly,' I acknowledge. 'No wonder he kept the shield in front of his face.'

The dead man has no teeth in his wide mouth. His nose is little more than a tiny stub end. I doubt he found it easy to breathe through that. But the inkings and scars on his hairless cheeks truly mark him out. He's been wounded before. Badly. The wounds had healed, but in their wake, ribbons of pink prick holes, where he must have been stitched together, march up and down his face, making it too easy to see where he was injured. One cheek was also pulled too tight, leaving him with an almost skeletal look to one side of his face.

'Poor bastard,' I mutter, pleased he's dead.

'That must have hurt,' Goda concludes with the detachment of a man who's been wounded many times in the past.

In the distance, I hear Icel shouting at the men. I wince at the strident tone he uses, but recalled to the here and now, I also spin and appraise my men. I see the horses under Hiltiberht's control. I raise my arm and beckon him toward me. I need a bloody drink.

'Who's wounded?' I shout, trying to move forward, grateful when Goda catches my inelegant stride, and rights me on two feet. 'Bloody hell,' I growl, sweat lingering on my forehead.

'Sit down, my lord king,' Icel shouts in my direction.

'Bastard has eyes in the back of his head,' I mutter but indicate to Goda that I want to get closer to the rest of my warriors. Oda's sitting on the ground, head slumped between his legs. Cealwin's lying on his back, breathing so deeply I can see his chest rising and falling beneath his byrnie, eyes focused on the sky. He's cast his helm aside, and a livid bruise is already forming on his right cheek.

'Bollocks,' I wince. Cealwin grunts in agreement but doesn't have the breath to say more. The enemy has fallen everywhere, some clearly trying to escape and lying on their fronts. Others fighting until the end, blades in hand where they lie cooling on the ground. Rudolf's already scampering between them, as is Hereman, checking they're actually dead.

Icel's encouraging a fire to smoulder in the ruins of one of the tents. I know what he means to do with that. I don't welcome the searing pain of a blade to my flesh, but at least it'll stop the wound rot. That way, I won't have to contend with my aunt's fury as well as Icel's.

The chaos of the battle fades to nothing, bird song filling the air. I turn, breathing harshly and observe my warriors. I count them as I survey the aftermath of this fucking stupid attack by the enemy. The whimpers of wounded men touch my hearing, but it's my warriors that concern me, not the Viking raiders.

I've killed six men, well, nearly six of them. They're lifeless. I struggle to where they lie, kicking the final man I killed, curious, despite myself, to determine who he was and why he was the last to die. Was he the leader?

I see the familiar inkings that cover his arms and upper body. This man felt some affinity with a bear, or so I think. Some might whine to see such a powerful emblem, dead and paling on the ground. I'm not some people. But it doesn't aid me in deciding upon this warrior's identity. A muddled shout of words, and I sight Hereman, intimidating the single Viking raider who yet lives. His face is a livid white against the bright red of the blood that pours from above his right eye.

'Wærwulf,' I shout. He stands, panting and nods to show he realises my intentions.

'Hold,' I shout. Everyone knows I mean Hereman. He's likely to kill the bloody man without realising how important he could prove to be.

Hereman grins and spins, spear raised to point it at the hobbled man's neck. The laughter that erupts is about as amused as a fork of lightning and, certainly, more menacing. The foeman lives, I realise, as I hobble closer, slapping my men on their backs or raising them to their feet where they sag to the mud and blood-churned ground, recovering their breath. The enemy warrior hasn't so much been allowed to live as he isn't quite dead yet. One of his legs is severed, his face turning ever paler. I consider if we could save his life with the aid of fire, as Icel means to do for me, but dismiss that. The attack has been fierce. It's better if the enemy all die. I might limp, but he won't ever stand on two feet again, even if we could save his life, which I strongly doubt.

Wærwulf speaks quickly to the man, and for a few moments, I believe the man will say nothing, lips stubbornly closed, resolve on his pain-streaked face. Hereman bends and grips his arm, and the blade he holds falls away. Hereman kicks it further. The enemy howls, clawing on the ground as though he can move to retrieve it. A nasty trick. It works every bloody time.

I'm there, and with my good foot on the blade, I speak. 'Ask him again. Tell him he can have his blade back once he speaks the truth about why he's here and who that ugly bear-daubed bastard is over there.'

The man looks from me to Wærwulf, and I can tell he tries not to look at Hereman, who glowers at him, bloodied spear in one hand and a war axe resting at his feet. I consider if he used that to sever the leg. Dispassionately, I conclude he did.

The enemy swallows heavily, licking his lips.

'Water,' I bellow. Hiltiberht scampers closer and offers me my water bottle. I grip it and trickle a few drops onto the dying man's lips. It won't matter how much he drinks, he'll die thirsty now. I'll provide some temporary relief. I beckon for another water bottle. I don't want to drink from that one, but I'm bastard-thirsty as well.

The foeman licks his lips. I offer him more, standing close enough that I can smell his piss and shit, the sharp smell of his spilt blood making the whole encounter as pleasant as the shits. I try to retain my balance, but sweat beads on my face. Fuck me, my leg pulses with pain.

'My lord,' Icel growls, coming closer, his face furious to find me so close to one of our enemies. From behind him, I catch the whiff of smoke. I realise the flames are slowly building. Not long, and I'll be in a whole new world of pain.

'He's fucking dying,' I state, instead of arguing with him.

'Ask him again,' I request from Wærwulf. The words rumble, and the man looks from me, to those who surround him, his gaze resting on the seax that still waits, just out of reach. As I sway, Icel bends to collect it into his huge hand, ensuring I remain upright with a hand on my arm, and holds it, handle extended, towards him. He reaches for it feebly. But Icel holds it just out of reach. It's cruel. But not as cruel as what these men wanted to do to us.

'I need to know who he fought for and who sent him here.'

The man licks his lips once more. They're becoming blue. His lank hair is sweaty, and his tunic is sodden almost up to his middle. I'm always surprised by how much blood a body contains. It doesn't half make a right fucking mess. I don't look to where my own trews are stuck to my leg. I try not to consider the squelching noise from my boot every time I move.

Abruptly, our enemy starts to reply, and Wærwulf holds up his hand to stop me from asking another question while he listens.

As he finishes speaking, I see his entire body shudder. The end's very near.

'Give him the bloody blade,' I order Icel. He does so without argument. The man grips it, bringing it close to his body, purposefully not looking at where his severed leg lies just out of reach. The lifeless limb is already growing stiff. I grimace at the sight of it. Hands are often lost, but an entire fucking leg? That's a new one for me.

'He fights for a Jarl Horic, who in turn fights for Jarl Guthrum. They were sent to scout for the Wessex warriors. The poor fuckers found us instead.'

'When did they kill these people?'

'During the night, but they only set the fire this morning, hoping to bring King Alfred here. He says Jarl Guthrum is within those walls, over there.' I nod at this. It doesn't surprise me that Jarl Guthrum has sought the ultimate protection from King Alfred's forces in Winchester.

'Anything else?' The soft gasps of the dying man are almost at an end. Wærwulf looks from him to me.

'He said thank you, my lord.' I nod. A strange sentiment, yes, but we've not been that cruel. Blood bubbles from his mouth, and he's choking. I bend low and run my seax along his throat. His death is quicker that way. I'm not a soft-hearted bastard, but there's only so much choking I can listen to until it makes even me count my breaths. I'd like to think that if I'm ever in the same situation, one of my enemies would do the same for me. We might hate one another, but men who fight to the death often hold respect for those they battle against. We're a rare breed. We recognise like from like.

'Now, my lord,' Icel's meaty hand rests on my shoulder, pulling me away. The dead man lies silent. Overheard, a lone cry of an eagle or buzzard fills the air, no doubt calling their fellows to join the feast.

'I'm coming,' I pant. Hiltiberht finally gives me another water bottle to drink from, and I tip it into my mouth until not a drop remains. I wipe the sweat from my face and allow Icel to guide me where he wants me to be.

'Not too close to the fire,' I urge him. If I get any hotter, I'll have to strip all my clothes away.

'Just here,' he invites. I nod, swallowing heavily. My leg's an agony of pain, and while I can sense the wound's sealing itself, and the bleeding has more or less stopped, it's not that which Icel means to guard against.

I lie down on what appears to be the only piece of grass unchurned by horses or feet, extending my leg, trying to distance myself from the pain I know is coming.

Wærwulf leers over me, as does Hereman. My forehead furrows in consternation.

'Apologies, my lord king,' Wærwulf growls. I belatedly realise why they're both there. They mean to hold me down. Icel's voice seems to come from far away, barking his harsh orders, but I try not to listen. I'm not a coward. I'll face any of the bastard enemies and fight them to the death, but a heated blade on my skin? I don't much welcome that.

I look up, focus on Rudolf's rushed words as he speaks to Pybba, distracting himself from what's happening to me, no doubt, as he talks about trinkets and coins and the wealth of weapons the enemy had. Then I sense Icel's heavy tread nearby. I try not to tense my body, try to breathe deeply in and out of my nose to guard against the coming bite of pain.

But it's all fucking useless.

'Hold him,' Icel growls. 'Fucking tight,' and Hereman and Wærwulf take my arms and my legs between them.

And then the blade touches my bloody flesh, and I scream like a fucking wounded horse, the sound high and almost piercing my ears, and then the sky shades black.

Chapter Twenty-Five

When my eyes open, Icel's peering at me.

'He's fucking awake,' he calls. I doubt much time has passed. Hereman and Wærwulf continue to hold me, although their grip's slacker now. I'll carry the mark of their fingers on my flesh for some days.

'Come on, my lord. Only little children cry when the blade touches their flesh.' I wince and huff, trying to sit upright. I glance at my leg, noticing the livid mark of his blade transposed into my flesh.

'Thank you,' I offer through gritted teeth.

'You need something to bind it. Do we have honey?' he calls. I realise he's directing this towards Rudolf. I've no idea if he has honey. What I do know is my thigh shrieks in agony. It hurts to move it. It hurts to sit up. I wish I'd not been such an arsehole as to get hurt.

'Now, my lord, let this be a lesson to you that you really shouldn't take on six of the enemy alone.'

'You said four,' I argue. 'I can see I'm to get fuck all sympathy from you, Icel, my friend.'

'Sympathy is for those wounded by accident. You, my lord, walked right into this injury. Perhaps you might learn some hesitation from this.' I glower at him. The sweat on my face is drying. I can sense it tightening on my flesh and feel the urge to dunk my face into water to clear away the smell and stink.

'Does anyone else need your tender ministrations?' I encourage Icel to leave me alone.

'Aye, a few of them do. I'll just pop my blade back into the flames.' I shudder as he speaks with such relish. He moves away. I watch his wide back sway to where the fire's rapidly dying down. There's not much left to burn. He'll need to be quick.

'Here,' Hiltiberht offers me a refilled water bottle. I drink thirstily again.

'Are the horses well?' I question. Anything not to focus on the pulsing pain of my leg.

'Yes, my lord. Haden was unsettled when you shrieked.'

I nod. 'I'll go to him,' I announce, using Hereman to stand upright. Icel hasn't removed my trews, but they gape around my wound. My sock and boot are still saturated with blood. I could do with changing my clothes.

Once more, I reassure myself that my warriors are hale. Rudolf stands from his pilfering to verify himself I'm well. He's not brought Icel any honey, so I assume we don't have any. I'll just have to contend with the pain. Not, I realise, that honey would ease the pain. Only ale would do that, or good wine, and I swore off both of them long ago.

I'm still hobbling, but now every step is an agony of a thousand searing pains.

'Be careful, my lord,' Icel calls forcefully, striding past me to get to Eahric. Eahric bleeds heavily from a cut on his forearm, his face pale. He welcomes the coming knife blade as much as I did. Mind he doesn't scream in pain but takes Icel's heated blade with a stoicism I admire. He makes me look like a child crying over a scraped knee. I might have to order him to shriek.

Haden walks towards me, sniffing the air, unhappy with the scent but determined to reach me. I slap his back and welcome having him standing there so I can lean against him.

I'm still wary of all the enemy man told us before his death. Jarl Guthrum, if he's to be believed, is seeking King Alfred. But we've not seen him since we split. I don't know where he is. He sent no messenger, even though he told me he would. Icel's told me Winchester isn't far from here, but he meant to take us somewhere else, with thick woodland and a river. We're not there yet. This place is beside a river, but it's open on all sides. Why King Alfred's men thought to camp here, I don't know. Did they intend to protect the river crossing? It makes little sense to me.

'I think this must be the man who was in charge of the West Saxons,' Rudolf points down. I can't see the body, but he holds a ring in his hand, an elaborate piece, the gems visible even from here.

'Why did the enemy not take it?' I call to him.

'He was lying on it. The daft bastards probably didn't even think to look,' Rudolf mutters. With the aid of Haden, who walks towards Rudolf because he loves him much more than he does me, I make my way to the dead body as the sharp stink of cauterised skin again fills the air. This time, Wulfstan allows Icel to burn him, and it's on his face. A deep gash. I see Wulfstan's eyes boggle at the pain, secretly relieved, when he flops backwards, unaware of what's happening around him for the moment.

'You're not alone, my lord king,' Icel, the bastard, calls. 'Not all men are the same as Eahric.'

'Fucking cock,' I mutter, aware Rudolf smirks at my indignant words.

'Do you recognise the West Saxon?'

'No, do you?'

'No. He wasn't at Cricklade, that's for certain.'

I'm aware some of the men have started to gather the bodies together. The West Saxons to one side, the Viking raiders to the other. There are a lot of dead men. Rudolf hasn't stripped them all. He's been joined by others who are able to stand without needing further time to tend to wounds or recover. My men know what's worth taking, and what should be left behind. I don't fancy having to bury them all. Neither, I realise, can we leave them to rot beneath the heat of the late summer sun.

'Icel,' I call to him, mindful he's abandoned the fire, content everyone who needed cauterising has been cauterised. 'Build the fire up again. We'll have to burn the bastards.' If Bishop Wærferth were he, he might object to the summary burning of the West Saxons, but if he were here, then we'd be at peace, and there wouldn't be a huge pile of stinking bodies in need of disposal.

Icel grunts, and my warriors understand the situation well enough not to complain.

The pile of bodies grows higher. I'm almost pleased I don't have to help haul them to either side of the encampment, but I'd sooner do that than wince with every step. Turning to Haden, I make my way around his side, and mount up, better to see the terrain, or so I tell myself, but really because I hope it'll be easier to ride than stand.

My right leg screams when I lift it to place it in the stirrups, but gritting my teeth, I make the transition from standing to riding and then look around me. The river's shallow here. We can cross it easily, the ford makes it even more accessible. But where, I find myself considering once more, is King Alfred? I try to dismiss my thoughts that this could all have been his doing. I don't believe he'd have sent the enemy to kill me. Or rather, I don't believe he'd have sacrificed his men to ensure I died. He's a better man than that. Admittedly, only just a better man than that.

'Where now?' I call to Icel. The sharp stink of burning hair and flesh rises from the pile of dead enemy. Icel has fired them first. The flames leap merrily, and the sizzle of burning fat makes me feel hungry. I swallow my disgust. Flesh is flesh when the fire has it, after all.

'We carry on along the Portway,' Icel calls, from where he's also about to set the bodies of the West Saxons aflame. We need to find King Alfred, and also, somewhere we can get our hands on a pot of honey, or you, Eahric, and Wulfstan will need the aid of fire again in less time than you might think possible.'

I growl at his words. I don't want that. Not again. I can't stomach him taking the piss out of me once more.

'Towards Winchester then?'

'Aye, my lord. Towards the bastard capital of Wessex.'

Chapter Twenty-Six

The men mount with grunts and groans. Well, some of them do. Others seem to show no evidence of injuries from their morning's work. I doubt it'll be the same later when our bodies have grown colder and have had time to absorb what's happened to them. Well, that's what I hope. I don't want to be the only one limping. I can already imagine the supercilious look on King Alfred's face when we meet him next.

Unless, of course, we don't because he's been captured by the enemy.

Admittedly, if that does happen, I'll have to try and rescue him, and I don't want to bloody have to do that either.

The enemy arrived on foot. We don't need to worry about their horses.

I direct Haden through the ford, the water reaching no further than his ankle. The water's low, and the stone slabs lining the stream also raise him somewhat higher. Icel and Hereman forge ahead. I can see that neither of them wishes to relinquish that duty, so I leave them to it. My leg throbs every time Haden steps. I try to banish it from my mind. And I know just who can aid me.

'Rudolf, tell me, anything of interest amongst the dead.'

'No, my lord,' he calls from Jethson's back. 'Well, apart from the ring. And some interesting-looking coins. Silver, I'd say. More of those strange designs you say come from far away. They like to hold on to their money, the tight bastards.' He laughs while speaking. 'Some had coins, some didn't. All of them had decent enough blades.' I realise then that he has a heavy sack on Jethson's back. It clinks enticingly.

'How many seaxes?'

'Thirty-one.'

'Spears?'

'No more than thirty. I left them, other than the ones Hereman took. They're too cumbersome.'

'Swords?'

'Just the one in the hands of the big bastard you fought.'

'War axes?'

'Twenty-three.' I chuckle at his precise reckoning.

'Any for anyone else?'

'My lord,' Rudolf sounds shocked. 'I only transport it for the good of Mercia.' Now Wærwulf laughs as well. Rudolf's long had the reputation of a young scamp who can exchange all kinds of battle loot for something that might be useful. He's never mean when sharing the proceeds, we all accept that. Now, he's one of my warriors, he should share his tricks with the young squires, especially Hiltiberht.

'There were also seventeen arm rings, nine silver, eight made of iron, five were elaborate, the rest were just cobbled together bits and pieces.'

'You should have found work in a mint,' Wærwulf suggests. 'You could have kept better reckonings than anyone else I know.'

Rudolf, nose high, retorts, 'It pays to keep a good record of everything. Numbers are a weapon to be employed against the enemy.' His words thrum with conviction, and everyone except for Icel laughs. That man would need a thousand feathers against his skin to make him laugh. And even then, he'd probably announce he'd been faced with men wielding ten thousand feathers and never even crack a smile. He's a hard bastard.

I watch him and Hereman ahead. We all ride with shields to hand and helms once more on our heads, even Eahric has managed to wedge his helm over his severed cheek. Poor bastard.

I'm alert but also in pain. I'm relying on my men to keep their eyes peeled for signs of the enemy, or for King Alfred and his missing force.

The road we traverse rises and falls over small hillocks. Ahead, I can sense that the land must end because there's a tall bank of white clouds. But I can't see the sea. I don't want to see it, anyway. It'll only reveal the extent of the enemy force.

There are clusters of woodlands close by, as well. Temporarily, they block the view of where we've come from. There are some small settlements. They've not been set ablaze, but their doors are tightly locked, and no one calls a welcome. The animals that should be in the fields seem to have been taken into the barns or perhaps even the houses to keep them safe. I notice some of the settlements have rudimentary defences surrounding them. This, then, has become a lawless land, no matter that King Alfred claims the kingship.

The only true sign of enemy destruction is the smoke drifting upwards from where Winchester must be in the distance.

Eventually, Icel calls the journey to an end.

'Is this it?' I ask him. He nods and surveys the landscape. We're being funnelled through two huge woodlands, rising on either side of a thin strip of road or, rather, trackway. The surface is far from even. No doubt, tree roots threaten the ground's integrity. In my pain-hazed mind, I imagine the limbs of the subterranean roots, trying to reach out from either side of the narrow expanse, to grab one another. This piece of trackway might not last. It could soon be overwhelmed by the slow march of vegetation. Ahead, the trickle of water can be heard. This place is Icel's river and woodlands.

I admit, as I rotate Haden, not wanting to risk dismounting just yet, that it's a good location to overawe the enemy. I'm surprised they're not here, waiting for us.

'Yes, here. We can watch or attack. We should split our numbers between the two sides of the woodlands?' Icel replies.

'Hum,' I grunt, unsure if I agree with that.

'Perhaps not tonight?' I feel, in my weakened state, that we should remain united. But Icel rides his borrowed horse towards me. He speaks in a low growl.

'We split the force. That way, we'll triumph when they come, for mark my words, they'll seek out those who've died, and want to exact their revenge.' Unwillingly, I assent.

'We split the force,' I call to my tired men. Some of us look decidedly rung out. We could do with a good night's sleep and warm food. I sense we're not going to get either.

'My lord,' Icel speaks before I can make my decision on who goes where. 'You should be to the north of the road. In case you need to ride for Mercia.'

I shake my head at him, already denying the words. He comes even closer.

'Remember, my lord, what we talked about earlier.' He inclines his head towards my leg.

'Fucking arsehole,' I mumble. He grins widely.

'I'll lead the men on the far side. I'll take those who were with me at Gloucester.'

I open my mouth to argue with him, but it's a good idea, and he knows it. They're used to obeying his commands.

'Do as he bloody says,' I mirror the orders. 'Tell me, Icel, do we set night watchers on both sides?'

'Of course, my lord,' he informs me in no uncertain terms. 'And you're to have none of the watches.'

He makes me feel like a petulant child. I'd continue to argue with him, but as I dismount, standing woozily on the road, I realise I'm weak. I'll be no good for anything if we're attacked during the night.

My men set to without complaint. It seems I'm the only one to be disgruntled that Icel has taken so much upon himself. I admit, I shouldn't be. After all, I appreciate Icel knows Wessex better than I do. All the same, I don't like feeling so out of control. I miss Mercia. I really bloody do. I wish I'd not come to Wessex. And, I wish I knew where bloody King Alfred was. If he's already dead, then I can return to Mercia. We need not linger here, and I'd welcome that.

* * *

Hereman takes the first watch, Pybba the second, and Wærwulf the third. I sleep through all of it—not that it's restful sleep. When I wake, I've sweated enough to have bathed in the stuff. I'm grumpy and in pain. The only thing that cheers me is the smell of pottage cooking. Admittedly, it has a sharp tang of burnt alongside it.

'I didn't think we were allowed a fire,' I call to whoever's cooking.

'I never said that,' Icel replies from seemingly far away, although his heavy tread is heard coming closer. He carries a bowl of pottage with him. I can smell whatever he's laced it with from here.

'Eat up like a good boy,' he croons. I snarl. 'It'll help you with the pain,' he adds, already retreating.

'Hiltiberht, bring me a fresh tunic,' I call. 'And some trews as well.' I didn't change yesterday, other than to remove my sock and cast it into the fire alongside the burning bodies. It was never going to be possible to remove all the blood from it.

I grit my teeth as the sharp stab of pain makes itself known. Not that it's really gone anywhere all night, but now it's alive and as though a hundred teeth chew my leg. I grimace.

Hiltiberht's quick with my tunic. He assists in stripping my byrnie and tunic and then pulls the cleaner one over my head before resetting my byrnie. Here, in Wessex, with the enemy all around, we must always remain armed.

Changing my trews is more difficult. I stay sitting and wriggle my arse free. My leg pulses, and I catch sight of the bright pink flesh and the edges of the deep cut. I've been fucking lucky, I know that, but right now, it doesn't feel as though I have much for which to be thankful.

Exposing my legs, I'm struck by another problem. My trews are stuck to me by my own dried blood.

'Yank them,' I order Hiltiberht. His wide eyes fix on mine. 'I bloody mean it,' I instruct, and he does as I ask, the horrible ripping sound of the wool coming away from my flesh about as comforting as a punch in the eye. I see where my white feet are bruised from the fighting. Indeed, while it's my spear wound that's most obvious, I am, in fact, covered in bruises and small cuts all along my legs. I really should take better care of myself.

Before I can wriggle back into my spare trews, which at least don't have a bloody great big hole in them, Icel reappears and slathers some obnoxious green lotion over my wound. It stinks worse than horse shit, and indeed, might well be horse shit. He also ties a makeshift bandage around my leg and walks away without saying more.

'Fuck me,' I wince. He's tied the bandage so tightly my wound's pulsing all the way to my head. I work at it with my hands. If he's not careful, I won't be able to feel my foot at all.

'Leave it,' Icel rumbles from some distance. I grimace in his direction, slip my trews back on, ask Hiltiberht to help me with my sock and boot on the right leg, and then moodily eat my pottage. It tastes like shit as well. I can detect the sharp bite of some healing herb. Not that anyone else is complaining, not even Rudolf, who likes to think he makes the best pottage out of anyone. No doubt, Icel has only added the herb to my pottage. If he wasn't trying to help me, I'd be pissed off about it.

'Anything during the night?' I query my guards, even though they'd have told me if there was a problem, but my leg hurts and so does my head, and I'm out of sorts.

'Nothing. Although, I think there might be a wolf nearby,' Wærwulf suggests. 'I don't believe it'll come any closer after last night.' I consider asking more, but I know Wærwulf has an affinity for the creatures. If he thinks there's a wolf, there's no doubt a wolf.

'Let's hope the beast stays away,' I offer, hobbling to my feet. I need to piss and see what's happening with the rest of my men. I should check on those who were wounded. No doubt Icel's already done so, but I'm the king, and these are my warriors.

With ill grace, biting my lip to ward off the throbbing that makes me dizzy once I'm upright, I go through the trees to a quiet spot. I empty my stream, one hand on a tree trunk to stop me from falling. My piss is a vivid yellow. I need to drink more. Indeed, my mouth, after the pottage, tastes as though I've dipped my tongue in the cloudy residue from ale-making. I swallow and bite back nausea, which I convince myself is caused by a sour belly and not the shock of my wound.

Putting myself away, I run my hand over the scar on my neck. The pulsing pain of the wound which plagued me for months after I was wounded hasn't troubled me for a long time, but the scar reminds me that I'm just a man. A single man. Maybe, I accept, Icel makes a fair point. It was all well and good when I was simply an ealdorman and had no one to answer to other than my warriors and my aunt. But I'm Mercia's king. I should be more careful with my person. After all, if I die, there would only be Æthelred to take my place, and so far, I've done fuck all to establish him as my brother's son. I'll need to do that when I go back to Mercia.

'Coelwulf,' the hiss of my name has me standing to attention, only to wobble precariously. I grab for the tree trunk once more, not wanting to land in the wet pool of my own piss.

'What?' I hiss back, hoping Rudolf will find me. My fingers reach for my seax, but it's absent from my weapons belt. I slept in my byrnie. I did take the precaution of removing my weapons, so that I didn't stab myself in the night. I've failed to return them. Bollocks.

'Where are you?' he hisses again.

'Over here.' I can't tell where he is. If I move, I'll make a racket, so I remain where I am, hoping he'll find me. And he does. His pale face lifts on sighting me, and he scampers towards me, his lips curling as he smells my piss.

'Bloody hell,' he whispers. 'Drink some water; you dried-out bastard.'

'What is it?' I demand, waving aside his complaint while continuing to whisper.

'There's someone coming.'

'North or south?' I'm struggling for balance—my head still pounds, and my leg throbs. I do need to drink.

'From the south,' he whispers, walking away and then pausing. 'Come on, old man,' he huffs when I don't immediately follow, and that makes me grit my teeth and follow the jumped-up little shit. One day, if he's bloody lucky and fights the way I've bloody well taught him, he can enjoy being a bit fucking older and hobbling because some shit tried to slice his leg from his body.

'Quietly,' he murmurs. I snarl again. He's testing me, and the way I'm feeling, if I had a blade to hand, he might just be trying to evade its reach.

Desperately trying not to fall while attempting not to drag my wounded leg, I follow him back through the trees. I didn't realise how far I'd come from the encampment. Now I wish I'd been a bit less shy about showing the bastards my cock when I relieved myself.

I can hear nothing above the thud of my heart beating and the shuffle of my feet. I realise Rudolf skips from side to side, almost as though he has wings to aid him in not touching the woodland floors with their many dips and hollows.

Just as I think I can see my men, I kick an exposed tree root with my left foot. I tumble, without the aid of my right leg to keep me upright. Pulling my arms into my body, I land in a soft jumble of my byrnie with my left knee hitting the ground. I bite down on the throbbing agony that drives all sound from my hearing and plunges me into a whole new world of discomfort.

I can't deny that tears form in the corners of my eyes. I'd like nothing more than to shriek in agony. I don't know how I hold it in, I really fucking don't.

'Have you fucking finished,' Rudolf glowers down at me when I open my eyes, shaking his head in disbelief. He's really boiling my piss. 'Come on,' and he offers me his hand. I reach for it, and then change my mind. This ain't going to be elegant, but I need to reach my feet in the least painful way possible.

I roll onto my knees, and then stretch my left leg out, hands still on the floor. I huff under my breath, counting to three, and then, on two, thrust upwards with my hands, hopping on my good leg while I curse my damn foot and the tree root, which threatens to tumble me once more.

I'm aware of others watching me, perhaps thinking I'm the enemy. I breathe deeply, jut out my chin, and limp towards the rest of my warriors. At least, I take some comfort, Icel won't have seen me fall because he's on the other side of the small roadway. Alas, Hereman has. He offers me a worried look. I hop by him with all the composure of a headless chicken.

'Report,' I demand from him in a harsh whisper.

'Warriors, we think, coming this way from the south, or that way,' and he points towards the west. I nod. I understand what he means.

'How many?'

'Enough,' he grumbles. I hop to where I slept last night, but my blades are missing. Rudolf hastens to offer them to me. He could have done that much sooner, but perhaps then I'd be missing a bit of belly or some such. I add them to my weapons belt. I can hear the horses from a little further away. I hope Hiltiberht has them under control.

'My lord,' Hereman begins, but I shake my head, aware of what he's about to suggest. And, despite my earlier thoughts, I know I can't allow my men to fight this battle without me. Even if I will be fuck-all use to them.

The others, I realise, have already taken up defensive positions, some much closer to the road. Goda and Gardulf are almost hidden by the trees. I detect their familiar backs as they focus, not on me, but on what might be approaching us. Rudolf, Hereman and Pybba remain near to where I stand. Beornstan and Cealwin have disappeared amongst the trees. I don't know if they're behind me or even further in front. Wulfhere, Wærwulf and Sæbald are just in view behind us. Where the others are, I'm unsure, but I sense they're not far away.

No doubt, I grimace, Icel has his half of the men much better prepared.

Silence fills the air, and not even the sound of small animals scurrying or birds flapping their wings in the canopy overhead breaks the deep quiet of the woodlands. It's too still, too quiet. Anyone worth their weapons will realise that someone lurks amongst the trees.

I wish I knew how big the coming force was. I lick my lips, taste my salt, and realise I've had nothing to drink. My pounding head is getting worse, not better.

Then we hear it, the sound of men moving along the road. There's a cacophony of iron and wood and the thump of footsteps, but more than anything, the men speak to one another, no thought of keeping their presence a secret. They speak not with the West Saxon tongue, or indeed any Saxon tongue at all, but the Norse of our enemy.

I look to Wærwulf. He nods, only too aware that he must tell us the content of the warriors' conversation.

His forehead furrows, his lips moving, mirroring the words he hears. I wait impatiently for him to tell me what he's heard, the conversation growing louder and closer, and still he doesn't speak. I don't want to ask him for fear he might miss something important. My hand clenches on my seax, my leg throbbing. I swallow and taste only the bitterness of whatever Icel laced my pottage with earlier.

It sounds as though a huge force walks along the woodland trackway, no thought for anyone who might be waiting to attack them from beneath the trees. My lip curls at the arrogance, my fury driving away some of the pain from my head and leg. Perhaps that's what I need, to kill a few of the fuckers and have done with it. Maybe that'll clear my headache up.

I grip my seax, wish I had my shield in hand, and almost rush forward, but a hand on my shoulder steadies and stops me. Wærwulf shakes his head, finger held to his lips. Then he speaks, his words so soft I have to lean towards him to hear.

'They're looking for the other force, led by Jarl Horic.'

'We can't let them find their dead allies,' I counter, fearing the delay will allow them to pass through this pinch point entirely, which Icel has insisted we adopt.

'Wait,' Wærwulf cautions. 'The force is huge.' As he speaks, Gardulf scampers back towards me, his face determined but pale, using the cover of the enemy warriors moving to obscure the sound of his movements.

'More than a hundred, perhaps four ships worth.' I growl at that. The number's too vast, even for us.

'We should let them through,' Wærwulf mutters. Gardulf nods fervently in agreement. I bite my lips again. If we let them through, we'll know there's an enemy force behind us, and also, no doubt, many more ahead of us. That's far from sound good military strategy.

But, of course, Icel and the men who stand with him are separate from us. Before I can make any decision, I hear a noise I don't want to hear: the cries of the Viking raiders caught unawares, being savaged by Icel and the other half of my warriors. I look from Gardulf to Wærwulf, noticing the scowls on their faces.

'There's only one way we can bloody win this,' I inform my warriors quickly. 'Get the fucking horses.'

I don't like this. Not at all.

Chapter Twenty-Seven

Rudolf hurries towards me, his focus on where the horses are being kept safe by Hiltiberht.

'Bring me Haden,' I urge him. I know I'll never get there and back quickly enough without painfully jolting my leg. He nods and rushes onwards.

'Tell Hiltiberht to stay out of it,' I urge Wærwulf as he, too, streams past me. 'And release the other horses. They might confuse the enemy or make it to Icel and the others and help them escape.'

All of my warriors hurry onwards without thought, leaving me alone. If the enemy found me now, I'd be fucked. I don't like it. But I like the sounds of battle even less. Bloody Icel. It's not like him to act so precipitously.

Awkwardly, I hop towards where I slept last night, scouting the ground to ensure I have all my weapons alongside the seax that Rudolf handed me. Quickly, I slip my double eagle-headed sword into its scabbard, even as I fight for balance, entirely reliant on my left leg to keep me upright.

I'm fucking hampered. I don't see that being on Haden's back will do more than give me a greater height from which to fall. I hardly welcome that, my thoughts tumbling back to the roof of Northampton's church. At least I won't have that far to fall, or so I console myself. But a sneaking thought reminds me that I had two bloody legs that worked well on the roof of Northampton's church.

The sound of the horses coming towards me quickly fills the air. As does the shriek and sharp commands of one of the Norse warriors. I need Wærwulf to tell me exactly what's said, but I can safely assume they're attacking my warriors.

Hereman's the first to return. His hands are busy preparing a spear and shield. I hold my hand up to stop him, and just then, the shriek of a wounded animal rings through the air. I gasp. It sounds like Eahric.

'Fuck this,' I mutter, pleased to see Haden's next, alongside Rudolf and Jethson. I hop to my horse. I sense him watching me, no doubt trying to decipher why I suddenly only have one leg that's worth a damn. I grit my teeth, place my throbbing right leg in the saddle, and haul myself onto his back. As I do so, I catch sight of his healing wound. It's not been long enough for the skin to be completely repaired. I have to bloody hope he doesn't earn another such injury.

I glance at my warriors. While I labour to mount, they're stuck behind me, the trees pressing in too tightly to be able to circumnavigate me easily. I eye the riderless horses. They don't have saddles, only reins, and they've been tied up high to prevent them from entangling their legs.

I bite my lip, trying not to focus on the sound of the fight, while I think about how best to do this. I look from Hereman's set face to Pybba's furious one. My men need to join the fight and quickly.

'We attack from this side. We use the riderless horses if we can to get them through to our fellow warriors. Whatever happens, keep your animals safe. We don't want to lose them to these bastards. We crash through the enemy line and join up with the rest of my men.'

As it goes, it's a shit plan, if I can even term it a plan. But it's all I have.

'Stay the fuck alive,' I order them and then release Hereman and Haden to follow the path we've made through the thick trees. Ahead, the sound of a bloody fight is intensifying. I'm surprised Icel doesn't shout for my aid, but then, he'll know, no matter what, not to inform the enemy his force isn't alone.

In no time at all, the branches part, and I can see the shit show taking place on the small strip of trackway. It's a good location for an ambush, but not when only half the force knows of the attack.

There are many Viking raiders. The bastards fight in a hastily formed shield wall, their back mostly to us. I can't see the emblem they fight beneath. I can't see much but arses and backs. I do see my warriors. The fourteen men are hard-pressed. They hold the shield wall against the enemy, using the tree line to reinforce them. It'll be only moments before they're overwhelmed or the enemy sends men to go around them.

'Fucking hell, Icel,' I mutter, wincing at a sudden sharp stab of pain along my leg as Haden's hooves hit the remnants of the trackway just slightly to the east of the fight. The shouts and shrieks of the enemy are so loud no one even notices the hoofbeats. I shake my head at that. I can't decide whether to be more pissed off with Icel for forcing this fight or more astounded that the enemy is so unaware of what's happening around them.

Hereman's taken his borrowed horse further along the line of enemy backs. The others follow him. I didn't order them that, but it makes sense. We're forging a shield wall with our horses, not our shields. I must hope the animals don't become as battered as our shields.

Another bellow of fury. I detect Icel's voice urging my men on.

There's no time to order my men further. They launch themselves at the Viking raiders, urging the horses into the rear of the enemy shield wall. I don't even consider how unlikely this is to be successful. I must protect my men, and then I'll fucking have it out with Icel. No doubt, determined to prove himself a better commander than I am, he's rushed into this. Bloody arsehole.

The road's narrow. Haden's hardly gathered his hooves beneath him, and we're ploughing through an adversary. I use my sword to swipe at heads or backs, anything to kill them or knock them insensible and relieve the pressure on the shield wall that faces them. Haden's a big horse. He doesn't stop to wait for men to move aside. I hear the sharp crack of breaking bones as he steps on feet and legs, even as others try to avoid their falling allies, unsure what causes them to tumble. Now, the enemy is crying in as much pain as my warriors, and the battle has only just begun.

A warrior with more sense than many others turns to face me, his war axe held in hefty hands, his lips cast down in a grimace of fury. Orders are being called by someone amongst the Viking raiders. I don't need Wærwulf to tell me what they are.

I swing my sword towards him, not yet aiming to kill. He jerks back, not keen to kiss my blade, but while he has eyes on me, he doesn't realise that Pybba and Brimman are just to the other side. Pybba, preferring his seax to a sword, is quick to stab into the man's exposed shoulder. But he doesn't twist to face Pybba, launching himself at Haden, the fucking bastard.

The war axe whirls. I watch it, coming closer and closer, but in the press of men and horses, there's nowhere for Haden to go. I try and get him to reverse his progress, because only by going backwards can he find clear space. Haden's having none of it.

'Fuck,' I mutter, bunching my legs and pressing fiercely into his sides, gripping the reins tightly with my left hand. Haden rears, a shrill neigh on his lips. He kicks out with his front hooves, a direct blow on the man's face and chest. He's down before completing the swing of his war axe that might have taken Haden from me. Another sharp crack of splintering bone and I realise Haden's finishing the task.

The initial panic of our arrival's starting to fade. The enemy continues to press against Icel and my fellow warriors, but some have also turned to face us. Our opponents are wedged between a shield wall and a line of angry horses, snapping teeth and hooves that kill. I don't fancy their chances, but to either end of the compressed line, some are streaming free from the tight quarters.

'Watch your backs,' I urge my men, sweat dripping down my nose, as Haden settles to the ground again. My leg's screaming at me. I'm astounded I can stay focused on the fight, but that's exactly what I need to do.

'Forwards,' Hereman calls from further down the line. He's scything his way through our foemen, stabbing with his spear, and all but lifting men clear of the ground as he impales them. Gardulf's just behind him. Already blood sheets his face and clothes, and a rictus grin touches his lips.

'Fuck me,' I mutter. I need to watch what I'm doing and not be distracted by my men. The other horses are as busy as those being ridden, the shouts of their riders urging them on.

'We need to break through,' I urge Pybba and Rudolf, who has my back.

'We're bloody trying,' Rudolf bellows.

Another of our opponents twists to face me. He has a seax in both hands but no shield. He lifts one blade and then another, already jabbing towards Haden's face. I don't like risking my horse like this, I really fucking don't. Blades are coming at me from every angle, and with my wounded leg, I rely entirely on my horse to maintain any forward momentum. I lift my sword to jab at my opponent, hoping to scare him with such a movement, but I know it won't work. He hungers for my death just as much as I do his.

A shrill neigh of pain, and I understand one of the horses is already wounded. This is going to shit, just as I feared it would.

'To me,' I urge whoever's listening, still slicing my sword towards the enemy, who steps closer. Haden jerks backwards, the flashing blades catching his eye, but I need him to go forward now.

I kick him onwards with my one heel, not liking to be so vicious. I can hear his teeth gnashing together. His head tosses from side to side, jerking my arms, which pains my leg. The bastard with the blades has unsettled my horse as no one else has. I need to break through to the other side, or we'll be overwhelmed, and I'll be able to do fuck all to help my stranded men. I'd blame Icel for such an action, but he knows, as I know, that in a similar situation, I'd have done the same.

Rudolf and Pybba come close, almost near enough that our legs touch. There's no room for the enemy to get between us. Wærwulf joins Rudolf's side. We should have done this from the beginning. Icel's mount attaches itself to Brimman's side, and more and more of my men follow, even as I continue to menace the seax-wielder, keeping him from hurting Haden while my warriors prepare.

The enemy nearest to us doesn't seem to realise what's happening, even the man who faces me. When as many of my warriors and horses are assembled as possible, Hereman entirely oblivious, I spin and meet the eyes of those close by, Rudolf and Pybba. They nod, resolve on what I can see of their faces beneath their helms.

'Now,' I order. Once more, I kick Haden roughly. He surges to a gallop, and men jump or fall beneath his hooves. At the last possible moment, I loosen my tight legs, well thigh, my right leg is useless, and bend low over his head. He soars above the final two rows of fighting men: my allies and enemies. He lands heavily, a loud wooden twang assuring me he's hit someone's shield with his trailing hoof.

I duck low, the boughs of the trees tight and claustrophobic, and turn Haden in as tight a circle as I can to reinforce my warriors. Many of the horses have made it. Hereman, Cuthwalh, and Beornstan still fight on the other side of the enemy. They have four of the riderless horses with them. I'd worry about them, but instead, I need to reinforce the shield wall that's suffered despite my intentions to aid my fellow warriors.

Two of the enemy surges through a gap between Ingwald and Lyfing. I raise my sword to drive it through their exposed throats, but as I do, I see the line of red that mars Haden's coat. The bastard cut him before we could escape. I don't think it's deep. I hope it's fucking not.

The two foemen are on me in the time it takes me to refocus. I counter the war axe with my sword and slip my hand through my shield to protect Haden and me from the spear the other holds. Its blade glistens wetly. The bastard's already wounded one of my Mercian warriors.

'*Skiderick*,' I shriek at him, the clatter of the spear point on my shield and the force behind it, assures me the bastard isn't pissing about. He means to kill me. With my sword in one hand and the shield in the other, I'm struggling for balance, my right leg doing little but making me fucking sweat with the agony of it.

I feel myself slipping. I pull my sword back and try to hold the reins more tightly. The saddle is in place, but it's been flung on Haden's back too quickly. It could do with being tighter. I don't feel secure. In a moment of brief respite, I kick my left leg free from the stirrup and wrap the hanging leather more tightly around it. I need more purchase on the reins as well, but my hands are full. I'd like to thread my arms through the reins, but I don't have the time.

The war axe comes at me once more, catching the corner of my vision. I lift my sword, even as I feel my leg slipping. I sense wetness there. I've reopened the wound, and now it bleeds, adding to the slickness of my body.

'Fuck this,' I glower, allowing a worm of fear into my belly, only to banish it. The spear knocks my shield. Ahead, I realise Ingwald and Lyfing have closed the gap in the shield wall. These two men are marooned, but it's not helping me much. My sword hand vibrates with the force of the blow. The bastard will take the edge from my blade if this continues.

I can't order Ingwald or Lyfing to help me. Rudolf's dismounted and added his force to the shield wall. Pybba's in the midst of doing the same. Some of my men remain mounted, and some of them aren't.

I could really do with some fucking help, I mutter to myself, not liking to admit it. If I could just kill one of the bastards.

The spear knocks me once more. At least, I realise, while he attacks the shield, he's not wounding Haden. Haden's moving forwards and backwards, doing his best to evade our foemen. But the two men won't take their eyes off me. I consider if they know who I am. All Norsemen look alike. I can't tell one from another, not when they're dressed for war, and these men are dressed for war. The weapons they have are fine and lethal.

Once more, the sword comes at me, but it deviates at the last moment, aiming for Haden's neck instead.

'Fuck,' I roar, kicking Haden the hardest I've ever done so. He rears. I fear he'll knock my own men. I hear the satisfying sound of a hoof meeting a blade, and when he's once more on all four legs, I appreciate the sword has spun out of our opponent's hands. Foolishly, he's scampered to retrieve it from beneath Haden's hooves. As he does so, I lean over, straining every part of my weak leg, praying I'll stay mounted, and slice my weapon into the gap between his byrnie and neck guard. He bucks, a horrible gargling noise coming from his mouth, before slumping. I yank my sword back, but the movement is too much.

Of everything I've endured, it's my own damn blade that sees me falling to the ground. I brace myself, curling my head, but I land on my back, wind-knocked from me, the agony from my leg the only thing that keeps my eyes open.

'Fuck,' I roar. 'Fuck, fuck, fuck,' I bellow. Haden steps back, avoiding standing on me, but I have no sword or shield. As soon as Haden's out of the way, the man with the spear leers at me, his blade almost piercing me as he steps closer.

Gasping like a gutted boar, I can't even move backwards. My leg's a dead weight. I've nothing with which to fight. My byrnie's ridden high over my belly, and my helm's been knocked askew so I can only see out of my left eye.

I watch him coming closer, time slowing.

'Fuck,' I mutter, 'my aunt's going to be pissed.'

I clench my left hand, my right pulsing with pain from where it's hit the ground. Then I smile, meeting his gaze as the blade approaches.

With a heave of effort, I lift my left arm. Just as he pauses to perfect his aim, I open my hand and fling the scrabble of dust and woodland floor I've managed to hold in my clenched fist into his face.

A cloud of dust, old leaves, and small branches temporarily blinds him. The blade still comes perilously close. I turn just in time to feel a slice of pain along my left arm, and then, right leg extended to the side, entirely reliant on my left, I suck in air. With a wild shriek of fury and fucking pain, I find my feet, surging up, my sword in my right hand where it's knocked against it as I rolled to avoid the enemy. The man dies, blinking crap from his eyes, with my sword wedged through his neck so far it sticks out his back.

The sudden sound of drumming blood assures me the bastard's dead, even while his body jerks on the edge of my blade.

'Fuck me,' I huff, drained, looking up to see the backs of my warriors as they battle the enemy.

Not one of the bastards has even seen my peril.

I'll berate them about that. Fine warriors they make, protecting their king, but first, first we need to overpower the enemy. And the only way I can do that is to mount Haden once more.

'Fuck,' I mutter, ordering my horse close. I mount, a whole world of pain allowing sweat to bead once more into my eyes, even as I correct my twisted helm.

Mounted, I eye the fight taking place just before me.

Fuck. I might have survived the two enemy warriors, who now lie, cooling below Haden's hooves, but I've been the lucky one. Hereman's beleaguered, and the shield wall faces ruin.

'Fuck,' I mutter, eyes wide as I realise this isn't even half-won.

'I don't bloody this like,' I growl.

Chapter Twenty-Eight

Not one of my warriors has the same oversight as I do. The men on the ground can't see how many enemies remain. Hereman, Beornstan and Cuthwalh can probably tell, but they and the four riderless horses are entirely surrounded by our foemen.

Once more, a slither of fear worms its way into my belly. On this occasion, I allow it to take hold. I need it. Without the fear, I'll never determine how to aid my allies.

Rudolf and Pybba are reinforcing the shield wall, their horses staying back beneath the trees. I eye Jethson, fearing he might panic, but he chews stray grasses plucked from the ground with his sharp teeth. He's not concerned at all.

Others have remained mounted, so they should realise what's happening. Gardulf and Goda are opposite, where Hereman, Cuthwalh, and Beornstan fight, trying to cleave a path through to them.

'That's not going to bloody work,' I admit, even though it pains me.

I brought the horses to aid my warriors, but at the moment, I believe the best they could do would be to gallop from this place with my men mounted on their backs. I don't like that thought. We don't run from the enemy. We're the warriors of Mercia, even if, right now, we're deep in the bloody West Saxon kingdom with King Alfred missing. I will find him. I assure myself of that.

I look left, I glance right, struck by how disorganised the enemy is. They determined to attack us by funnelling their way between the line of horses and shields. But now most of the horses have gone over to stand behind our southern shield wall, they're standing around, scratching their fucking arses. However, it won't take long for them to reinforce their fellow warriors, especially as my men are battling well. The number of wounded is growing amongst our opponents. A shimmer of bloody rain seems to hang in the air, the shouts and shrieks of our enemy cursing in whatever tongue they speak so loud it's as though I don't hear it at all.

All it'll take is one of the enemy mounting one of the few riderless horses to the far side of the shield wall, and they'll realise how close they are to victory if only they change tactics.

'Sæbald, Wærwulf, Wulfhere, to me,' I roar above the tumult, directing Haden eastwards. We don't want the enemy escaping to ravage the interior of Wessex, or reaching the River Thames, with easy access to London. I certainly don't want them getting anywhere close to Reading, from which they've previously assaulted Wessex.

Surprised by my orders, it takes them too long to obey me. I'm almost in position by the time Sæbald even brings his horse under control to follow me. I wait for him, watching. Before me, Eahric and Lyfing fight with wild abandon, working together to defeat the enemy who surge against their shields. Behind those enemy men, there's a collection of about twenty or so foemen, milling around, jeering and encouraging their allies and showing no interest in joining the fight. Cocky fuckers. I sense one or two of them looking at me uneasily. And well they might. Not that they do anything to defend themselves. Their weapons aren't even in their hands.

Finally, Sæbald is close, an apology on his lips that I ignore. The press and push of the shield walls are intense, with men fighting to the death, but not all men.

'What?' Sæbald huffs. He runs his hand along his mount's upper right leg, perhaps reassuring himself that all is well.

'We need to stop them from getting further east,' I announce, jerking my head towards the enemy. Haden's restless beneath me, shuffling forwards and backwards with the movements of Eahric and Lyfing.

'We take them from the side,' I urge him, as well as Wærwulf and Wulfhere as they get close enough. They nod. None of them thinks to argue. They can tell how desperate the fight is. My decision is unconventional. It doesn't mean it won't bloody work.

Without seeming to notice, Wærwulf slices one of the foemen who thinks to run to the back of our shield wall, taking advantage of the last of the men in line. I'm sure I can detect others walking through the trees behind us, but I'm not about to expend my time chasing them down. That'll come later when the rest of the bastards are fled or dead. Preferably bloody dead.

The man falls lifeless at the feet of his borrowed mount. Wærwulf quirks an eyebrow at me. 'We'll do it, Coelwulf. You're wounded,' now he references my leg, which hangs lifeless and throbbing with pain.

'I'll help,' I rejoin quickly. 'I can fight from here, but not on the ground.' Lips pressed tightly together, he nods and says nothing further. He knows there's no point in wasting his time arguing with me.

'Two ahead, two behind. We plough through them like we're churning the fields for the crops. Kill as many as you can.' The three men nod, resolve on their familiar faces. God, I love my warriors. They're brave bastards. All of them.

'We'll take the lead,' Wærwulf informs me, nodding to Sæbald. I'd argue about that, but we need to take action. Now. If not, the shield wall will be overwhelmed, as another thinks to try his luck and again dies on Wærwulf's blade.

'Fucking get on with it then,' I grunt with ill humour. Sæbald smirks. Wærwulf smiles, and then they urge their horses onwards, rounding the end of the shield wall, weapons drawn, their horses calm beneath them even though the stink is overwhelming. Dead men never smell good.

Now the twenty or so foemen who were standing around, doing very little, spark to life, realising our intentions. One calls to another, his words tripping over his tongue in the haste to voice them.

Wulfhere joins me as we bring our horses around the end of our shield wall. I can see along it, noting where men are winning and others are struggling. It's not so much a firm, straight line as the crooked hind leg of a dog in sleep. Every so often, it moves forward of its own accord and then strops.

'Fucking come on,' I mutter. The pain in my leg is almost unmanning me. Only the perilous nature of the fate of my warriors has me struggling on. That, and a real desire to kill as many Viking raider bastards as possible.

Abruptly, my uninterrupted view disappears as Wærwulf and Sæbald set to work. They move their horses together, both carrying shields in opposing hands. This'll be uncomfortable for Wærwulf, as he usually fights with that hand, but protecting the horses and themselves is better. They carry a sword each, stab down or slash with them as the horses move through the mass of the enemy.

The twenty idle warriors shout in dismay, almost falling over themselves to stop us, or so I assume. They rush towards Wærwulf.

'Come on,' I urge Wulfhere. We need to stay close together, but not too close. Wærwulf and Sæbald absorb the brunt of the threat from the front, but we'll have it from behind. Five of the enemy men are hastening towards us, their intentions clear as they finally pull weapons clear from their belts. They intend to divide us. I won't fucking have that.

'Fucking come on,' I urge Wulfhere again. He's to the right of me. He's as hampered as Wærwulf by having his shield and sword arm swapped, but at least he protects my wounded leg. I can't really argue with him. He'll also have to counter the threat from those who aren't yet in the front two lines of the enemy shield wall.

Haden tosses his head at once more finding himself amongst the heaving mass of the enemy. Even I don't like it. The smell of blood and shit, the scent of fear and sweat. It pervades everything.

Eahric must realise what we're doing.

'Kill 'em all,' Eahric roars, face red with exertion as I sweep my sword across the helmed head of the foemen in the second row of the shield wall. His shield is held high above the man he protects, but no one defends him. I stab into his exposed neck. He bucks and twists, not realising I'm behind him. As the fucker rotates, he forces the blade deeper and deeper, killing himself with little more effort from me.

'Stupid bastard,' I glower, aiming for the next in the second row of the shield wall. Eahric has one man to fight now. I hope he'll kill him quickly.

Haden's buffeted by those attacking Wulfhere. Stilton walks into my wounded leg. I grimace, temporarily losing the grip on my sword. A shout of pain erupts unbidden. I feel tears forming in the corner of my eyes. I redouble my grip and, again, slice it down into the neck of the unprotected man in the second row of the shield wall.

'Fucking die,' I mutter. He obliges me by doing so, not by turning, but because my blade bites deep as Haden rushes forward, keen to evade a blow coming from behind us. Lifting the bloodied blade, I eye the bastard who thinks to wound my horse.

He leers at me, dirty, long beard trapped beneath his byrnie. I can't stretch out to reach him, but when his war axe next comes at Haden, I stop it by using my sword almost as a spear, stabbing it towards him, my right arm straining with the effort. I sense myself falling once more. I can't allow that. Not here. I grimace, but Eahric's overpowered the man he was fighting. Eyes glinting with malice, he hacks into the man behind me. Blood flies through the air, the war axe landing heavily on the ground. The man I've killed falls back, lying over the axe, and the dying man, bucking as the foeman beneath him gasps his last breaths.

'Bloody hell,' I mutter, spitting to ward off the evil of such a bad death.

Eahric grins, showing me his blood-stained teeth. Now he's with me, following me and Wulfhere along the line of enemy hacking into our shield wall. Wulfhere's dealt with two of the enemy warriors who thought to stop us from reaching Wærwulf and Sæbald, but the other three still menace him. I'd welcome Eahric at Haden's back, but Wulfhere needs him more.

'Aid Wulfhere,' I urge him, sure that Lyfing will have killed his enemy soon and can join me.

Our progress is slow. The horses are mired in the press of bodies, as though a river, but filled with sharpened blades instead of fish.

Lyfing must call his horse to him, for the next thing I know, he's mounted and assisting me to finish the second line of the shield wall, dividing the men who battle there from anyone who might reinforce them, leaving a solitary figure to fight against my warriors.

I see Icel next. He grimaces at seeing me, steadfastness writ into the sharp strikes he inflicts on his opponent. The second man in the shield wall falls with a shriek, shouting loud enough that I sense the eyes of others on us. All have finally seen our slow advance.

Shouted words amongst the enemy, and I'm aware that the men are panicking. They thought they'd won this and had overpowered Icel's small force. They didn't realise there were others. They perhaps don't even understand from where we came. Frightened eyes look my way. I smirk, even as my blade flashes wetly, and the crunching of breaking bones rings through the air where the horses step without thought. I'm jostled from side to side, but this time, the pain doesn't unman me. If anything, it makes me more fucking angry. My men and I are closing off the chance of escaping eastwards, or northwards if that's how you think about it, along the Portway. The enemy will soon die, or they'll run for it. I hope we kill them all before that happens.

Icel's quick to mount his borrowed horse, and the line of the shield wall is almost halved. Hereman and his allies are getting closer and closer to us. We'll meet soon, and then the enemy, who lack horses, will have nowhere to run. The twenty men who thought to do little but call words of encouragement to their allies are dead or dying. If I look behind, it'll be as though the road's been covered by an expensive carpet or tapestry, only woven with the blood, broken bones and blades of our enemy, skin greying in death, bright eyes fading as though left in the sun for too long.

I grin, and it twists to a grimace as Haden missteps. I'm jolted forward, rearing up against his neck, a mouthful of sweating horse hair almost choking me.

I right myself, trying to determine how many enemies our small force still faces. Too many of the bastards remain, but we are prevailing.

'Stay behind me,' Icel rumbles. I'd tell him what I think of that, but abruptly, the pain in my leg returns. Sweat beads on my face, and nausea gurgles in my throat. I've done too much. And yet, it's not yet enough. I spit aside the sourness of my mouth but allow Icel to take my place, moving Haden back to ride beside Lyfing.

He grins at me, eyes flashing with delight beneath his helm, which still shows the sign of when it was dented by a horse standing on it. It's lucky he wasn't wearing it at the time.

I also try to grin and find delight in what we're doing, but my strength's leaving me. I don't want to leave my men to the fight, but I think I must. Either that or risk falling and causing even more chaos.

I blink and focus on the way ahead. The small force that Hereman fought beside has met up with Sæbald and Wærwulf. The number of foemen is growing ever smaller. Only then, I hear the shout from whoever is in nominal command of our enemy. I know what they mean to do.

I grip my sword and shield more tightly. I can't withdraw. I must continue to fight because the enemy is about to make a run for it, and with Haden beneath me, we can really do some fucking damage to the bastards.

Chapter Twenty-Nine

One moment, the battle is deadly and bloody; the next, my warriors who still stand in the shield wall have no one to fight.

'Halt,' I command them. I know exactly what they're about to do. I can't have them running all over the countryside with no thought for maintaining a formation that will aid them if the enemy thinks to form a counterattack.

'My lord?' Icel bellows.

'Wait,' I urge him through tight lips, fighting my nausea. I'm glad I wear my helm, or he'd see how weak I feel. No doubt my face is whiter than virgin snow.

'Wait,' I order once more, Hereman echoing my cry. Eyes glance at me. I see fury and blood lust, and also too many cuts and eyes lacking focus.

'We need to do this sensibly,' I explain.

'We never do anything bloody sensibly,' Icel counters angrily. His fingers curl on the horse's reins. Any moment now, the bastard will be gone.

'Then we'll fucking surprise everyone, won't we?' I remark with heat. I glance down at the dead and dying men. There are many of them.

'Icel, tell me what lies ahead,' I point where I mean.

'Winchester,' he admits unwillingly. But that's not what I mean.

'Any more tight passes like this one?'

'I can't remember everything,' he huffs.

'Then we ride as two groups. No one is to rush off alone, and I include myself in that before you argue with me, Hereman.' He grins as I look at him. Daft git.

'We'll keep the same divide as last night. Men, get to your horses and ride together. We'll not be entering Winchester today, but if we can stop more of them from reaching it, that's to the bloody good.' As I speak, more and more riderless horses are claimed until only one remains. I glance around, a thrum of fear in my belly for my missing man if I can call him a man. He's still a boy to me.

'Where's Gardulf?' I shout, knowing I'll not bloody forgive myself if he's dead.

Hereman swivels his head from side to side, seeking his nephew, but I can't see him and Kermit's nibbling at the ground.

'Bollocks,' I glower. Rudolf dismounts and quickly begins to rollover the dead bodies, seeking his fellow young warrior. Hereman does the same. Icel glowers at me, chaffing at the delay.

'Fine, those with Icel go now. The rest of you, see if you can find Gardulf amongst the dead.' The words slip from my tongue too easily. He better not be bloody dead.

'Aye, my lord.' Icel's already moving, those warriors who've already fought a bloody and long battle, keen to be on their way to resume their task of killing the enemy.

'Blood-thirsty bastard,' I mutter, peering over Haden's shoulder to look down at the corpses.

Most of the enemy have died with their faces pressed to the ground. Only a few of them look upwards, and none of the fuckers I can see are young Gardulf. Hereman and Rudolf move quickly, others joining them, although Sæbald and Wærwulf stay mounted, close to me, eyes peering both ways along the road.

'My lord,' Wærwulf's words are quiet. 'Are you sure you're well?'

'I'm not, no,' I surprise him by replying, his lips compressing, not enjoying my honest assessment. 'But I can't stop here or now. If I have to tie myself to Haden's saddle, then that's what I'll bloody do.' He nods, respect on his familiar face.

'Just don't fucking fall,' he cautions me. 'That'll get bloody messy.'

'He's not here, my lord,' Rudolf rushes towards me. 'I'm sure of it.'

'What, you've checked all of the dead?'

'Yes, all one hundred and eight of the fuckers.' I see that Hereman's already shaking his head.

I peer into the surrounding woodlands, biting my lip and thinking of the noises I heard earlier.

'It's possible he's hunting down those who thought to attack us from behind.'

'It is, yes,' Hereman admits. I'm torn now. I've sent half of my men on and we need to join them. But I don't like leaving Gardulf if he is beneath the trees.

'We ride on,' Hereman states, wincing as he speaks. 'We take Kermit, and we either find Gardulf, or we don't. If he's here, alone, he'll seek us out. It's not as though he doesn't know where we're going.'

'But he doesn't know Wessex?'

'No, but Icel made it clear this trackway leads to Winchester. That's the way we're going to go. If we can, we'll come back later and seek him.'

Uneasy, I turn, wishing I had time to find Gardulf. I can't lose him and Edmund so close together.

'Do it,' I urge Hereman, decisively. 'Ensure Kermit's reins are tied tightly.' He nods, and while I watch him, Rudolf takes a final look at one of the bodies. I notice him jerk away, and then his seax blade plunges into the man's neck.

'There's always one of the bastards that's not quite dead,' he mutters, wiping his blade on the very dead man beside the one who wasn't quite dead and returning to Jethson.

'Stay the fuck alive,' I glower at my men.

I hear Wærwulf's answering cry. 'And you, my lord.'

* * *

Clear of the woodland, the view stretches out before me. There's a trail of dead enemies all along the roadway. The bastards thought to run for it, but their wounds, or more likely, Icel's blades, have killed them all.

I don't push my warriors. We've fought a hard battle. The horses have been sorely used as well. Many of them have cuts on their bodies. They'll all need tending to when this is over.

I muse over Gardulf's whereabouts. I take comfort in knowing he's not amongst the dead, but what if he crawled away to die? What if he was taken captive? The fact Kermit's there isn't reassuring at all. I'd curse the bastard, but fear makes me loath to do so. I'll not forgive myself if I name him everything under the sun and then discover he's dead.

Wærwulf keeps a wary eye on me. I'd tell him to fuck off, but actually, it's better if one of my men realises I'm severely compromised. I can't feel my right foot, which worries me. I can feel my right thigh, which also concerns me. What a time to take a bloody wound, I curse myself.

I can't see my fellow Mercians, only the dead Viking raiders. Free from the trees, I realise the sun is bright, but the horizon remains clouded with smoke.

Hereman's far from his usual jovial self, and he's not alone in peering over hedgerows and into deep ditches that line the trackway. I pray Gardulf's not dead. I don't like the fact he's disappeared. Him, King Alfred? Where are the bastards? Mind, I care more about Gardulf than Alfred.

And then, up ahead, we join the rest of the men. The horses have slowed, and for a moment, I'm unsure why. But then, I look further, as opposed to at my hands or my men, and I realise there's a settlement up ahead, one almost enclosed by walls, but perhaps not fully. They don't glint with the brightness of London's remaining ancient walls. But many banners are hanging over them, showing the familiar emblems of the Grantabridge jarls, or so I imagine. I can more decipher the colours than the emblems.

I push Haden through to where Icel has stopped his forward advance, and it's not just because a river blocks the way, and the bridge there is also heavily guarded. The rest of my warriors mill around, watching the trailing end of the survivors surging through a gap in the wall only for a solid-looking gate to slam shut on them.

'Winchester?' I question, although it seems obvious even to someone who's never seen it before.

Icel nods, his expression unreadable, even when he removes his helm so I can see the whole of his face.

'Aye, my lord. Winchester, the home of the kings of Wessex. Or so it used to be. It seems, my lord, that the bastard Viking raiders have truly taken it, and so far, I can see nothing of the Wessex ealdormen or their damn king.' His words thrum with fury, and I share it.

Where the fuck is King Alfred, and where are his ealdormen?

I'm bloody and wounded, and I might have lost young Gardulf, and for what? If King Alfred can't bestir himself to protect his settlement, then why the fuck should I?

I spin, looking back the way we've come, as well as at the imposing settlement and the bridge blocking our path.

I don't like this, not at all.

And then, I don't like it even fucking more.

Chapter Thirty

They come at us from the south. There are more than we've just fought, and they're fresh and ready to engage.

I sigh deeply.

'Fuck,' Icel glowers. 'They've come from the south west gate.'

The only thing we have going for us is that they're not behind us. The trackway's clear. I turn to glance at it. I don't want to retreat from this fight, but perhaps there's no choice this time.

'We go,' I urge my warriors, alert for their complaints. 'Even I'm not fucking stupid enough to battle that when we're already compromised with many wounded amongst us.'

'I agree,' Icel growls and my jaw drops.

'Fuck, it must be bad if even Icel agrees,' I admit, already redirecting Haden to race back the way we've come. The feeling in my foot has returned, but it's not a pleasant sensation. Far from it.

'Hurry,' I order my men, not even Icel lingering.

'What if they chase us?' Hereman huffs.

'Then they chase us, and we'll have to go faster.' This isn't at all how I thought today would play out. I didn't believe there were so many Viking raiders within Winchester and prepared to die to keep hold of it. I thought we'd break through the gate, or the walls, and hand Winchester back to King Alfred as though he's the damn arse who couldn't beat a child at *tafl*. But, if these are the odds he faces, I'm unsurprised he's struggled as much as he has.

Wærwulf stays close to me. I grip Haden's reins and hold on tightly with my left thigh. I've forced my right foot into the stirrup, but it's uncomfortable. Sooner that, though, than being skewered by the enemy.

The jeers of our foemen can be heard even above the pounding of the horses' hooves. I risk looking behind and realise the enemy have far from given up their chase, and there are more men, standing on the remnants of the walls, the flash of bare flesh assuring me they're showing us their arses. Not that we need to bloody see that.

'Bastards,' I glower, sweat streaming down my face. I've really arsed this up, and I've lost Gardulf in the process. It's far from my finest act.

Hereman and Sæbald ride to the rear. Icel's streaming away in front, not because he's a coward, but because he knows the way. It could be as simple as following the trackway we've taken to get here, but I hope he knows something else that I don't. I can sense the enemy gaining on us, well some of them. Not all the foemen have horses, but certainly, a good number do, and they're chasing us. If they're good animals, their horses will tire long after ours. That's not a comforting thought.

Once more, along the trackway with the hedges and ditches, I keep my eyes moving, keen to focus on something other than the pain in my thigh. If we can find Gardulf, that would make today's poor showing more bearable.

'Hurry, my lord,' Hereman huffs, his horse coming closer and closer. I risk another glance and see he's correct to be fearful. The enemy is gaining. I can almost see the colour of their mounts. Still, Haden's steady beneath me. My horse could canter at a good speed for much of the day. I wouldn't be able to gallop him for so long, and the enemy is galloping, which means their horses should tire more easily.

I see no sign of Gardulf, but we pass the scene of the earlier fight more quickly than I think possible. The stink of the dying is intense, the scent of decay already fouling the air. The bastards need burying or burning. We disturb a flock of black birds as we race through the pinch point. I also see other animals skulking away. The smell of decay will be more enticing for them than it is for me.

Icel presses onwards. I lick my lips, wishing there was time to drink or even eat. It's been a long time since my burnt pottage. I can sense myself weakening. I've not tied myself to Haden's stirrups and saddle. I should have done so. I risk falling.

The pinch point quickly fades behind us, and slowly, the enemy starts to drop away. Soon, there are only a few hardy individuals maintaining the chase, but once the horses recover, it'll be easy enough for them to find us. We're hardly evading them by keeping to the trackway. But, for now, even as ruined as it is in places, it's still the quickest route away from them.

Eventually, I realise Hereman's calling us to a halt. My head throbs, my leg's agony. I've retreated within myself, focusing only on Haden's steady gait and my hands on his reins.

'They've all stopped,' he shouts. 'Some time ago. I don't think we'll have long.'

Ahead, Icel reins in, and I focus on my men and horses. Apart from Kermit, who has no rider, the horses are sweating, their bellies heaving. We don't look much better.

'Where from here?' I question Icel as my warriors take the chance to dismount and allow their horses to drink sparingly from a spring close to the road.

'We could make it almost to London,' he suggests. I shake my head.

'They'll expect that.'

'Then we should veer off northwards and try and find the path we took to get here.' This seems like the more sensible option, but I still don't like it. It was slow going. If the enemy realises what we've done, they'll be on us quickly.

'If only we had a larger force,' I huff, dismounting carefully on the left side of Haden. I need to piss, and he needs a rest. But I'll fall if I'm not careful. This really was a shit time to take a wound.

'The ealdormen will be days away,' Icel huffs.

'I know. And we don't know where the fuck King Alfred is.'

'No, we don't,' he concurs. I shake my head. This is a fucking mess, and so am I. I stand firm just on my left leg, but Icel's appraising glance assures me he knows how much I'm struggling.

'We can't rest all night.'

'No, we must keep going.'

'And it'll be quicker to follow the trackway?'

'It will, but there's a point further north where the true decision must be made.' If Icel thinks this will console me, he's wrong, but it does give me pause for consideration.

'Then we take what sleep we can and continue along the trackway.'

I spin to assess my warriors. They're all exhausted, and Hereman's fiery with his fears for Gardulf. I feel the same way. I don't see how Gardulf will ever find us, not now. I consider whether it would be better for him if he were dead. Potentially, but I hate the fucking thought.

'Pybba and I will keep watch,' Icel informs me. 'We're old men. We've spent many a sleepless night and can afford another one.'

'Only for half the night. Then you must wake us all, and we'll resume.'

'My lord,' he inclines his head, which I take for agreement. 'Now, will you let me look at your wound?'

He makes it sound like a question, but it's not.

'Aye, if you must. But I need a moment.'

Hobbling and hopping, I make my way to the side of the stream and the road and release my stream into some long grasses. Better to piss here than piss myself when Icel tends to my wound. Even just releasing my trews sends fresh waves of agony down my leg. Whatever Icel does to me is going to hurt like a bitch, but if he doesn't look at it, the chances of it taking the wound rot are high. I'd rather hold my pain close today than die a slow and lingering death.

It hurts so much when Icel forces me to remove my trews that I lie, sweat-soaked, as his fingers prod at the wound in the last of the daylight. I bite my lip, place my arm over my head, and grip my fists tight. None of it helps.

'Concentrate on your breathing,' he suggests. 'In through your nose, out through your mouth.' My befuddled mind struggles to do as he suggests, but it's a means of distraction, which works well enough until he prods my wound and a thousand hurts make themselves known. He grunts as I stuff my fist into my mouth.

'It's not bleeding,' he announces, sounding pleased about that. 'The bandage has stayed in place. I think it's merely the pain of healing. It can be like that sometimes.' His words contain some consolation, but it doesn't stop it from hurting like a bastard.

'Here, I'll change the bandage, which should keep it cleaner. I take it we didn't find any honey?'

'No,' Rudolf agrees. I consider where Icel thinks we might have found honey today, my gaze flicking between them.

'Just a thought,' Icel counters, almost grinning, as he works quickly and then stands and walks away. Rudolf remains, helping me sit upright and wriggle back into my trews.

'You stink,' he complains.

'Aye, we all do,' I agree, grateful to have Icel's inspection done. I'm exhausted, my leg throbbing, but at least my head has stopped pounding.

'Here,' Rudolf offers me a water bottle, and I drink deeply. 'You might want to chew this as well. Mind, it'll taste like shit, but it'll help with the pain.'

I take the leaves and gag at their smell. Rudolf shrugs his shoulders but lingers.

'Where's Gardulf?' he questions softly.

'I wish I knew, Rudolf, I really do, but I don't. I don't believe he's dead. He's somewhere, doing something. Let's hope he finds us or returns to Mercia alone.'

Rudolf's face furrows in thought, the coming night half-shadowing him. His eyes remain bright. 'We should all have stayed in Mercia,' he mutters unhappily. I don't reply. I know he's correct, and he knows he's correct; what more is there to say?

'If King Alfred weren't such a fucking arse, we wouldn't be here,' I mutter, but even I know the argument is poor. It's his meddling and my pig-headedness that have brought us to Wessex. Yes, it made sound political sense to ally with King Alfred, but it was my desire to beat him in his own kingdom that allowed this shit show to persist. I realise Rudolf hasn't asked about King Alfred.

'Where do you think the bastard is?' I question. Rudolf wrinkles his nose.

'I wouldn't be surprised to find him sheltering in Mercia while you do all the work.' I chuckle at Rudolf's dire prediction.

'Maybe. But he was supposed to send word to us, and he didn't. Perhaps he's already dead?'

'If he is, then Wessex is yours to claim, my lord king,' he grins, his worries for Gardulf temporarily dismissed. 'In which case, you need to do a bloody better job of keeping it free of the bastard Viking raiders.' I growl at that. Rudolf's never been one to honey-glaze his thoughts on my skills, or lack thereof. In this, he's once more correct, which has me thinking as I finally close my eyes and snatch what sleep I can get.

* * *

When Icel shakes me awake, it's still dark and my eyes burn with grit and lack of sleep.

'Bloody hell,' I mutter.

'Aye, my lord. That's your lot.' His words lack all sympathy but don't snap with his usual tone. He's tired. I wish he could rest.

'How's the leg?' he questions. I wince.

'I'm trying not to think about it.' With as much grace as a three-legged dog, I stagger upright, the pain fierce but bearable. I hurry to piss and mount up, the rest of my warriors hastening to do the same.

'Anything?' I question Pybba, as he's already mounted and ready to go. The moon overhead is half-shadowed. There's enough light to see by, but only just.

'No, quiet. Perhaps too quiet.' I nod, hauling myself with my left foot into Haden's saddle. He's half asleep as well.

'Which way,' I call to Icel when we're ready—well, apart from Osmod, who's as slow as ever. I'd curse him, but it would do no good. With darkness coating the land, at least the enemy can't see us.

'This way,' and he leads his horse along the trackway. 'But not for much further. Have you decided?'

I shake my head. I haven't.

'We'll see what the day brings. Try and get some sleep.'

Icel huffs at that. I don't force it. If he doesn't sleep, he'll be useless to me. But for now, I need him because he knows the way. Hopefully, he'll get some rest because we're not cantering in the dark, but we do need to keep moving.

I pull my cloak tight around my shoulders. I can't tell if it's cold or if I'm cold. I don't ask. After my days of sweating, it's nice not to feel too hot. Icel leads on, but I eventually sense him slow, and Hereman and I replace him, ensuring the horse keeps following us while Icel slumps in the saddle. Pybba does the same.

Full daylight finally floods the landscape in a flurry of pinks, yellows and reds. It would be nice if we weren't stuck in Wessex. We've remained on the trackway, following its path. The horses are sure-footed. I have to fight my own exhaustion at points, but we can't all bloody sleep.

I don't hear the enemy following on behind, but I suspect they do, all the same. Once more, I consider where King Alfred is. Has the enemy killed him? I don't sense they have, but I don't know him well enough to feel any worry at the thought, unlike Gardulf. I keep reassuring myself that he still lives wherever he is. I sense his absence as a hollow in the centre of our group. I've hardly managed to get used to Edmund being gone.

When Icel speaks, it's as though he expects us not to know he's been sleeping.

'Well, my lord. The decision is upon you.' He points ahead. I see nothing different in the trackway or surrounding landscape, certainly, it's not familiar to me. 'Here is where we either continue to London, or rather, to the south of London, or we cut across and make it to Mercia.'

I turn and look back at the way we've come. I can see a surprisingly long way, and nowhere on that road are black dots moving.

'We're not being chased?'

'No, my lord. Not yet. They might have given up after all.'

I bite my lips, deep in thought. It doesn't feel as though we're running, but all the same, the loss of Gardulf plagues me, as does not knowing King Alfred's fate. The men take advantage of my lack of decision, dismounting and tending to their horses.

Icel waits patiently beside me. He offers no suggestions. That should worry me. He's always so free with his opinions.

'We need to join up with the rest of the Mercians,' I announce. 'We can do fuck all with so few of us. So, we head towards Cricklade, and hopefully, we'll hear news of our allies.'

Icel twists a startled glance at me.

'That's very sensible, my lord,' he mutters, the shock evident in his voice.

'Oh, fuck off, Icel,' I rejoin, but I'm laughing.

Chapter Thirty-One

We ride alert and armed, but the countryside we pass through is quiet. We see men and women about their daily tasks, heads popping up from fields they're tending. Once more, it seems idyllic. They appear fearful at our passage, but one or other of us always shouts a greeting, and they soon call for news. We tell them what we know, which is very little, and they share what they know, which is even less. Their demeanour is either frightened or defiant. The men and women of Wessex are no different to those who live within Mercia. They despise the Viking raiders. It seems they also have reason to hate them.

A sense of anticipation hangs on every word we share. We all know something's going to happen, but when remains a mystery.

My leg continues to plague me, but Rudolf sweet talks a kindly matron to share some of her honey in exchange for Mercian coinage, and with that slathered on it, I rest easier, despite the pain. I know the power of honey. The wound is clean, pink and fiery, where it starts to heal. The honey will keep the wound rot at bay if I'm lucky. The others also get some as well. I'm not about to hog the honey, as it were.

Undisturbed by any sign of the enemy, we sleep that night beneath a low-hanging oak tree, sheltered from the gentle wind and the occasional raindrops. The men take guard duty while Icel, Pybba, and I get to sleep all night. I'm so exhausted I hear nothing until I'm woken in the morning by an incessant shoving on my shoulder.

'Come, my lord,' Rudolf hurries me. 'We can't bloody stay here.' He grins on speaking, but worry clouds his eyes. I'm also thinking of Gardulf. I wish I knew where he was. If he was with us, this would feel much less like a hurried retreat in the face of overwhelming enemy numbers.

'How many days has it been?' I question Rudolf. I've lost count of how long it's been since we left Cricklade. Rudolf purses his lips while thinking, but it's Icel who answers.

'Five, my lord.'

'Enough for the ealdorman to be coming this way.' He shrugs his wide shoulders.

'Depends. It could be.' His noncommittal response has Rudolf grimacing. We'd all feel better if we knew where Ealdorman Ælhun and Kyred were.

'Surely Kyred?' I state more confidently. 'He doesn't have as far to travel.'

Once more, we ride alert, but the closer we get to the border with Mercia, the less fear I feel despite my leg wound. Others who took cuts and blows are also starting to recover. A few have livid bruises marring parts of their body. Hemming looks like a bloody rainbow.

And then, just as the day's starting to draw in, we hear the sound of hooves over the ground, coming towards us.

'From the north,' Hereman's quick to reassure.

'We'll wait,' I order my men, the animals coming to a stop in a jangle of harness and soft whinnies. I stay mounted. It's still easier for me to use Haden as my legs than try and get around using my wounded leg. I hope it'll be fully healed before I have to face my aunt's fury. I don't object to fighting the enemy with the wound, but my aunt? She really will deliver the most crushing of blows, and all without saying a word.

I squint into the distance, aware whoever comes this way is visible, but my eyesight's too poor to make out the details.

'It's Kyred,' Rudolf reassures me, alert to my failings.

'Good.' I mutter, already feeling the tension ease from my shoulders. He comes at the head of a good-sized force. Not thousands, but certainly hundreds.

Kyred's forehead furrows on seeing me.

'My lord king,' he questions, even while assessing my force. Some of his men dismount and quickly offer to share food. I'm grateful for the smell of only recently baked bread.

'Kyred, it's good to see you,' I offer, staying mounted. He brings his horse closer, and a gap opens up around us. Pybba speaks loudly to the other Mercians, sharing information and asking for an accounting of his family, reunited now at Kingsholm, allowing us some privacy.

'A fierce battle, not far from Winchester, three days ago.'

'Not a victory?' he surmises.

'Not a loss either. We were chased by a bigger force. We retreated rather than be overwhelmed. Reinforced by you and your men, we can return.'

'Is that wise, my lord king?'

'King Alfred has disappeared, and young Gardulf's missing.' Understanding covers his face, and he offers a brief grimace.

'You should know Ealdorman Ælhun isn't far behind. We met him earlier. His men had travelled all night and needed to rest. They should be with us by the morning.'

'How many do you have?'

'We have the might of Worcester and Gloucester. All told, just over two hundred warriors.'

'And Ealdorman Ælhun has a similar number?'

'Perhaps more. He's come via London, and taken half of the force who once served Bishop Smithwulf.'

'And news from Wessex?'

'Nothing, my lord king. You know more than we do. My lord king,' he says slowly, and I know where his thoughts have taken him. Mine have gone there many times during this journey as well. I don't force him to say it.

'We must do what we can for Mercia will be the enemy's next target if King Alfred is dead. Is there another route?' I question Icel. 'Perhaps to the far side of Winchester? We know the enemy holds it. They'll expect us to come at them from the same direction we left it.'

'They might, my lord,' Icel admits, looking uneasy. Perhaps he hopes I'll ride for Mercia, but Icel has never been a bloody coward.

'We could take a different route, abandon the Portway to this side of Winchester. If King Alfred lives, I suspect he'll have sought shelter at Old Sarum.'

'Where's that?'

'To the west of Winchester, not far, but it's ancient, very ancient. I'm surprised you've not heard of it.'

'Why would I have heard of it?' Icel smiles then.

'You'll realise, my lord, when we reach it.'

I furrow my brows, but he offers nothing else. I scowl at him, but I must consider his suggestion instead of being annoyed by his evasiveness.

'How many days travel?'

'More than it took us to get here, perhaps only by one day. We'll need to travel west from here, and then find a road or track that leads to Old Sarum.' Kyred says nothing, and I suspect he's never heard of the place either.

'We'll wait for Ealdorman Ælhun. With our forces combined, we should have enough to counter the enemy, if not to take back Winchester for King Alfred.'

Both men nod, neither offering any complaint. I eye the men Kyred's brought with him, my heart sinking to see old Tatberht amongst them. He was with my aunt when they left Cricklade. I hoped he'd stay with her.

With our strategy meeting over, he comes towards me.

'My lord.'

'What are you doing here?' I question perhaps more forcibly than I should.

'Aye, well, Lady Cyneswith bid me to protect her nephew,' he rumbles. I growl at that. 'I always had a hankering to visit Wessex,' he continues.

'My aunt is well, and my nephew?'

'Yes, well, your aunt is uneasy at your little trip to Wessex, but young Æthelred's a fine boy. Now I know I can see much of your brother in him. He's not as timid as he was, either, now there's been constant food in his belly and warm clothes on his back.'

'You'll get yourself killed,' I complain. He chuckles once more.

'I've lived a good, long life, my lord. I don't plan on dying yet, and certainly not in defence of Wessex, so don't worry yourself on my behalf.' And with that, he rides Wombel amongst the rest of my warriors, and the sound of men preparing for the night fills the air.

For a moment, I regret my determination to continue assisting Wessex. We've no formal accord with them. We're so close to Mercia that I can almost smell it. But what point is there in ensuring Mercia is protected if the bastard enemy is simply going to march through Wessex and then take Mercia, as they tried to do with the kingdom of the East Angles?

Bastard Viking raiders. Fucking King Alfred.

I feel like I have to protect this island alone. Thank fuck I have my loyal warriors to aid me. I'm going to need them. I pray they don't die for Wessex.

* * *

As Kyred assured me, Ealdorman Ælhun arrives in the morning. I greet him warmly, eyeing the yawning men.

'My lord king,' he glowers, noticing my pronounced limp. Pybba's suggested I use a stick to aid my balance. I've told him where he can bloody shove that. His laughter still echoes around my head.

'It's healing,' I reassure him, reaching out to grip his forearm when he dismounts. 'Have you ridden all night?'

'No, my lord. We woke early. I wanted to join Kyred's force today. It seems we've found you as well. But where is everyone else?'

'King Alfred has disappeared. We've lost young Gardulf and Winchester's in the grip of the Viking raiders.'

'And what do you mean to do?' he stands taller while speaking, releasing the grip on my arm. He's a brave man. I've grown to admire him in the last year and a half.

'We intend to go to Old Sarum. Icel assures me King Alfred will be there, if nowhere else.' A faint smile touches the ealdorman's grey-flecked whiskers at that.

'And has he told you about Old Sarum?'

'No, he's not. Why, what do you know?' But Ealdorman Ælhun shakes his head, smiling.

'Ah, well, it's to be seen to be believed, so if Icel refuses to inform you, I'm not going to spoil his fun. Be assured, it's worth waiting for.'

'Very well,' I grudgingly concede. 'And you will join us?'

'As you command, my lord king. As you command.'

'Tell me of Northampton first.'

'The encampment remains, but there are no more than fifty Norse within it. They don't attempt to take Northampton. No one has seen any sign of Jarl Halfdan since just after you left Worcester. He's gone from there.'

'Um, yes, I fear he's now in Wessex.'

'But that was your intention, was it not?'

'It was, but there are more of the bastards than just owe allegiance to the Repton and Grantabridge jarls.'

'As long as we prevent a recurrence of a few years ago,' the ealdorman cautions.

'Yes, we must,' I acknowledge, not wanting to admit to how much I don't know about that period. I was safe in my drunken haze and days filled with manual labour. All the same, the repercussions of those years and years of attack have left a deep impact on those who were involved.

'And we will,' the ealdorman's words are reassuring.

'King Alfred isn't a great warrior.'

'No, he's not, my lord king. He's a man of politics and religion. You'll have to perform the task for him, and we must hope you can get it done once and for all.'

I nod but realise the ealdorman is very much mirroring my thoughts on the matter.

'No one but you, my lord king, has the ability to do what must be done to permanently evict the Norse from our island. It's a great deal of responsibility. I've every faith in you, as do your warriors.'

I don't respond this time. The ealdorman surprises me by laughing.

'Think about it less. I always find the problem comes when you think about things too much.'

I smile then, eyeing my warriors and reassuring myself of Mercian strength and vitality.

If Mercian warriors must save Wessex, then despite all my assertions to the contrary, that's what we're going to have to bloody well do.

'Come on, you lazy bastards,' I call, limping to Haden. 'Time we were on the way. We've got Viking raider bastards to kill.'

A ragged cheer greets my words. I allow myself to grin.

Perhaps we might even have some fucking fun doing so.

Chapter Thirty-Two

True to his word, Icel picks his path to the north of Wessex, and finally finds a trackway he's confident will take us to Old Sarum. But it's only when we pass a strange circle of stones that Icel announces he's sure we're on the correct route.

'What is this place?' I question. He shrugs.

'Old,' he offers.

'How old?'

'Older than me,' he rumbles, as we ride our horses down a short slope and through the collection of stones. I eye them, a sudden chill running down my back. Whatever this place is, it's ancient and exudes an atmosphere I don't much like.

'I wouldn't like to be here in the dark,' Rudolf calls, eyes wide as dishes.

'Scared of a few stones?' Icel taunts, but without his usual acerbic tone.

'I think we probably all are,' Hereman suggests. Only the horses seem immune to whatever the place is. I'm pleased to be through and out the other side.

'A decent enough marker,' I confirm, looking to Icel.

'Not too bad. Permanent,' he acknowledges, encouraging his horse to pick up the pace. We're cantering, not galloping to Old Sarum. The horses have already been tested. It's time to make sure they can keep going without us having to worry that they'll be winded and unable to gallop northwards at the first sign of trouble.

Despite Icel's assurance he knows where we are, his face clouds as the day advances.

'I thought we'd be there by now,' he growls. I look at him. Of us all, he's the only one who knows this area at all well, well apart from Cuthwalh and he's already announced he's got bugger all idea where we are.

'We stop for tonight,' I announce when it's too dark to see. 'In the morning, we should find our way.' I don't much like the thought of being lost in Wessex, but what more can we do?

With guards set for the night, we sleep. The morning greets us with rain and a cold wind, and I glower as it sheets into my face.

'Fucking wonderful,' I mutter, limping towards Haden. We ride in sullen gloom, men ahead scouting the way. Eventually, Rudolf returns to my side.

'There's another collection of standing stones,' he points where he means. I turn to Icel. His eyes furrow in thought.

'Didn't know there were two of them,' he mutters, no doubt hoping that explains everything. 'Shouldn't be long now.'

And this time, he's proven correct. Eventually, the rain clears, the clouds lift, and even I can see the strange structure in front of us.

'Is that a hill?' I mutter, trying to make sense of what I'm seeing.

'Come on, my lord,' Icel calls, encouraging his horse onwards. 'You're going to like this.'

The closer we get, the more my forehead creases. I almost forget we're seeking King Alfred so astounded am I by what I'm seeing. Of course, I know there are old structures in Mercia. The hills close to the kingdoms of the Welsh are liberally splattered with what people tell me are old ramparts, visible now only as grassy banks in the landscape, and a few scattered stones as well. This is altogether different, but also the same.

Smoke billows from within, and I realise people are inside what seems to be a hill, if that's even possible. From ground level, it does appear that the *hill* could be hollow.

Icel chuckles as he rushes forward. Now I pick out one or two people standing on the hillside, if that's the correct word for it. The sullen sun glints from weapons.

'The enemy?'

'I doubt it, my lord, but we'll discover soon enough,' he bellows joyfully. I shake my head and turn to eye Ealdorman Ælhun. He wears a look of faint amusement on his lips, but I think he's as amazed as I am, even though he knew more about this place than I did.

Icel leads on, circling around the strange creation until we meet the remnants of an old road, complete with a stone and weed-crusted surface. From here, I look to the south and almost think I can see another settlement. I try and orientate myself, but I'm entirely perplexed, and then Icel reins in.

From an opening within the hill, almost to the east, warriors pour forth. I recognise the emblem they carry, the wyvern of Wessex, and nod towards Icel, impressed. True to his word, he's found our missing King Alfred and his warriors.

I ride to greet them.

'Good day,' I call, not recognising the faces of the fifty or so men who obstruct the path. There's a more temporary structure blocking any access within the hollow hill – I can't think of it as anything else. The smell of turned earth is ripe in the air. 'I'm seeking King Alfred of the West Saxons. Tell him that King Coelwulf of Mercia has arrived with his warriors.'

Startled looks pass between them, but one steps forward from between the turned earth and stakes embedded in the ground.

'My lord king. I'll have King Alfred informed immediately.' As he speaks, he flicks his wrist and a warrior sprints within. Behind the reinforcements, I see more Wessex warriors ceasing in their preparations. It appears they were prepared to fight to keep this place if not for Winchester.

I sit back on Haden, eyeing Old Sarum. Through the opening, I can see there are steadings within. The walls are so tall they far overtop my head, and they're steep as well. I can't imagine any horse being able to run up them. I can't imagine a warrior would find it easy.

'What is this place?' I demand from Icel. Despite being in Wessex and our proximity to King Alfred, he wears a broad grin, entirely pleased with himself.

'Old Sarum, my lord. A place that even the Romans were in awe of, for all they mostly lived closer to the river, along that way,' he points to the west. I follow where his finger points, but I can't see a river.

'But what is it?'

'An old settlement, defensive, I would assume, from before the Romans. Not bad,' he questions me, his lips downturned but in awe, not unease.

'Aye, not bad at all.'

Just as quickly as the man ran to find King Alfred, I see him coming back.

'Allow them entry,' he calls. 'All of them,' he huffs just in case the guards are unsure.

'Indeed,' the man who speaks to us mutters. 'Then King Coelwulf of Mercia, welcome to Old Sarum.' He steps aside, as do others, but I allow Icel and Hereman to precede me. While Haden follows the other horses, I twist my head from side to side, trying to take in as much as possible about this strange place.

I can't help wondering why, if the West Saxon kings have such a settlement that could shelter them, they've made Winchester their capital. It seems most strange to me, even as the sense of being enclosed washes over me. This place reminds me of Northampton, and the defences built there, and now at Worcester and Hereford, only constructed of earth and sod, not wood and earth. There is a permanence here that's missing at Northampton, Worcester and Hereford.

I have to admit, I'm fucking impressed.

Only then does King Alfred come into view, his familiar face uneasy.

I should have remembered why I came here. The thought of protecting Wessex is one thing, but doing it for bloody King Alfred is quite another.

He appraises me on Haden's back, and I can't tell whether it's with displeasure or unease.

'My lord,' his words are well-oiled rather than pleased. 'We thought to have lost you when you didn't come at our bidding. Did you make your way back to Mercia? How are my wife and son?' He watches Kyred and Ealdorman Ælhun. I notice he makes no mention of his daughter.

'My lord king,' I reply, aggravated that he still doesn't name me as a king, gripping my fists tightly to prevent me from saying something I shouldn't. 'Alas, we received no messenger from you but did discover an encampment that had been set upon on the Portway. No one survived.'

I sense men turning startled eyes to one another at my words, and even King Alfred looks perplexed.

I notice he's wearing the clothes of a court day—not at all the byrnie and weapons belt I would expect to see around his waist, which, indeed, encircles mine.

'That would have been Lord Æthelstan,' he mutters sadly. 'He was protecting the western road from the enemy. They have Winchester firmly in their grasp,' he bemoans, 'only a day of hard riding from here, although more likely to be two, if I'm honest. Still, it's an unpleasant feeling. Come, dismount, we'll talk within. I can offer food and drink for you and your men. The horses will overwhelm the stables, alas.'

'The horses can be held in a temporary paddock, perhaps to the north,' I suggest, pointing to where I see an expanse of well-tended grasses.

'Yes, of course,' he confirms, as though the thought would never have presented itself to him.

'We can't leave them without,' I comment, chuckling darkly. 'That would risk them being taken and these are Mercia's finest horses.'

Preparing myself to dismount, which will be tricky, but not as hard as on past occasions, I slide down Haden's left side, grateful he stays still.

'Ealdorman Ælhun, Kyred, Icel and Pybba, escort me inside to discuss affairs with King Alfred. The rest of you, tend to the animals and ensure they have water and fodder. With the enemy so close, we might have need of them very soon.'

Despite the surety in my voice, as soon as I try to walk, I know I'm going to limp. I grimace but stand as proud as I can. I shouldn't be shamed by my wound. After all, I gained it fighting for King Alfred.

While the rest of my warriors move aside, King Alfred watches them with an unsettled look. Once more, I consider why I'm here. I don't trust him. He seems to have done fuck all but use Old Sarum's walls to keep him safe. I see then that there are guards along the walls. I wouldn't enjoy having to climb them in all my equipment. I wouldn't even be able to do so today. It would be beyond my leg's capability.

Hiltiberht hurries to take Haden's reins. Alone, without the support of my horse, I step forward, unsurprised to find Icel and Pybba shadowing me. No doubt, they mean to mask my wound from the sharp eyes of the West Saxon warriors. I'm grateful King Alfred's turned his back and entered his hall.

I seek the ealdormen of Wessex that I met at Cricklade, but find them absent. I wonder if King Alfred has them fighting for him while he hunkers behind these walls. It wouldn't surprise me.

Gratefully, I settle on a chair that's been brought forward for me. King Alfred's been sitting close to the hearth, absorbing the heat. It's almost too hot for me. I've been outside for days, just the lack of wind on my face warms me.

'Now, Lord Coelwulf, tell me what's befallen you and your men?'

'We did as was arranged, travelling west along the Portway, or close to it, at any rate. We received no message from you, and so prepared to make our way to Winchester. We encountered your dead men close to a river crossing, and then we fought the enemy. We moved closer to Winchester, and overwhelmed another collection of Viking raiders. When we tried to make it to Winchester, we were driven off by a far superior force. I determined to wait for reinforcements and then seek you out. It seems, other than one collection of West Saxon warriors who are dead, there was no sight of any others throughout much of the parts of Wessex we travelled through.' I speak blandly, reciting the events of the last few days quickly. Here, before him, my fury's reignited. I can see why Icel believed King Alfred would be within Old Sarum. My suspicion he's been here all along while I've been risking my warriors and losing Gardulf in the process angers me.

'You've had some adventures,' King Alfred responds, as though I talk of a jaunt across the River Thames for pleasure. 'It's unfortunate my messenger didn't reach you. It's thrown all my plans into disarray, and I've been forced to retreat to Old Sarum.'

'Where are your ealdormen?'

'Detaining the enemy at Wareham and protecting the road that runs from Winchester to Old Sarum.'

'And what plans did I disrupt?' I question. I think he's talking shit. As soon as we let him out of our sight, I suspect King Alfred rushed to Old Sarum.

'Why, an attack to reclaim Winchester, of course. It was set to take place four days ago.'

I narrow my eyes at this. I've given him no indication of how long ago I was close to Winchester. I look to Icel. He nods slowly. He's thinking as I am.

'Did the attack not proceed at all?'

'My ealdormen and warriors were there, of course, Lord Coelwulf. When you didn't appear, we were unable to advance.'

This astounds me.

'I had only a small force. How did you think we would sway it to a victory?' A flicker of uncertainty over his face, and I realise he's failed to appreciate my force was so small before meeting up with Ealdorman Ælhun and Kyred.

'You would have held the western exit,' he dissembles. I scowl. I don't so much want to call him a coward as assert that he's one. But I must remember his importance. If nothing else, he is Wessex's king and commands her ealdormen and warriors to help him defend the kingdom from the Viking raiders. And that's what I need him to do.

'And what are the plans now?'

'Now?'

'Yes, to rescue Winchester from the enemy?'

'I've sent word to my wife, asking her to return while informing the Mercians you were lost.'

'How would that have helped?' I spin to Kyred. He's shaking his head. If there's been a messenger, he's not encountered them. Admittedly, I imagine a Wessex messenger would know the landscape better than Icel. We've probably come via a very circuitous route.

'The Mercians will know to send reinforcements.'

I shake my head.

'It seems unlikely. Not even my aunt would worry about my whereabouts.'

'I've demanded Lady Ealhswith return to Old Sarum with my son. I know a Mercian force will accompany her.'

'I doubt that,' I mutter, but he doesn't seem to hear me. 'Why would you want your wife and son here when Wessex is so overrun?'

'The ruling family should be together and united. My nephews are here. And my brother's wife.' Only then do I twist and meet the gaze of a small huddle of people the king indicates. The woman is regal, where she sits with two lads about the age of young Æthelred. The three of them watch me with varying degrees of interest. I incline my head towards her. She holds my gaze, assessing me. I detect something in that cool gaze. It might be fear. The boys have the look of King Alfred about them, only somewhat taller, already. They watch me with all the interest young boys give to warriors.

'So, now I've reappeared, have your intentions changed, or should I return to Mercia and leave you and your wife to battle the enemy for Winchester?' I detect a dark chuckle from Icel, but focus on Alfred. It's a low blow, but fuck, his battle tactics are shocking. Why he'd want his wife and son here, I don't know. I doubt, as well defended as Old Sarum is, he can stay here for the rest of his days. There isn't enough land to farm. There isn't enough land to graze animals.

'My lord,' King Alfred begins, his tone slightly censorious. I shake my head.

'You asked for Mercia's assistance. You sent no messenger to seek me, just assumed that what, I'd turned tail and fled to Mercia? I assure you, my lord king, it's not my way or that of my warriors. Now, what are your intentions?'

'Winchester and Wareham must be reclaimed, perhaps by a treaty.'

My eyes narrow at that.

'What sort of treaty? You aren't in a position of strength, unless I misunderstand your current predicament.'

'Well, one where Wessex pay the enemy to leave.'

'Pay them? For attacking your kingdom? My lord king, that seems somewhat counterproductive, does it not?'

'You made an alliance with them,' he retorts.

'I had their leader in my hands. I was in a position of strength.'

'But you're not now, are you? I understand that Jarl Guthrum is the man who holds Wareham. He understands the potent symbolism of the place as a religious centre.'

I chuckle darkly at the attempt to rile me.

'So, you mean to make an alliance with a man who shares your religion, and hope he'll leave Wareham and Winchester.'

King Alfred's eyes are fiercely bright.

'We share a religion. He'll be willing to reach an accord.'

I can't help myself, I laugh aloud, the noise harsh and filled with disdain. He was angry when he learned that Guthrum had become a Christian. Now, he means to rely on it.

'In that case, my lord king, my men and I will rest this night and then return to Mercia. You have no need of Mercia's support when you're determined to make peace with the enemy.'

'Now, my lord, I think you forget how much help Lord Æthelwulf provided at Gloucester.'

'Ah, yes, Lord Æthelwulf, where is he? I'll summon him back to Mercia. He should be protecting his properties, not those of the West Saxon's.' Once more, King Alfred doesn't like where my thoughts have taken the conversation.

'Lord Æthelwulf's holding the road from Winchester.'

'He's protecting you?'

'He is, Lord Coelwulf. He is, after all, my brother by marriage. He's bound to me as much as to Mercia.'

I don't understand King Alfred. I really don't. He'd rather argue with me about Lord Æthelwulf than discuss the shit he and his kingdom currently wallow in. I open my mouth to debate with him, but I'm interrupted by the sound of running feet over the floorboards. I turn towards the doorway, somehow knowing exactly what the messenger will inform his king.

I'm not to be disappointed.

'My lord king, the enemy have ridden through Lord Æthelwulf's force. They're coming to Old Sarum.' The voice is almost hysterical. I sigh uneasily, waiting to hear what terrible idea King Alfred will devise next. All of my sympathy for his predicament has disappeared. He does nothing to help himself.

'Then we'll defend it,' he announces. 'Summon the warriors. Have the guard redoubled on the entrance.' He rotates to me, a faint smile on his lips.

'It seems, Lord Coelwulf, that you'll have to fight for Wessex anyway.' But I'm already standing, my Mercians following me.

'Tell me, are they at the entrance?' Frightened eyes look my way, but the West Saxon quickly shakes his head.

'No, not yet. They've not been sighted.'

'Then, King Alfred, if you'll excuse us, the Mercians will distance themselves from this. After all, you've everything you need here. I'll return to my kingdom and ensure your wife, son and daughter,' I growl that because he's failed to mention Æthelflæd, 'are protected until such time as you can be reunited with them.'

With barely a bow, I stand and limp my way out of the hall. Icel's gone ahead. I hear him shouting for the men to prepare themselves. Ealdorman Ælhun and Kyred make no comment. It falls to Pybba to speak what we're all thinking.

'Fucking hell. He couldn't defend himself from an attack with a wooden sword.'

'Lord Coelwulf,' King Alfred shouts from behind me, his voice filled with panic, but I don't spin or let his fear infect me.

There's a time for the protection of mud walls and ditches, and there's a time to get the fuck out of what will be a place of entrapment. I know what I'd rather do.

Just as I'm about to mount Haden, I hear the frantic footsteps of someone else. I turn and meet the fearful eyes of the woman I take to be King Alfred's sister by marriage.

'Take us with you,' she urges. 'Please, take us with you.'

'Do you have horses?'

'Yes, yes, we do.'

'Are they fast?'

'I don't know. But, yes,' she staggers, her sons hurrying to catch her while a servant throws cloaks at them.

'Then, if you can keep up, we'll protect you. Hurry.'

With that, I limp to Haden's side and mount up, my eyes peering all around me.

The news that the enemy is coming has the few men there

hurrying to protect the entrance, but the number is tiny—far too few to protect against the horde of men we saw holding Winchester.

'Fucking arse,' I glower, encouraging Haden to ride on, forging a path through the scant collection of warriors available to defend Old Sarum's entrance.

'He really is a bloody arse,' I mutter to myself, taking in all I see and then streaming back the way Icel has just brought us.

King Alfred will fucking lose everything.

Chapter Thirty-Three

It's Pybba who catches me as we veer towards the west.

'We're not really leaving him, are we?' he demands, a perplexed expression on his face.

'Hurry the fuck up,' is all I respond. In truth, I'd love to leave the bloody useless bastard. He would deserve it. He has too few men and those he does have are fuck all use to him. He should lead by example. Admittedly, I know few kings as warlike as me. I recall stories of my childhood when Mercia's kings fell like wheat beneath the scythe. Subsequent kings have been less desperate to meet the same fate. I blame them for this predicament, just as much as I do King Alfred.

Haden's fluid beneath me. His cut from Gloucester has finally healed. I confess, with rage and fury cursing through my body, I can hardly feel my leg as anything more than a dull twinge. Long may that continue.

Icel's the next to catch me. No doubt he intends to lead us away from here.

'Don't get too far ahead,' I roar at his broad back, casting a glance behind me. King Alfred's sister by marriage, I don't even know her name, is amongst my warriors. She and her sons have good, fast horses, but this is so unexpected for them that I doubt they've thought to ensure the saddles sit perfectly, or that they're comfortable. They have cloaks, but evidently not much else.

They're a problem I could do without. But being inside Old Sarum when the enemy arrives is no place for her and her young sons. King Alfred should have thought of that long ago. He should have sent them to Mercia rather than thinking to recall his wife and son.

What sort of man stands behind women and children when the bastard Viking raiders and their fucking warriors are coming.

I work to temper my fury, to drive it from my body. Fury never won a man anything, only led to their death much sooner. I won't allow my rage for King Alfred's ineffectiveness to place my warriors and I in jeopardy.

Pybba hurries Brimman, almost as fast as Icel and his borrowed horse. If Samson were here, I imagine Icel would have been far ahead. I consider if he suspects my intentions.

I think quickly. The jangle of harness and weapons is reassuring, but I lack warriors, and now I have the woman and the two boys. I don't know their names either. What should I do with them? I don't believe they'll be able to endure this pace, but perhaps they will. Fear can make even the weakest strong.

Again, I glance behind me. We're almost out of sight of Old Sarum. Certainly, the opening is long out of view but I continue onwards. We won't go as far as the old stones Icel showed us. We won't need to do that.

I sense the glowering fury of my warriors. The consternation that Ealdorman Ælhun and Kyred feel at being asked to come all the way here, only to hasten for home. Do they think me a lesser man because I've abandoned King Alfred? If they do, they'll have to hold their tongues, like those who show allegiance to King Alfred. It can't be easy for men who see weakness in their leader.

Abruptly, a terrible roar of rage reverberates from the south. It has me bringing Haden under control, slowing him with an uneven canter before he walks. I bounce in his saddle, hurting my leg more than galloping. Fucking thing. It frustrates me.

'Icel, Pybba,' I roar to my men. They look behind and eventually slow. The pair circle back to me. Icel has a gleam in his eye. Pybba's forehead is furrowed, but it's the woman who speaks first, breathing heavily.

'Why have we stopped? The enemy are close.'

'They are, my lady, but you and your sons are safe.' I sweep a quick look at their young white faces, relieved to see no tears on them. They might be terrified, but they're also brave. All the same, it's what's happening behind that absorbs my attention.

If King Alfred is within Old Sarum, and I see no reason why he'd have left, then he's entirely trapped, but also, holds somewhat of a position of strength. The enemy won't be able to get within quickly, unless the single entrance is compromised.

'I need ten warriors to escort the lady and her son north, towards Mercia.' I don't want to order anyone to this task. I'll see if someone steps forward first. Ealdorman Ælhun and Kyred have also joined me, as have the rest of my men. I hope they know I don't want them to accept the task, although, if they do, I won't deny them. This is going to be fucking difficult.

'Why?' the woman cries. I wish I knew her name. 'What are you going to be doing?'

'My lady?' I question.

She glowers at me. 'Wulfthryth, although now isn't the time for introductions.'

She's really quite beautiful when furious, I appreciate and quickly dismiss the thought. Now isn't the time for admiring a fine woman.

'Lady Wulfthryth,' I incline my head towards her feeling Haden's chest rising and falling beneath me. He's almost recovered his breath. 'I can't leave your brother by marriage to fall before the Viking raiders.'

'Why, I have two sons, they can rule in his place?' I grin at her fierce resolve. I like the way she thinks.

'They are but boys. A time will need to come when they can rule in place of their uncle. It's not now. So, why the Viking raiders are out in the open, and sense an easy victory, my warriors and I will do all we can to kill as many of the bastards as possible.' I catch a glimpse on the face of one of her sons, the older one. No doubt he finds it funny that I name them as bastards. Lady Wulfthryth makes no indication she's even concerned by such a term.

'Then what of us?'

'Ten of my men will escort you northwards. You'll either make it to Mercia, where my aunt will welcome you, and you'll be reunited with Lady Ealhswith.' A downturned cast of her lips assures me of what she thinks about that. 'Or, Wessex will be freed from the enemy, and you'll be summoned back.'

'My lord king,' Ealdorman Ælhun eyes me with concern at my suggestion, but Icel's nodding, I hope with approval.

'It's the only way, Ealdorman Ælhun. We know how powerful Northampton can be when holding against the Viking raiders. Perhaps we've grown too used to having such protection. We need to counter them, now, while they scent victory. It won't be easy, but we can't not try.'

He grunts, but offers nothing further. I look to Kyred. He swallows heavily but nods once, decisively.

'I'll have ten of my older warriors escort you to Mercia, Lady Wulfthryth. They're good men, but are perhaps, a little slow these days.'

I can tell she's unhappy about my change of plans. Not that it is a change. It was my intention all along. If anything, she's complicated it by running from Old Sarum. I think her choice was a good one, all the same.

Like Mercia, the future of the West Saxon ruling family must be ensured by separating them from King Alfred. He means to kill himself.

'My thanks,' she grudgingly admits. Kyred turns his horse and summons ten warriors to his side, quickly directing them. If they're surprised, they mask it well. Lady Wulfthryth appraises me for a little longer. 'You know Alfred isn't worth it, don't you. He's an arse who can't fight to save his own life, let alone his kingdom. My husband, and his older brothers were the warriors. Alfred has been coddled since he was a child. While his brothers practised their shield and sword work, Alfred was within, studying the holy texts and doing anything but learn how to fight. He's a bloody liability. The sooner he's dead, the better for everyone. He says he rules for the day when my sons can claim the kingship, and yet, he manoeuvres so his young son can take their place. If you save him, you'll rue the day.' I hold her gaze, seeing much truth in what she says.

I bring Haden closer to her mount. The animal she rides is tall and handsome, and has the measure of Haden, which brings a smirk to my lips.

'I don't do this for your useless brother by marriage, I assure you. He is, and I know it only too well, as much use as a shit in a bucket. I do this for Mercia, and for the future of the other Saxon kingdoms on this island. The Viking raiders are everyone's enemy. If we can kill them here, or at least decimate their numbers, then perhaps our kingdoms will survive. If I allow him to be overwhelmed, and for the Viking raiders to hold Old Sarum, they'll never leave, and your sons will have fuck all to be king over, when they're older.'

She doesn't flinch at my words. She doesn't even look disgusted at my self-interested approach.

'Then, I wish you well, King Coelwulf, the second of his name. But mark my words. You'll get fuck all thanks from King Alfred for this.'

'And from you?' I arch an eyebrow.

'Perhaps even less,' and with that, she turns and encourages her horse onwards, quickly being absorbed into the group of Kyred's warriors, alongside her two sons.

I watch her go until Pybba coughs.

I twist and meet his gaze. He offers me a smirk.

'A fine mare,' he suggests. I really don't think he's talking about the horse.

A chuckle breaks out amongst my warriors who watched my war of words with Lady Wulfthryth. It's a reminder of why we do what we do. After all, King Alfred isn't Wessex, even if he occasionally forgets that himself.

'How are we going to do this?' Icel recalls us to the matter at hand. The roar of the nearby battle's growing in intensity. We probably need to hurry and help, or Alfred will have lost Old Sarum before we can do anything to assist him.

'I suspect the Viking raiders will throw all they have at the defences Old Sarum boasts. As they do so, we attack them from behind.' I look to Icel, Pybba, Ealdorman Ælhun and Kyred but it's Hereman who speaks.

'Is that fucking it?' he mutters unhappily.

'What did you expect me to say?'

'Not that.'

'We can't crest the mound surrounding Old Sarum.'

'Not easily, no. By the time we got up there, we'd be worrying about how we got down.' Icel confirms.

'Then what would you have me do?'

For a moment, Hereman narrows his eyes.

'Shouldn't we aim for Winchester, while the fuckers aren't within.'

I had considered this.

'It seems the greater risk. It's over a day's ride from here, and Wareham's close. If Jarl Guthrum has Wareham, then he'll be able to send his men to Winchester. He might already have done so.'

'So, Old Sarum then?' Icel breaks the sudden tension.

'Yes, Old Sarum. We'll split the force. Half coming from the east and half from the west. I fear those from the east will have the harder time of it. There's no certainty that the enemy will throw all they have at Old Sarum. If they've got any sense, they won't.'

'Which they don't,' Hereman interjects, warming to the idea.

'They won't send every able-bodied warrior at the same time.'

'Which they will,' Hereman announces with certainty.

'Who'll lead which force?' Kyred questions. A gleam in my eye, and he's already shaking his head.

'My warriors and I, alongside Kyred and his remaining men will take the east.'

'No, my lord king,' both Kyred and Ealdorman Ælhun complain, while Hereman nods in fierce agreement.

'And Ealdorman Ælhun and his men will come from the west. We'll deploy against them but with the intention of stopping them from retreating and taking Old Sarum for themselves.'

I sense Rudolf working out the strength of our force in his head. I know I'm not going to want to hear what he has to say.

'So, no more than four hundred against the might of the Viking raiders?' he queries. There's no fear in his voice. There's not even surprise. Perhaps he's merely highlighting the point that we know the enemy have many ships, and no doubt, many more warriors if the archbishop's intelligence is to be believed.

We either have similar numbers, or much less.

'That's it,' I agree. 'I've always told you that one Mercian warriors is worth at least five of the bastard Viking raiders. Today, you'll see that for yourselves. Now, let's get to it, and remember all of you, stay the fuck alive, or I'll have to kill you myself.'

Laughter greets my words, and we ignore the underlying thread of fear that makes the sounds too sharp and harsh.

'We will prevail. We're the bloody Mercians, and we'll overwhelm every single bastard Viking raider. I promise you.'

With no further words, I bend to ensure Haden's saddle is firm, and that he's recovered from our initial gallop from Old Sarum.

Now we need to go back. We must overwhelm the bastard Viking raiders. And, I confess, if King Alfred meets his death in the coming fight, I sure as fuck won't mourn the bloody weasel.

Chapter Thirty-Four

In the near distance, I watch Ealdorman Ælhun take command of his warriors. His men have fought for Mercia before; they're used to my orders and expectations. While they look back towards Old Sarum with an appraising glance, they don't deny what Ealdorman Ælhun's instructing them to do. I admire their resolve.

I turn to my warriors. Icel's staring at Old Sarum, almost as though if he looks hard enough, he'll be able to see through the huge mound walls and determine what King Alfred's doing and how his warriors are faring against the might of the Viking raiders.

'We take the horses to the east. Then we leave them and move on foot. The enemy will realise we're not Viking raiders if we all have horses.' This occasions some nervous looks from those who are a little slow, Osmod amongst them. 'We don't need the horses to break through a barricade. We need horses to escape, and we're not going to do that,' I advise them.

'We split the force, half come from along the road, scything their way through any enemy who might think to try their luck, facing towards Winchester. Kyred, will you and half your men do that.'

'Aye, my lord king,' he reassures.

'The rest of us will advance from that point towards Old Sarum and prevent the bastards from retreating. We'll press into their backs and kill them when they think we're bloody allies.'

Mutters and nods greet my words.

'If it goes wrong, we'll go back for the horses and retreat towards Mercia, ensuring the enemy doesn't get any closer to our kingdom. We'll also have half an eye on Ealdorman Ælhun and his warriors. If this works, we'll join together and leave a swathe of destruction. They'll have to be fucking content with Wessex because I'm not giving them Mercia. We've fought too bloody hard and lost too many men.'

'Aye, my lord,' my warriors mutter, Kyred echoing the sentiment. I raise my voice then, for Ealdorman Ælhun has yet to move off with his force, and it's important they hear what I have to say.

'Brave men of Mercia,' I shout. 'Let's kill us some bastard Viking raiders.' They're not my finest words. I detect a smirk on Pybba's face, but I'm already urging my horse onwards, Haden eager to be moving once more.

Now, I have to hope we have the ability to overwhelm the enemy.

Who am I fucking kidding? I know we do.

We'll kill the enemy. We might even enjoy doing so.

With no further conversation, I turn Haden and lead him around the side of Old Sarum we've yet to explore. I keep us close to its encircling defences, mindful of a handy collection of trees, no doubt specifically tended to ensure the local inhabitants have a ready source of wood and forage for their animals. It's within those trees we'll leave the horses. The entrance is tilted to the east. We'll encounter the enemy before Ealdorman Ælhun. We must be wary of not being seen.

Eyes ahead, I focus on where we need to go, ensuring I can't see the enemy. Quickly, we reach the trees. I dismount, tying Haden's reins high so he won't tangle his feet. I don't tie him to a branch. He'll either stay or leave. The horses are used to this. Fuck it. On occasion, they've realised our need even before we did.

'Come on,' I urge my men, suddenly desperate to face the enemy. I step fully on my right leg, and it hurts, but not as much as earlier. The honey Rudolf bartered for has done the work of keeping it free from the wound rot. It's done nothing to restore my strength there, but I have my seax, shield and sword. I'll fucking kill the enemy with them.

As we get closer, the sound of the fight taking place gets louder. So noisy is it that I don't need to step carefully. They're never going to hear me over the roar of voices and the shrieks of those doing all they can to overwhelm the king of Wessex. The distinctive Wessex-tilt of our language spoken here in the south is distinctly lacking. The enemy either so outnumber them that they won't be heard, or, and I suspect this, King Alfred is holding his men in reserve. He knows his strength is in retaining possession of Old Sarum. Perhaps he's finally made a good strategic decision. Either that, or he's a fucking coward, and he's on his knees, praying within the small wooden church I saw to the north of the hall.

When the dense foliage starts to thin, I pause, holding my warriors back. Kyred's close to me, ready to veer towards the east. Icel and Hereman are almost stuck to me they're so damn near. I twist and offer a complaint, but before I can do anything about it, I really notice what's taken place.

There's a small settlement outside Old Sarum's walls. The Viking raiders have moved through it, setting ablaze to anything that can burn, and slaughtering anyone who's not retreated inside the defences of Old Sarum. The smell of blood and smoke is sharp in the air. I feel my fury beginning to build once more, and bank it.

The smoke blocks my view, as it buffets in the wind, sometimes coming close to our hiding place, and sometimes not. What I notice is the small collection of horses, and the large quantity of Viking raiders. I can't see around the corner of Old Sarum's walls from where I stand, the angle too sharp, but almost all of the enemy look that way.

'Rudolf says he can count at least a hundred of them,' Pybba informs me. I nod. I've made the same deduction. If there are that many of them here, then their numbers are much larger than I thought they would be. But, again my eyes look to the horses, these men have mostly walked here. They'll be tired and grumpy, and desperate to win because they won't want to run all that distance back to Winchester.

'Go, lead your men through the woods before you take the road.' Kyred nods, but pauses, his expression unreadable.

'Are you sure about this, my lord king?' I offer him a grim smirk and nod.

'I am, Kyred. We will prevail. It might not feel like it, but we have the skills if not the numbers.'

He grunts and turns aside. 'Stay the fuck alive,' I caution him and his men. I allow them to leave before I do anything else.

The fifty men who owe allegiance to the bishop and Kyred eye me a little sullenly. Perhaps they don't like being separated from Kyred. Maybe they don't want to fight for Wessex.

'Remember, for every one of the bastards we kill here, they can do no harm to Mercia.'

I hope to inspire them, but morose faces still look my way. I turn to Rudolf, and grin at him.

'Cheer the miserable bastards up,' I ask him. He smirks, and spins to those who wait to advance on the enemy.

'He's a right fucking bastard, but he's usually right,' Rudolf offers, and now more and more of my proud Mercians grin, while my usual warriors chuckle darkly. This is more like it.

'We wait a few moments longer, and then we go. Every man here should have a partner. Fight together. Protect one another's backs. Shout for help if you become overwhelmed. We'll slip through the trees and emerge behind that burning building. And then we'll work through them. I don't like to stab men through the back, but when there are so many of them, it's good to cull the numbers before the really dirty work starts.' My words thrum with conviction. 'As soon as you can, take a shield from one of the enemy. That way, we'll blend in better and the fuckers won't realise what's happening until it's too late. And, make sure you don't stab one of your bloody allies,' I add as a final caution.

Another swirl of smoke as the familiar crash of a roof giving way is heard, and I know the time has come. The smoke blinds us, but it'll also mask our approach.

'Come on then,' I urge my men, and with Icel and Hereman, I slip through the trees, hand over my mouth to stop me from coughing on the smoke.

Icel strides ahead. He's seen what I've seen, and now moves us into position.

The enemy horses are uneasy. They've been picketed too close to the burning building, and none of the stupid bastards has thought to release them. While their whinnies are shrill, we slip amongst them. I cut their tethering ropes free. There are no more than twenty or so animals. It takes no time. The animals slip away, some running for the trees. I imagine we might find them, and our horses, enjoying themselves when the fight's over.

The few houses are little more than burning ruins, the smoke occasionally cloying when the wind drives it towards us. Icel furiously beckons me f, his eyes keen. I hasten to join him, as do the rest of my warriors. Almost as one, with a look over our shoulders to ensure Kyred and his men have performed their task and prevented more from coming this way, we emerge from behind the smoking ruins and immediately stand tall as though we belong there.

My eyes sting from the smoke. When I can see again, having blinked fiercely, we're almost on the enemy. For some reason, they're staying true to the track, or road, that runs through the small settlement. Ahead, I can't see the fight, but I can hear the shouted order of my enemy, and the men at the rear hurry to get involved in the altercation, not wanting to miss out on winning battle glory.

'Keen to die, as fucking usual,' I mutter.

Icel, Hereman, Wærwulf, Rudolf, Pybba, and I are the first to encounter the back of the enemy. The roadway's tight, only six or seven men can fill it. Those at the rear die with barely a whimper. Not one of them having the time to yell in fear and alert their enemy.

I lower the man carefully to the ground as he stills in death, taking his shield from his hand, and immediately blend into the crowd ahead. Goda bends and drags the body out of the way. Others do the same for the enemy Icel, Hereman, Wærwulf, Rudolf and Pybba kill. We won't do that for every dead man, but for now, we need to practise stealth.

With the shield, a horrible heavy thing that's too large and unevenly balanced, we merge easily with the Viking raiders. Sæbald worms his way between my shield and Wærwulf's. Cuthwalh, Eahric, Ingwald and Cealwin do the same. They stoop to retrieve enemy shields. Now we're really starting to get somewhere.

Those ahead are so focused on what they mean to do that they've no idea of how exposed they are to the rear. They must be expecting more of their allies to join them. They're certainly not surprised others are behind them. They'll be alarmed when someone realises we're the enemy.

It seems too easy. In no time, we all have an enemy shield to hand, and the number of dead behind us has severely depleted those ahead, although we're still far from the entrance to Old Sarum. Not that it's been entirely peacefully achieved, but the cries of those who've realised they're being attacked from the rear have been subsumed into the noise and shouts of those ahead.

I lick my lips, taste the salt of my exertions and hope Kyred and the rest of his men continue to hold the enemy. I don't want to be caught between two enemy forces. I intend to trap them between the few warriors King Alfred has, and my warriors.

We emerge from the smoking ruins of the settlement. I note the slashes of blood on staring eyes and curse the bastard enemy and bloody King Alfred. He should have protected these people much better than he has.

Icel comes close.

'I can see Ealdorman Ælhun's men. They're pressing in behind as well.' I step away from the advance, and peer towards the west. I appraise Ealdorman Ælhun's men. They've also adopted the enemy shields, but I recognise them all the same. How the enemy don't realise we're there, I've no idea. I hope I'm never so focused on accomplishing one task that I don't realise what's happening before my eyes.

I feel some unease that this is occurring too quickly. Someone must have overall command. If the Grantabridge jarls are ordering the fighting, then they know to expect more from the Mercians. Are the West Saxon warriors truly so shit that the enemy believes themselves invincible? Admittedly, Kyred and his warriors must be in position by now. They'll be endeavouring to ensure no more of our foemen can get close.

Soon, all of my warriors and Kyred's men, who are with me, have taken an enemy shield. We blend in with the bastards, even though it pains me to realise how much we resemble one another.

The shouts from ahead assure me that the enemy is unaware of our presence and mean to continue their advance on Old Sarum. That suits me fine.

I turn to my warriors, a nod to those who'll weave a path through the jostling, stinking warriors. While our presence remains undetected, we'll kill with guile.

Icel and Hereman press close to me. I keep Pybba back as well. But the rest slink their way through the enemy line. I watch Rudolf stab into a man's back. He stumbles and falls, and no one else notices, not even when they trample on him. Goda walks up to another of the enemy and with a glance in my direction first, juts his helm into the back of his foeman's head. He judders and half turns, no doubt to complain, but Goda merely slices his blade across his belly. He could still talk, but Goda thinks of that and, just as quickly, jabs into his mouth. The enemy warrior dies, gargling on the blade. But both of those men are the final line of attack. Others of my warriors move forward and take greater risks.

Ingwald and Leonath work together, sliding to either side of one foeman, jabbing into his side simultaneously. The warrior crumbles.

The stink of blood and sweat is rank, mingling with the buffeting smoke from the almost destroyed settlement. I can't see exactly where the enemy aims their attack, but the imposing sides of Old Sarum are visible. I can't determine how many men there are ahead of us. Enough. Too many. Who the fuck knows.

I want to follow my men, but Icel and Hereman ensure I don't. They're no doubt correct to keep me at the back. When we're discovered, and we will be discovered at some point, I can't be lost amongst the swell of heaving men. And I'm hardly doing nothing. The four of us are busy working our way through the back markers. Some of these men jeer and holler, but drag their steps. They want the rewards without the terrible risks—such brave men.

They die like the craven bastards they are.

From ahead, I hear West Saxon voices directing the defence. One voice I don't hear, is fucking King Alfred's. Again, I consider what he's doing. He might be fighting, but I think he's more likely trying to escape. How he'll do that, I don't know. I do wish Wessex had a better sort of king to protect her. I might have to question Lady Wulfthryth about her husband. Or my aunt.

Norse voices urge their warriors on. I'm astounded no one has realised we're quietly culling the back of their attack. How long will it take for someone to notice? How many of these useless bastards will die before they do? Hopefully, more than I anticipated. I'd like the odds to be more even than they were initially.

'My lord,' Icel mutters, his head twisted to where Ealdorman Ælhun and his men are fighting. I realise why he's worried. A few of our enemy to the rear are starting to look about them. We don't have much longer, and one of the stupid bastards will realise what's happening. Then, this will get nasty.

I grin at Icel. His eyes glitter with anticipation. I check on Pybba.

'Is your shield firmly tied on,' I question him.

'Aye, my lord. Rudolf helped me.' He lifts the heavy enemy shield to show that yes, he does have his protection in place.

'Not long now,' I mutter, pleased that neither of them has taken too great a risk. 'Any fucking moment now,' I repeat. I seek the Mercians through the throng of the enemy. Right now, I think they need to return to me, rather than be isolated amongst the jostling warriors.

'Now,' I urge Hereman.

'Aye, my lord,' Hereman offers with a grin. And with absolutely fuck all care for where the thing will land, Hereman rears back and flings his spear above the fighting. It's the signal for my men to retreat. It's not as though we can shout to them. And quickly, many of them start to slide their way back to us. The jostle of the enemy swells, and any moment now, I realise we'll be doing more than fighting the backs of our enemy.

I eye my warriors, noting those with bleeding cuts and bruises, and then lean back to look towards the west.

That's when the cry erupts amongst the enemy.

That's when they turn and face us.

And we're ready for the fucking bastards.

Chapter Thirty-Five

The fear on the faces of those who spin to see us brings a rictus grin to my lips. Those who yet stand have been lucky bastards. Their allies haven't been.

'Attack,' Hereman roars. I do as he says, blade busy, enemy shield before me. The bloody thing is heavy and huge. I don't appreciate the feeling of it on the end of my left arm, but I need it to defeat our adversaries.

They don't know if they fight the Mercians or the West Saxons. I don't think they fucking care.

A pounding thud on my shield has me holding it firmly before me. We've not formed a shield wall to defeat them. We'll fight them as individuals as part of a bigger, interconnected group. I lower my shield and swipe my seax across the enemy one. It does little but assure my enemy I'm not going down without a fight.

I press in closer. The foemen have so far been allowed the room they need to swarm forwards while also being able to retreat if needed. We're not going to allow that any more.

Ealdorman Ælhun and his men have made their way around the back of the Viking raider force so there's no means of our foemen escaping our advance unless they erupt from the sides of the attack. We must be wary of that happening. At least Kyred and his men have ensured there's no one behind us. We have more freedom.

The man I face drops his shield below his chin, fury on his twisted face. I knock into his nose with the hilt of my seax. His head jabs backwards with the blow. He hits the man behind him with his head, even as blood surges from his nose.

In retaliation, he jabs his shield at me. I lift my shield and duck behind it. He'll have to do more than that if he means to overwhelm me. I use my shield as a weapon, moving it forward and backwards until I meet his shield as well. I crash against it, arm straining with the weight of the bloody thing. I'd like my own shield in hand, but that would have given us away too soon. Now, I'll have to contend with the ungainly thing.

I see Pybba battling to the side of me, using his war axe to pull down the shield of the man he faces, while Rudolf stabs into the man's open mouth. I witness Hereman running at his foeman as though there are no shields between them, and the man loses his balance, pitching backwards, Hereman's seax in his throat.

I lower my shield and assess my foeman. He has his shield in front of his face now. I eye his boots, but my shield prevents me from bending low. I can see almost nothing of him, but I catch sight of the leering face of the man behind him. Wild-eyed and spittle-breathed, he snarls to be allowed close enough to attack. I step forward, hammering my shield against the warrior who faces me while the warrior behind him steps to meet the assault. A strangled cry erupts from my enemy's throat while frantically trying to find the air he needs to breathe and keep going. I grin at the man behind him, jabbing my blade between his teeth. The fucker snaps his teeth down on my blade. With a horrible shriek, I force my blade deeper and deeper. He could step back. I don't think he realises that.

My blade widens, cuts forming on the join of his lips. He lifts his hand to punch into my face. I duck beneath his extremely long arm and feel the man between us forcing all his weight behind his shield.

I step back, abruptly releasing the pressure that kept him upright. He clatters to the ground. I bend and stab into the back of his neck, shield before me to protect me from the daft bastard who ensured his ally died.

He grimaces, blood dripping from his cut lips into his blond beard. He has a war axe to hand and moves to swing it in my direction. I thrust my shield between us. The sharp bang reverberates along my arm. I sense movement below and realise the first man still lives. He reaches towards my feet. I stamp down on his hand, dropping my shield atop his hand with a crunch of broken bone.

'Die, you bastard,' I huff even as I slice my seax across the blond-bearded man's throat. He veers back to avoid the cut of my blade. I use his distraction to jab the heavy shield into his throat. He gargles, blood spurting from his mouth. This time, there's nothing he can do to stop me sliding my blade through his bleeding lips.

I think to take a moment to relish the victory, but our opponents are furious. Angry eyes glint my way as they decide to fight me and my warriors and not the West Saxons blocking the entrance into Old Sarum. I suddenly realise I may have made those at the front even more desperate to triumph, but there's fuck all I can do about that now.

The West Saxon warriors will have to fight all the harder if they mean to live through this.

I glance to the left and right, reassured that my men are fighting well. It's not easy to determine where everyone is. The huge enemy shields block the view, but I decide that those labouring against the back of the enemy force are my warriors. Those fighting them are the bloody enemy.

A crash on my extended arm holding the enemy shield, and I face the next bastard who thinks to kill me.

His face is narrow, his chin almost narrowing to a point, from which a long, straggling black beard droops. With eyes that glitter with menace, he snarls, and then surprises me by speaking my name.

'King Coelwulf of Mercia, what the fuck are you doing here?'

I don't recognise him, which shouldn't surprise me. All of these bastards look alike.

I snarl and step to ram my blade across his exposed throat, but he steps back. I know what his next intention is as his mouth opens wide. I rush him, dropping the shield in the process. It's more important to kill the fucker than defend against his war axe.

He must realise my aim. With hardly a flicker of his eyes, he rotates and crashes his way back through the heaving mass of the enemy.

'Bollocks,' I glower, following him, mindful that I probably shouldn't. At the last moment, I turn.

'Icel, with me,' I roar. I see him lower his shield and see me. He shakes his head, complaints on his lips, but I'm following the lank hair of the man who knows I'm here. It matters that the enemy doesn't realise my men fight them. I don't want them to think I'm here, helping King Alfred. They'll think me a weak bastard. They might even start to reconsider the events within Gloucester. Shit, shit, shit, I mutter beneath my breath, forcing my way through the rows and rows of fighting men. I'm jostled and punched, kicked and winded, but not one of them realises I'm not who I seem. Neither, it appears, do they understand I'm not one of their number.

I hear Icel following on behind. He makes no secret of his identity.

'Out of the fucking way, cocks,' he roars. His words elicit a swell of angry responses. I don't need Wærwulf to translate them for me. And behind Icel, I sense more and more of my men are following him, ploughing a path through the enemy.

I reach out and grab the shoulder of the man who knows who I am. I don't know where he's going, but his intention is to let whoever directs the battle know of my presence. I don't want that. The Viking raiders need to think King Alfred and his West Saxon warriors won this fight, when we prevail. I don't want my part in it to become widely known. That would undo the aim behind my involvement. Just like at Gloucester, my enemy can't know I'm here.

The man twists, and a seax is in his hand, which he jabs towards my hand. I snatch it aside at the last moment, hoping he'll skewer himself, but there's no such luck.

Another enemy warrior knocks into me, his stink making me gag. Momentarily, I lose sight of the man ahead. I shove into the enemy who knocked me, a glancing slice with my seax running around his belly, forcing a roar of anger from his throat. The words are gabbled, no doubt calling me all the names he can think of to explain why one of his own has stabbed him. But, of course, I'm not one of his own.

I escape from him, and catch sight of the black-haired man once more. He's only managed to make a little more progress. I can still get to him, but the press of bodies here makes moving anywhere all but impossible. I need to make more headway.

With my seax in my right hand, I stab into those around me, and they move aside, keen to be away from my wild strikes. Angry shouts greet my actions, but with Icel rampaging like a bull behind me, it doesn't really matter. None of the bastards are intelligent enough to determine what's happening. No doubt, they think one of their numbers is desperate to smash their way through the West Saxon defence.

I reach out and grip the arsehole trying to evade me. This time, my grip's firmer. Again, he tries to jab his seax at me, but I punch with my left hand, knocking into his shoulder, and just managing to keep him upright with my seax hand and the support of those around him.

He swings wildly, eyes glazed with pain. I offer him a crooked smile.

'Going somewhere?' Again, he opens his mouth to shout, his seax held before him, but I've had enough of this, and launch myself at him. Or rather, I would, but at the last moment, something knocks me, sending me, my arms spiralling into the press of bodies. Men shout and shove me so that I regain my feet. I spin. Icel has the black-haired man. Or he did. The man's limp and falling to the ground, his eyes flecked with rage momentarily, until they blank and he sees no more.

'Get away with you,' now Icel's meaty hands are on me. He uses his huge fists to forge a path back through the enemy. Shrieks of rage greet his action. I feel like a small child being propelled onwards.

'What the fuck was that?' he roars as we finally win free. My warriors continue to fight their way through the enemy. The trail of dead and dying is remarkably long. I see where we started and where we are now. There are more dead than there are Mercians, which pleases me.

'He recognised me,' I rotate and huff, shrugging Icel's hands from my shoulders.

For a moment, I think he'll argue with me, but then the held air expels from him, and he nods.

'Well, that was well done then.' With no further words, he turns and launches himself at the enemy again. I shake my head.

'He really is a fucking cock,' I mutter, pleased all the same to be free from the tight press of the enemy. Men will die in there, and not thanks to blades but because there's no order, and every man is either desperate to kill or desperate to live. Those desires aren't necessarily compatible.

'Coelwulf,' I twist as Rudolf shouts for me. I see that he and Pybba fight well, but it's not that which Rudolf wishes me to see. No, he's pointing over his shoulder.

Chapter Thirty-Six

'Bollocks,' I exclaim. Through the smoky haze, enemy warriors are once more flooding in from behind. I fear for Kyred and his men. I hope they're not fucking dead. They better bloody not be. I look for a moment longer, trying to decide who these warriors are. Are they the enemy or our allies? I narrow my eyes, still unsure. This could be about to get fucking nasty.

And it is. It's the flicker of light over one of their emblems worn around the neck that tells me what I need to know.

'Bollocks,' I exclaim. We have the chance to move aside. But we need to do it quickly.

'Icel, Hereman, to me,' I shout. They revolve and quickly realise what's happening.

'Get everyone, and move to the west,' I order them. I'm already running to knock on my men's shoulders and alert them to the danger. To the far east, Sæbald and Goda battle their enemy, but the new influx of warriors will reach them first.

'Sæbald,' I roar, 'To me.' He turns, confused, before noticing the danger, but as he does, his foeman lands a huge blow against his chest, and he drops his shield. Sæbald goes down in a clatter of iron and wood.

'Shit,' I explode, already running to help him. Goda's also fighting an enemy and he can't aid Sæbald. This is my fault. I must reach my downed warrior before the enemy gets him.

'Get out of here,' I shout to those I encounter. They aim shocked eyes at me. This wasn't part of the plan. Kyred's men are confused by this sudden change. My warriors are quicker to obey me, running where I point even though I'm going the other way, hobbling but with a reasonable amount of speed.

I see Sæbald tussling with the man who menaces him from above. He twists and spins, stabbing up with his seax, while the enemy warrior bends over him, jabbing with his blade. I don't see him land a blow, but I imagine he'll eventually succeed. Sæbald doesn't have his shield, and his foeman has cast his aside. Sæbald kicks and bucks, and then I'm there. I crash into the man trying to kill my friend and ally. We go down in a cacophony of legs and iron, the air knocked from me as we plough into the legs of more Viking raiders, pain exploding from my wounded leg. Somehow, we avoid Goda.

I come up stabbing and punching, mindful that my leg's hurting, but this is no time for weakness. Behind us, the rumble of running feet can be heard. Our time's limited, and we need to get away from here. A lucky blow, and my blade impales the man through his eye, his helm knocked askew by my running tackle. I hurry back on my hands and knees, desperate to be free. A hand on my shoulder. I surge up with my seax, but it's Goda, his face white, breathing deeply.

'Come on,' he exclaims. I grip his hand, grateful not to be alone. Sæbald's also scampered to his feet, but those coming from behind have formed up between me and the rest of my warriors, who rush to reach Ealdorman Ælhun and his men.

'Quickly, back through the smoke,' I urge both. Goda's limping. Sæbald has blood on his left arm, and he holds it with his other hand.

'Bollocks, we've become separated,' I exclaim, stating the obvious.

I can hear Icel's roar of fury, but I keep my view on trying to evade capture.

The smoke helps us, but makes me cough, as I support Goda under his shoulder. Sæbald helps on the other side. We're breathing deeply, and coughing. We need the smoke, but we also must get away from it.

'This way,' I urge, mindful that Goda's a heavy weight. My running and fighting has jarred my thigh. I'm also limping, although not as badly as Goda.

'What will we do?' Sæbald huffs through tight lips.

'Get to the horses,' I decide. It's the only solution. If we knew where Kyred was, we could go to him, but we don't. I'm fearful for my warriors. There was a huge force of enemy, almost enough, I think to replace those we've just laboured to kill by attacking their rear. Where are Kyred and his men? I hope my warriors continue to fight the enemy. All is not lost. We live, but now we need to reach them.

The fury of the fight behind us seems to rumble to a raging torrent once more, but we're free from the smoke, almost at the trees.

My eyes sting from sweat and smoke, but I stay focused. It might take us a while, but we can reach the horses. Only then Goda stumbles and I can't stop him falling forward.

'Arse,' I huff, already bending to get him upright once more.

Sæbald's swaying on his feet, and for a moment, I fear that of us three, only I can defend us if we're seen. I don't look behind. The odds of being discovered are overwhelming. I can't allow that to happen.

'Get up,' I huff at Goda. 'Sæbald, walk on, beneath the trees. Get deeper under them.' My words resonate with conviction. Sæbald staggers onwards, swaying alarmingly. Goda looks up and meets my eyes.

'Help me,' he demands. It takes all my strength to get him upright once more, but we manage it.

'Come the fuck on,' I mutter. We must make it under the trees. They'll protect us as we find the horses. Goda tries to keep upright. Sweat beads on his face. I can tell how much this is hurting him. He bites his lip, keeps his focus ahead, and does what needs to be done.

'Come the fuck on,' I urge, as much to him as me. Finally, we disappear beneath the trees, and I sense we won't be seen by the enemy.

'Now, to the horses.' I can't hear the animals but know they'll be there. They wouldn't leave us. Haden's too damn stubborn.

'Nice and quiet,' Goda manages to complain. I'd smile at the bastard, but he's right. I need to be quieter. It doesn't help that Sæbald seems to bounce from tree trunk to tree trunk, and Goda and I, held tightly together by our grip on one another's shoulders, are hardly better.

'It can't be much further,' I announce as the sound of the fight diminishes behind us. Here, I can't see Old Sarum or the roadway running to the east of it. Eventually, I hear the whinny of one of the horses. I almost sag with relief. Goda and I are more damp with sweat than if we'd gone for a bloody swim. Ahead, there's a small break in the low-hanging boughs, and that's when I see Haden. He's looking this way as though he can recognise my heavy tread. Perhaps he can.

Sæbald's already seeking out his horse while Haden walks towards me, bumping me with his inquisitive nose so I almost fall over. Somehow, Goda and I remain upright. Magic must also recognise his rider because he nudges his way through the rest of the horses.

'Can you mount?' I question. I'm unsure how bad his wounds are.

'Aye, my lord. Can you?' the taunt is what I need to hear. With a low growl, I force myself into Haden's saddle, unwrapping the high reins to direct him where I want to go. But, of course, the other horses are also looking for their riders, which leaves me with a problem. There are a lot of horses, not just those belonging to my warriors.

There are Kyred's warriors as well. All of them look to me and then away, no doubt wondering where their riders are. I intended to ride around the rear of Old Sarum to join with Ealdorman Ælhun's men. If I do that, and the horses follow, I might deprive the Mercians of their mounts at a time they need them.

'Arse,' I exclaim. Goda winces and doesn't look at me. Sæbald has finally managed to mount, but it's been painful. Perhaps I should leave him here, with the horses? I don't think he'll be able to fight. He proves my point by bending over his horse's neck and vomiting loudly onto the ground. He looks white and green and every shade in between. Poor fucker. I know what it is to try and ride with that sort of head wound.

'Sæbald, stay here with the horses.' He looks at me, eyes running from voiding the contents of his belly onto the floor. But he nods rather than argue.

'What about you Goda?'

'I can fucking ride,' he asserts. His fury is clear to hear. He doesn't like being questioned. I waver. I don't know if I should take him with me.

'It's my choice, my lord. And I'm coming with you.'

'Fine, but if you get yourself killed, I'll fucking kill you,' I mutter. He surprises me by chuckling.

'You never spoke a finer threat. I don't want to be killed by you, my lord. It would be a poor death.' His eyes flash, and I find myself grinning.

'You're a fucking cock,' I inform him, turning Haden.

'Sæbald, remain here. Dismount if you need to, but keep the horses here for the others. I'll come for you.'

'Aye, my lord,' he slurs. I don't like to leave him but there's no alternative.

'Stay the fuck alive,' I instruct him. He doesn't even smile at my oft-repeated phrase. I think he's almost out of it, but as I encourage Haden to retrace our steps from earlier, he surprises me.

'You do the same, my lord. Or, mark my words, I'll haunt you every damn night.'

'Daft git,' I mutter, but then we're moving. Magic and Haden are fairly evenly matched. Even with Goda far from secure in his saddle, we're soon clear from the trees. I rotate towards Old Sarum. There's smoke rising in a thick grey patch into the sky, but where it's coming from, I'm not precisely sure.

'Come on.' I allow Haden to gallop as fast as he likes, even though it pains me, and a swift glance behind, assures me that Goda's holding on more by stubborn determination than anything else. Poor bastard.

From within Old Sarum, I can just detect terrified cries from those trapped. I consider if that includes King Alfred. Is he praying? I suspect the church is just to the far side of the mud bank wall. If only there were a tunnel through it, but there isn't, and that's probably for the best. The people within might be fearful, but they only need to defend the entrance until we can drive the bastard Viking raiders away. I hope it won't be much longer.

Haden gallops swiftly, the sweat on my face drying, although it makes me shiver beneath my byrnie. Quickly, we're around the rear of Old Sarum and making our way towards the entrance. Because it bulges outwards on this side, I can't see anything, only the walls above us.

I feel myself growing impatient. The smoke's billowing black now, and the sound of the ongoing fight grows in intensity. Suddenly, I fear that I'm arsing this up. I've been separated from my warriors. They might be panicking about where I am. They might be pressing towards the east. What if they're not even where I thought they were, and now all I have is Goda, Haden and Magic to aid me?

'Fuck,' I mutter to myself, wishing Haden could go even faster than he currently is. I need to know where my warriors are. I need to know they're well, despite fighting the enemy.

'My lord,' Goda calls, and I glance at him. He's struggling, Magic going so fast he can hardly stay mounted. I slow Haden. Neither of us like it. Level with Goda once more, I bite down on my impatience.

'Don't go alone,' he urges me, working to stay mounted, trying to find the rhythm of his horse because it's defeating him.

'Hurry the fuck up,' I growl. He snaps down his angry reply, which pleases me.

Finally, we round the bend of Old Sarum. The hum of the battle is all-encompassing. The curling black smoke, I discover, is from some sort of building, the thatch wet, if it's thatch at all. It could be straw or something else. It's choking. I consider what the building is used for. Could it be a blacksmith or some other sort of industrial use?

At last, I see my warriors and the Mercians. They're still fighting, but I also sight Icel to the east, his expression almost frantic. I hope he'll realise I'm here.

The enemy has been reinforced, but not by as many warriors as I feared. They do cover the road, and Icel can't get through them. I detect Mercian voices coming from the east. I hope Kyred and his men are there, fighting the enemy just as fiercely as we did before being overwhelmed by the reinforcements surging through our rear.

Ealdorman Ælhun sees me first. He's standing to the rear, sucking in deep breathes, and I sense his confusion, even though all I can see are his eyes and chin beneath his warrior helm.

Haden whinnies at the sudden stink of blood. The smoke concerns him less, which surprises me. I consider dismounting but realise Goda can't fight on his feet, and it might be better to take advantage of the elevated view to direct my men.

I sense Icel looking my way, his expression unreadable at such a distance.

I eye my warriors. They're doing well. I can see some of them are wounded, but as far as I can tell, everyone still fights, even Ealdorman Ælhun, who thrusts himself back into the thick of it, Icel doing the same. They'd realised I was missing.

'We need to conclude this quickly,' I inform Goda. He nods, Magic moving forward and backwards with agitation. How to accomplish that remains a problem. We're outnumbered, even if we do seem to be prevailing.

I urge Haden to the rear of the fighting, keeping to the roadway running southwest towards the river. The fighting's on the side closest to Old Sarum's entrance. For a moment, I consider if the enemy could use the river to cut us off from behind, but if that was going to happen, I think they'd have done so already. No, the enemy comes from the east from Winchester.

I see the entrance to Old Sarum. The defences are holding, but the press of the enemy is increasing. Angry shouts from those being crushed fill the air. I turn east and see my men there, led by Kyred, pressing into the enemy as well. From behind, there's little to see but smoke from the ruined buildings the Viking raiders set aflame when they started their attack.

'What to do? What to fucking do?' I muse. The more we assault the rear, the greater the enemy try to crash through King Alfred's defences. I even see some Viking raiders attempting to crawl up the steep sides of the mound, but that's never going to work. They can't make it with their heavy equipment. It's a stunning fortification. The only weakness is the entrance.

That doesn't help me determine what to do next.

A sudden commotion in front of me, and I realise Rudolf and Pybba are temporarily overwhelmed by the enemy. I pick out their familiar stances amongst the Viking raiders. I can't dive into the heaving mass to rescue them. I can't force Haden through the enemy either because he would be too vulnerable.

'Hereman,' I bellow, pointing where I mean. He's standing back, heaving air into his body. A murderous set of his jaw, and he rushes to aid Pybba and Rudolf.

I catch sight of Kyred eyeing me with relief from the east. I try to ignore Pybba and Rudolf now, focusing on what needs to be done. My eyes narrow. I don't know who leads these enemy warriors. The men and a few women, or so I think from the higher pitched grunts, who fight do so for someone, but who, I'm unsure. If I knew, it might help me decide how to proceed.

Hereman stamps from the fighting, dragging Pybba and Rudolf

with him. Rudolf hurries my way, while Pybba's slower, limping, and holding his good arm tight to his chest.

'My lord,' Rudolf shouts when he's close enough. 'We need to press them. In the middle, they're weakest. That's where the two forces meet, and the bastards don't like one another, I assure you.'

I survey the fighting and realise he's correct. Down the middle of the enemy attack, there's almost a visible line all the way to the West Saxon defences. We need to rush down it and drive the two forces apart.

'My thanks,' I shout to Rudolf. He bends over, hands on his knees, to suck in much-needed air.

'Goda,' he's not far from me. He nods anticipating what I'm going to say next.

'Order half of Kyred's men to infiltrate that area, down the middle. The other half will move to the east, down the line, and through the enemy.' He grunts and moves Magic aside. I beckon Ealdorman Ælhun to me and explain the same.

'We'll divide the bastards, and kill 'em that way,' I growl. He agrees and runs to order his men aside. Icel and my warriors will forge their path through to the West Saxon defences and then begin to scythe their way to meet Ealdorman Ælhun's warriors to the west. My problem now is, what to do with Haden. I can't risk him. I can't see Ealdorman Ælhun's horses. I don't know where he's left them.

I can't fight on horseback, not amongst these bastards.

Quickly, my warriors are preparing themselves. If I want to be involved in this, I must decide what to do with my horse. I twist left and right. The only trees nearby are those we've hidden the horses within, and to get there would involve going around the fighting once more. That's sure to reveal my presence.

'What do you think?' I question my horse. Haden's moving forward and backwards, but he's not uneasy. He doesn't even seem to notice he's alone, aside from me.

Maybe, for once, I should sit this one out and allow my warriors to fight on my behalf. But no, that's what bloody King Alfred's doing, tucked up nice and tight behind the impenetrable walls of Old Sarum. I can't do that.

To the east, Goda's reached the other Mercians. He speaks urgently to them. He won't be able to fight, I'm sure of it. I should have sent Haden with him. And then my eyes alight on something that might just aid me.

To the rear of the fighting, there's a shallow stream. I consider if it also runs through Old Sarum. Perhaps this is where they get their water from? But I can lead Haden down to it, and he'll drink. He might even walk along the shallow bed. It would take him away from the fighting. It's far from fucking ideal, but I need to do something to protect him until Goda can return and take command of him.

I redirect him quickly, and we disappear down a small ditch only visible to me when I'm mounted. Haden bends his head and drinks eagerly, while I cajole myself into dismounting. I should have done that first. It pains me, but not as much as when I was first wounded. I hurry to tie his reins high, tying it and then tying it again to ensure the leather doesn't slip. I slap him on the arse, reaching for my shield from his saddle.

'Haden, stay here,' I urge him. 'Or go that way,' I point. He watches me with his wise eyes. I think he understands as I revolve to move back up the slope, only for him to follow.

'No,' I caution, aware that the sound of the fighting has suddenly grown in intensity. My warriors are already pushing through the enemy. I need to join them.

I take Haden back to the water. He looks at me again. I turn his head towards the stream's source, or so I assume. He pauses, perplexed. I am, as well. I could tie him to a stone, but I don't want to risk him becoming trapped. Then he'd be easy prey for any of the enemy. He dunks his long nose and starts to drink once more. I move away from him, and he doesn't raise his head.

I surge up the slope, spinning to make sure he won't follow.

'Stay fucking there,' I huff, forced to misstep to keep my balance. With a parting shot, which sees him dipping his hooves into the slow-flowing water, I race to join my friends and allies.

We will overwhelm the bastard enemy. We will save King Alfred. And my fucking horse better behave himself until we've accomplished that.

Chapter Thirty-Seven

I notice quickly that the fighting's well underway. I can't watch from ground level as well, but I can see my warriors surging through the enemy's lines.

Someone amongst them has realised the difficulty, and a harsh voice barks orders. I can't tell if anyone heeds those words from here. I scout for Goda, but he's out of sight. I don't imagine he'll have abandoned Magic. He'll be directing from the rear. He's a sensible man, but sense has never beaten the bastard enemy.

Rudolf and Pybba fight at the end of the line of men to the west, splitting the enemy force, as I ordered. I hurry to join them, gripping my shield tightly. But, some of the foemen are alert to what we're doing. While Ealdorman Ælhun and his men press in from the west, Rudolf, Pybba and the rest of my warriors are deep in the heart of the bloody business, splitting the force more effectively than a blade through hard cheese. Those who can, run free from the fighting, fear on their faces, although they're hardly bloodied.

'Fucking cowards,' I curse, stopping my advance to counter them. I don't want the bastards running from here. This is their last fight, and they'll die here.

There's a howl of fear from the first man, old and long in the tooth, as I drive my seax before me, holding the shield to protect from any attack he might attempt. He wears a byrnie and helm, but his weapon flashes with the sunlight, no blood marring its edges.

I rush into him, seax striking his neck. Only seeing me at the last possible moment, he's dead before he can defend himself. The enemy warrior next to him is shorter and much faster, but my shield knocks into his chest while his eyes are on what's happening behind him. As he drops to the ground, I stab into his back. He bucks like a fish out of water.

Another tries to evade me by running far to the back of the fighting before rushing eastwards. I think he'd do better to go west, but I run after him, well, I hobble after him and push him forward with the weight of my shield. His legs fail him. He goes down with a crash and whimper of pain, which quickly fades. I bend, seax to hand, but the bastard's already dead, his forehead oozing blood where his helm came askew, and a handy rock smacked into his forehead. I wince at that. Standing, I see another one of the bastards coming for me. His teeth are rimmed with blood as he grimaces. I see he's wounded, his byrnie dark with blood. He dies like the others, with a seax wound to his neck. But while I kill him, one of them makes it past my guard, running onwards towards the east.

'Bastard,' I mutter, hoping one of my warriors over there will see him and finish him. I don't want a single one of them to survive.

More and more of the enemy are becoming trapped, and the two sides of my warriors are meeting in the middle. Rudolf moves towards one of Ealdorman Ælhun's men, and unless the enemy thrust their way through the shield wall, they'll die in there. Hurrying, I rush to complete the circle, my shield held before me. I skip over those already dead, noting the wealth of their byrnies and arm rings. These men already had so much. Why fight to the death for more?

My lips curl with displeasure as I merge into the line of Mercians beating the enemy. My shield protects me, and soon, men are dying beneath my blade while the shields Rudolf and I carry merge together, and then Ealdorman Ælhun's joins mine as well.

Sweat beads my face. My arms and feet are busy, although I'm wary of using my right leg with its healing wound. It's not as strong as it should be. Rudolf roars and bellows as he fights with neat, concise movements. I could weep at his beautiful skill with a blade. I taught him that, I remind myself, allowing a slither of pride. Ealdorman Ælhun's less vocal, but his cuts and strikes are just as lethal. He fights with more flare.

A frantic enemy pushes against my shield, his chin bleeding heavily, half of his reddish beard sheered away from someone's blade, his eyes pain-hazed and crazed.

'*Skiderick*,' he mutters, time and time again, as I hold him in place. He's trapped between me, Rudolf and Ealdorman Ælhun. His swings with a war axe are frantic and lack the force to haul one of the shields down. He dies with a soft sigh as Rudolf drops his shield and stabs into his underarm.

I'm breathing heavily, wincing every so often as I put too much weight on my right leg, but we're fucking winning, which makes me joyful. The enemy no longer fights against the West Saxons and their defences protecting the entrance into Old Sarum. They've realised the fight is behind them, not in front. As the circle of Viking raider warriors grows ever smaller, and the Mercians vie to hold our shields without bashing one another, I consider if King Alfred will finally send his men to join the fight.

'We surrender,' a rough voice calls, tripping over the unfamiliar words. I lower my shield to see there are no more than fifteen enemy warriors before us, standing amongst a carpet of their bleeding and lifeless allies. The man who talks isn't familiar to me. He speaks our tongue with a harsh bite, as though he doesn't wish to sully himself with our words.

'There is no surrender,' Ealdorman Ælhun growls. But the man hasn't finished yet.

I can see all of my warriors, where they hold their shields lower.

Not one of the foemen attacks us. Some are evidently wounded, and bloody noses and missing beards are perhaps the least of their problems. They all stand firm, taking the chance to recover their breath. Hemming and Wærwulf are closest to the West Saxons. I imagine, if they weren't there, I'd be able to see King Alfred's warriors watching on from behind, perhaps fearful, perhaps triumphant. Not that this success is down to them. Well, some of it is. They've held the bastards. I'm impressed by that.

'Surrender, we surrender.' The man calls again, fumbling at his neck. I sense what he's about to do, and I'm not surprised, although I'm bloody disappointed.

'I surrender. As a brother in your faith,' he burbles too quickly. The words run together but I understand them well enough. I consider what I should do. I'd like to know more about how this attack came about. Equally, I vowed to kill all of the fuckers.

Ealdorman Ælhun eyes me. Hereman and Wærwulf both wear murderous expressions on their faces. Wærwulf speaks to the man asking for surrender in their language, while his fellow foemen eye us uneasily, also revealing they wear crosses around their necks.

'Bollocks,' I mutter, but determine to wait for Wærwulf to tell me more before I decide. I turn, and realise the same's happening to the other side. Well, the circle of shields is small, and only a few still stand. I don't know if they also seek to call on our shared faith in the act of surrender. I think the Mercians might take their go to finish off the stragglers.

'He says they're the men of Jarl Guthrum. He says they worship our Lord God and don't wish to die like this. They'll repent their crimes and willingly serve the West Saxon kingship.'

I crack a smile at that. It's not as though the West Saxon kingship are responsible for this defeat. As I'm considering how best to respond, I see movement behind Wærwulf and Hereman. I'm immediately on my guard, but I relax as I recognise the Wessex wyvern on the shields held before the men streaming from within Old Sarum

Perhaps they've come to kill some of the enemy, after all. Maybe they need to be out in the open to take pride in their accomplishments.

But no. I lower my shield, eyes narrowed, as a familiar figure appears. Fucking King Alfred. He's dressed for war, and he's mounted on his fine horse. But no man with a byrnie that shiny has ever actually killed anyone. The fucking arsehole. I glower at him, aware I'm covered in the filth of the enemy, sweat beading my face, my right leg trembling from all it's endured. I look like a warrior who's fought for his people and who's risked his life to ensure they live.

King Alfred doesn't even glance at me, or seem to note those who fight with Mercia's eagle emblem on their shields. Instead, he brings his horse towards the enemy warriors, men keeping him protected to either side, shields displayed, eyes daring the enemy to attack. King Alfred notes the wooden crosses on display with a flicker of something I don't recognise on the parts of his face I can see beneath his elaborate warrior helm, complete with white horse hair on its crest. Fucking arse. That would be seen from a good long distance if he wore it in the scrum of the shield wall. I would never wear such a thing, apart from before my loyal subjects at the witan. And even then, I wouldn't want to bloody wear it.

'I will accept your surrender,' King Alfred intones, as though this is his decision to make. Wærwulf gabbles the words into the heavy silence because none of the West Saxons move to speak. I thought him a man of learning. Does he not think to know the language of his enemy? While I admit I couldn't converse fluently in it, I'm surprised by King Alfred. Some say he speaks the awful garbled Latin of the holy texts.

'I will accept your surrender,' King Alfred repeats, waving his hand as though he's progressing through his loyal subjects, shouting his acclaim. More of his warriors rush to take the surviving men under their control, casting aside blades and roughly tying hands in front of them with strips of hempen rope. King Alfred stays mounted throughout this, watching all with satisfaction I believe he's done fuck all to earn. But I hold my tongue. I'm intrigued to see how another king thinks to rule. I can say I don't fucking approve. Only when the men are devoid of weapons and have their hands tied does he even flash a look my way.

The revulsion on his familiar face on recognising me has me thinking I've probably been killing the wrong fucking enemy.

'My lord, King Alfred,' I call, pitching my voice so that it carries well. Apart from my warriors, every single man there jumps at the roar of my voice. I see a smirk on Hereman's blood-stained face while Icel scowls. 'We warriors of Mercia have won you freedom from the Viking raiders.' I see him open his mouth to argue with that, but I don't allow it. 'Now that you see how easy it is to do, we suggest you get your fucking arse off that horse and blood your bastard blade.'

So spoken, I stamp forward and grab the first of the enemy. The man bucks beneath me. I hold my blood-encrusted blade to his throat while the West Saxon emits a small shriek and scampers away from me.

'Come,' I urge the West Saxon king. 'This man is your prisoner. Now, show me you can kill him.'

King Alfred's face blanches of all colour, and even his fucking chin wobbles uncertainty.

'The man will die anyway,' I mutter, wrinkling my nose as the prisoner pisses himself with fear. I don't like doing this; I really don't. But King Alfred has shown himself to be a craven coward. I will know that he can defend his kingdom, or I will have no choice but to take it from him. And, from what I've seen, it's not a bad place, but it doesn't call to me as Mercia does. I know I belong among Mercia's roadways, trackways, high peaks and sweeping landscape.

'If we're to be allies, I must witness your ability to kill.'

King Alfred's rage washes from him. I stand firm against him. His warriors say nothing. I consider what they think of us. Do they look to King Alfred and see a true warrior king, or do they look to me and see the image of a man who will risk his life for what he believes in?

'I have killed,' he calls, but his wobbling voice assures me that's utter bollocks.

I don't move. The enemy before me doesn't fight me, which surprises me—the poor bastard.

'Then show the Mercians of your battle prowess and earn the alliance of Mercia's king.'

Silence stretches out. It's not uncomfortable besides the smell and the itch of my sweat-drenched skin. I could stand like this all day. I probably will have to.

'I'll do no such thing,' King Alfred announces, jutting out his bearded chin with defiance. I laugh at him, the sound deep and mocking. I move the blade to slice the man's neck, but I don't need to show I can kill. Instead, I release him, kicking him to the ground, where his bound hands do nothing to prevent his face from meeting the hard ground.

'Then there'll be no alliance,' I call, turning to wall away. I'm not angry. I'm not surprised either.

'King Coelwulf,' King Alfred calls, finally naming me as his equal, I notice, but my men hurry to join me, all of them. The other half of the fight is well and truly over as well.

'King Coelwulf,' King Alfred shouts once more. He sounds like a petulant child who'll stamp his feet until he gets his way. But I'm looking for Haden. I hurry down the slope, seeking my horse, forehead furrowing to allow more sweat to drip into my eyes when I can't see him.

'Bollocks,' I exclaim, hobbling back to the flatter ground once more. I look for Goda and Magic. I need them to find my horse. This is hardly the way I intended to take my leave from King Alfred and his warriors. I eye the carpet of dead bodies with a smirk. We did this. I'm proud of what we accomplished, but I can't ally with a man who'll not do this work to protect his kingdom and family.

As I've always suspected, King Alfred is weak.

He brings his horse towards me, but the animal refuses the command, even as the enemy who live are led inside Old Sarum.

Poor fuckers. I'd sooner have died on the slaughter field than surrendered to King Alfred.

'Find Haden,' I urge Goda, on seeing him. He nods and directs Magic down to the stream.

King Alfred still calls my name, but my focus is on where Pybba and Rudolf, amongst others, pilfer the dead for all their wealth. Rudolf's never one to let such an opportunity go by. I think he must have a box filled with such treasures somewhere. One day, he'll be a wealthy man, and not just because as one of my warriors, he's paid a pittance for risking his life.

I only realise King Alfred has dismounted when his voice comes closer. I'm checking with Ealdorman Ælhun and Kyred to determine who's wounded and making sure no one is dead.

King Alfred's face is filled with fury, his eyes flashing as he stamps towards me, his warriors leaving him to pilfer the dead as well. He's alone, and the image of him as a querulous child is impossible to ignore. He wears all the finery of a warrior king with none of the skill. Fuck, I hate the bastard.

Only then, before him, one of the dead enemies is not quite as dead as he should be. He rears up, war axe to hand, and fuck me, King Alfred fumbles his blade to hand, eyes wide, a startled shriek erupting from his mouth. There's no one to help him, not at all. I sense my warriors twisting to watch, and suddenly, all eyes are on King Alfred.

While he waves his seax around as though a banner to be displayed, I realise the bastard is going to prove me wrong after all.

With absolutely no skill and a lot of luck, all helped by the fact that the enemy warrior is weakened by the loss of his left hand, which pumps blood over him, King Alfred finally lands a killing blow.

His blade bloodied at last, I watch him realise what he's done, horror writ into the lines of his body, as he jumps back to avoid the spraying blood of the man he's just killed.

I sigh heavily.

'Fuck,' I exclaim, but I'm an honourable man. King Alfred might be worth fuck all, but the people of Wessex are Saxons. We share blood and ancestry. I won't allow them to be ruined by the ineffectiveness of King Alfred. With my aid, I know I can make Wessex strong enough to stand firm against the enemy. And I'm going to have to do so.

I grip his shaking arm, blade bloodied, and raise it into the air while a few men show their acclaim, all of them West Saxons.

'It appears, King Alfred, as though we have a fucking alliance, after all.'

A slow smile spreads across his face, even while he keeps glancing at the man he's killed.

'It'll be an alliance of equals,' he announces, chest puffed up. 'Warrior king to warrior king.'

'It most certainly will fucking not,' I reply quickly. 'But, if you do as you're told and listen to what I say, you'll save the West Saxons from the enemy. But first, first, my lord king, you really need to learn how to fucking fight.'

Chapter Thirty-Eight

'My lord,' I see Goda coming towards me, Haden with him, but another figure slumped on my horse's back.

Goda's unaware of what's just happened. I don't think to tell him. I'm more concerned with Haden and whoever Goda's found. For a moment, I fear it might be Lady Wulfthryth or one of her sons.

I hobble towards my horse, Icel, Ealdorman Ælhun and Kyred shadowing me. Goda looks somewhat better, but he relies on Magic to keep him moving. I notice his face is dripping with sweat and water. Has he taken a dunk in the stream?

'I found him,' he huffs. My eyes switch from Goda to Haden, and a slow smile spreads across my lips as I realise what he means.

'Gardulf,' I exclaim, already rotating to call for Hereman to come closer.

'He's in a bad way,' Goda cautions me, but I can already determine that. His face is pale, and a livid black bruise has formed on his left cheek. I'm perplexed by his presence here, but perhaps I shouldn't be.

'Gardulf,' I say his name and one of his eyes opens.

'My lord,' he whispers.

'Bring him water.' Rudolf hurries to obey.

'What happened?' I question him, and now he smiles.

'I know what the bastards intend,' he says, eyes widening. 'I was looking for you.'

'And what is that they intend?' I prompt him.

Gardulf's silent momentarily, but when he speaks, I know my time in Wessex is far from done.

'They mean to take Canterbury.'

'Fuck,' I mutter, already regretting my hasty acceptance that King Alfred might be a warrior after all.

'It seems,' and I twist to include King Alfred in this. 'That the fighting is far from done. Make Old Sarum secure. We ride for Canterbury.'

Cast of Characters

Coelwulf's Warriors

Æthelred – a youngster adopted by Coelwulf's war band

Ælfgar – one of the older members of the war band

Athelstan – killed in the first battle in The Last King

Beornberht – killed in the first battle in The Last King

Beornstan – one of Coelwulf's warriors

Cealwin – one of the older warriors from Kingsholm, first appears in The Last Shield

Coelwulf – King of Mercia, rides **Haden**

Cuthwalh – one of the older warriors from Kingsholm, rides **Aart**

Edmund – rides **Jethson**, was Coelwulf's brother's man until his death. Brother is **Hereman**. Dies in The Last Seven.

Eadberht – one of Coelwulf's warriors, now dead

Eadulf – one of Coelwulf's warriors, now dead

Eadfrith – one of the older warriors from Kingsholm, first appears in The Last Shield

Eahric – one of Coelwulf's warriors, rides **Storm**

Eoppa – rides **Poppy**, dies in The Last Horse

Gardulf – first appears in The Last Horse – Edmund's son, rides **Kermit**

Goda – one of Coelwulf's warriors, appears from The Last King onwards, rides **Magic**

Gyrth – one of Coelwulf's warriors, appears from The Last King onwards, rides **Keira**

Hemming – son of Beornberht, a young warrior from Kingsholm, rides **Perry**

Hereman – brother of Edmund, rides **Billy**

Hereberht – dies at Torksey, in The Last Warrior.

Hiltiberht – a squire

Ingwald – one of Coelwulf's warriors

Icel – rides **Samson**

Leonath – first appears in The Last Horse, rides **Petre**

Lyfing – wounded in The Last King

Oda – one of Coelwulf's warriors

Ordheah – one of Coelwulf's warriors

Ordlaf – one of Coelwulf's warriors

Oslac – one of Coelwulf's warriors, dies in The Last King

Osmod – one of the older warriors from Kingsholm, first appears in The Last Shield

Penda – first appears in The Last Horse – Pybba's grandson

Pybba – loses his hand in battle, rides **Brimman** (Sailor in Old English)

Penna, his daughter

Beca, his granddaughter

Higuel, his daughter's father-in-law

Rudolf – was a squire at the beginning of The Last King, rides **Dever**

Siric – now dead

Sæbald – one of Coelwulf's warriors

Tatberht – first appears in The Last Horse, normally remains at Kingsholm. Rides **Wombel**

Wærwulf – speaks Danish, rides **Cinder**

Wulfstan –, rides **Berg**
Wulfhere – grandson of Tatberht, rides **Stilton**
Wulfred – one of Coelwulf's warriors, rides **Cuthbert.**

The Mercians

Bishop Wærferth of Worcester
Bishop Deorlaf of Hereford
Bishop Eadberht of Lichfield
Bishop Smithwulf of London, dies in The Last Seven
Bishop Ceobred of Leicester
Bishop Burgheard of Lindsey
Ealdorman Beorhtnoth – of western Mercia
Ealdorman Ælhun – of area around Warwick
Ealdorman Æthelwold – his father, Ealdorman Æthelwulf, dies at the Battle of Berkshire in AD871.
Ealdorman Wulfstan – dies in The Last King
His son – (fictional) dies in The Last King
Werburg – (fictional) his daughter
Ealdorman Beornheard – of eastern Mercia
Ealdorman Aldred – of eastern Mercia
Lady Cyneswith – Coelwulf's (fictional)Aunt

The Northumbrians

Archbishop Wulfhere of York
King Ricsige of Northumbria

Viking raiders

Ivarr the Boneless – dies in AD870
Halfdan – brother of Ivarr (above)
Guthrum - one of the three leaders at Repton with Halfdan. Baptised as Æthelstan in The Last Viking
His sister, who dies outside Northampton
Oscetel - one of the three leaders at Repton with Halfdan
Anwend – one of the three leaders at Repton with Halfdan

Anwend Anwendsson – his fictional son

Jarl Sigurd – dies in The Last King

His wife, now dead

The royal family of Mercia

King Burgred of Mercia

m. **Lady Æthelswith** in AD853 (the sister of King Alfred of Wessex)

they had no children

Beornwald – a fictional nephew for King Burgred

King Wiglaf – ninth-century ruler of Mercia (827-840)

King Wigstan- ninth-century ruler of Mercia

King Beorhtwulf – ninth-century ruler of Mercia

King Coelwulf II– ninth-century ruler of Mercia from AD874 (the main character)

Coenwulf – his older brother, died 10 years ago

Lady Cyneswith – his aunt

The royal family of Wessex

King Alfred of Wessex

m.**Lady Ealhswith**, a woman of the Mercian royal family in AD864

Æthelflæd, their older daughter, born c.866

Edward, their older son, born c.974

King Æthelred of Wessex, Alfred's older brother, died 871.

m. **Lady Wulfthryth**

Æthelhelm, their son

Æthelwold, their son

The West Saxon Ealdormen

Ealdorman Eadwulf - of Somerset

Ealdorman Garulf – appears in charter S345 without location

Ealdorman Bucca – appears in charter S345 without location

Ealdorman Cuthred - of Hampshire

Ealdorman Wulfhere - of Wiltshire

Misc.

Wiglaf (now dead) and Berhtwulf – the names of Coelwulf's aunt's dogs, Lady Cyneswith

Wulfsige – commander of Ealdorman Ælhun's warriors

Kyred – oathsworn man of Bishop Wærferth of Worcester

Turhtredus – Mercian warrior

Eanulf – Mercian warrior

Places Mentioned

London – more strictly the twin settlements of Lundenwic (a market site) **and Londinium** (Roman ruin) **at this time**

Gainsborough, in north-east Mercia.

Northampton, on the River Nene in Mercia.

Grantabridge/Cambridge, in eastern Mercia/East Anglia

Gloucester, on the River Severn, in western Mercia.

Worcester, on the River Severn, in western Mercia.

Hereford, close to the border with Wales, on the River Wye

Repton, important Mercian mausoleum. St Wystan's was the name of royal mausoleum.

Gwent, one of the Welsh kingdoms to share a border with Mercia.

Powys was one of the Welsh kingdoms to share a border with Mercia.

Gwynedd, one of the Welsh kingdoms to share a border with Mercia.

Warwick, in Mercia.

Torksey, in the ancient kingdom of Lindsey, part of Mercia

River Severn, in the west of England

River Trent, runs through Staffordshire, Derbyshire, Nottingham and Lincolnshire and joins the Humber.

River Avon, in Warwickshire

River Thames, runs through London and into Oxfordshire

River Stour, runs from Stourport to Wolverhampton

River Ouse, leads into the Cam/Granta, runs through Bedford (Bed's Ford)

River Nene, runs from Northampton to the Wash

River Welland, runs from Northamptonshire to the Wash

River Granta/Cam, runs from Cambridge to King's Lynn (East Anglia)

River Great Ouse, running from South Northamptonshire to East Anglia

Kingsholm, close to Gloucester, an ancient royal site

The Foss Way, ancient roadway from Lincoln to Exeter

Watling Street, ancient roadway from Chester to London

Icknield Way, ancient roadway from Norfolk to Wiltshire

Ermine Street, ancient roadway from London to Lincoln, and York.

The Portway, ancient roadway in Wessex

Old Sarum, in Wessex

Winchester, in Wessex

Wareham, in Wessex

Historical Notes

Not historical, but in case you wondered, the breathing in through your nose and out through your mouth is something my dentist tells me to do to distract me from needles and drills. I'm very grateful for her calming, reassuring manner because although I loved the dentist as a child (yes, I was weird), I bloody hate it these days. I thought it fun to write it in to try and sort out Coelwulf.

I did not intend to take my warriors to Old Sarum, but having listened to a fascinating discussion on recent fieldwork at the site in a Society of Antiquaries public lecture presented by Alex Langlands in March 2024, I couldn't resist it. The lecture was called 'New Perspectives on the Archaeology and History of Old Sarum,' and I hope it's available on the SOA YouTube channel here, https://www.youtube.com/watch?v=iFhXatc--lg&list=PLGOCpw7BaRwUMnUhv_EG-5acBUYNjwkmV&index=5

Once more, this novel attempts to explore the 'other' scenario regarding the relationship between Wessex and Mercia at this time, hinted at through the surviving coin evidence and by 'reading between the lines' from the 'official' 'Wessex-centric' interpretations we've accepted for a long time without further thought, and which only started to be written 15 years after the events they describe (from about 890) onwards. The inclusion of Lady Wulfthryth, the widowed wife of King Alfred's brother, reminds us all that King Alfred's son, Edward, was, it appears, not intended to claim the kingship after his father's death. One of his nephews should have done so. Alfred, it seems, was not quite the honourable king he's often portrayed as being, in stark contrast to King Athelstan, who, it's said, purposefully didn't marry so that his younger half-brother would rule after him, and equally, as Edmund's brother, Eadred did, leaving the kingship to Edmund's sons, who were too young to rule on their father's murder.

I'm also grateful for a talk I attended virtually at 2024's Jorvik Viking Festival presented by Dr Gareth Williams regarding the second (or first) recent hoard, The Leominster/Herefordshire Hoard, of ninth-century coins discovered, including the 'Two-Emperor Coins.' The legal case has also brought these ancient coins into a contemporary setting, which is an intriguing facet to the story. The coins are fascinating, and Dr Williams' presentation has led me to make more of the character of the Archbishop of Canterbury. It's so interesting that both the Watlington (2015) and Leominster hoards (2015) have been found so close together in time, when previous to this, only one example of the Two-Emperor coins had been found in the Cuerdale Hoard discovered in 1840. It's almost as though 'someone' wants the story of this period rewritten😊 As you might know, I'm fascinated by the Saxon coinage system (apologies if you're not quite so enamoured).

The River Thames – I've discovered that the River Thames might not have been as navigable as perhaps thought. The inclusion of Lechlade/Cricklade is my attempt for both this series and the Eagle of Mercia Chronicles to find a means to travel from Mercia to Wessex and vice-versa. It was both a barrier, and it appears the further west you travel, not a barrier.

Coelwulf and his warriors will return. Soon.

What to read next?

I hope you've enjoyed Coelwulf's newest tale. If you'd like to keep reading about Saxon England, and Mercia in particular, then please consider this series of interconnected titles, which I term 'The Tales of Mercia.'

<u>Gods and Kings (Seventh century)</u>

Pagan Warrior
Pagan King
Warrior King

<u>The Eagle of Mercia Chronicles (Earlier ninth century)</u>

Son of Mercia
Wolf of Mercia
Warrior of Mercia
Eagle of Mercia
Protector of Mercia
Enemies of Mercia

The Lady of Mercia's Daughter (Tenth century)

A Conspiracy of Kings

The Earl of Mercia Series (End of the tenth century)

The Earl of Mercia's Father and subsequent titles (please note, perversely, I began this series first).

Enjoy

Meet the Author

I'm an author of historical fiction (Early English, Vikings and the British Isles as a whole before the Norman Conquest) and fantasy (Viking age/dragon-themed), born in the old Mercian kingdom at some point since AD1066. I like to write. You've been warned! My first non-fiction title is also now available.

Find me at mjporterauthor.com. mjporterauthor.blog and @coloursofunison on twitter. I have a monthly newsletter, which can be joined here. All subscribers will receive a free ebook short story collection.

https://dashboard.mailerlite.com/forms/699265/105452112446489757/share

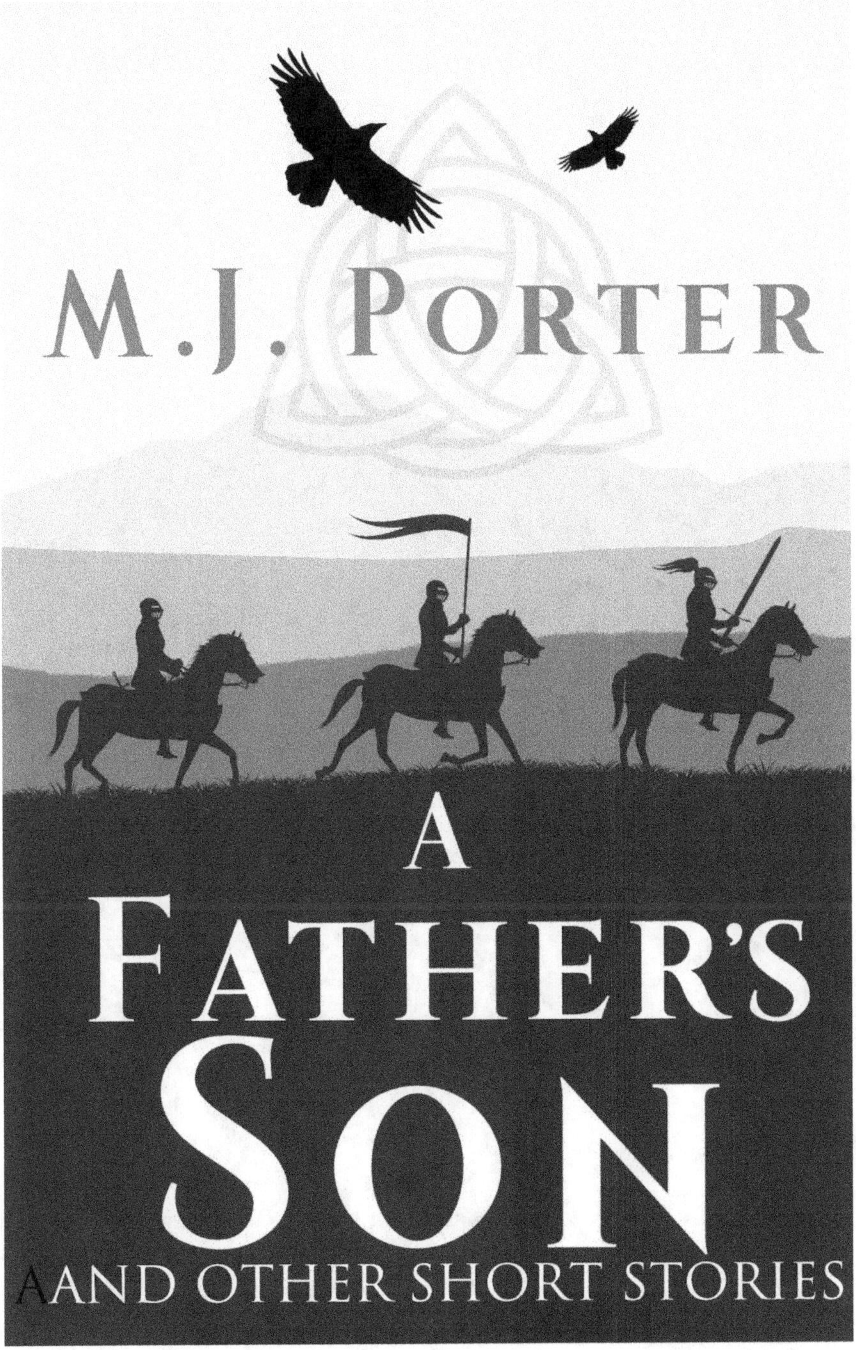

M.J. PORTER

A FATHER'S SON

AND OTHER SHORT STORIES

Books by M J Porter (in chronological order)

Gods and Kings Series (seventh century Britain)

Pagan Warrior

Pagan King

Warrior King

The Eagle of Mercia Chronicles

Son of Mercia

Wolf of Mercia

Warrior of Mercia

Eagle of Mercia

Protector of Mercia

Enemies of Mercia

Betrayal of Mercia

The Ninth Century

Coelwulf's Company, stories from before The Last King

The Last King

The Last Warrior

The Last Horse

The Last Enemy

The Last Sword

The Last Shield

The Last Seven

The Last Viking

The Last Alliance

The Tenth Century

The Lady of Mercia's Daughter

A Conspiracy of Kings (the sequel to The Lady of Mercia's Daughter)

Kingmaker

The King's Daughter

Non-fiction title

The Royal Women Who Made England: The Tenth Century in Saxon England

The Brunanaburh Series

King of Kings

Kings of War

Clash of Kings

Kings of Conflict

The Mercian Brexit (can be read as a prequel to The First Queen of England)

The First Queen of England (The story of Lady Elfrida) (tenth century England)

The First Queen of England Part 2

The First Queen of England Part 3

The King's Mother (The continuing story of Lady Elfrida)

The Queen Dowager

Once A Queen

The Earls of Mercia

The Earl of Mercia's Father

The Danish King's Enemy

Swein: The Danish King (side story)

Northman Part 1

Northman Part 2

Cnut: The Conqueror (full-length side story)

Wulfstan: An Anglo-Saxon Thegn (side story)

The King's Earl

The Earl of Mercia

The English Earl

The Earl's King

Viking King

The English King

The King's Brother

Lady Estrid (a novel of eleventh-century Denmark)

Fantasy

The Dragon of Unison

Hidden Dragon

Dragon Gone

Dragon Alone

Dragon Ally

Dragon Lost

Dragon Bond

As JE Porter

The Innkeeper (standalone)

20th Century Mystery

The Custard Corpses – a delicious 1940s mystery (audio book now available)

The Automobile Assassination (sequel to The Custard Corpses)

Cragside – a 1930s murder mystery (standalone)

www.ingramcontent.com/pod-product-compliance
Lightning Source LLC
Chambersburg PA
CBHW070434170726
48291CB00002B/492
9781917374040